TREASURE

TREASURE

A Peachtree Street Chronicles' Novel

Sam Biondo

iUniverse, Inc.
New York Lincoln Shanghai

Treasure

A Peachtree Street Chronicles' Novel

iUniverse books may be ordered through booksellers or by contacting:

iUniverse
2021 Pine Lake Road, Suite 100
Lincoln, NE 68512
www.iuniverse.com
1-800-Authors (1-800-288-4677)

ISBN-13: 978-0-595-36555-5 (pbk)
ISBN-13: 978-0-595-67390-2 (cloth)
ISBN-13: 978-0-595-80986-8 (ebk)
ISBN-10: 0-595-36555-8 (pbk)
ISBN-10: 0-595-67390-2 (cloth)
ISBN-10: 0-595-80986-3 (ebk)

Printed in the United States of America

CHAPTER 1

▼

BEGINNINGS

Evening, 06 December 1958
Plantacion El Pinar, Guanahacabibes Peninsula, Cuba

Senor Pedro Martinez, *Patron* of *Plantacion El Pinar,* took the hard slap across his sweaty face, the pain bursting through the calm expression he was fighting to maintain.

Before he could recover, a second slap crossed his face in the reverse direction, and his sight exploded in white light, as if a flash bulb had gone off just inches in front of him. Salty tears stung his reddened cheeks.

The short, stocky man felt his knees begin to buckle as he fought to maintain his regal bearing. His breathing was shallow, and he nearly collapsed.

His wife, Maria, dark haired with a deep, honey colored complexion, nearly a head taller than her husband, and much thinner, stood with their three children, a boy, twelve, and two girls, six, and four, huddled in the doorway of the plantation house, sobbing noisily. Martinez willed himself to remain stoic, holding back tears, trying to ignore the sting of the attack. He would not show weakness in front of this miserable coward and his henchmen. He heard their laughter. It made him stand to his full height and he forced himself to stare down his attacker.

Threatened as he was, Martinez knew, as he stood on the veranda of his hacienda, here among the rich tobacco fields his family had owned and cultivated for generations, these rebels were not here to kill him and his family. Not yet. Other followers of the renegade, Fidel Castro, had come this way before from their mountain hideouts, stealing food, clothing, livestock, even the magnificent tobacco from the curing sheds. Twice they had coerced some of his field hands to join them in "overthrowing the ruling class that makes you work their fields, but will not allow you to own your own land."

This was a lie. He knew it, the other landowners knew it, and he went to great pains to try to tell his workers so. Yes, it was true that the government had many corrupt officials. What government was not corrupt? But he had always been fair to his workers, had he not?

So he and his family and his magnificent plantation had been visited by this scum before, but with every success of this rabble against the inept government army of *El Presidente*, Fulgencio Batista, the visits became more threatening, more violent. Yet he knew that only in the event, which still seemed outlandish to consider, of the Batista government's fall to the rebels, would they truly be in mortal danger.

His assailant moved even closer, and Martinez could smell the man's stale sweat, his dirt encrusted clothes. The fetid breath swamped him. Suddenly, he realized he knew this man. *I know you, you pig! You have worked my land. You earned your bread in my fields, until you disappeared in the dead of night! And now this, you stinking pig!*

"Your days are numbered, *Patron*," his tormentor sneered. "You filthy bastards must no longer oppress our people! You will die *Patron!* You and all the oppressors of the people will be gone forever!"

Martinez could hardly breathe. His world was spinning out of control.

The rebel looked past him to the woman crying in the doorway. He turned to his men, giving them a gap-toothed grin, and said to Martinez, "Maybe we keep your bitch for a while, eh? Maybe we pass her around before we kill the bitch, what do you say?" He and the others laughed. Pedro Martinez could take no more.

"You dog! You will keep a civil tongue in your hea......"

The words were smashed from his mouth by the rebel's fist. This time, Martinez went down hard, and blackness engulfed him. He never heard Maria's scream.

*   *   *   *

He came awake with a start, feeling the pressure of the cold, damp cloth across his forehead. As his vision cleared, he stared up at the slowly turning ceiling fan which made him feel like he was spinning around and around. Finally, Pedro Martinez sat up with the help of Maria and his young son, Carlos. They were inside the house, in the entrance hallway. Somehow, his family had dragged him inside. They sat around him on the floor, a pillow, and some blankets strewn around them.

Maria's eyes were dry now, but worry still showed on her face. He was fully awake now, but felt great pain at his temple, and down the left side of his jaw.

Pedro Martinez, patron of *El Pinar*, the great plantation of over five hundred *hectares* located in the center of Cuba's premier cigar tobacco growing region, struggled to his feet. He took still a minute to regain his balance and his composure. His daughters Anna, and little Maria, held on to him as if to steady him, but really, he knew, it was because of their fear. Their apprehension was fully visible in their tiny faces. Their father smiled through his pain and reached out to them, stroking their beautiful, deep black hair.

"Do not be afraid, my darlings," he said. "Papa is fine. Everything is going to be fine."

He looked into his wife's eyes, and they both knew he was lying.

*   *   *   *

Later that night after the children were calmed and put to sleep, Pedro Martinez lay in bed with his wife. Maria was lying with her back to him, but he could hear her softly weeping, and a feeling of helplessness engulfed him. Pedro lay on his back, staring at nothing, a million thoughts playing through his mind.

A man was supposed to protect his family, his land, his way of life, he thought. At this moment, surrounded by darkness and the palpable fear his wife was suffering, Martinez had no idea how to accomplish this.

Evening, 13 December 1958
The Habana Road

Jose Garcia stood on the gas pedal of the black, 1956 Buick Roadmaster, and the big machine jumped forward. He had just left the village of *Santa Cruz de los Pinos* behind, and the two-lane road was again wide open before him. Garcia, now forty-four and for twenty years known as *el Jefe*, the chief, in his position as foreman of all field workers at *Plantacion El Pinar*, his thick, black hair blowing in the wind rushing through the open windows, was hurrying back to beat the curfew recently imposed by the provincial governor. *By order of those fools in Habana,* he thought.

Garcia had an even more important reason for returning to the plantation at the earliest possible moment. He had news, and it was not good news for him, or for *de obreros,* the boss, as he affectionately called Senor Martinez, whose family he had served for so many years.

There was great danger for them all. Once again, the forces of El Presidente, and the foolish louts who commanded them had been decimated by a handful of rebels, high in the *Sierra Maestra* Mountains. Ten thousand government troops had, since August, been defeated time after time in small battles and harassed by guerrilla attacks. Much weaponry had fallen into the hands of Castro and his chief, Che Guevera, the Argentine doctor turned *comunista.* Now the rebels were moving on the capital, and thousands of fearful residents were making their way out of the city.

There was no love lost on Batista or his government. He had taken control of Cuba not once but twice, by military coup. But, he had brought millions of dollars in American investment capital into Cuba and kept order, if somewhat oppressively, in the country. If he and his compatriots had tasted a little of the fruit of this prosperity, it was probably a necessary, and mostly harmless, sin. If these *"pecados,"* these sinners, were removed from power by the agitator, Fidel Castro and his band of thugs, the patrons, the wealthy, and the civil populous of Cuba would have their lives changed forever. Jose Garcia liked his life as it was.

The dark of night was closing in much too quickly for Garcia's liking.

He slowed the big automobile as he approached the small village of *Consolacion del Sol.* He entered the town and, as he drove through, he searched the faces of the villagers. *Were they staring at him? Were they waiting to attack him with rocks, or worse?* He knew he was reacting to unreasonable fear, but it unnerved him, just the same. Garcia was glad to pass the last ramshackle buildings, and again pushed the Buick down the roadway. He was less than an hour from the plantation, and safety.

*   *   *   *

When the "Great Explorer" made his second landfall in the New World, late in the Year of our Lord, 1492, Christopher Columbus and his men came ashore near the very eastern tip of the island which became Cuba. The spot of this landing was known by the native inhabitants, *los indios,* to the Admiral of the Ocean Seas, as *Baracoa.* It was not Japan, as he had hoped.

The invaders found no treasure during their short stay on the island, as they had not at their first landfall, at the island of *Guanahari.* What they found was a peaceful tribe of natives known as the *Tainos*, who cultivated and smoked the cured leaves of a plant known to them as *tobaco.*

It was this now-extinct tribe, which introduced the rolled logs of tobacco to the Spaniards, as cigars. The Spanish invaders showed their appreciation by decimating the tribe with physical abuse, Old World illnesses for which they had no defense, and tortuous death. The Tainos, before dying out, got a modicum of revenge on the Spaniards by infecting them with syphilis, which they then unwittingly introduced to the rest of Europe.

Columbus went on to bigger and better things, but Cuba, which means "barrel," or "crate" in Spanish, had been established and the village of *Santiago de Cuba* on the eastern coast became the Spanish colonial capital.

Cuba's future changed forever in 1522 with the arrival of the first slave ship from Africa. Over the next three hundred years, nearly one million Africans sold by their own tribal chiefs to white slavers, were sent to the island's shores. Two hundred thousand never made it across the ocean, their bodies, riddled with smallpox, measles, and other communicable diseases, were unceremoniously dumped overboard.

But those who made it across the Atlantic to the fledgling plantations where tobacco and sugar cane were the main crops changed the face of the Spanish colony forever.

These crops, along with the fortuitous discovery of great quantities of silver and gold in Columbia, Peru, Mexico and other parts of Spain's New World holdings, were shipped from Cuba in the holds of great treasure ships and merchantmen, making the island a prize coveted by the British, French and, eventually, the United States. Throughout the seventeen hundreds the Spaniards battled the British, losing the island for a year in 1762, but regaining it later in an exchange for Florida.

It was during this exchange of colonial holdings that a young corporal of the Spanish army, having served his time in arms, made a drastic decision, which would lead to the founding of a family of Cuban landed gentry. With stories of vast treasure and land for the taking lodged in his brain, Pablo Martinez became the first member of the Martinez family to enter the island and stay. His face pock marked by a battle with smallpox, and his body wasted by bouts of malaria, he decided his future was in the New World. Along with the remnants of Spain's Florida garrison, he sailed in the small, waterlogged gunboat *Santa Clara*, bound for the town of Habana, which now served as capital of the Spanish colonies in the Americas.

Although riches of gold, silver, and jewels were not awaiting Pablo on the docks of Havana, he quickly saw the opportunities which lay before any man willing to work hard and save his *pesos*. The lure of the azure waters and a climate seemingly healthier than that of the Florida swamps sealed the decision for him. When Pablo Martinez' remaining fellow soldiers boarded the larger vessels which would carry them home to Spain, he bid them farewell from the dock.

Two years working the burgeoning waterfront of Havana returned him to his former health, and as the town continued to grow in importance, Pablo's prospects grew with it. His lust for land began to grow as he saw the carts, bursting with their blocks of tobacco leaf, coming with greater frequency to the boarding ramps of the merchant ships. Sugar cane, increasingly becoming the main crop exported from Cuba, shared one major similarity with tobacco. They both required rich soil to grow.

Land.

Land. *Tierra,* would make him rich. But, how could he acquire some? Working the docks put a roof over Pablo Martinez' head. It put food on his table. It would never, he knew, put his own soil under his feet.

The second great decision of his life came on a day late in April of 1766. Following a breakfast of bread flavored with the pungent olive oil imported from his native land, he packed his few belongings and left his small room behind the cantina where he had lived since the army had released him. Instead of heading to his job on the docks of Havana, he turned south, heading for the fertile fields of his future glory, and never looked back.

In 1771, as the American colonies to the north began in earnest their drive to win independence from the hated English King, Pablo Martinez, who, while becoming an extremely competent *cultivador*, a grower of tobacco was working hard to win the hand of Maria Theresa Gonzalez. He had worked for her father, Arturo since the day of his arrival in the village of *El Pinar*. She was beautiful, and an only child, but it was the land, and the art of growing the long leafed plant, that he fell in love with first. He learned his craft in the fields, working hand in hand alongside the *patron* and his *esclavo,* his African slaves.

Arturo Gonzales took note of the talents of the young man, and nurtured his education in plantation arts, as well as his education in the art of winning Arturo's only daughter's hand.

Their wedding, attended by all the newly founded *aristocrata* of landed gentry, led to the beginning of the Martinez aristocracy when his father-in-law died six years later. As Maria Theresa's husband, Martinez inherited her father's land and personal wealth, including paintings, heirloom furniture, religious icons, and jewelry brought from Spain.

In the coming years, their family grew, as did their holdings and the quality of their tobacco, which included the growing of the rare, oily *Carojo* wrapper that would grace the fine tobaccos of some of Cuba's greatest cigar brands. The ascendancy of Pedro Martinez and Cuba was well on its way.

In the early years of the eighteen hundreds, Mexico and the other South American countries won their independence from Spain, leaving only Cuba and Peru in her grasp. And Cuba was now the world's largest producer of sugar.

The slave trade ended in 1865, and in 1868, the first war for the independence of the island began. It lasted ten years, and failed. Showing extremely good sense, Arturo Carlos Martinez, then patron of the plantation, stayed out of the fray and suffered no ill consequences when the war ended. The second war for independence began in 1895 and finally ended with the victory of the United States in its short, and suspiciously started, war against Spain. The treaty ending the conflict saw the island ceded to the winners. The Martinez family, whose plantation was nearly a little country of its own, welcomed the victory over their ancestral land. Now, truly, Cuba was a part of the New World.

The Martinez family, *formerly* of Madrid, was now a long-standing member of Cuba's land holding aristocracy; growing the pungent, strong tobacco for which they would become famous throughout the world. Independence, achieved in 1902, seemed to Senor Carlos Martinez, grandfather of Pedro, good reason to look forward to great things for his country.

But the Cuban experience as a new republic was strewn with rocky government dictatorships, coups, and the entrance into the political arena of the *Partido Comunista*, the Communist Party. The fraudulent presidential election of Fulgencia Batista in 1955 was looked on with great disdain by the lower classes of Cuba, as well as some of the more liberal patrons. In an effort to garner support for his stolen election, Batista released political Prisoners, mostly communists, from jail, in May. Among those released was Fidel Castro, an agitator and guerrilla, who had been captured by the Batista government and for some reason, jailed instead of being executed, on the Island of Pines, now called *Juventud*. The patrons were horrified by his release, suspecting bribery.

Castro used his unexpected freedom to flee to Mexico and from there, he directed his remaining comrades in Cuba as they began to put together another insurgent army. This band of communists made their first coup attempt against Batista at *Playa Las Coloradas* in the *Oriente Province*. They were easily repulsed and Castro, his brother Raul, Che Guevera and a few others who would become his *capitans*, his captains, escaped into the *Sierra Maestra* Mountains.

Right thinking Cubans celebrated the demise of the rebels. Surely, this would be the end of them. No more would they threaten the peace and prosperity of the country. Or so it seemed.

Now, barely a year later, the communists were on the verge of taking Havana and Batista was secretly planning his escape from Cuba. American "investors," made up, in large part, of American mobsters, were about to lose millions. And the lives of millions of Cubans' were about to come under a Marxist controlled government.

＊   ＊   ＊   ＊

3 A.M., 17 December 1958
Plantacion El Pinar

Pedro Martinez could not sleep. His mind would not let loose of the information that Jose Garcia had brought to him two nights before. He could not bring himself to believe that the government was about to fall to this Marxist pig, Castro. How could anyone believe that Castro's purpose was a better life for the people of Cuba?

The night was warm and the air thick with moisture, but Martinez felt a chill he could not escape. Maria slept fitfully beside him. It was still very early, and he did not wish to wake her with his own restlessness while the children still slept. Every day his wife and children were less at ease, and the slightest noise or rush of wind through the trees set them on edge.

The news from the mountains, and now from the very streets of Havana was ever more troubling, and the fear among his neighbors was palpable. Pedro Martinez slipped quietly from the bed. Taking his robe from the chair and grabbing a pair of slippers from under his dressing table, he left the sleeping Maria and padded down the steps to his office on the first floor of the hacienda.

Sitting at the big, ornate desk that had been his father's and his father's father before him, the room, still hours from accepting the light of another day, was ghostly dark. Only the small desk lamp broke the gloom. Martinez was quickly lost in thought. Facing the large shade covered window overlooking the south fields, Pedro Martinez took stock of the situation and considered his options, in the event the rebels succeed in pushing out the government in Havana.

What had been inconceivable only a few short months ago now seemed all too real. The Americans were a large part of the problem, he thought with disgust. He knew that many in the United States saw Batista and his cohorts as dictatorial buffoons, but the main tourist businesses of Havana, including prostitution and gambling, were controlled by Americans, many tied to organized crime lords in New York. What to do? Surely, those making money from these "industries" would not let their good times end.

The big grandfather clock that his wife's family had brought to the New World so many years ago chimed three times, snapping Martinez back from his musings. When the chimes faded away, the room took on a heavy silence again, broken only by the tick-tock of the clock. Pedro Martinez felt the life that generations of his family had built was also ticking away.

An idea began to form. He detested the thought of it immediately as it entered his mind, but he knew the validity of it just as quickly.

But first, his family must be safe. He had to get them away from Cuba while he figured out a way to protect the plantation. Get them away until the country came to its senses and the danger passed. Batista's armies were too preoccupied to protect the plantations.

There would be others who would want their families safely away from here. Surely, he could find a way to get them out of the country; to Mexico, Brazil, even the United States. Once Maria and the children were safe, he and the other patrons would find a way to intervene between the government and the rebels. This madness could not be allowed to continue and bankrupt the country.

Yes. With help, he could do this.

Martinez sat back in the big leather chair. He closed his eyes. He needed sleep, but did not want to go back to the bedroom and risk waking his wife. He would rest here.

But his mind would not let loose of his thoughts. What would his father say about all this—his grandfather, and all those who came before him—who had built this beautiful and productive place? Would he be considered a coward by those noble souls for risking the loss of his heritage? Maybe, but why should this be so? Was it not his sacred duty to protect his family? Pedro Martinez knew that he could not cure Cuba's ills by sacrificing his loved ones. What he now contemplated in this dark room, might be the only way to salvage the life he and his ancestors had sacrificed so much for.

Through his eyelids, he slowly began to notice light flooding into the room. Too early, he thought, opening his eyes. A weirdly fluctuating light of varying hues spilled through the ornate cloth shade covering the window—red, orange, white hot. Suddenly the pungent aroma began to engulf the room.

Pedro Martinez jumped from the chair and grabbed at the shade, pulling it sharply away from the window. The entire room was immediately filled with a blinding light. Outside, a hundred meters away, the largest of the curing sheds blazed uncontrollably, flames shooting high into the dark sky. The smell of burning tobacco permeated the air.

Upstairs, running feet pounded against the heavy oak flooring. The patron of El Pinar could hear only the piercing screams of his children.

*   *   *   *

Dawn, 08 January 1959
Havana

Jose Garcia had been hiding in the bell tower of *Iglesia del Santo Angel Custodio*, the Church of the Guardian Angel, for the better part of five days. He lived on food and drink brought to him daily by Father Ignacio, the only soul who knew of his presence high above the church, and used a slop pail which was becoming riper by the hour, for his bodily functions. Only the early morning breeze, passing through the bell tower, kept the small space livable.

He put down the bread and sausage he had been chewing on and crawled back to one of the openings in the wall through which the sounds from the bell chimes would escape on the wind to spread over the city.

Down below and across the *Avenida de las Missiones* stood the Presidential Palace, occupied, since the fifth of January by Manuel Urrutia, the former judge who had assumed the presidency five days after Fulgencio Batista had finally fled the country, in the wee hours of New Years Day.

The street below, bathed in the early morning light, was quiet, with the exception of the unusually large contingency of army guards around the palace. Garcia took another bite of sausage and followed it with a swig of the blood-red *vino tinto*. He leaned farther out the opening.

"Careful, my friend," a voice came from behind. "That is not sacramental wine. It will not protect you from a soldier's bullet!"

Garcia pulled back from the edge, turned, and sat against the wall as his friend came up the last steps, into the small room. He looked at the black robed Jesuit, a short man with a pleasantly round, cherubic face and sandy brown hair. He was a younger man than Jose, but with leathery skin that gave away his years of working in the outlying, rural missions. "I did not hear you, *padre*. If you were any quieter, you could be one of that bastard Castro's slinking spies."

"Such language in the house of the Lord, Jose!" The priest said, with mock horror as he knelt down next to Garcia. "Anything of interest?" Garcia took another drink, and wiping the rim with his sleeve, passed the jug to his friend. The priest declined the offer and peered around Garcia to sneak a peak outside.

"All is quiet. What are you hearing from your parishioners?"

"Nothing but rumors, although the reports that said Batista is now in the Dominican Republic with his friend in crime, Trujillo, appear to be true." Jose Garcia mulled over this information. The priest said, "You know Urrutia is Castro's man, Jose. This new presidency is nothing but a sham!" He sighed with disgust. "There is no legitimate government in Cuba, now."

"The newspapers all say that the people are happy to be rid of Batista," said his friend. "If they are so happy, why are they so quiet? Where is their joy?"

The two sat, lost in thought, for several minutes. Father Ignacio said, "When do you return to El Pinar?"

"My instructions were to wait until there was some news of extreme importance." Garcia thought a moment before deciding to confide in the priest. "The Patron does not share all his thoughts with me, but I hear things on occasion, and I think he and others are planning something of a drastic nature."

Father Ignacio looked deep into his friend's eyes. "But what can he do, Jose?"

"I cannot speak for him" Garcia said. "If it were me, I would leave Cuba as quickly as possible."

The Jesuit was stunned by these words. "Leave?" He looked away from Garcia. "But Jose, leave everything he has built? Everything his family has built?"

"If he believes it will all be taken from him against his will." It was a statement. It was exactly what Martinez expected would happen, with the communists in control. "Are you not afraid, my friend? The *comunista* are not friends of the church, you know." Garcia was pensive again. "If Senor Martinez leaves, I do not think he will leave alone."

"Castro continues to say he is not a communist." The priest's face took on a look of distaste, as if what he had said was too ludicrous to consider. "And some of my parishioners believe him. They are so hungry for change, Jose," he said, as if to excuse them for their stupidity. "They *want* to believe him, because they want a better life! But I agree, I think you are right about the patron leaving," he said, sadly. "In any event," he went on, "I am not afraid. Cuba is very Catholic, and I doubt the communists could as easily influence the people of Cuba about religion as they did those in Russia."

The silence between the two was deafening, each lost in their own thoughts.

"So, you think others will follow him?" Father Ignacio said finally, beginning to consider the ramifications of an exodus by the country's wealthy families. "This could destroy our homeland, Jose."

"The communists will destroy Cuba, padre!" Garcia spit out the words. "Senor Martinez is under no edict to allow his family to be destroyed with it." Outside, the suddenly audible growl of an automobile engine could be heard. Garcia rolled onto his belly and crawled back to the opening in the wall, the priest followed, peering over his shoulder.

A drab-green painted army truck sat at the curb near the Palace, six soldiers sitting in the open back. Moments later, two identical vehicles approached down the *avenida* and pulled up behind the first. The occupants of all three trucks sat motionless. With their engines turned off, the silence was again palpable.

What was happening? There was something else. What was it? Instantly, Jose Garcia knew. The soldiers who had been guarding the Presidential Palace were gone, and the street was deserted, except for the army trucks. Was this a changing of the guard, perhaps? No, that did not seem right.

Suddenly the passenger door of the first truck opened, and a soldier wearing a dark green beret hopped down. Again, something was not right. Garcia pulled back and looked questioningly at Father Ignacio. "Those are rebels, my friend," the priest said with resignation. "That man down there is Che Guevara, and," he looked over Garcia's shoulder, "and that one, getting out of the second truck, that, Jose, is Fidel Castro."

The doors of the presidential palace swung open. Two men emerged and walked down the steps and out to Castro and Guevara, who stood beside the lead truck. El Presidente, Manuel Urrutia extended his hand to Fidel Castro, who took it in both of his. The two men embraced.

Garcia was struck by the irony of it all. For years, armies had chased the rebel leader without success. Now, with a rifle, Jose Garcia could have changed the future of Cuba. Of course, he most certainly would have sacrificed his own life, and maybe that of his friend Father Ignacio, but this bastard would be dead, and the name of Jose Garcia would have echoed through future histories as the savior of Cuba. He felt his trigger finger tighten and sighed. What a shame for his country.

Father Ignacio, sensing the thoughts going through Garcia's mind, sat back on his haunches. For the first time, a hint of fear was in his eyes. "I think, my friend," he said, "it is time for you to return to El Pinar."

*   *   *   *

Midnight, 01 April 1959
Isla de la Juventud, Golfo de Batabano, Cuba

It was done.

It had taken the better part of a week for the wealth of six families to be vaulted in secrecy on the island. It had been the idea of Pedro Martinez, but one quickly approved by his neighbors among the tobacco growers. Those wealthy enough to lose their fortunes, and maybe, their freedom, to the government controlled by the newly installed Prime Minister of Cuba, Fidel Castro, knew it was time to leave.

But what of their belongings? What of their artwork, heirloom furnishings, religious icons, jewelry, the things that tied them to the generations that had come before? What of the precious tobacco seed which was the source of their wealth? There was no way to safely take their family mementos and other valuables from the country undetected, in small boats. They would be leaving illegally, in secrecy, under cover of darkness.

The government allowed no citizen to leave the country, only the tourists and foreigners stupid enough to still be in Cuba.

Martinez knew this.

He devised a plan to safeguard their valuables where no one would find them until they could return to their homes, after the communists were thrown out. If this did not happen in a reasonable time, then they would have to sneak back into the country to remove their belongings.

Surely, the Cuban people would come to their senses, and they would return to their homes again soon. In the mean time, at least their families would be safe. It would be necessary to take whatever seed they could with them, for the seed was their safeguard for the future.

In February, shortly after Castro was proclaimed Prime Minister by the puppet Urrutia, Martinez sent Jose Garcia, his trusted foreman, to visit five nearby plantations. His plan depended on stealth, and he feared involving too many others in his plan.

Garcia visited the tobacco plantations of the families Castillo, Azpiazu, Bacallao, Prado, and Ortiz. His message was simple. The patrons' were asked to meet with Pedro Martinez in private, at El Pinar the evening of 23 February. The meeting was to be kept secret, even from their families.

At the meeting, Martinez found no opposition to his plan to leave Cuba, but much despair about what would be left behind.

There was good reason why no one objected to the plan. It was called the First Agrarian Reform Act, which would take effect in May of 1959. Simply put, all plantations of over four hundred hectares, including those of these particular families, would be nationalized. This Act would also affect the holdings of big American corporations, like the United Fruit Company, potentially further eroding the economy.

Their fears had been realized. Their lands would be taken from them in the name of the government.

The plan was simple, yet ambitious. Each plantation would send two of its most trusted male employees, family members if possible, to Plantacion El Pinar. They would be taken to a secret location, where they would construct a concrete underground bunker in which to safeguard the valuables until they could be retrieved. Jose Garcia would visit a different plantation every night in revolving order for two weeks in a truck which would appear to be loaded with bales of tobacco. In an open space underneath the bales they would load up the treasures of six families, to be taken to the little seaside village of *Cortes*, on the southern coast, and hidden there in the basement of the small church, since churches were mainly ignored by Castro.

There, Martinez and Garcia would direct a few most trusted souls of their choosing to pack the valuables in waterproof crates, and the crates would be hidden in the vaults below the church until ready for transport to the bunker. Once the valuables were hidden, everyone would return to their homes to gather their families. The patrons and their trusted workers would transport the families by car, truck or any means available to the little fishing village of *San Rafael* on the northern coast of Cuba, meeting at the home of Maria Martinez' brother.

Three fishing boats hired by Pedro Martinez at an exorbitant, but necessary, cost, would take the refugees, for that is what they were about to become, across the ninety miles that separated Cuba from the Florida Keys at the very tip of the United States. They would only be allowed some clothing, as much cash and jewelry as they could carry, and no more than three small casks full of the precious tobacco seed. The exact location where Martinez proposed to build the bunker would be kept secret for now.

Many of the patrons gave little chance of success to the plan, but to a man, they understood the necessity of trying. And, they had little more than a month to pull it off.

∗   ∗   ∗   ∗

Pedro Martinez watched the sweating men cover the last of the hole over the concrete bunker which was capped with layers of thick wood planks. He looked over at Manuel Ortiz and Jose Garcia, who were urging the workers to finish their job quickly.

Afterward, the ground, in an opening amidst the wild tall palms would then be covered with greenery. In a short time, the dense vegetation would obliterate all traces of their work. It had taken three weeks to complete the hiding place and deliver the valuables.

Sweat dripped down Martinez' face. Everything was under control here. Now the families would be reunited on the mainland, and the next step in their journey would begin.

Thirty crates, waterproofed to maintain their contents in pristine condition, were brought here, three at a time, over a period of several days, and were now buried nearly ten feet below them, encased in concrete and covered by layers of heavy, wooden beams. Only those present, the six patrons, who had affixed their family crests to the trusted, and their trusted workers from their plantations would know this location. They would return for their belongings together soon.

Their wealth was safe for the time being. Now they must protect their families.

There was a thrashing sound behind Martinez. He turned to find Salvator Ortiz, eldest son of Manuel Ortiz, patron of *Plantacion Compostela*, working his way through the brush. "Senor Martinez," the boy was breathless, "the boat has arrived to take us to the mainland!"

Pedro Martinez signaled to Jose Garcia to hurry the workers along, and quickly followed the young man back nearly a kilometer through the palms. They wound their way down the path he and the others had worn through the jungle-like terrain with the little handcart that they had used to transport the crates through the heavily forested route from the cove, where they had hidden the boat that had made so many trips from Cortes. When they reached the cove on the western end of island, they found the rest of their party boarding the fishing trawler.

Soon, Jose Garcia, last to leave the burial site, joined Martinez and the others.

An hour later in the darkness, they were crossing the fifty kilometers of water back to the village of Cortes. There, they would find two trucks waiting to return them to their homes.

All went smoothly. At 4 a.m., Martinez jumped from the rear of the vehicle and, watching it drive away in the predawn light, he entered the *hacienda*.

Martinez quickly and happily found Maria and the children packing a few small bundles. It had been three days since he had seen his family. Maria hugged her husband. Tears streamed down her cheeks. "I was so afraid while you were gone! Oh, Pedro! Leaving our home, this is the most difficult thing I have ever done!"

At precisely 5 a.m., Jose Garcia pulled up in front of the house in a truck loaded with bales of straw. It was the same truck he had used to spirit away the family valuables. This time, it would be the Martinez family which would be hidden in the rear, inside a cave made of wood, surrounded by the straw. Garcia's wife and child, a boy of six, would ride up front with him. The two men quickly loaded the bundles and the children into the hollowed out truck bed, then Maria and Pedro scrambled up. Garcia handed Pedro three small casks known as "cubas" which contained the precious seed, the life's blood of El Pinar, then he replaced the straw bales to seal up the truck.

"Maria," said her husband when they were moving down the road from El Pinar, "we are together, we are safe, and the children are safe." He smoothed back her dark hair and lightly brushed away her tears. "We will survive these troubled times…together. Now, my dearest, keep the children calm. We will be traveling for many hours, and there may be road blocks between us and our destination."

*   *   *   *

Everyone was finally aboard the three fishing boats that Martinez had hired to take the families on to the small key in Florida's extended group of islands at the very end of the United States. From there, they would be met by two buses, and transported to the small Spanish-speaking colony in Miami, where arrangements had been made to house the new arrivals.

To his relief, all three owners of the boats had decided they would not only take the refugees to the United States, but would also take their own families along and stay, if Senor Martinez and the others did not object. They did not, and were actually relieved, since this would insure they would not be given up to the authorities by the fishermen.

After they had brought Martinez and the others from the island to the mainland, just close enough in the darkness for the men to jump overboard and wade to shore, the boat had been joined by two others, and had put back to sea, taking a westerly route around the coast, but keeping well south of the tip of *Guanahacabibes* Peninsula.

They pushed farther west and then turned northerly along the coast, appearing to be fishing as they passed near other fishing boats heading out of *Playa San Pedro* and other coastal villages.

Long hours out from their starting point, their fishing lines out, and traveling slowly to appear to anyone who saw them to be trolling their lines, the boats passed by the barrier islands on the north coast of Cuba, and eventually reached the small harbor at *San Rafael*, there, to await their passengers.

✳   ✳   ✳   ✳

Over several tense hours, the patrons and their charges arrived by cars and trucks and were hidden until the last of the refugees were accounted for. That evening, as the sun fell below the horizon, the boats were loaded and pushed off from the dock.

Traveling slowly to keep the noise of their engines down, the boats pulled slowly away from shore, picking their way through the little islands along the coast and out onto the roiling sea. As it grew darker and the sea and sky merged into one deep shade of blue, then black, the coastline of their homeland disappeared from those standing against the rail. The waves pushed up, and many of the passengers were sickened by the motion of the overloaded boats.

Pedro Martinez was too overcome by the enormity of the decisions he had forced upon his family and friends to notice their discomfort. Cuba was, for the moment, in their past. A place where they would be unwelcome for whatever time it took the Cuban people to get rid of Castro and his henchmen. He was lost in thought. Would they ever come back to the life they knew, or did their future lie to the north, in a country that felt, at this moment, as foreign as any place on earth?

Later, he stood at the rail of the boat looking back to where the place of his birth had been visible only a few hours before. Then, he turned away from where Cuba had been to see, in the dim light of dawn; the coastal islands of Florida begin to appear out of the foggy shadows.

He pulled his children close to his side. "We are almost…home," he said.

CHAPTER 2

▼

7 A.M., 27 September 2002
Atlanta, Georgia

How in hell did I wind up living in a two-room hovel above a bar in Atlanta, Georgia?

It's a good question, one that I ask myself every morning. I mean, there is a very logical explanation, a hundred very clear-cut reasons. And yet I lie in bed with a pillow over my head, a three-day beard on my face, a hangover squeezing my gut, and wonder what went wrong.

My eyes are open, but I'm staring into the pillow pressed tightly against my face, so that the white linen is like a movie screen on which to show my very short life story. *This is a bad idea,* I think to myself.

The official program for the Ohio State University's opening football game of the 1998–99 season, a copy of which I keep in the bottom of a dresser drawer under old socks, listed me as follows:

> THOMAS J. PATRICK: True Freshman, wide receiver, St. Ignatius, Cleveland, Ohio. Height 6'1", Weight 185. "Tommy" brings blazing speed and great hands to the Buckeye receiving corp. The coaching staff sees great things for this record breaking, high school All American.

Pretty cool? The only thing it didn't record was that while going up to catch my first and last pass for the Buckeyes, I would be hit by two very mediocre defensive backs, who would never have had a chance in hell at a pro career. We all came down in the most awkward way possible. Crack…two broken bones, and a destroyed knee in the same leg.

Checkmate. Season over. And, career over.

Sadly, my football-ending injury which left me with a slight limp and a left leg which would never match the right in strength didn't come against our archrival Michigan Wolverines. Oh no, not against Penn State or Iowa. No, I didn't win the big game with my sacrifice. We beat Toledo 49-zip that day in one of those non-conferences, early season, warm-up games that no one remembers. They don't remember me, either, and that may be the worst part. I've always been tough, took a black belt in Karate, boxed three years in the Northeastern Ohio Golden Gloves, all to increase my reactions and hand and foot speed for football. But this was not about being tough, this was about dropping from three feet with my leg exposed to the falling weight of a defensive back. This was about the beginning of pain, and the death of dreams, and I took it hard.

Oh yeah, Atlanta.

Okay, so this is the story. My academic career went the way of my athletic career. I had been a good enough student in high school, and I guess a degree at OSU would have come, in Political Science or Home Economics or something, but my chosen major had been "NFL."

I admit that the life went out of me when the cast went on.

Even slathered in plaster, I found it comforting to visit the campus area bars with great regularity, where I majored in alcoholism, with a minor in "crying in my beer." I knew the location of every watering hole in a mile radius. I did, however, forget the locations of my classes on most days. I found it easy to accept the opinion of the university that I probably didn't need to return for my sophomore year.

Its funny how, once it was decided I would walk but never play football again, my life became progressively lonelier, except for the companionship of my drinking pals. Of course, they would be friends with Hannibal Lecter if he was buying. And, by the way, you become less attractive to the sorority babes, too. Go figure.

Anyhow, in September, when the Buckeyes and every other college team were playing for glory, I was tending bar at my Uncle Jerry's Irish pub in Solon, Ohio, outside Cleveland, and undergoing rehabilitation at the Cleveland Clinic's Sports Medicine Department twice a week.

If you don't know Cleveland, let me tell you, it is the All American City, made up of all the worlds' people. It is an ethnic, hard working place, where grandmas and grandpas came as children years ago, to make their dreams come true. As you might imagine, all these different people settled in neighborhoods that quickly came to resemble the human make up of their former countries. Dad's people settled west of downtown in the Irish community, and mom's parents settled and raised six kids to the east along Murray Hill, in the area called "Little Italy."

In one of those strange twists of fate, these two people of diverse backgrounds, both first generation Americans, got together during the summer of '72 at Geauga Lake, an amusement park south of town. According to my dad, it was his charming, Irish ways, which had won my mother's heart. His friends always said that she must have been a glutton for punishment to pick him for a boyfriend.

So, they fell in love and married soon after. Dad had followed his father onto the Cleveland police force two years earlier, and mom had three kids in the first six years of marriage, me being the last of the brood.

My brother, Patrick, was the first football star in the family, followed by a much better looking me six years later, when I followed him to Columbus. My sister Rosie's claim to fame was that she hated boys until she was ten years old, and then quickly changed her mind.

Anyway, so I'm back in Cleveland, living the life of luxury in my old bedroom, drinking too much and doing too little, feeling sorry for myself, and unable to watch a football game on TV.

One Monday, I was working the day shift at Jerry's and business was pretty slow. More time for me to sneak a little drinky-poo. The few daytime regulars were sitting around at their usual places at the bar. I sat on a stool as far away as possible, so as to not involve myself in their musings on the latest college games.

Staring at, but not reading the comics in the *Cleveland Plain Dealer*, I was able to reduce their conversation to a droning buzz in my ears until the words "Ohio State" were blurted out by some unfeeling swine. Immediately, the buzz became an achingly clear roar, like it was coming out of earphones glued to my head.

My uncle walked in the front door, took in the scene, and came over to my little island.

Jerry: "So, boyo, you look like a man who has found his life's work."

Boyo: "How can you tell?"

Jerry: "Come on, kid, you're miserable here! I can get anyone to pump beer. You need to get out of here and do something with your life!"

Boyo: "Join me in a shot?"

Things went on that way for a while. I was going nowhere fast, although I had recovered enough strength to begin working out. The limp eased, but was never going to disappear. Dad took his shot at getting me interested in law enforcement, which didn't seem right for a guy with my obvious talents. As you might expect, it was my mother, who started the process of straightening my ass out.

She was waiting up for me one Friday night as I returned from several hours of drinking with my pals. I always seemed to drink a little harder the night before the weekend football games.

I came in bleary eyed and making more noise than necessary at 2 a.m. She was sitting at the kitchen table in semi-darkness, as all Italians do when they have something important to discuss.

I stumbled through the kitchen door in search of cold water, saw her sitting there, tried very hard to ignore her presence, poured and swallowed a whole glass in one gulp. I noticed that my father had had the good sense to go to bed, and leave the dismantling of his problem child to his wife.

"You look tired (drunk)," Concetta Rose Patrick said. I mumbled something even I didn't understand, but she let it pass. "Sit down." Dark eyes bored through me. She is still a beautiful woman, I know, and very intelligent, and most men can't resist the opportunity to be in her presence. Uncle Jerry, three years my father's senior, had been the first to be blindsided by her jet black hair, deep brown eyes, and inner strength, and welcome her to the bosom of the family. Best guess, he had been speaking with her about his nephew's propensity for getting shit-faced of late.

Mom got up and poured a cup of hot black coffee for me and topped off her own cup, while I waited miserably for what would come next.

"Thomas," she started, "everyone has a right to feel sorry for their self for a while, but you cannot live like that forever." I made to speak, but she put her hand on mine, and went on. "You are not going to play football anymore. You are not going to be in the Museum of the Best......"

"Aah......Hall of Fame," I said, trying to build a sickly defense.

"......and your father is not going to be the chief of police or the mayor. But he is a good man, and a good policeman," she said with obvious pride. "What he does is important. It is time for you to take your place in society and do something with your life."

I burped, loudly.

"Or, at least, *pretend* to be among the living," Mom said, with a bemused look on her face as she rose from her chair and smacked me lightly on the head with the dish towel that always seemed to be in her hand. "Don't annoy me, Thomas."

"I don't want to be a cop," I said forcefully, but without conviction.

"Did I say you should be a policeman?" Then slowly, "You could go back to school." My silence answered her. But she was busy making me a sandwich of cold, sliced eggplant, smothered in tomato sauce, and grated cheese, which I didn't believe for a minute I would be able to get down. She was quiet until she returned to the table with the food. "You're going to Atlanta," she said suddenly and decisively. "Your brother and Charlotte June need help with the restaurant."

I stared at her, dumbstruck. "Excuse me? I must have blacked out for a minute there."

"You heard me." She was reflective. "I think you need to be away from here. It's too close to your pain, Thomas." And then she continued in a brighter tone, "Besides, they have a good business there for you to help out at until you get started."

"Ma, get started at what?" I was not believin this conversation. I could almost feel the alcohol bleeding out through my pores, but I was sobering up fast.

"The restaurant is your brother's business," she went on as if I had never spoken. "You need a career of your own." She pushed the untouched sandwich away from me and took a piece of paper out of the breast pocket of her housedress. She laid it in front of me. I tried to unscramble my eyes and bring the print into focus.

"Private Investigator? Private…what, you want me to carry a gun? You want me to go to this community college and get a license to be a Private Investigator?! So I can take pictures of guys cheating on their wives? *This,* is the career you want for me? Jesus, Ma, where did this come from?" I wanted to say this in a loud and belligerent voice, but my throat was suddenly very dry, and I hardly got the words out.

"Don't swear," she said. "They have other courses of study at this school, but this would be good for you! You have policemen in your family, so it's in your blood," she said, as if this statement made perfect sense.

"Ma," I said, "blue eyes are in your blood! Black hair is in your blood! Being a policeman is *not* in your blood!"

She ignored me some more. "Thomas, you need to do this."

I suddenly began to feel very small. "Ma," I said again, "you want to throw me out?"

"No, of course not," she said in a soothing voice, the same one she used when I had been an injured child in pain. "I want you to find yourself. And you will always be close to me, here." She placed her hand on her heart.

I picked up the square of paper and stared at it as if some life-changing answer was going to pop up and fix this. "Private Eye?"

Five months later, PI license in hand and a .38 caliber hand gun, which I supposed someday I would wear on my person, but for now was kept in the locked glove compartment of my '89 Ford pickup, I was on my way down I-77 through West Virginia to Charlotte, North Carolina. There I would pick up I-85 to Atlanta, to a room above Pat Patrick's "Ireland's Own" Pub.

So I'm here, what, thirteen-fourteen months now, got my license to operate as a private investigator in Georgia and my little business has seen six cases of little consequence and less money. So, I continue to live in and operate from, two small rooms overlooking Peachtree Street, above Pat's bar in the nightclub zone of Atlanta, known as Buckhead. It's a ritzy area of expensive homes, apartment complexes, massive office buildings, restaurants, and bars of every style and class and high-class hotels. Atlanta really has a string of three downtown areas, and Buckhead, stretching toward Atlanta's wealthy northern suburbs, is the fun one.

I work more hours at the bar than I do as a PI, but I meet, and even date, some of the gorgeous Georgia Peaches who frequent the establishment. Pat gives me whatever time I need off to allow me to cover whatever small amount of PI business I dig up, although not without some good-natured grousing concerning my "flex schedule." Not so bad.

Until the morning. Every morning, I still wonder if this is where I'm supposed to be. At least I don't see myself in a football uniform whenever I look in the mirror anymore.

My pillow/movie screen fades to black as a yell penetrates my subconscious.

"Hey, asshole!" That's how my brother pronounces "Thomas."

"Y'all get down here, man. We got work to do!"

Y'all? Pat has become a southerner quickly. He had some pretty good help. My brother met Charlotte June Hemphill, of the West Paces Ferry Road Hemphill's during his fifth and last year as a linebacker with the Falcons. She is as close to the ideal of the southern belle as one can imagine; beautiful, smart, a great mom to the twins, and, I think, the brains behind the business. Don't tell Pat I said so, although I expect he knows it.

The Falcon players were involved in a children's cancer research event at the Scottish Rite Hospital, in Atlanta. Charlotte's family was one of the sponsors of the annual three-day program, and she was serving as a hostess the night of the dinner dance finale.

Pat saw her across the room, and he was immediately dazed and demented. They danced every dance and were inseparable from then on. It took me and the rest of the family a full five minutes to fall in love with her, the first time Pat brought her to Cleveland. It probably took slightly longer for the Hemphill clan to accept the Yankee footballer, but things had evened out by the time he gave up the game to open the restaurant and become a "legitimate" Southern businessman. At six-five, two fifty, a very *big* Southern businessman.

Anyway, having been screamed at by the owner of Georgia's premier Irish bar and grill, the time has come to put aside wistful thoughts and return to my main employment, which consists mostly of dragging cases of beer up from the basement storeroom. On good days I get to stock the coolers.

CHAPTER 3

▼

A half hour later, I was getting dressed in the little bathroom which made up the third room of my "suite," when there was a knock at the door.

"Hey, Yankee Tom, you decent?" The sweet voice of the very lovely Charlotte June. I smiled to myself. A great way to start the day. Patrick is a very lucky man.

"Yeah," I yelled back. "But give me a minute, and I'll get naked!"

"Oh, yuck! Naked Yankee skin is quite upsetting to us Scarlett O'Hara types." came back through the door. I heard C.J., as she is known to all except for my mom who still calls her by her first and middle names, come in. I finished dressing in jeans and a golf shirt, and came out of the bathroom to greet her.

She was sitting at my two-seater kitchen table. As usual, she was impeccably dressed in white slacks, blue, sleeveless top, open-toed pumps, perfect hair and that beautiful face. On the table sat a soup dish containing two huge biscuits ladled over with steaming, creamy white, sausage gravy. An Irish pub doesn't serve biscuits and gravy, so I knew this was home made. It looked delicious, and I was suddenly very hungry.

"Jeeesus!" I said with a horrified look on my face. "How do you people live over twenty years eating that crap every day?" It was an old joke between us. She knew I'd be wolfing the food down in less than a minute.

"Yankee Tom," she said in an exaggerated southern drawl, "this 'crap' as you call it, is the reason we have such longevity in the South. That stuff is the glue that keeps our body parts from falling right off. With the help of mint juleps, that is." We both laughed. Like everyone else, I'm very comfortable with this woman. It's not that she reminds me of mom, except that there is that solidness there, that is very reassuring. *Life will work out, somehow.*

I kissed her on her cheek and sat down across from her. "Girl, where were you when I was looking for the love of my life?"

"Hell, boy, I was planning my coming-out cotillion when you were in short pants!"

"There's only six years' difference between us," I retorted. "Besides, I like older women, long as their not, you know, drooping." I gave her an appraising look and did a Groucho with my eyebrows. "You could have waited for me to grow up. Instead, you wound up with that big lug brother of mine."

The bell-like laugh came easily. "True," she said. "He is a big lug, but he has his good points. Besides, Yankee Tom," she said, wistfully, "you will never grow up!"

"Jeez, I hope not," I said. I like when she calls me 'Yankee Tom'. It's much better than what her husband calls me. I dug into the biscuits, making sure to sop up as much gravy as possible with each bite. "How are the kids, Big Foot and Monster Boy?"

"Don't you dare insult my future Pro Bowlers," she laughed. "They just love their Uncle 'Yankee Tom' to death, and you insult them 'cause they're a little big for their age! But, since you asked, they're fine. Grew a foot taller overnight, as usual. I took them over to my Mama's while I run a few errands this morning."

I looked at my watch. 8:20 a.m. "This is weird," I said. "The lug hasn't yelled for the hired help to come to work."

"I told him growing boys have to eat. Anyway, I think he is satisfied that he can work you to death all afternoon. How's the private eye business going?"

"Slow," I said. "Actually, let me rephrase that. It's a good thing this palatial palace is free, or I'd be living with you."

"Uh uh, bud. I have one too many children in my house, now. Three kids, to be precise, including your brother. Besides," she said, "it will happen, if you just give it time." She watched me for a reaction. Then C.J. said, "You believe that, don't you?"

"Honestly? I don't know." I answered. "I'm trying my best, but I see what Pat has, and I can't figure where I go from here, sis."

"Hey, Tom," she said sternly. "You caught a bad break! We all know where you would have been a few years from now if you hadn't gotten hurt. That doesn't make you a 'lost child' like my little brother, Bobby. This isn't about what Pat has, or what you expected to have. It just means you are going to do something else, just as great. Got it?"

"Yeah," I smiled. "Got it."

"Good. Besides," she said, her eyes twinkling. "Luckiest thing to happen to the big lug was me."

She watched me finish the food. "By the way," she said with a sly smile, "I've got a friend I'd like you to meet."

I pushed the dish away from me and leaned back in my cheap chrome and plastic chair. "Come on, sis, you're not playing matchmaker again, are you?" I rolled my eyes. "You remember what your last friend looked like?" I puffed out my cheeks like a blowfish.

"Come on, yourself," she laughed. "There is no such thing as an unattractive Southern girl."

"Uh huh. Besides, you know I lost interest in all women when you went off the market."

"I'm sure you did, you poor thing."

"Actually," I said seriously, "I've been kinda' seeing someone. But right now we're just good friends."

"Do tell," she said in a surprised tone. "Details, please!"

"No, really, I like her. In fact, I like her a whole lot, but it's just friends for now. In fact, I haven't seen her in a few days. She's nice. It hasn't really been a *date* thing. Mostly I see her at the pub, but we've had a few dinners together. She comes in with her roommates from Tech."

"Well, Romeo, I'm excited for you! I guess I'll just keep my friend in reserve."

"And, I guess I better go downstairs and earn my keep," I said, feeling strangely uncomfortable.

CHAPTER 4

▼

4 P.M. 27 September 2002

Ireland's Own opens at 10:30 in the morning and does a decent lunch business, but it's happy hour, the late night crowd, and weekend party animals that puts the big bucks in the till.

The place seats around a hundred and fifty, but on the best nights, the fire department allows about two hundred elbow-benders at a time. On Friday and Saturday nights, there is every bit that many customers inside, and a line waiting outside. The food is standard American bar menu with burgers, steaks, sandwiches, salads and more, with a smattering of dishes from the "auld sod" of Ireland, like lamb stew, Scottish eggs, which are hardboiled eggs encased in ground sausage and deep-fried, corned beef and cabbage, and the like. Sixty beers from around the world, a decent, affordable wine list, and good food, works. My brother and C.J. have done it right.

This Friday night was typically busy up and down the Buckhead strip. It's an interesting place. The north end of Buckhead is filled with high-end shopping and expensive hotels and restaurants. Also, some of the most expensive housing in Atlanta surrounds the area. The mid-section, where Ireland's Own resides is loaded with sophisticated, expensive restaurants adjacent to middle-of-the-road Yuppie fern bars, which are next to twenty-something, brew 'n barf establishments. The southern tip, an area of more useful, everyday shopping for the area residents, leads into the "Midtown" area of theatres, the symphony, and museums, with loads of condos' and lofts. At the south end of midtown is the true downtown of Atlanta. Monster office buildings run throughout all three areas, and through the center of it all, like an artery carrying life's blood, is Peachtree Street.

I was working the main bar along with Freddy Neil and Robby Sedgwick. Every bar stool was filled, as were all the tables I could see. It's standing room only. Pat was in the office, a small room off the kitchen. People were coming in as fast as others left. It's a completely different atmosphere than Jerry's place in Solon, what with all the noisy, happy, well-off patrons doing their best to party 'til 4 a.m. every weekend.

That's the way it is tonight. Since Georgia Tech's campus is just a few miles away and, with a home game coming up tomorrow, we were being inundated with alumni in town for the game. Georgia has two major universities: the Tech campus, here in Atlanta, and the University of Georgia, located about sixty miles away, in Athens. Like Michigan State-Michigan or Virginia-Virginia Tech, the yearly game between the Georgia schools, even though they are in different sports conferences, is the big game for bragging rights. But this Saturdays' games are warm ups for that match up later this season, so most of the college crowd tonight is made up of Tech fans.

I had just delivered some appetizers to a couple at the bar when a seat opened up, and Bobby Hemphill grabbed it and signaled for a beer. C.J.'s younger brother is about five ten, rail thin, handsome enough with dark wavy hair, and with just a touch of his big sister around the eyes. A good guy but, at twenty-one years old, he reminds me of myself, a little lost and unsure of what comes next. Lately, he has been bugging me about taking him on and 'teaching' him the PI business. I knew what was coming even before I delivered his Coors.

"Hey, Columbo! What's doin' man?" He is pink faced and red eyed, and speaking loudly. This wasn't his first stop tonight.

"That's 'O'Columbo' to you, sport." I said. No laugh, not even a smile. Over his head. I tried again. "How've you been, Bobby?"

"Okay, I guess. Hey, I been waiting to hear from you, Tommy." Bobby was slurring his words a bit and repeating himself, which is not a good sign. "You think about it? I wanna come work with you, man. I can get a license like you, you know. Have a career, like you!"

I went over to the cooler to grab some brews for a group of guys who were standing on the other side of the bar stools, waiving money at me to get my attention. "Bobby," I said when I came back, "look at me, man." I waited until a thought he might actually be listening. "Bobby, I'm working behind a bar. I've no idea if I can ever get this to work for me. How am I going to hire you or any one else?" Bobby looked down at his empty beer bottle. I sighed and got him another. "Hey," I said getting close to him to get his attention. "Hey, you hearing me, Bobby?"

He pulled a big swig. "Yeah, I hear you." He was getting sullen, now. This would not be the last time we have this conversation. I'd do anything for C.J., but egging on her lost little brother about a nonexistent job wouldn't be doing anyone a favor. I figured I'd better try to mellow him out a bit, and monitor his alcohol intake too, at least as long as he was here.

"Besides, I thought your sister said you were going back to school, right?" Bobby had spent a few messy semesters at Georgia State, a predominantly day school, but one undergoing a growth spurt into a major university. He looked at me and smiled unpleasantly.

"You have any idea, man," he said, "how a Harvard graduate, 'big time' attorney father, a Smith educated mother, and a highly educated, model gorgeous sister look down on the son who barely made it into a state school, quits, and still doesn't know what he's doin' three years later?" His head hung down, again.

"Hey, come on, man. I mean I don't know your folks that well, but no way C.J. looks down on you! Besides, an education is an education." I know this better than most. "You should go back. Don't worry about what anyone else thinks. Bobby."

"Shit, that's easy for you to say!" Not so easy, really. "Nothin' ever goes my way. Your folks don't think you're an asshole," he said, in a whiney voice. "Tommy, think about it, okay? I'd be good at this, man, I know it!"

"Sure. Okay, Bobby, I'll think about it, but no promises. Okay, Bobby?" I said again. I was lying, but I had no more patience for this conversation. I moved away. A few minutes later when I went back to the other end of the bar, Bobby Hemphill was gone, a twenty-dollar bill on the bar all that was left of him.

*　　*　　*　　*

About 11 p.m., three coeds from Tech came in, and grabbed a table in full view of the bar. One was the girl I had mentioned to C.J. a few days earlier up in my room. I noticed their entrance because I had been watching for Abby Barrett, and hoping she would be with her girl friends, and not some guy and my heart fluttered happily when I saw her. We had talked off and on for a few months when she came in to the bar before finally meeting for lunch once or twice in the last month. Three weeks ago, we had our first real, if necessarily cheap, date. I enjoyed her company. Abby is petite, maybe five foot five, with a lovely shape and very pretty.

Abby is very smart and easy to be around. She has jet-black hair and a clear, creamy complexion. Abby is beautiful, and appears to actually find me attractive, too.

She immediately sought me out with her dark eyes and offered me a beautiful smile. I smiled back and felt a warm tingle. Abby excused herself from the table and came over to the bar. "Hey, Thomas," she said, simply. Her voice was melodic and soft.

"Hey, Abby. How you doing?" Smooth. But I quickly got comfortable. I was very glad to see her, and I wanted her to know it.

"Sorry I've been out of touch," she said, although I had no intention of asking why I hadn't heard from her in almost a week. "I had to take a few days off from school to travel with my mom."

"Just get back?" I brought her a glass of chardonnay that I knew she liked.

"Yeah," she said, a bit distractedly, not offering where she had been. "Just some family stuff we had to do." She brightened. "So, how are you? Been busy?"

"So—so," I said, thankful that the bar trade had slowed down enough for Freddy and Robby to handle it, and free me up to spend a minute with her. I leaned on the bar and tried to look into her beautiful eyes without appearing to stare. "You look great." I was wishing I had the money to take this girl out for a real dinner—maybe the Dining Room at the Ritz Carleton or, maybe, Seeger's.

I can't honestly say I know Abby all that well, but she had hooked me from the first time I saw her. I had waited on her table, passing a smile, then later, exchanging a few words, then longer talks at the bar which were often interrupted as I took care of other customers. She was still there whenever I could come back to her.

We met outside the bar for the first time at the Varsity, the famous, and gigantic, drive-in across the interstate from the Georgia Tech campus, downtown. The chili dogs and burgers are great and, although a cheap place to eat, it's acceptable for a date because of its location and varied clientele of students, ageing alumni, businessmen, tourists, and locals.

She had time to kill between classes; she's a Junior, studying architectute, which makes me feel a little inferior, but she is so down to earth that she puts me at ease, and we had a very pleasant hour and a half together.

I learned that she has a brother and sister, and that her father died in a car accident when she was ten. She is very close to her mom and the other kids in the family, both of which are younger than her. I tell her my life story, and Abby is surprised that I'm working at Ireland's Own while trying to get my little business off the ground. While I'm talking, her face is being burned into my memory.

Subsequent dates were even better as we started to feel more and more comfortable around each other. I find that I think about her a lot when I don't see her or talk to her for a few days. "Anything wrong? With your family, I mean?"

She thinks about this for a second. "No, it's taken care of, for now. It's really not worth talking about." Abby changes the subject. "Are you working until closing?" She asked the question briskly.

"Actually, I'm off in about twenty minutes. Can you stick around for a drink?"

"Sure," she said. "But I was wondering if we could maybe go up to your place." Abby put her hand on my arm and gave me a shy smile. I was surprised by her suggestion, but not stupid enough to show it. I wasn't completely sure that I understood what she was suggesting, but I wasn't about to ask, either. Besides, I wanted very much to be alone with this girl. I nodded, afraid my voice would crack if I spoke. Abby Barrett slid off the seat and, giving me a last, sidelong look over her shoulder, rejoined her friends to await the end of my shift.

*   *   *   *

Later that night we stood in the center of my room, struggling to get each others' clothes off. I kissed her forehead, her lips, her neck, her shoulder, and lower as she tore at the buttons of my shirt. The smell of her hair and skin was intoxicating and, as I got her shirt and bra off, I stood back for a moment to look at her. Her breasts were perfect, the color of fresh cream with a rosy glow around her hard nipples. She had wide, strong shoulders that tapered down to her tiny waist. Her skin was flawless. Abby stared up at me as I took in her beauty, and slowly unbuckled her form fit jeans and let them drop to the floor.

I couldn't believe she was standing in front of me like this. I wanted to say something to her, but I was tongue-tied. She stepped out of the jeans and moved up against me, and we kissed again. I could feel her fumbling with my belt, then my zipper. Abby's hands were working quickly, as if she desperately needed this intimacy. I chose to believe it was me and me alone, that she wanted. I couldn't get enough of her, and when she looked at me and softly said, "Tommy?" I took her by the hand and led her to the bed, hoping she wouldn't notice that the maid hadn't been in. As it turned out, neither of us cared how the room looked.

For a long time, we kissed and touched, exploring each other as first time lovers do. She gave herself to me openly and passionately. For the first time in my life, I felt I was making *love* to someone. It was very different, very exciting, and emotionally exhausting.

Eventually, we drifted off to sleep, although my mind was so full of her, I can't swear to having slept deeply. In a while, I felt Abby move against me, and I came awake. She slid on top of me. My face was instantly hot, and I felt myself responding to the weight of her. She straddled me and guided me into her body again. It was almost as if I was living in a dream. In time, I felt myself tense again, and then the sudden, excruciating release came. Abby, her skin glistening and hot against my chest, reached up and gave me one last, long kiss, and slid off me to lie in the crook of my arm. I fell into a coma-like sleep.

In the morning, she was gone.

CHAPTER 5

▼

30 September 2002

My brother's friend and attorney, Max Howard, occasionally threw me some mercy work which was much appreciated. I spent Monday up in Hall County, traveling up I-85 north of Atlanta, digging up some background info for a case Max's firm, Howard, Jones & Axelrod, had pending against a nursing home operator.

Max had set up two meetings for me with former employees of the Crystal Harbor Nursing Home, who had come forward after the suit had been filed. My job was to meet with these two almost certainly, disgruntled people and asked them a list of questions prepared by Max' firm. The place is located on a finger cove of Lake Lanier, and the claims against the owner were concerning the loved ones of four families who had suffered severe injuries while in the home's care. I thought it might make sense to check in with some of the local agencies, maybe the sheriffs' office, to see if there were any other kinds of complaints about the home on file.

Max Howard had thrown other work my way. Little stuff, for sure, but I hadn't come to him with a raft of sterling references, either. I was happy for the work, and I appreciated his generosity. I wanted to do a good job. My pickup was sounding its age, but it got me out to the Crystal Harbor Nursing Home. I had decided to stop there before interviewing the former employees, just to get a feel for the place.

Before doing so, I called Abby's apartment on my pre-paid cell phone. I hadn't seen or heard from her since my night with her. No answer. It was the fifth or sixth time I'd called in two days. I was wondering if she had come to her senses, thinking about how she had ever wound up sleeping with a bartender.

It was a crisp early autumn day, but the leaves were still very green, and they hung tight to the tree limbs. It would be November before there was a big change in the scenery. The grounds looked well cared for, but there were few cars in the lot located on the east side of the building. No one was outside. I pulled into a space and got out.

I was dressed in tan slacks and a pullover sweater. I figured I looked inconspicuous enough and decided to take a look around before going inside. I walked along the side of the low rise, clapboard structure. There were tiny windows spaced evenly, maybe ten or twelve feet apart along the wall. I was probably walking along a wall of patients' rooms. At the rear of the building, a pretty panorama opened up, with pathways meandering down to a little dock by the water. Lanier is a major reservoir for the metro Atlanta area, and is over thirty-five thousand acres. It is dotted with expensive houses and marinas. This is a very valuable piece of land that this building is sitting on.

The day was perfect; about seventy-two degrees and clear, but the grounds were empty of people. The place was tomb quiet. You would expect to see patients out there, enjoying the fresh air, but there was no one around. I walked down the slight hill to the water, maybe a hundred fifty feet from the nursing home building. There was a dock at the shoreline, and the water looked deep enough for a sailboat with a three or four foot draft, but the cove was empty. The water was dark, but placid.

Overall, it was a very pleasant spot, very quiet, with million dollar views. I could imagine retiring to a spot like this, but the idea of being dependent on someone else for a chance to enjoy it leaves me cold. And then there is the neglect, poor nutrition, the open sores, broken bones suffered in needless falls; the very things I was investigating for Max. And all the while, checks sent by families who thought they were doing right by their elders. A sad situation. And, then there is the infirm and aged who were parked here by families who could no longer be bothered, or worse, were financially unable, to care for them.

I shivered a bit with that thought and headed back up toward the building. I got about thirty steps up the hill when I found myself face to face with a tall, older man wearing blue coveralls. He was nearly bald, with scraggly long tendrils of hair around his ears, and a little slovenly in appearance. He was carrying a pickaxe slung up on his shoulder. He may have been as surprised to see me as I was to see him, but he didn't show it.

"You lost, sonny?' His voice was cigarette gravelly with a heavy southern accent, a real country boy. He turned his head and spit noisily.

"Uh, no, no I was just looking over the place," I tried to keep my voice steady and act as if my being here was the most natural thing imaginable. "I'm checking out homes, you know? I'm looking for a place to put my granddad. I'm Bob Perry." I stuck out my hand.

He seemed to relax a little, but didn't offer a name back, letting the nametag on the soiled blue shirt that said "J.T." speak for him, I guess. I saw no reason to tell this guy what I was doing here. I dropped my hand.

"What's wrong with him?" He asked the question like it was his right to ask, and pulled out a half-empty pack of unfiltered Camels. I didn't know they still sold those things.

"Sorry? Oh, just old age," I said. He didn't offer me a smoke. "This place comes highly recommended."

He laughed a short bark of a laugh. "What dumb-ass told you that?" Interesting response.

I took the plunge. "You disagree? You work here, don't you?" I waited a moment to see if he would bite, but he just stood there. "I was told about this place by a doctor..."

"Musta' been Rogers, maybe Doc Ebersol," he interrupted. Was I on to something? Why would a handyman know so much about doctors who sent patients to Crystal Harbor?

I walked up the hill a bit until I was on the same level with him. I kept the conversation going. "Yeah, Rogers," I said. "Was he wrong?"

"That old fool is always sending folks here, but, shit, he ain't been here himself for two, maybe three years. I always figured he had some deal with old man Kline, or some such. Mighta' been okay here when the old man run the place." He took a long drag on the Camel and coughed out the blue smoke.

"You're saying I should look elsewhere?" I tried to keep his attention without seeming to be too nosy.

"I'm sayin' people don't do too well here bub, since Junior took over." Another drag on the cigarette, "Folk's been known to get hurt...or worse."

I feigned surprise. "Pretty strong accusations, don't you think? I doubt your boss would like hearing you say stuff like that!"

"Fuuuck hiiim," he said, dragging the words out. "He's planning to close the place anyways." Was this news? If Max knew about this, he hadn't mentioned it.

"Why's he closing it down?" I pressed.

"Too many questions bein' asked," he said. "Anyways, this land's too valuable for a nursin' home. Nope, they ain't takin' any new customers, sonny. Best look elsewhere, I was you." He tossed away the butt, not bothering to put it out, and seemed to lose interest in me.

"Thanks," I said, and moved on up the hill. I didn't think anyone inside the building was going to help me out better than my new friend, so I decided to stop back later and go check out the former employees first.

* * * *

Jack Martin lived about a half hour away from Crystal Harbor and he was waiting for me when I got to his place. The house was small and pretty beat up, maybe two bedrooms, once a cream color by the looks of it. Probably about thirty years old.

"Come in," he said without introductions, as if he didn't want anyone to see him talking with me. I walked into a shabby room with even shabbier furniture. The stale odor of thousands of smoked cigarettes hung in the air. Martin was tall, about six two, maybe forty, a heavy, full head of medium brown hair. He was unshaven and wearing an open checkered shirt over a dirty white tee, and jeans. A jury would hate the looks of this guy.

He seemed prepped for what I was doing here and started talking without preamble from me. "This guy, Junior? He's bad news."

"Hold on, Mr. Martin," I said. "Junior is Henry Kline, the owner of Crystal Harbor Nursing Home, right?"

"Yeah, him. His old man turned it over to him a couple a years ago. Senior died last year."

"And, you understand that I'm a private investigator working for an attorney named Maxwell Howard, who is suing Crystal Harbor on behalf of the families of four patients' who were injured there?" I wanted to be sure Martin could never say he had been deceived by my questions.

"Shit," Martin said, sliding into a brown velour recliner. "Just four? Hell, I seen lotsa' old folks gettin' hurt around there. Even had one or two die for no reason at all, you know?" He was quiet, and I let him alone a minute to collect his thoughts. "Just neglected, and it's a damn shame," he said, almost to himself. He got up and left the room.

I heard the refrigerator door open and close. He returned and handed me a beer, taking a swig from his own new bottle. I put mine on the table next to the couch without drinking, but he didn't seem to notice.

"Mr. Martin," I said, breaking the silence. "Why did you leave your job at Crystal Harbor?"

He sat upright in the chair, and his face reddened. "I didn't leave, I was fired. Junior fired me after ten years, 'cause I was complainin' about what was going on."

I wasn't sure whether he was mad or embarrassed. "He says you were drunk and didn't do your job."

"He can fuckin' lie all he wants," he said with conviction and more than a little anger. "I seen what I seen mister."

For the next half hour, I read off names of patients and Jack Martin told me what he knew. It matched up with the complaints of the patients' families. Then he gave me the names of other patients that I should contact. He even volunteered the names of nursing home employees that he said were responsible for many of the injuries. "I'm tellin' you, man, that asshole Junior, he's bad news." I left with more information than I had expected.

My next stop was the home of Jose Arroya. On the way over to his house, I called Abby's apartment again. Three more times, but there was still no answer.

*   *   *   *

Arroya was a short, squat, Mexican immigrant. He lived on a dead end road near, but not on, the lake. Another older dwelling, but, unlike Jack Martin's place, it was evident Mr. Arroya took pride in his home. He was working on his small porch, replacing some flooring planks when I pulled up. I guessed he was about Martin's age, but his work clothes were clean, his face shaved except for a moustache which matched this jet black, wavy hair.

A woman of about the same age, also Mexican, came around the corner of the house as I got out of the truck. She was plain clothed but neat as a pin. His wife, I figured. She saw me, looked at her husband, and walked into the front door of the house, never saying a word to me. Jose Arroya stood, put down the hammer he was holding tightly in his hand, and, with great dignity, walked out to meet me.

I offered my business card and we shook hands. His grip was strong, and his hand felt calloused and dry. "Mr. Max, he sent you here, yes?"

I nodded.

He motioned me to the porch and his wife met us with a tray of iced sweet tea, the "wine of the south," which is served everywhere.

Arroya gave me time to thank the silent woman and sip some tea while he studied my card. She quietly went back into the house and left us alone and I took out my little notebook.

"You want to know about the old ones," he said. "There were many, senor. There were many who were treated very bad. Senor Kline, he let the others take care of the old ones. He don' come to the home too much anymore."

"The others," I stopped him. "You mean the nurses and assistants who worked there?"

"Si, senor, the nurses, they are all men. They could be very hard on the people when they need too much help, like, you know, maybe they, uh…soil themselves, or they cannot eat by themselves." He watched me for a reaction. "These men, they can be very bad," he said again.

I asked Arroya questions about some of the particulars reported to the law firm by the families. He was able to confirm some, but not all. He had started working at the home almost fourteen years ago for the senior Mr. Kline. Arroya, like Jack Martin, also thought highly of the old man, but thought very little of the present operator. "I work there sometime at night," he went on, "you know, after the *horas de visita,* the, how you say…visiting hours, are done. This, senor, is when the people were at great risk."

"Why would Mr. Kline let these things happen?"

"Senor Junior," Arroya made a face, "he don' care about these people! This was his father's life. He don' want it, ever." He stopped and thought a minute, as if deciding to tell me something else, I waited. "I work there one night. I see these men, three men, come at eleven at night. No one comes so late. They go to the office and knock on the closed door. I don' even know Senor Junior is still there, 'cause he never there so late anymore. But he is there. He open the door and the men, they go in."

"How long were they inside the office?" I asked.

"Oh, it was a long time, senor. In a while, I hear them, they are talking very loud, and then, I here many shouts. They argue. They are very mad. My work is near the office, and I hear this!"

"Did you hear what they were saying? Did you know any of them?"

"No, senor, I don' know them, and not clear so that I know what they say." Arroya looked as if he wanted to say he was sorry. I didn't want to ask the obvious question about being able to recognize them if he were to see them again.

"What happened then, Mr. Arroya?"

He thought a minute. "This was very strange, senor. The men, they come out with Senor Junior. They see me there, and Senor Junior, he look very mad that I am there. The next day, I am told my job, she is no longer needed. I cannot work there no more!" He stopped, looking sad and confused. "I work very hard," he said, "I know I do my job well. But they give me twenty five hundred dollars, and I am told to leave. I don' even see Senor Junior no more."

"Then who let you go?" I asked.

"Senorita Ellen," he said. This was a new name to me, and I made a note.

"She is the *directora adjunta,* the manager, you say. I think," he said slowly, "that Senor Junior, he and Senorita Ellen, they very close!" He lifted an eyelid, and I had to smother a smile. "She was very nice, but she says 'Jose, you cannot work here no more.' Just so," he looked back toward the door to his house. "My Rosa, she is very sad for me. She know I work very hard to do my job." He paused. "She is very sad for me."

I asked a few other questions while already putting my notes on today's events in order in my head and got up to leave. I shook hands with Jose Arroya and headed for my truck. "Senor," he said behind me, and I turned. "There is a man," he said, "his name, he says, is John Edwards. He is new at the home, maybe eight months. He is a very bad man, senor. He is responsible for much trouble there." Arroya looked around as if expecting this Edwards to come around the corner. "This man, he would be very angry to know I tell you this. Be careful, Senor Patrick." I smiled my thanks, and tried to hide the slight shiver that went up my spine.

CHAPTER 6

▼

I stopped at the Hall County sheriff's office in Gainesville on my way south to Atlanta, but there were no records or warrants outstanding on any John Edwards. Max Howard might want to investigate him more, but I had basically completed my assignment. The former employees definitely had information pertinent to the case, and they would probably pass muster in court. Chances are, this thing never makes it to court, as there is definitely something going on at Crystal Harbor. Junior Kline wasn't going to want to let this thing fester.

At least for now, there is no way to put too much emphasis on Jack Martin's comment about "some dying," unless some other family member came forward with questions about a loved one's death. But, that's Max's call. My best guess is that Kline is more interested in becoming a seller of commercial real estate.

I was much more concerned about Abby. Our night together had embedded her in my mind and heart which, it appeared, might mean I took it much more seriously than she had. Why else would she have gone silent?

I tried her phone twice more before arriving in Buckhead. I parked in the lot behind Ireland's Own, and headed up to my room. It was two hours before my shift, so I computerized my notes on the PC Max had loaned me, including my chance meeting with J.T. on the grounds of Crystal Harbor. I called Max, but he wasn't in, so I took a shower and changed into fresh jeans and shirt. Being that Max was a regular, I figured he might be in tonight, so I put my notes in a brown envelope and took them downstairs with me and stashed them behind the bar.

The place was full of customers and Pat was helping bus tables. C.J., the kids, and her mom and dad were having dinner at one of the riser tables along the wall.

Bobby Hemphill was conspicuous in his absence. I had a few minutes before my shift, so I walked over to the table to say hello.

As I approached, Charlotte June and her parents all shouted "Hey!" at the same time. 'Hey!' is the universal greeting in the South. It is cheery, genderless, and absolutely does away with the need to remember anyone's name. I think they even put it on cemetery headstones, as in "Hey!—1920–2000." It's the Great Southern Equalizer.

I answered, "Hey!" and didn't feel the least bit silly, and took a chair. Monster Boy was on me in a minute while Big Foot slept away against his grandma's shoulder.

The twins, real names being Taylor, for the Deep South side of the family, and Timothy, for the Irish side, are three years old and great little guys, but big for their age. Grandma is a tiny thing, but she handles the little porker like he is weightless.

I sat there with Taylor on my lap watching him play with the silverware and listened to the idle chatter, but my mind was on Abby Barrett. I wanted to try her again before work, so I needed to do it now. C.J. turned to take the boy from me.

"You seem preoccupied tonight," she said. "You haven't said a word. Everything okay?"

"Sorry," I said. "A lot on my mind, I guess. How's with you?"

"Oh, we're fine. If I can ever get your brother to leave this bar and come home," she laughed. She took Taylor and he cuddled up against his mom. On the other side of the table, Timmy stirred, but remained asleep. "Listen," C.J. leaned over and spoke softly, "Bobby stopped by the other night. He says you guys are getting together?" She looked at me questioningly. "You sure about this, Thomas, or is Bobby jumpin' the gun?"

My pained expression gave her an answer to the question. "I swear, sis, I haven't been leading your brother on. He hears what he wants to hear. I keep telling him I can't even support myself. How can I take on a partner? He won't hear me, so I guess I told him I'd keep thinking about it." I'm sure my expression was sheepish, but C.J. tried to ease the situation.

"You know that isn't the only reason you shouldn't do this, Thomas!" She looked over to her parents to make sure they were not listening to our conversation. They were still preoccupied. "I wish I could help my little brother, but Bobby's different. He has a grudge on his shoulder a mile wide," she shook her head. "Daddy's given up on him. I haven't, yet, but he doesn't make it easy to stay on his side. He comes up with some crazy get rich quick scheme every week.

Daddy can't keep funding his silly notions." She stroked her son's hair. "Don't you let him box you in, Thomas."

I leaned over and gave her a peck on the cheek. "I know something about having people around who want to help you get your life together. I know something about making it hard for them to keep caring. He'll be okay, sis." I stood. "I better get to work." I smiled to her parents and went behind the bar.

As usual on Monday nights, things started to slack off around ten. The Hemphill's left with Charlotte June some time around eight, and there were several empty seats at the bar when Pat finally broke loose of his duties and threw himself onto a stool. I pulled him a draft Harp Lager.

"How's it goin' Sherlock?"

"Well," I said, "I found out who killed Kennedy."

"Ted Kennedy's dead?" He burst out laughing at the tired old joke.

"Irish humor really can suck," I said. "Things are okay."

"I hear Bobby's been on your ass again."

"Ahh, it's nothing I can't handle. Seems like Charlotte June is worried about him though." Pat sat back and shook his head.

"That asshole!" Pat pushed his glass forward, and I topped it off. "Came over the other night while C.J. was trying to get the kids to bed. He'd just had a fight with his old man about something. I think he was looking for some sisterly comfort, but he was stinkin' and wound up yelling and scared Timmy." Pat knocked back a good bit of the Harp. "She's getting tired of always having to referee those two, you know?"

"You think he's doing anything besides booze?"

Pat got up and drained the last of the beer. "I wouldn't be surprised. Not at all. Don't let him talk you into anything, bro."

"You're the second person to give me that advice."

"'Cause it's good advice, Tom. By the way," Pat said, "Max got your message. Said to tell you he'll be stopping by for lunch about noon tomorrow. If you're not going to be here, he wants you to leave your report on the nursing home thing with me." I grabbed the report from behind the bar and tossed it across the bar top to Pat. "He'll leave you a check," he said.

"I should be here, but if not…" He took it and headed for his office.

I was wiping down the bar and taking stock of what liquor bottles needed replacing when the door opened and Abby's two girlfriends walked in and grabbed a table. Theresa, I think, and the other ones name I couldn't remember. Abby wasn't with them. I tossed my bar rag to Freddy and walked over to their table. "Hey," I said. Theresa looked up to give a drink order.

"Oh, hi," she said, no recognition on her face, then, suddenly, "You're Abby's friend." She smiled slyly. "Thomas, right? She was waiting for you the other night." She gave her friend a raised eyebrow and giggled.

"Yeah," I said, with a little blush in my cheeks. It makes me look vulnerable. "Is she coming by tonight?" I motioned to the chair and Theresa nodded. I sat. "I've been trying to reach her at the apartment all weekend with no luck."

Theresa looked at her friend again. She looked confused. "Why would you be calling her there?" How many confused people can you have at one table?

"Well," I said, "because she lives there. I got no answer all weekend. I was concerned."

"It's my place, and I was away all weekend." Theresa said. "Abby hasn't lived there all semester." She and her friend looked at each other. "You didn't know?"

"Then, where the hell is she living?" I said, more forcefully than I should have.

"She's living at her mom's place," the other girl blurted out, drawing another raised eyebrow from Theresa. I could read her thoughts. *If Abby didn't tell him...*

"Look," I said calmly, before they could get spooked. "We've had a great time together. I don't know why she didn't tell me, but I just want to talk to her and make sure she's okay. Honest."

Theresa looked at her friend a hard minute. She was uncomfortable with this, and I couldn't blame her. Why would Abby stay with me all night and pretend I didn't exist the next day. I wasn't comfortable with this either, but I had to know why.

Finally, Theresa said, "Look, I don't have her number, but I know her mom lives east of town. Somewhere near Emory University, I think," Emory is Atlanta's other major university, and is heavy in the medical arts.

"If you see her on campus," I stood and smiled at them. "Please ask her to call me, okay?" *And, please don't think I'm a murderer or something.*

Theresa smiled back, and nodded.

CHAPTER 7

▼

01 October 2002

I'd had enough for one day.

I left Abby's friends, had Robby send over two beers to their table, and went looking for my brother.

I guess the look on my face spoke volumes. Without a word leaving my lips, he said, "See you tomorrow. Don't forget Max is coming in for lunch." I nodded my thanks and closed the door behind me.

The door from the restaurant kitchen which led to the hallway and the stairs to my room also led to an exit to the parking lot behind the building. This is where deliveries were made to Ireland's Own.

I decided to step outside and clear my head of the lingering smell of cigarette smoke, and the irritation I was feeling over my conversation with Theresa and her friend.

It had been a good day for me, one of the most satisfying I had experienced in my budding career. I learned things that would be helpful to Max Howard's case against Junior Kline and Crystal Harbor, and I learned that I enjoyed the process. I might, I thought, actually make this work.

But I really care for Abby, and tonight's revelations left me with an empty feeling. I hadn't realized that I was so hungry for a relationship of a higher intensity. I care for Abby in ways I had not experienced before, yet she is keeping things from me. Things that would seem too mundane to keep from someone who is important in your life

I wanted much more than friendship, or sex for the sake of sex with her, and I had no idea where I stood. But I knew my feelings for her were strong.

I took a couple of deep breathes of the crisp fall air. The parking lot, usually full at all times of the evening, had several empty spots. Buckhead was closing down for the night, and so was my brain. Suddenly, I felt very tired. I went back inside.

I needed sleep, but I needed a shower first. I went into the bathroom and turned on the shower faucet. The pressure was strong and it took only a minute for the water to heat up. I undressed slowly and stepped into the stall, feeling the hot needles hit my skin. It was like a tonic, as a hot shower had always felt to me during my athletic career.

Standing with my back to the flow from the showerhead, letting the water beat against the back of my neck I let the soap rest in my hand a good five minutes before lathering up.

The tension in my muscles eased and I hated getting out of the shower, but fatigue was creeping up on me.

Toweling off in my bathroom, I heard a rap on my door. I figured Pat had decided to give me some crap about quitting early, or maybe he just wanted to check up on baby brother. In any event, I was in no mood for it tonight.

I wrapped a towel around my waist and, still dripping, I went to the door and threw it open, ready to give as good as I expected to get.

It was worse than I had thought. A disheveled Bobby Hemphill stood in my doorway.

"Tommy Boy!" He blurted out too loudly.

"Bobby," I said, "what are you doing here? It's a little late. I was just going to bed."

"I just stopped by for a minute, okay," he said, apologetically. He looked over my shoulder, as if willing an invitation to come in. I sighed and pushed open the door a little farther, and turned away. He followed me in.

I was not ready for this, but I motioned him to a chair and sat across from him. "What's up, Bobby?" I didn't really want to know.

He seemed to ponder my question, or maybe he wanted to consider his answer before speaking. He looked nervous and his hands were in constant motion. Bobby was wearing a blue sport coat and dark slacks, but his collar was open, and his tie, the one he was wearing earlier at the bar, was gone.

He looked at me finally. "Hey, man, I got this great thing, this opportunity, you know?" He was speaking very fast, as if afraid I would interrupt him. "This friend of mine? He's got this place, this restaurant space out by Gwinnett Mall. It's a great place for a restaurant and bar. It's even got all the kitchen equipment!" My face must have remained blank. "It would be great for Pat to put another pub out there. I could run it for him, you know? It would be great, man. Maybe you and me could run it together, Tommy!"

"Hold it, Bobby," I finally got a word in. "You know I don't own this place, man. You're gonna' have to talk to Pat about this." I knew Pat would never consider his proposal, but it was up to him to tell Bobby. "Just go talk to him, or at least talk to C.J., okay?" I was tired, and probable more brusque than I needed to be.

Bobby sat there for a minute, his shoulders sagging. "Nothing works out for me, man. I can't get a break!"

Suddenly, it was clear to me. Bobby *had* talked to his sister, and that conversation had not gone well.

"I…uh…could you talk to him, Tommy? I mean, he's your brother, you know? I know he'd listen to you, man."

Bobby was pleading with me. I needed to end this, but as nicely as I could. "I don't think I can do that," I said, gently. "I don't know anything about the restaurant business. You really have to discuss this with your sister and Pat."

Bobby Hemphill sat there, staring into space. "I can't get a break," he said resignedly. "C.J. won't help me with the old man anymore. He just don't believe in me, man. How am I supposed to get through to him? Even mama won't help me with him."

"You've tried a lot of things, Bobby. Look, why not give your old man what he wants?" I figured I might as well be straight with him. "Go back to school, get your degree. Maybe he figures you would have a better chance with some of your ideas with a degree behind you. What's the worst that happens? That you get a good education?"

He wasn't buying. "Shit, Tommy, I got ideas! Stuff I can make money at! What I got to waste time going to school for?" He got sullen again. "You got anything to drink, man?"

"You don't need it," I said.

"Come on, Tommy, just one. Please, man." Pleading, again.

I got up and went to the kitchen cabinet. A whole God damned bar downstairs! I grabbed a shot glass and a bottle of Sauza *Tres Generations* Tequila, my only financial splurge. I poured a shot and placed it on the table next to Bobby. He paid no attention to it, continuing to stare straight ahead, seeing something in the distance. I said "Bobby?" and got no response.

I went over to my closet and grabbed a pillow and blanket. I threw them on the couch across from where he sat. "It's late, man. You had better sleep here tonight. You're in no condition to be driving." There was still no response. "I need to get some sleep. We'll talk in the morning." I left him sitting there and went to my bedroom. Sleep did not come, and I tossed and turned, short cat naps about the best I could do. I don't do well when things are on my mind at night. It was frustrating, but I couldn't turn my brain off. About four, I got up and used the bathroom. I thought I had better check on my guest, and quietly opened the bedroom door and peered out. The pillow and blanket were exactly where I had thrown them on the couch. Bobby Hemphill was gone. The untouched glass of tequila sat on the table, right where I had put it last night.

CHAPTER 8

▼

7:30 AM, 02 October 2002
Peachtree Street

If I had been drinking all night, the condition I woke up in would have been classified as a Grade "A" hangover. I hadn't been, and it wasn't, but I was physically and mentally exhausted from lack of sleep, and I had a headache to beat the band.

I finally staggered out of bed and double-checked to make sure I had been right, that Bobby Hemphill really had left my apartment during the night. The shot glass of Sauza still sat on the table.

It was time to rid my mind of Bobby's problems and concentrate on my own, like, finding Abby Barrett.

I took a quick shower and threw on some sweat pants, leaving the towel draped around my shoulders. Max Howard wouldn't be in for lunch for hours, so I had time to crank up my four cup Mr. Coffee, and sit and stew over my situation. I kept reliving my night with Abby. I know that in the throes of passion, I had told her that I loved her. Had I scared her off?

Abby did not impress me as someone who scared easily. Besides, this is 2002. People…any people, men or women…were not afraid to say something when a situation was uncomfortable. I didn't think that was it. But I don't know what it is. I do know that Abby is the only one who can tell me what *is* going on between us.

Sitting at my dining table, slurping up a cup of sweet black coffee, I glanced to my left and caught sight of the heavy training bag suspended in the corner over by the window. I had hung it there my first week in Atlanta as a reminder to keep up my exercise program. This is especially important for my damaged left leg, doing karate leg kicks to strengthen and stretch my muscles. Needless to say, I hadn't kept up the regimen the sports doctors in Columbus and Cleveland had designed for me.

I put down my cup and wandered over, and ran my hands down the rough leather skin of the bag, finding the cracks and scuffed areas. My dad had bought the bag for me when I was in the sixth grade and beginning to show some promise as an athlete. I used it initially to build upper body strength, hand speed, and eye coordination. It got a lot of use during my Golden Gloves boxing days, and even more as I practiced my karate lessons. But not much since then.

My injury had affected me in a bad way. I had felt cheated from the moment I lay in the emergency room and they were cutting off my uniform pants around my swollen, distorted knee. I never could figure out how to get past it, and I hadn't felt like an athlete in a long time.

I stepped back and looked down at my balled up fists, and took a tentative jab at the bag. I heard the satisfying noise that popping leather makes, and took another swing. In close, jab, jab, jab, slowly, lightly, then harder, with more speed, moving my feet in time to the punches, feeling the bag dent deeper as I swung harder and faster. I began to breath deeper, hitting harder and harder.

I lost track of how many times I had struck the bag. I felt my skin dampen; sweat beginning to bead on my forehead, dripping into my eyes, the salt stinging. My breathing came faster and faster. I was gulping air as I stepped back and leveled a kick to the side of the bag with my right leg. My injured leg took the weight and I stepped back in with more jabs. I kept up the pace, even as I began to hear my jagged breathing ringing in my ears. I pulled back again and this time, I kicked with my left leg. I felt the tightness even before the twinge of pain in my knee. It wasn't an excruciating pain, but enough to snap me back to reality.

I gasped and grabbed hold of the bag with both hands, slamming it against my chest and holding on tightly while my breathing slowed. I came down from the adrenalin rush and got myself under control.

Finally, I was able to loosen my grasp on the bag and pushed back away from it. I stood there, wiping my sweating face with the towel that was still around my neck. I took a tentative step back, then another. My leg took the weight of my steps without further pain. I couldn't remember the last time I had broken a sweat, but my attack on the bag or whatever I had been attacking in my head, left me completely exhausted.

I staggered back to the bed and sat down heavily. Before I knew it, I had lain back and drifted into a heavy sleep. Two hours later, it was all I could do to get to the bathroom and douse myself in the hot water of my shower for a good twenty minutes.

*   *   *   *

Just before noon, I showed up downstairs at the bar. There was no sign of Max or my brother. I sat down on a stool and Chris Tucker, one of the day shift bartenders, saw me, pointed to the beer trough where a dozen brands of beer bottles were stuck in mounds of crushed ice. I waved her off and mouthed "Diet Coke" and she brought me one.

"Wow, it must have been a bad one last night, honey. You look like you've been slapped around by a keg of 'Bud.'"

"Well, just thank you all to hell," I said, giving her the evil eye. Chris is a very attractive blond, maybe twenty-four or five, around five-seven and well built, with a great smile and a mouth full of Georgia Peach teeth, which makes her a real attribute if you're looking to build a bar trade. She's worked for Pat since he opened the place. "Actually, I haven't had a drink in three days, if you don't mind," I said.

"Takes talent to look like that without a snoot full," she laughed.

"Smart ass," I said, and pushed my glass back to her for a refill. "Pat around?"

"He took off with C.J. about a half hour ago. He left this for you." She kept up the conversation while filling several orders along the bar, and for the waitresses working the tables, a real pro.

Pat had left my report with her. He must have planned to be away for a while. I nursed the second Coke while watching Chris. Actually, I was hoping I could finish my business with Max quickly. I had it in my head that I would try to find out where Abby Barrett's mom lived. I didn't know how Abby would react to my showing up on her doorstep, but it was something I figured I had to do. I reached behind the bar and grabbed the phone book with the residential listings from a shelf underneath. Before I could flip through to the B's, Max Howard came through the door, moving his big, wide body quickly through the busy room to the bar stool next to me, his huge hand stuck out to take mine in his strong grasp. He about shook me into the next county, which did little good for my headache and sore muscles.

"Son, you look like you been rode hard and slapped around on the way to the barn!" His jowly, flushed face exploded in laughter as he sat down heavily next to me and grabbed the draft Coors that Chris had slid across to him, all in one fluid motion.

"That seems to be the general consensus around here," I said, glaring at Chris.

"Uh huh," Max said, draining the beer glass.

I laid my report on the nursing home investigation in front of Max. He placed it under his quickly refilled glass and said, "Tell me what you saw, Tommy."

I've seen him do this before. He can always read a report. He wanted to know what was in my head that I might have forgotten to put in the written report. People don't always put their sense of a certain situation in writing. They tend to stick to facts.

"Well," I said, "let me start with the interviews. You'll have to clean Jack Martin up and calm him down a little. He's somewhat rough around the edges, but his story rings true, and he was able to back up your clients' claims. Jose Arroya is fine. He's believable, and a sympathetic figure. He lost his job, but not his dignity. He doesn't come off bitter."

"And he can back us up, too?" Max was digging into a newly arrived basket of chicken wings basted in honey BBQ sauce. He never put in an order, so I guessed that Chris was very familiar with Max's tastes.

"Neither one can speak to every instance of abuse in the brief you gave me, but they got some of them right on, and knew about other instances of neglect, or worse."

That stopped Max for a second, and he looked at me closely. "What do you think is *really* going on up there, sport?"

I figured Max knew more than he was saying, and was really fishing for my thoughts about the situation at Crystal Harbor in order to solidify his own perceptions. He's a very smart attorney of about fifty years of age, wrapped in a mish-mash of conflicting clothes, with a balding head, and a "good ol' boy" persona. But you'd better not underestimate him.

The place was filling up, and I had to speak louder to be heard.

"Well, I see a few different scenarios. One, maybe it's all a big, sad mistake. Kline loses interest in the place, the help gets out of control, and bad things happen. Two, Kline is way deep in something, maybe drugs, or maybe something less troublesome, but it still takes up too much of his attention, and he loses control…"

"Like?" Max asked, as he licked his fingers.

"Arroya said his boss had at least one late night, closed door meeting with a bunch of suits. Said there was a lot of yelling inside Kline's office. Most likely, this meeting wasn't to discuss the health care industry. I think he's looking to sell out to the real estate crowd, and, maybe, the deal isn't going down so smooth. He has long-term contracts with the residents. He might be trying to break the contracts and get rid of those old folks so he can sell. It's a pretty valuable piece of property, and it looked like Kline hadn't spent a penny on the place in a long time."

"Hmm," he said. I wasn't sure if this was a comment on what I had told him, or on the food. "Or?"

Chris dropped off another diet for me and a chili cheeseburger plate for Max. He tore into the sandwich and signaled for another beer. I was getting full just watching him.

"Three," I said, "there is something so bad going on, that Kline feels it's necessary to fire long time employees that *might* have seen or heard something they shouldn't have."

"Bingo. I agree, but what?"

I sat back. "I'm not sure, Max, but there are some other things you need to know. I was walking around outside the building, and ran into a maintenance man who told me Kline was intending to close the place, and wasn't taking on new residents. He thought I was trying to put a relative in the place. Also, he named a couple of doctors that had been sending people to Crystal Harbor for years, but hadn't been there personally in a long time."

Max took a pull of the Coors. "Anything else?"

I told him about John Edwards, and how he didn't exist, at least as far as the Hall County sheriff was concerned. "Arroya says the guy is dangerous. Says he caused a lot of the problems up there. I think Kline must have hired him as his enforcer, to maybe get rid of the residents. And then, there is Senorita Ellen."

He looked at me questioningly.

"Evidently, she's the daytime manager." I smiled. "Mr. Arroya seems to think that she and the boss are 'very close.' Kline got her to fire Arroya the morning after he was found outside the office door where he might have heard Kline arguing with his after hours visitors. She gave him twenty-five hundred and told him he was done there."

Max Howard finished his beer and wiped his mouth. "All this stuff in your report?"

I nodded.

"Sport," he said, "why don't you take another ride up yonder and see if you can have a word with this Edwards and the lady. We got our preliminary hearing next week, and if it's best to try to settle this thing, I want all the ammunition possible to throw at this here Kline's attorney. My folks don't need to get in some protracted lawsuit with possible criminal aspects. What say?"

"Sure Max, I can head up there now." Abby would have to wait. I owed Max that.

He slid off the stool and threw thirty bucks on the bar, which was much more than the bill and a twenty per cent tip would total. Maybe that's how you get this kind of personal service. Max took an envelope out of his jacket breast pocket, handed it to me, and slapped me on the shoulder. "You need to eat somethin' son. You're gonna' waste away!"

He barked out a laugh and headed for the door. I watched Max leave, opened the phone book, and, finding the page with the "Barrett" listings, I tore out the page, folded it and stuffed it into my pocket, and went upstairs for my truck keys.

*   *   *   *

I met my brother and sister-in-law in the parking lot behind Ireland's Own. Pat immediately took on an aggrieved look.

"Looks like I'll be calling in a replacement bartender," he wined to C.J.

I shrugged and gave him a pained expression. "Sorry, got to do something for Max," I said. "Besides, he pays better."

"Well, Hunkster, you can't argue with that," C.J. said to Pat.

He grumbled, and waived me away good-naturedly. In a few minutes, with surprising ease considering that Atlanta is a drivers' nightmare, I pulled onto the northbound ramp of I-85 at Lenox Road, and headed toward Hall County.

I had just crossed over I-285, the perimeter highway surrounding Atlanta when I hit the first slowdown. Two additional slowdowns later, I finally reached I-985 and took it northwesterly to the Friendship Road exit. Friendship is the main access road to Lake Lanier and the Lake Lanier Islands. There are two major resorts, golf, and boating facilities, and a water park on the islands. It's a very pleasant place, about thirty-three miles from Buckhead.

The weather was perfect again; mid-seventies and sunny, so the trip, even with the traffic, is nice enough. Heading west on Friendship, I found the turn off to Crystal Harbor Nursing Home, and finally reached the place about 1:15 in the afternoon.

There still was no one outside enjoying the perfect, southern fall day. I parked, grabbed my little notebook, and went in. I figured there was no need to hide my reason for being there today, so I kept the notebook out in the open and went inside. I wouldn't get the kind of information Max needed by pretending to be looking for a nursing home for grandpa.

The interior of Crystal Harbor was old, ugly, and depressing. If it were a home up for sale, it would be classified as a "fixer upper." The main hallway was deserted, but I could pick up a cough here and there in the distance, and a door closing somewhere nearby.

I decide to snoop around for a while before announcing my presence at the managers' office.

The hallway was dark and dingy, with lay-in ceiling tiles stained and bulging from the effects of years of a leaking roof. The floor tile was, at best, badly scuffed, and torn up in some places. The tile was that creepy speckled brown color that was so popular in the '50's. I couldn't imagine how they could ever pass a health inspection. I didn't even want to think about the kitchen facilities.

At the first turn, I went down another hall which was obviously a residential area. All the doors to patients' rooms were shut, which seemed unreasonable at this time of day. People should be out, visiting each other, maybe in the dining room finishing lunch, and there was a moldy, unclean smell that pervaded everything.

I still hadn't run into any employees. Halfway down the hall, I found a door open, maybe an inch. I looked around and, seeing that I was still alone, I pushed the door open, little by little.

The stench hit me like a kick to the face. Urine, feces, and odd medical smells escaped into the hallway. I pushed the door open farther, and saw the old woman. She was strapped to a hospital bed that was practically lying on the floor. She was disheveled and her hair was matted and scraggly. The woman appeared to be asleep, or drugged, and moaned softly.

Suddenly, as if she was aware of my presents, her eyes opened, and she turned her head quickly toward the door.

But I could tell she didn't see me. The old woman was blind. I closed the door, and took a deep breath to expel the smells that permeated the room.

I backtracked to the main hall and turned down another hallway. More patients' rooms, and all those doors were closed too. It was almost as if these people were being forced to stay out of sight. There wasn't even a pretense of a working nursing home. I picked out a door and knocked, but there was no answer. I opened the door. Inside, an elderly man sat in a chair in front of the window, the room was in disarray and stiflingly hot. He sat in the chair facing away from the door, and when I called out a greeting, there was no recognition. I tried again with the same results, and walked over and put a hand on his shoulder. That's when I noticed the shaking, and heard the sound of trickling water as he lost control of his bladder, and the urine ran down the chair leg. "Please," he said in a tiny, fearful voice. "Please," he said again.

I felt my stomach convulse, and forced back the bile that rose in my throat. I stumbled out of the room, and closed the door. My heart was pounding in my ears and sweat poured down my face. For the first time since my last football game, when part of my pre-game ritual had been to build a hatred for the other team, I was wholly and truthfully angry. I took a minute to regain my composure, but the anger wouldn't leave me. It was time to talk to whoever was in charge of this nightmare.

*   *   *   *

I ran back to the main entrance and found the door marked with a rusty plaque that said, "OFFICE." I felt winded and needed a minute again. I braced against the wall to try to calm myself, but the anger and disgust would not go away. I'm sure that in the back of my mind, my heritage, from two nationalities that revere their elderly, could not comprehend that people could leave family members in such a situation.

There was no window in the door, or window in the wall, so I grabbed hold of the knob, ready to brace against the door and break it in, if necessary. From what I had seen, it wouldn't have surprised me if no one in authority was on site.

I twisted the knob, and the door popped open.

The small room, maybe ten by ten, painted a dingy hospital green with the same floor tile as the hallways, was set up for a receptionist, sparsely furnished with a desk, two side chairs for visitors, and several tan colored file cabinets against the far wall. No one was there, as I had expected. Two doors, going, I guessed, to other interior offices were closed.

Not one piece of paper, not a file folder, not even a pencil was visible on the cheap desk. I went in and walked over to the first cabinet, intent on rifling the drawers. Every one was empty. I slammed the last of the drawers closed and started working on the desk, pulling it apart, in search of any piece of paper, any scrap of information.

Suddenly, the door to the inner office on my left flew open.

"My God!" A high pitched, female voice exploded behind me. "Who are you?! What are you doing?!"

I spun around to find a plumpish woman, maybe mid-thirties, with a bookish, librarian kind of face, staring wide eyed at me. She was dressed in a kind of silly, multi-colored outfit, with ruffles around her sleeves, and a wide open neck line that showed deep cleavage in the middle of two full, heavy breasts, that I think was meant to make her look desirable, but didn't.

"You must be Miss Ellen," I said in a rough tone as I rushed past her into the inner office she had come out of. I pushed her out of my way, and her startled look turned fearful.

This room was also empty, and looked exactly like the first. I started through the file cabinets in here, while the woman stood staring in the doorway, no longer willing or able to question me.

"Where's your boss?!" I yelled, as I pulled the desk apart, and flung the drawers to the ground. She stood stock-still; wringing her hands, and shook her head, as if to say that she didn't know. I must have looked like a crazed animal, for that was how I felt. If I had been able to think about what I was doing, I know I would have stopped, but my adrenalin was pumping out of control. I stopped my frenzied search, not even sure of what I had expected to find, and went to her, grabbing her by the arm and dragging her stiffened body into the outer office. I went back around the desk to the door, grabbed the woman roughly by her arm, and threw the now fully frightened Ellen into the visitor's chair in the front office. I took hold of both chair arms, pushing my face down into hers. I could feel the sweat running down my face.

Tears spread down her cheeks, her fear palpable. "Where is he, Ellen?" I shouted into her face, my nearness taking her breathing room away, making her gasp and struggle to keep control of herself.

She wouldn't, or couldn't answer, and I shook her by the shoulder. "I said..." There was a crash behind me.

"Hey! What the fuck!" I turned, my anger so great that I could feel no fear at being found here manhandling this woman. A short, mostly bald man, as dumpy a figure as the woman, and dressed in cheap clothes of miss-matched hues of blue stood in the hallway door. A brown bag lay at his feet, a puddle forming under it. The smell of cheap scotch flooded up from the floor.

"I said, what the fuck...!"

He started into the room, and I pushed Ellen's chair away and turned into him. I grabbed him and spun him away. He landed in the other chair with a crash, barely able to keep from falling to the ground. He started to get up and I shoved a finger into his face. "Stay there, pal. Just don't move." I said menacingly.

He thought better of it and remained in the chair. Ellen hadn't moved, but her eyes gave it away. This was Junior Kline.

I could feel the heat rising up the open front of my shirt, and my face was still flushed and damp. I must have looked a formidable opponent to Kline. He took hold of the arms of the chair and kept his mouth shut, staring at me sullenly.

I was suddenly unsure of my ability to remain upright much longer. My adrenalin levels were falling off, and my legs were weak, and I struggled to maintain my intensity. I needed to keep the upper hand for whatever I was going to do next.

I sat down in the chair behind the desk, leaned back as the spring squeaked. It was the only sound in the room. I folded my hands in front of me. "So," I said with exaggerated friendliness. "How are you kids doin' today?"

Junior started to bluster again, and I looked at him hard. He stopped.

I turned back to the woman. "Where are all your records, Ellen," I said, as if we had been properly introduced. She was still shaking a little, and she wasn't talking. I sat upright abruptly, and she jumped in her chair. Still, not a word, I asked again, louder, and she shot a furtive look at her boss.

"Don't look at him, Ellen!" I shouted the name, sprung from the chair, and grabbed her arm. I pulled her away from the seat and she squealed.

Junior jumped up. "You son of a bitch…!" Veins were popping up all over his piggish face.

My left leg shot up and caught him squarely in the chest while he was in mid-rise. My muscles stretched and my knee popped, and it was the most satisfying feeling I'd had in a while.

Kline tumbled backward, off balance, missed the seat, hit the seatback with his butt, and he and the chair went over in a heap. He hit the ground hard, and my kick had taken his breath. Junior Kline decided to stay on the floor for a while.

Ellen was sobbing quietly in her chair, legs tucked up, almost in a fetal position.

I was spent, and slumped back down.

What, in God's name was I doing? I was terrorizing these people like some common criminal, acting like a madman. This wasn't some TV show, or "*Spenser*" novel. Only yesterday, I thought I was on the right track; doing business professionally, helping a legitimate attorney make a case. Today, I'm a thug dealing among thugs, and I have no idea how to get out of this without destroying Max's case.

We were silent, except for her sobbing, while Junior collected himself. Finally, he stood, and without a word, put the chair upright, and sat down, heavily.

"You through being a tough guy, Junior?" I said, quietly.

"What the fuck you want?" He said, in a voice barely back to normal. "I told Mr. Mitchell when I got the money, I'd call. Sendin' some asshole strong arm to roust me, scarin' women, ain't goin' to get him paid any sooner!"

I kept my mouth shut and stared at him, as if I knew what he was talking about.

"That shit don't grow on trees, you know? It takes time to get money from the insurance companies and the Feds. Shit!" He took a deep breath.

So here it was. I sighed. "So you keep skimming to pay your debt, boosting false medical bills. No luck betting on the horses, Junior, or football? How the fuck you leave those folks back there like that, man? Where are their relatives? Who checks this place out?"

He sputtered out a laugh. "Shit, you are a dumb fucker," he said. He was getting back his nerve. "Half these people got dumped here, and nobody gives a shit! They stick me with carin' for 'em, pay a few months, and they never come back. My old man spent a goddamned fortune taken care of these fucking people. He stuck me with this place and died broke. The stupid bastard."

"Poor you," I said. I looked at Ellen. I still didn't know her last name. I didn't care to know it.

"What do you see in this asshole? How deep you get in this mess for this pile of shit?"

It struck me, the moment she looked up at Junior Kline. It was in her eyes. She would do anything for him. He was, possibly, the first man to show any interest in her. It would never occur to her that he might simply be using her to help him scam money from insurance companies, and the government.

I said to Junior, "Where is John Edwards?"

I caught the quick look that passed between them.

"What?" He got very wary, again.

"We gonna' have to do this in sign language, Junior?" I looked at her. "Ellen, where is John Edwards?"

She looked about to speak, when Kline said, "He don't work today."

"Then, how do I find him?"

"I got no idea. He don't tell us what he does when he ain't here. Besides, Mitchell should know where he is. That crazy animal belongs to him!"

I looked at the woman. "You know where he lives, Ellen?"

She started to answer, and Kline said, "Shut up, Ellen!" She cringed.

"Ellen," I said, ignoring him, "if you want to get rid of me, I need you to do two things. First, get me John Edwards' address, and second, get me a few clean sheets of your stationery. Please." I spoke calmly. It was time to get her cooperation.

She returned in a minute, with a small slip of paper with a phone number and address printed in a small, clear hand, and the writing paper.

Softly, Kline said, "Jesus."

I put the stationery in front of him, and took out my pen and handed it to him.

I said, "Write it out, Junior."

He looked at me questioningly.

"Write out what you've been doing here. Spell it out, and I want to know exactly how you have been stealing the money, and what you're doing with it."

He looked at me like I was crazy. "Are you nuts? Why does Mitchell want that? He turns me in; his ass goes down too, for Christ's sake!" The veins on his forehead were about to burst.

"Just do it. Let's call it 'insurance.'" I looked at Ellen, who seemed calmer. "Please get me a list of the names of every resident." Again, she looked at him. "Do it, now," I said, tightly.

Junior picked up the pen, stared at the paper for a full minute, and finally started to write.

Twenty minutes later, I had a list with twenty-two names, and had just finished reading Kline's statement. It was all there. "You have Mr. Mitchell's phone number?" Junior looked at me funny, but had it in his head and gave it to me. I wrote it down, along with Mitchell's name on the bottom of the statement, right under where I Kline had written that he had given the information contained in the statement freely, and without duress. A bit of a stretch, for sure.

Then, I wrote "Witnessed by…," and put the date at the very bottom of the last page, and placed the papers in front of Ellen.

"Sign it as a witness," I said. "Read it, first." She looked at her lover, but hesitated only a second. I heard him sigh, but he kept quiet. She read the statement, and signed. "I'll need two copies, Ellen," I said. She walked into the other office, and I heard the copier running.

I had no idea whether what I had done was legal. I didn't know if my actions would help or kill Max Howard's case. I had been winging it since I had walked in here.

What was done was done.

I stood, picked up the papers, and walked around to the outer door, and stopped to face them. "Listen to me very carefully. This is very important." They both looked at me. Junior was expecting a deadly threat, I was sure. "I want you to start cleaning this place up. Start now, this very minute. You get those people cleaned up, keep them medicated as ordered by a doctor-a real doctor-, and get them fed properly, until I can get them out of this dump. You do whatever it takes, and do it now. I will be sending people here very soon. If this situation is not rectified, I will see that you are prosecuted far beyond you're monetary crimes." They were silent, pitiful creatures. "But first," I said, as I threw my business card on the desk, "I will come back here and punish you myself." I turned, and over my shoulder, said, "And, tell that bastard, Edwards, I'm looking for him." I walked out of the building and took my first breath of fresh air in what seemed like forever. I felt dirty. I got into my pick-up, turned the key, and drove away, hot tears running down my face, my mind, and body totally spent. I picked up the phone, took a deep breath, and dialed Max Howard's office number.

CHAPTER 9

▼

9:00 A.M., 03 October 2002

"You done good, son."

Max Howard and I were seated at a four-top table in a very crowded 'Jimmy's Bayou Restaurant' on Peachtree, down in Midtown. The place was a favorite morning stop for Max. As usual, he was getting the star treatment. We were up front near the window, which I had been staring out, while he went through a plate of six beignets, the square, puffy, Louisiana style donuts, which were covered with powdered sugar.

The day was clear and sunny and unseasonably warm, and Max's tie was sprinkled with the sugar.

"Thanks," I said. "And I hope I never have to do that again."

"Well, *that* one you're gonna' lose," said Max. He bit into another beignet, and I took a sip of coffee. I hadn't eaten since before my session with Kline and Ellen. I just had no taste for food. The smells that had permeated the Crystal Harbor Nursing Home had burrowed into my sub-conscience. Even the air tasted and smelled like that place.

"Look, Tommy," said Max between bites, "what you do is tough, nasty work. Nothin' tougher but, maybe, skip chaser, you know? See, you're like a cop, but different. Cops got laws they have to live by." He smiled. "Of course, you got laws too, but PI's break 'em all the time. Have to 'cause you got to deal with some pretty lousy excuses for human beings. It ain't like on TV, kid. Cop kills five bad guys on the tube, he's a hero. Real life, he shoots over the head of some guy he's chasing, and he winds up on leave, waitin' for a hearing. You people carrying private badges are sometimes the only one's who can get to these creeps."

This was the longest sustained speech I had ever heard from him. "I know what you're saying Max, but I'll let you in on a little secret. I've been an athlete all my life. But I've never been in a plain, old-fashioned fistfight. I never punched anyone in anger, and it made me sick to push those people around."

Three more donuts appeared on a fresh plate. The waitress offered us more coffee. I declined; Max pushed his cup toward her.

"Well, boy, you most certainly are not a Southerner!" Max laughed, then said seriously, "Made you pretty sick to see what was going on around there too, right?"

I knew he was trying to ease my mood. We sat without speaking while he finished eating.

Finally, Max went on. "After you called me, we went to work to help those old folks. We alerted the Hall County sheriff's office, and I had Grady Memorial and Hall County Hospital send over every available ambulance to Crystal Harbor. My boys and girls at the office got your list of patients' names, and started researching family members." He drank the last of his coffee, and waived away the waitress, who was on her way over. "We've started gettin' those people to hospitals. The sheriff arrested Mr. Junior Kline and his lady friend, and carted them off to the Gainesville jail. Arraignment should be this afternoon. Looks like they're gonna' need a public defender. The sheriff and his folks are tearin' the place apart, but they aren't finding much in the way of records. Junior's house is next."

The breakfast crowd was thinning. "What about this John Edwards?" I asked.

"Well," Max sat back in his chair. "There's an all-points bulletin out on him, right now, he's wanted for questioning, and if Mr. Edwards goes near his apartment, he's gonna' have a houseful of Bluecoats the minute he shows. But I don't think he will. Junior Kline isn't going' to want us talking to Edwards, and neither will this Mitchell character. No, I think Mr. Edwards is long gone."

"What do we know about this Mitchell guy?"

"Charles Mitchell," he said, leaning forward in his chair and half-heartedly brushing off his tie. "Charlie is well known to the Atlanta Police. He hides behind a real estate development business; apartment complexes, town homes, big, expensive homes on the lake, even some downtown lofts, but he is a long time bookie, well known, but hard to finger. Your little talk with Kline's gonna' help put a collar on his operation."

"So," I said, "he gets Junior deep into debt, so deep he can't get out. I bet he settles by taking over Junior's property."

"Good guess," Max smiled. "Kline was working' hard to keep the place so he could sell it for big bucks."

"I don't get the girl," I said. "She didn't look like a criminal. She looked like some school teacher, or secretary," I shook my head. "What would make her do this for a shit for brains like him?'

"Had to guess?" Max looked thoughtful. "He's probably the only guy ever showed her the time of day. She gets sucked in by his attention, presto she falls in love. Girl like that, lonely all her life, she just fell in love. Now she's gonna' go to jail, unless she gets offered a deal to tell what she knows about this mess."

"Could that happen?"

"Maybe, but the question is whether she learned her lesson, and rats Kline, Edwards and Mitchell out," Max said.

I had created a real mess. Of course, I knew in my heart that I wasn't the bad guy in this case, but it was still hard to believe things had gotten to this point. I stared out the window. The morning traffic was beginning to clear. It was a beautiful day outside. Inside the noisy restaurant, I felt like there was a cloud hanging over me. Just me.

I asked the question I dreaded asking. "What about your case?"

"Well," Max sighed. "I surely want to get my folks a large settlement, but I don't know if it's gonna' be possible now."

I cringed. "Christ, I'm sorry, Max."

"About what?" He motioned to the waitress. "Look, kid, there's gonna' be a long, drawn out criminal case. Chances are, the court will have to confiscate the property. Probably got some taxes due on it anyway. Long shot, maybe we'll get something. But, you saved lives, Tommy. Two of those people are on life support as we speak. That could have happened to a lot more of them, things stayed like they were much longer."

Max Howard reached into his coat pocket, and handed me an envelope. "You did well and I'm proud of you." The waitress dropped off a check and a small, white bag.

"You're learning, kid," Max stood, dropped a twenty dollar bill on the check, and pointed to the bag. "Now, have some beignets before you waste away!" He laughed, and walked out, leaving me to finger the folded page from the phone book in my shirt pocket.

*   *   *   *

My truck was parked behind the restaurant. I picked up the bag of donuts and headed out the door. It felt good to have the clean, October air hit my face, the bright, southern sun making me squint.

I went back to Ireland's Own and parked in the lot. When I made my entrance, Pat was tending to getting the bar ready for today's lunch crowd.

"Sorry, sir," he said. "We aren't open yet."

I laughed. "Message received. I've got the next shift."

He tossed me the towel he had had on his shoulder, and smiled back. "Max said you did a real good job up there," he said.

"Yeah, well, Max is pretty easy to please."

"Don't kid yourself, pal. There's nothing *easy* about Max Howard."

"Jesus, Pat," I said. "I really thought I had blown his case."

He poured me a Diet Coke. "Must have been a real sad scene at that place, huh?"

"It's gonna' stick with me for a long time."

"Hey, remember, you made the bad stuff stop. Ma would be proud, kid." I took over behind the bar. Pat slapped me on the shoulder, and went to his office.

The lunch crowd started arriving about 11:15 a.m., and for a while, at least, I was too busy to think about my experiences of the last two days. The thought that still stuck in my head was finding Abby. My shift would end about three, and afterward I would be free to try to locate the Barrett home. I touched the phone book page, which was still in my shirt pocket. Over the last day, I had tried to convince myself that there was nothing wrong with showing up at Abby's mom's house. I was a friend, and I was worried about her. I couldn't find her at the university. She hadn't been around.

It all sounded suspect, of course, but I was going to do it anyway.

Business was brisk until about one thirty, then fell off. By the time my shift ended, we were pretty much empty. I threw my bar apron into the waste can we used for towels and aprons needing cleaning, and ran upstairs to shower, change, and grab my keys to the truck. I was out of there and on my way in less than forty minutes.

I headed north on Peachtree against light traffic to Druid Hills Road and took a right. I was now on my way east bound toward Decatur.

The area where Abby's mom lives, is a wealthy, close-in suburban area of Atlanta. In the center of the area was Emory University, an extremely well thought of school, the world class Emory Clinic and Hospital, and the CDC, the Centers for Disease Control. This organization is the country's main defense against worldwide diseases and plagues.

When I got close, I pulled out the page of phone numbers and pulled into a McDonald's, grabbed a Diet Coke and a cheeseburger, for I was suddenly very hungry, parked and went through the "Barrett" listings. With the help of a map book I kept behind the passenger seat, I was able to figure out that six Barrett's lived in a roughly three-mile area around where I sat.

My first call, to a Lloyd Barrett, went unanswered, but the voice on the answering machine sounded black. I didn't know what Abby's father's name had been, or whether her widowed mother would even still use his name in the phone listings. Some women did, even years after becoming widows, feeling that it was safer against criminals who might use the phone book to find potential female victims who lived alone.

The second and third phone calls went through, but no one knew Abby. My fourth call went unanswered, with no voice mail.

That left two Barrett residences to contact. There was a "William T.," at 663 Tremont Road, and a "Richard J." at 25560 Abercorn Terrace.

I looked up both locations, and found one to be on the very outskirt of my three mile search zone, but the other, Abercorn Terrace, was only a half mile away, and very close to the Emory campus.

It was approaching 7 p.m., and I was still a little hungry. Maybe I was just looking for a way to stall off what I felt was inevitable contact with Abby's mother, or Abby herself. I wanted to believe this was not going to be a bad scene, but I admit I was beginning to feel a little foolish about it all.

I pulled out onto Druid Hills Road, and headed east toward the campus and the CDC. On the way, I tried William Barrett, and spoke briefly to a woman who sounded elderly. It was the wife of an attorney, William T. Barrett, and no relation to Abby.

Still hungry, although it might have just been nerves, I pulled into an Arby's drive-thru and ordered a roast beef sandwich, fries and a diet, and pulled into a parking space to eat, leaving the truck engine running, so that I could run the heater against the cool evening air.

When I finished, about ten minutes later, I pulled back out of the parking lot and headed east again.

Emory University sits about a mile south of Druid Hills Road, surrounded by tree-lined streets, and middle to high-income houses. It's a pretty place that looks like it has grown from time to time. Not to mention it's a leader in the continuing fight against AIDS, and reoccurring illnesses long thought to have been eradicated, like smallpox.

The campus is large, but would be dwarfed by the Ohio State University 'city' of about fifty thousand students. I remember a bumper sticker that was big around school that said "Welcome to OSU, home of Columbus, Ohio." They don't call it the Buckeye Nation for nothing.

I passed through the area, and using my map, finally tracked down Abercorn Terrace. As I had expected, Abby's mother lived on a very high-class street, completely lined with homes that looked to be between five thousand and eight thousands square feet, with highly landscaped lots. A few gates blocked entrance to some of the bigger homes.

Now I was starting to feel self-conscious about my relationship with this well to do girl. But there was no turning back now.

I slowed and continued down the street looking for the address. When I found it, I had to fight the urge to take off. The house was huge, and beautiful, sitting in the center of three or four acres. Everything about the place spoke of wealth.

I wasn't sure why I was here. Now that I had a good idea that this was the right house, I could just pick up the phone and call and ask for Abby. She would be here, or not be here, want to talk to me, or not want too talk to me. Why chance finding out face to face that she didn't want to see me?

The night was getting colder, and I was about to find out whether I was going to get the cold shoulder, too. Luckily, I had had the good sense to dress nicely. I had on my best slacks and a charcoal V-neck, and black loafers.

No sense putting it off any longer, I thought.

I walked up the stone walkway, up the steps, took a deep breath, and pressed the doorbell.

*   *   *   *

I hardly had time to take a breath when the door opened, and I was face to face with a young woman of about five-four in height, with jet-black hair, and deep chocolate skin. My heart sank. I must be in the wrong place.

She said, "May I help you?" in a lilting, island accent. I realized she was wearing a uniform. She was a maid or housekeeper.

"Yeah…I mean, yes, please. I'm looking for a friend, Abby Barrett. I was told her mother…"

A voice came from behind her. "Who is it, Patrice?"

In a moment, I was staring into Abby's beautiful face.

Except it wasn't Abby's face. It was older, darkly beautiful like hers, but mature, stately, I couldn't think of the words to describe the similarities or the slight differences.

She smiled Abby's smile, and said, "May I help you, young man?"

I found my voice. "I was wondering if Abby Barrett's mother lived here. I can see she does," I smiled back, trying not to look as idiotic as I felt.

"You are a friend of my daughter's?"

"Ah, well, yes, ma'am. We've sort of had a few dates, but I haven't heard from her in a while. Her friend, Theresa, said she was living back home. I was a little worried about her."

"You would be Thomas Patrick, yes?"

I was both pleased and thunderstruck that Abby had actually mentioned me to her mom, and then hopeful that it had been in a good way. I was surely blushing, and hoped she couldn't see it. I nodded.

Mrs. Barrett nodded to the other woman, and the maid left us. "Please come in, Thomas," she said, and pushed the door open wider. "My daughter has spoken of you many times." She turned and led me into a large reception room which was painted a sky blue, with high ceilings, a heavy molding at the top of the walls. The furniture was ornate, but not overpowering. Above the fireplace, a large painting depicting a farming scene commanded the room. A black grand piano stood at the other end of the room.

She motioned me to a couch, and sat across from me on an identical couch, a coffee table between us.

"I'm sorry," I said. "I didn't mean to intrude on you so late. I hope you will forgive me, but I wanted to make sure Abby was okay."

"You are quite welcome here, Thomas," she said. "Abby speaks very highly of you. You are an investigator, I believe Abby said."

She made it seem like a real job. "Well, ma'am, I'm working to establish a private investigation business, but I work at my brother's restaurant, too."

The maid wheeled a cart into the room. There were a gleaming silver coffee pot and china cups and saucers for two. Mrs. Barrett said. "Would you prefer something cold? A beer perhaps, or iced tea?"

"No thanks, coffee is fine," I said. "It smells great."

I took the offered cup. The coffee was steaming hot. The maid offered me cream and sugar. I took two cubes with a small silver tongs.

She took a sip from her cup. "I'm glad you found our house."

"It's beautiful," I said, looking around the room.

"Thank you. But it is just a house. It is the family that makes it a home. You are not a native of Georgia?"

"No. I've been here about a year and a half." I said. "My brother married a girl from Atlanta while he was playing for the Falcons."

She offered me a platter of cookies from the cart. I took one that reminded me of the biscotti my grandmother made us every weekend when I was growing up.

The cookie was crisp, with a slightly chocolate taste. Everything she did was with a stately, royal-kind of motion, yet without seeming to be presumptuous.

"I'm afraid Abby is away for a little while longer," she said. "I have asked her to handle some pressing family business in Miami for me. She should return in a few days, Thomas."

"She mentioned taking a trip to Miami not long ago. Do you have much family there?"

"My sister's family, and many old friends. It was our home for many years. I grew up there, my children, except for my youngest, were born there." She took another sip of coffee. "My family arrived from Cuba with many other refugees, when I was only four years old. My father was a planter in Cuba, following in the footsteps of many generations of his ancestors."

I hoped surprise did not register on my face. "I didn't know." I put my cup on the coffee table. "I guess Abby has never really discussed her family much. I didn't know you had come from Cuba originally."

"Escaped, really. My father was a major land owner, a *Patron*, as owners of large estates were called." Abby's mom was quiet for a moment, as if remembering. Then she said brightly. "His land was about to be confiscated by the new government of Fidel Castro, so he and other land owners arranged to smuggle their families to this great country."

"That must have been terrible for you."

"I was very young," she said, adding "And we were lucky. We left little family behind. Only my mother's brothers and their families stayed in Cuba, but they were fisherman, living far from our home. They suffered no reprisals due to our escape."

She offered me more coffee and cookies. I took both. I knew I was imposing on her hospitality, although she gave me no reason to feel that I was, and I found that I wanted to stay in this woman's presence. It was like being with Abby.

"You say my daughter has not spoken of her family?"

"Well," I said, I'm afraid that much of our time together hasn't left us much time for long discussions. "I realized immediately that that might sound funny to a mother. "I mean," I said quickly, "We meet a lot where I work, and it's kind of busy and very noisy."

She smiled, and put me at ease. "Let me show you a photograph of my family," she said, rising and walking to the piano. She motioned for me to follow, which I did. The piano's top was covered with silver and gold frames full of pictures spanning the Barrett family's life.

There was Abby and her siblings at all ages. As I expected, she was even beautiful as a child, with and without braces. Her mom looked at the photos with great love in her eyes.

She picked up a family portrait in a gilded frame, and handed it to me. She pointed to the little boy. "This is Carlos, and Nina, and, of course, Abby," she said. "And, my husband Richard."

I started to hand her back the picture.

"I am afraid Richard is away on business," she said. "I know he would like to meet you."

That startled me, and it must have shown. She looked at me questioningly.

"I'm sorry, Mrs. Barrett. I was under the impression that ahh......that Abby had lost her dad when she was young."

"Yes," she said, a little sadly, I thought. "My first husband, Abby's father, died when she was ten years old. Richard is her stepfather." She put the photo down, and picked up a small frame that held an older image, slightly frayed around the edge. "This," she said, "is Abby's father."

✳   ✳   ✳   ✳

I had been at the Barrett home almost two hours by the time I had kicked the pickup into gear, and started back to Buckhead.

Abby's mom was a beautiful and gracious person. She had treated me like an old friend, and I had enjoyed every moment in the house on Abercorn Terrace. But, I was troubled by the things I had learned about Abby. Maybe I was way over reacting. Her mom never did explain the trips to Miami, but neither was there a good reason why she should have.

It came down to worrying about little revelations that Abby might easily explain at some later time, or being happy that she obviously had some feelings for me, and had shared them with her mother. I chose the latter, and drove home in a better frame of mind that I had felt in a long time. I glanced at my watch. It was nearly ten, and I was actually starting to feel like I might get a restful night's sleep.

I made it back to the restaurant about 10:20, and pulled into the parking lot, winding my way back to the three spaces Ireland's Own kept reserved near the rear door.

My window was down a little, and I rolled it up, and opened the door. Out of the corner of my eye, I caught sight of the little bag of beignet's Max Howard had bought for me early in the morning. I reached back to grab it.

Suddenly, I felt an iron grip on my arm holding the door, and I was jerked hard toward the opening. At the same time, the door was slammed hard against my left shoulder, and I heard, rather than felt, the "pop" as my arm pulled away from its socket. My head exploded in pain as my face smacked against the door, and I was suddenly on my back on the seat, and being spun around so that my head was being pulled down toward the ground.

A guttural voice said, "You been fuckin' with the wrong people, asshole!"

The door slammed again against my face and chest, and I lost control of my breath.

I was gasping for air. My nose must have been broken, as I could feel hot sticky blood flowing back down into my eyes. In a fog, I thought I heard yelling. It seemed to be coming from miles away.

The door of the truck swung open, and the pressure was suddenly gone from my left wrist.

I could feel myself slumping out of the truck down toward the ground. I couldn't stop myself, and my head cracked against the pavement.

It was the last thing I remembered.

Thinking about it later, while lying in my hospital bed, I guess I had just not understood that this was a business where people could get hurt. A business which required total vigilance. I also realized that my personal life had been the only thing on my mind as I pulled into the parking lot that night. It was now evident that the job came first, and never really ends as long as the bad guys are on the street.

It also seemed to me that my assailant could only have been John Edwards, or whatever his real name was, or one of the other minions of Charles Mitchell.

I had stirred up a hornets' nest, and someone wanted me to pay. I couldn't bring myself to believe that this attack had been a simple mugging. Nothing was taken, and in the back of my mind, I had a fuzzy recollection of a voice telling me that I had interfered with something that I shouldn't have stuck my nose into.

Speaking of my nose, it was broken, and I had some facial lacerations, but they were healing. My shoulder had been separated, and my arm was heavily taped to my torso. That and a couple of cracked ribs were the most serious damage, but luckily, no punctured lung from the rib injuries.

My psyche may have taken the biggest hit of all. For the first time, I had felt helpless, and in absolute fear for my life.

I had lost conscientiousness during the attack, which was probably a good thing. The second good thing that happened was Robbie, the bartender, coming out of the back door at the end of his shift, and seeing what was happening thirty feet away. His shout for help scared my assailant away.

Waking on a gurney in the emergency room with my eyes glued shut by my own blood, and intense pain in my shoulder and chest was not a good thing. I was confused by the noise around me, I guess, and I struggled to sit up. I immediately felt my arms gripped by somebody, and one of the nurses or doctors ordered me sedated.

Before going out again, I thought I heard Pat's voice calling my name.

I remember thinking, *I should be dead. Why didn't he just shoot me? Why am I still alive?*

I didn't wake up again until sometime the next morning, and then, only partially. Everything was fuzzy, and the few times I heard voices, they sounded muffled. I realized later that my head had been bandaged over one ear because of some cuts.

I think I saw Pat and C.J. in my room, but I couldn't swear to it.

I guess I went out again, because the next time I opened my eyes, lights were on in the room and the shades on the windows were pulled down. C.J. was there, rubbing my arm above the IV needle that was stuck in it. I looked up and she smiled. Then I saw the metal stand holding a drip bag of clear fluid that was obviously being pumped into me.

My voice squeaked, and my mouth felt like a sock was stuffed in it. "I prefer ale, or maybe an Irish red."

"How sweet," she said. "Even near death you Patrick boys can still be endearingly weird." And she kissed me on the forehead, with her cool lips.

*   *   *   *

The next day I woke feeling a little more clear-headed, but I was loaded with painkillers, which was for the best.

C.J. was napping in the one lounge chair in the room, which looked totally uncomfortable. Her bare feet were pulled up under her, and an open paperback lay face down in her lap. She was sound asleep although it looked to be mid morning. I figured she had been there all night. Pat was not around.

The tray which folded over the bed when they feed you was parked alongside the bed on my "good" arm side, and I was able to grab a cup of water that was on it without asking for help. The cool water slid down my parched throat tasting like the best drink I had ever had.

The TV, perched high on a rack on the wall near the ceiling, was on, but the sound was muted. I left it that way.

I twisted a little, having been in the same position for a long time, and felt a twinge of heavily masked pain. Not bad enough to make me cry out, but bad enough to tell me that I had some real injuries.

I closed my eyes. What made me think I had any business being a PI? I couldn't remember any class in the community college curriculum entitled "Protecting Yourself from Getting Your Ass Kicked, 101." On the other hand, I did spend a good part of my youth watching TV. I guess I never made the connection between TV Private Investigator, and Thomas Patrick, Private Investigator.

I made it now.

The question now was could I handle the future possibility of violence. And, did I even want to try. I reached for the water pitcher to refill my little cup.

"Let me get that for you, Thomas."

I turned to see C.J. rising from her chair. "Sorry," I said, "did I wake you?"

"No, I guess it was just time to wake up. Lovely accommodations you have for guests," she said, looking back at the killer chair.

"Only the best for you."

She put her hand on my forehead.

"No temperature," she said, and smiled, looking like she just walked off a fashion show runway, instead of having spent a night on that chair. "How are you feeling?"

"That's the good part," I answered. "I don't feel much of anything."

"No temp's a good sign. Probably means no internal bleeding, but they are going to want to keep you here a few days."

Damn," I said. "I guess dog sledding across the frozen tundra is out this year."

"Hmmm, near future, anyway."

"Where's Pat?"

"He left about an hour ago. He's picking up your mom and dad at the airport," she said.

I winced. "Not good," I said.

"We had to tell them, Thomas. You were hurt pretty bad."

I knew she was right, but I was sure my mother would blame herself for talking me into this. It wasn't her fault, of course. She was just the first to realize I had to do something with my life, before I sank too low to get my head back above water.

"How bad do I look?"

"Well, better than you did when they brought you in here, for sure, still pretty messed up, though." She sat on the edge of the bed. "The blood was the worst," she said, and her eyes were moist. "You scared us pretty good, Thomas."

I felt guilty about that. "I'm sorry, sis. I scared myself pretty good, too. It was stupid, I know, but I never even had a thought about being in danger."

"Are you sure about this?" she said after a minute.

I knew what she meant. "No," I said. "I mean, I'm in the wrong profession if I can't train myself to look around every corner as if danger should be lurking there, or look at every person as if they are a danger to me. But hell, I don't know if I can live like that, anyway."

She was silent for a minute. Before either of us could speak again, a nurse stuck her head in the door to let us know the doctor would be around in a minute.

That broke the morose spell.

"By the way," I said as brightly as I could, "Where the hell am I, anyway?"

"Grady Hospital," she answered. Grady was right in the middle of downtown, running along the I-75/85 highway that split the city.

We didn't go back to our conversation, but I knew there was going to be a lot of discussion about all this once my folks arrived.

For now, Abby was in my thoughts, and as much as I wanted to see her, I hoped she would not return until I was out of the hospital, and on the mend.

I didn't want to worry her, or scare her away for fear that I would wind up here again some day.

CHAPTER 10

▼

11:30 AM, 07 October 2002
Peachtree Street

Everyone has seen old war movies in which the hard-boiled sergeant sends the young recruits into battle, and then spends the rest of the movie lamenting their deaths. Or the TV cop who sends a rookie through a door, and sees him blown to bits by the bad guys.

Luckily, my stupidity had gotten only *me* hurt.

After some time in the hospital, mostly to make sure I hadn't sprung an internal leak, I had come to the realization that I didn't have a clue about this business I was in.

My parents and Pat came in as the doctor was leaving. Mom took one look at me and tears ran down her cheeks. She came over to me and touched my swollen face. I took her hand and kissed it.

"I'm okay, Ma, really." Dad came to the other side of the bed, and shook my free hand gently. He was looking at me intently, and his face was set.

"Not too bad, boyo," he said, and pointed to my shoulder. "That the worst of it?" He hadn't let loose of my hand.

Dad was use to seeing Pat and I bandaged up during our playing days, and as a cop, he had seen more than enough injuries, but I could see he was shook up.

"This, and a couple of cracked ribs," I said. "Otherwise, I really am okay."

"Of course you are, cauliflower boy," Mom said, staring at my enlarged and rather ugly ear, and looking at me with that deep-in-your-heart stare that said she didn't believe you. But she was back in control of herself, and finally found time to hug her daughter-in-law. It was good to have them here, I found myself thinking.

We talked for a while, mostly about the grand kids, who were with their other grandma. Things calmed down considerably, although I knew we would speak of this again.

The door popped open, and Max Howard plopped his plump face around the jamb. Pat motioned him in and introduced him to my parents.

"Don't mean to intrude, folks, but I wanted to see how my star investigator was doin'."

As always, Max took over the room, and filled everyone in on the Crystal Harbor case, and how his "star investigator" had saved the old folks, and caught the bad guys, red-handed.

I blanched at his tale, but I could see dad puff up with pride, and my mom was feeling better, knowing that some good came from all of this.

"Your boy, he did good, ma'am. Y'all should be proud of him, that's for sure."

Mom said, "Thank you," in a tone that said, *but don't you dare give him any more dangerous assignments, mister!* But I don't think Max caught on. Or maybe he did.

"I hear you're outta here in a day or two, Tommy. I may have some news for you, but I'll let you get better, and I'll see you at home." Max bowed his way out, and Pat followed him into the hallway.

"I am going to let you all spend time with Thomas," C.J. said, as I winced at the thought of the lecture I was about to receive. "I need to rescue Mama, before the boys tie her up and put her in the closet again." She made plans with my parents for dinner later, and left, giving me a 'sorry' look on the way out.

Once we were alone, my mother said, "Seamus, you need a cigarette." And, as if by magic, dad got up from the chair that had been C.J.'s bed last night, and said, "I think I will go down stairs for a smoke," and walked out of the room.

"How long did it take you to train him to do that?" I said with the best smile I could give in the present circumstances.

"Don't annoy me, Thomas," Mom said, just as I had heard a thousand times, and sat on the bed beside me. She stroked my hand, and said, "This is all my fault, isn't it?"

"Damn straight!" I smiled again, and said to her hurt face, "No Ma, it is not your fault. I did something stupid, because I'm still learning about this job, and what is expected of me, if I'm going to be smart about how I do things. This was my first case with any possibility of danger, and I just didn't recognize that danger." I squeezed her hand. "I will next time. I promise."

"I don't want to worry about you being hurt," she said.

"You've done it with Dad for how many years?" But I realized that worry was in her eyes. How had she managed to hide it from us all this time?

Now it was her turn to smile. "I miss you so very much."

It was a simple statement, not needing an answer, but I said, "Me too, Ma, me too."

*   *   *   *

Two of the three most important women in my life are driving me crazy. Since coming home from the hospital late yesterday, I've been treated like an invalid. At least I *have* been allowed to use the bathroom without help.

There have been times when I felt lonely in my little apartment above Ireland's Own. Today I'm trying to think of a way to send everyone home. But it has been decided that mom and dad will be leaving tomorrow, after some very tense (on my part) conversations about mom staying a "few" weeks more. I'm glad they were here for me, but I'm feeling a lot better now, and it's time to resume life.

My face is almost back to its normal size, but the stitches on my two deepest cuts near my ear will remain for three more days. My ribs are sore, but I escaped the internal bleeding the doctor was concerned about, and a heavy tape job and pain medication is all I needed. My shoulder was now supported only by a sling, and even that came off at night. Nothing hurt as much as my ego.

I was sitting in the living room, which was open to my little kitchen area, watching mom and C.J. cleaning up, and marveling at how their constant comments about what slobs men were, were almost identical and simultaneous.

There was a knock on the door, and I yelled, "Come in," above the din in the kitchen, and Max Howard and a man I didn't recognize walked in.

Max' tie was tight against his neck, so I figured this was a business call.

"Lookin' good, Hoss," he said. "This here is Lt. Jake Berger from Vice down at the 14th Precinct, Tommy."

I shook hands with the big man. He looked to be mid-forties, about six-two, heavy, but all muscle, with an all business face. The two sat down, the lieutenant in the chair Bobby Hemphill had used a few nights ago, and Max pulled over one of my chairs from the kitchen table set.

"You ladies will excuse us if we talk a little business?" Max said. Mom perked up, looking a little concerned, but C.J. got her talking about the kids, and she seemed to lose interest in us.

"Jake here's an old friend, Tommy. He's been handlin' this deal since your buddy at the restaurant gave the police a description of the guy that jumped you." He looked at the cop as if to turn the discussion over to him.

Berger looked apologetic. "Hate to bother you with this now," he said. He sounded like he was maybe from New York, or Jersey, but a long time ago. I nodded for him to go on. "The description we got from…," he looked at the notebook in his hand, "…from Robby Sedgwick, got a few of the people on my team thinking. We pulled some prints off your truck, and sure enough, they matched prints for a Melvin Udall, an enforcer-type wanted in Chicago."

"Uh huh," Max chimed in. "They've been lookin' for this guy for a long list of mob crimes up north." Max spoke in a low voice, so as not to alarm my mother. "And, here it looks like he's been plying his trade in our fair city."

"How does a guy that works for the mob in Chicago wind up working for a small time bookie in Atlanta?" I asked.

"We wondered that too," said Berger. "Our best guess is that this Charles Mitchell may be part of something bigger, maybe multi-state, and that means the Feds can get involved."

"This Udall might have been on loan to Mitchell from Chicago, maybe to help him get a bigger scam started for a more powerful group."

I thought about that for a minute. "What do you want me to do?"

Jake Berger took a picture from his breast pocket, and handed it to me. "Is this the man who attacked you?"

I took the picture from him. "I have no idea." I said. "I'm sorry, but I never saw his face."

They both looked disappointed.

"Max, there are two people in jail and two former employees of Crystal Harbor that you could show this to who can verify that this is a picture of the guy they knew as John Edwards."

"We done that, Hoss, and its him. But they don't know if this is the guy who attacked you."

"If it's not, why would his prints be all over my truck?"

"They shouldn't be," said Berger, "but we need to be sure."

"I sure as hell can't prove it," I sighed. "But I know in my heart it was. I do think I heard him say that I had gotten involved in somebody's business that I shouldn't have, and I wasn't dealing with any other case at the time."

Berger stood up. "Well, let me know if anything comes to mind." He handed me a card, shook hands, and he and Max got up to leave.

"One good thing," Berger said. "Not much chance Udall would stick around, knowing we're looking for him. I think you won't have to worry about seeing him again."

I hadn't even considered that. I did now, and I hoped he was right.

CHAPTER 11

▼

5:00 P.M., 11 October 2002
Peachtree Street

I had slept off and on during the night, plagued by dull but persistent pain in my shoulder and in my chest. About noon, having dosed myself again with pills, I dozed off in my living room, the TV droning on with mundane daytime programs.

A knock at the door woke me. I felt groggy and my mouth was dry and sticky. I croaked out a "come in," and C.J. entered, carrying in a tray of food, and a pitcher of iced tea.

"Well," she said. "Don't we look like shit?"

"And feel like it too, thank you very much."

She smiled, and put the tray down next to me. She poured a glass of the tea, and I gulped it down. The fog began to lift somewhat.

I looked at the burger and fries. "Hey," I said, "This doesn't look homemade!"

"Hey, yourself! You're back on regular rations, sport. I've got a house to run, and in case you've forgotten, there's a whole big restaurant downstairs."

"Jeez," I muttered. "The good times didn't last very long."

"Eat something, and then we'll take a little walk."

"Sounds good," I said, needing to get out of this room for a while.

I was half way through the sandwich, a little surprised at how hungry I was, when the phone rang. C.J. answered, and then handed the phone to me.

"It's a lady," she whispered.

I took the phone as a lump came up in my throat. "Abby?"

"Thomas," the smooth voice said. "It is Maria Barrett, Thomas."

"Oh," I said, a little disappointedly. "How are you, Mrs. Barrett?"

"Thomas, I must see you. I have need of your help." There was apprehension in her voice. It was hard to imagine this woman in a state of distress.

Suddenly, I feared for Abby's safety. Why else would Maria Barrett call me?

"My help? What is it? Is there something wrong with Abby? Is she back home?"

"Please," she said. "I can explain much easier in person. May I come to see you?"

I thought for a moment, concern, and fear welling up. "No," I said, "I'll come to you, if that's okay."

"Yes, of course. But, it would be best if you come by this evening. Would 8 p.m. be all right?"

I tried again. "Mrs. Barrett, please, can't you tell me what is going on?"

"Tonight, Thomas. I will tell you tonight."

The line went dead.

C.J. was standing over me, watching my face intently. "What is it?"

I took a moment to collect myself. "That was Abby's mother," I said. "Something is wrong with Abby, I think. She wouldn't tell me anything over the phone."

C.J. took the tray that was still on my lap, put it on the table, and sat down next to me. "I wondered why Abby hadn't been by to see you."

"She's been away, in Miami, some kind of family business."

I stood and wandered around the room. "Why couldn't she tell me what's going on over the phone?"

"What did she say?"

"She asked to see me tonight, said she would explain then. I said that I would come to her house." I looked at my watch. "Hell, that's over four hours from now." I picked up the phone. "I've got to call her back."

"Wait, Tommy," C.J. said. "Do it her way. There must be a reason. Look, you'll need a ride. I have to run to Mama's, but I'll come back and pick you up at 7:15, unless you need some help dressing?"

"Thanks, sis, but I hate to take you away from the kids. I don't know how late I'll be out there."

"Thomas, you know you can't drive yourself yet. Mama will be glad to stay with the kids, and Pat will be needed at the restaurant tonight."

She kissed me on the cheek, and said, "I'll see you later."

*   *   *   *

Night had fallen, and the air had turned crisp and cool. C.J. maneuvered her SUV through the remnants of rush hour traffic on Peachtree to Druid Hills Road, and turned right.

Neither of us had said much. I wasn't sure what to say, and dreaded what I feared I was about to hear from Abby's mom. I gave C.J. directions to Abercorn Terrace after we reached the Emory University area, and we pulled into the Barrett driveway three minutes early.

On my first visit to the house, and that seemed like a month ago, the whole property had been lit up…the porch, the driveway. Now, the house and yard were in pitch black. Not even an inside light showed through a window.

"You sure this is the right place?" C.J. said, staring out the windshield, up at the dark house.

"This is it," I said.

"You want me to wait in the car?"

I was already out and moving toward the porch. "No," I called back to her. "Please, come with me." I couldn't shake the feeling that I was going to need family around.

I started up the front steps, and when I had nearly reached the top, the front door opened a crack, but the lights stayed off.

A soft voice said, "Thomas, is that you?"

"Yes, ma'am."

Mrs. Barrett caught the shadow behind me. "Is there someone with you?" she said, a slight sound of alarm in her voice.

"Yes," I said again. "It's okay, ma'am. My sister-in-law drove me here. I hope that's all right."

The door opened wider, and we went in. As she closed the door, Abby's mom turned the foyer light on, but only dimly.

"My God!" She was staring at my stitched-up face, and the sling on my arm. She touched my face with her cool fingertips. "What happened to you?"

"I'm okay," I said, not wishing to explain. "Just an accident." I turned to introduce C.J., eager to get the attention off myself. Mrs. Barrett shook her hand.

"Would you prefer I wait outside?" C.J. asked. "I don't wish to intrude."

"Of course not, my dear, you are most welcome as Thomas trusts you to be here."

I was losing patience; even though I wasn't sure I wanted to hear what might be said. "Mrs. Barrett, please, where is Abby? Is she home? Is she okay?"

"Thomas," she said, touching my arm. "Abby has been kidnapped." A tear welled in her eye. "She was taken while in a cab on her way to the airport in Miami."

I was sure I had misunderstood. This was impossible.

"What do you mean? What do you mean kidnapped? By whom? Why?"

"Come with me," she said. "Please, Thomas, and we will explain what we know."

I caught the "we" but kept quiet as we walked down the hallway to a heavy wood door. I could feel C.J. close behind me.

"This is my husband's study," Maria Barrett said.

We entered the dimly lit room covered with heavy, dark paneling, and bookshelves surrounding the room. A large, ornately carved desk sat opposite the door. On the desk, a lawyers lamp, one of those small lamps with a green, glass shade sat, the only light on in the room. Behind the desk, rising and coming around to greet us, was a man of medium height, with a full head of starkly white hair.

It was the man from the picture on the piano, the family portrait with Richard Barrett. He appeared older than I had thought, maybe ten years older than his wife. He walked with the aid of a burled walnut cane.

Richard Barrett's right leg was withered; two or three inches shorter than his left. He wore a built-up shoe.

"I had hoped to meet you under happier circumstances, young man," he said warmly, and shook my hand. He looked at my injuries, but refrained from asking me about them. He introduced himself to C.J., as I explained who she was, and motioned to the chairs in front of the desk. Mrs. Barrett pulled a chord hanging from the ceiling, as her husband brought another chair for her. A moment later, the maid, Patrice opened the study door.

"Coffee, please, Patrice." Maria said. The girl nodded, and left silently.

When she closed the door, I said, "Would you please tell me what is going on?"

They both sat down.

"Three days ago," Mrs. Barrett said, "a man came to see me. Richard was away and I received our visitor alone. He said he was a representative of the Cuban government. I doubted the credentials he presented, but what could I do, but listen to him?"

Her husband leaned toward her, and touched her hand, urging her on.

"He said that he had come on behalf of the Castro government, to confiscate the family valuables left behind in Cuba, when my father and his friends… 'gusanos,' worms, the man called them…, 'deserted' their homeland."

"Wait," I said. "I don't understand what this has to do with Abby."

"Please be patient, Thomas. You must understand the whole story if you are going to be able to help us."

I sat back and waited for her to continue, wondering how I could possibly help.

"He said that these valuables were the property of the Castro government, and had been abandoned by certain families, including my own, when we had 'abandoned' our mother country. I feigned ignorance and the man said he had expected that I would be uncooperative. He said he was sure my memory would improve if Abby were to 'visit' him as a 'guest' of the Cuban government. At least until I gave him the information he wanted. That's when he showed me a picture of Abby, tied to a chair, gagged and blindfolded."

She fought her tears again. "He wouldn't leave. He just sat there staring at me, then at Abby's picture. Finally, I relented somewhat and told him that I remembered stories about buried valuables left in Cuba, but that I was a very small child when we left, and no one had ever confided in me as to what had occurred those last days in Cuba. You see, my father was a member of the landed gentry of Cuba. He and his closest friends were anti-Castro, and they decided to take their families to the United States. They buried their treasured belongings that they could not spirit out of Cuba, in a secret location unknown to but a few.

"The plan was to return after Castro was thrown out of power and retrieve their valuables, and to reclaim their plantations."

There was a light knock at the door, and Patrice wheeled in the serving cart.

"I will serve, Patrice. You may go." Mrs. Barrett poured the coffee and set delicate cups before us. She seemed relieved to have a moment to collect her thoughts. I fought my impatience and could barely drink my coffee.

"Of course, Castro is still in power, and over the years the few who knew the location of this secret place began to die off. There are few alive who might be able to help."

"And your father never told you the location?" C.J. asked.

"If he meant to tell me, he didn't have a chance. My father died suddenly, at a young age. He never had a chance to tell me or anyone that I know of."

"How about your mother?" I asked. "Didn't she know?"

"If she did, she never told me. After my father died, the life seemed to go out of her. I think my father was so obsessed with returning to the plantation that he took himself away from us mentally. You must understand that he began to feel that he was responsible for talking the others into leaving Cuba. He went into fits of depression, and mother felt she had lost him. We began to believe *el tesoro,* the treasure, was just a legend."

"Did anyone try to go back for their belongings?"

Richard Barrett leaned forward, and spoke, giving his wife a break. "Several of the family members who were involved in hiding el tesoro went to Cuba with the liberation army at the Bay of Pigs in April of 1961. None were ever heard from again. It is unknown whether they were killed or captured. But they were never accounted for, I'm afraid.

"Of course," he continued, "I was not in the picture then, but I've heard the stories over the years that Maria and I have been married."

"But, why did this guy, whoever he is, single you out to harass?" I asked.

"I can't know for sure," Mrs. Barrett said, "but my father planned the burial site and the defection. My sister never was involved with family business, and my brother is a doctor working with the poor in Central America for many years now. I think he assumed that I was most likely to know the location."

"But you don't know," C.J. said. It wasn't a question, as much as a declaration.

"No, I'm afraid I don't."

I was losing patience. "Look, you've got to call in the police," I said, "or the FBI. Mrs. Barrett, you can't handle this alone. You are endangering Abby's life every minute you wait!"

"No," Richard Barrett spoke forcefully from behind the desk. "That is precisely what we cannot do."

"Thomas, if we bring in the authorities, they will certainly kill Abby," his wife added. "This man made it very clear to me that I must not contact the authorities, and I believed him."

I sat back, feeling defeated. "What do we do?"

Maria Barrett said, "I made a deal with him."

Her words hung in mid air.

"A deal?" I said, stunned by this simple admission. "What kind of deal could you make with the Cubans?"

"I told him that I might be able to get the information he wanted from some people still alive in Miami. He wanted to know who, but I refused to tell him. I said that not telling him would be my way of protecting my daughter." She drank a little coffee and her hand shook a little. "I was buying time, of course, but he said that my position was reasonable. I told him that I cared nothing about el tesoro. It was lost to us a long time ago and we didn't need any of it."

Her husband reached over and squeezed her hand. "We have no need for more money," he said. "We just want our Abby back, unharmed."

"Then what?" C.J. asked.

Maria Barrett continued. "He told me he would give me ten days to get him the information he required, and that he would return here at the end of that time."

I stood up, the pain shooting through me. My adrenalin started pumping now and I moved forward. "You mean this son of a bitch is just going to walk in here, in the open, and demand this information?"

"Thomas, remember that Abby is not with him. If he doesn't leave here safely, then my daughter will be in the gravest danger."

She was right. I knew that. I felt suddenly spent again, and braced myself against the side of the big leather chair. "What do we do?" I said quietly.

"I said that we needed your help, Thomas," Mrs. Barrett said. "We need someone to go to Miami, make inquiries of certain people who might give me the location of the burial site. We need someone who can get to Miami without being followed, who can make contact with individuals who might help us without seeking to take the treasure for themselves," she said. "I cannot make contact by phone because the calls may be traced. I cannot go there as surely I will be followed. If the identities of others who might know the location that my father picked were revealed, the Cubans might abandon asking me for information and threaten them instead. We cannot protect Abby's safety if that happens, Thomas."

"And you think her life is safer with me involved than with the FBI handling this?" I shook my head. "This is crazy, ma'am. With all due respect, this is absolutely crazy."

"The FBI would be easily spotted and there might be political consequences to their involvement," she said. "In any case, Thomas, the FBI doesn't love my daughter."

*   *   *   *

Sometime later, I was reading over a letter that Maria Barrett had prepared for me as an introduction to her sister in Miami, as well as a list of three individuals she thought most likely to be willing and able to give me information that would be helpful. The letter asked her sister to assist me in locating the families on the list.

C.J. and Maria were speaking quietly to each other as I read. Richard Barrett leaned over the desk and said, "Maria has great faith in you, my boy. I want you to know I would pay any amount to get Abby released, but I get the impression that any sum that I would offer would be a pittance to what the Cuban's think the treasure is worth. And, physically......" he looked down at his leg. "Well, I'm afraid I cannot be of much help to you."

"Mr. Barrett," I said, "I don't know if this is the best way to handle this. In fact, I think it's a horrible mistake."

"Thomas, I'm prepared to trust Maria's intuition about you," he said. "You should too. By the way," he opened a drawer, "we don't know, but we must assume, that our telephone conversations may be subject to listening devises." He took two cell phones and a charger from the drawer. "These phones are from my office. There is no reason to think the numbers are known to anyone but me." He handed me a phone and the charger unit. "I suggest we communicate only with these cell phones."

I took a phone and the charger.

"Thomas," he said gravely. "You must not be followed to Miami. And......" he added unnecessarily, "...time is critically important."

*   *   *   *

We were on our way back to Buckhead. C.J. was thinking. I could tell from the way she scrunched up her brow. My head was spinning.

Finally, my sister-in-law said, "I'll call Pat. We need to meet tonight and help you plan a way out of Atlanta."

"C.J., this is crazy. Why would the Barrett's trust me with their daughter's life? They don't even know me!"

"They know that Abby is important to you."

"That doesn't mean I'm capable of handling this!"

"I can understand their reasoning," she countered. "You care for their daughter, you have investigative skills. You'll go the extra mile to help because you care."

I didn't answer, but I saw her point. I was just afraid I'd screw up, which could have deadly consequences for Abby.

"But," she said, "you will need help driving down there, and getting around."

"C.J., I can't ask you and Pat to get involved in this any further. As you can see," I looked at my arm, "shit happens."

"I was about to suggest......actually, ask......that you consider taking my brother, Bobby, along."

I gave her a troubled look. "I don't know. I wouldn't want him to get the wrong idea, like it's a job offer or something."

"Thomas," she said quickly, "we can make it clear he's just helping you out. It would be up to you whether you even tell him what this is all about. Please, he needs to do something with a purpose. Think about it, okay?" she added in her gentile accent.

After a moment, I said, "Sure, I'll think about it. How could I say 'no' to such a cutie?"

We both smiled for the first time that night, but my face went set again, and after a moment C.J. said, "What is it?"

"Nothing, really," I said. "Except, the Barrett's never did explain what Abby was doing in Miami all this time, anyway."

CHAPTER 12

▼

9 P.M., 12 October 2002
Ireland's Own

I was in Pat's office next to the kitchen, where C.J. was wrapping a Falcon's team jacket around my shoulders. I was wearing a ball cap, jeans, and Air Jordan's. I looked like any student or sports freak who ever walked into the bar.

On the chair next to me was a backpack with some extra clothes. Pat came in to check on us.

"Tom, you sure about this? Taking Bobby with you, I mean?"

"We'll be fine," I said. "Is it busy out there? I want to walk out with a crowd."

"Busy enough. You really think someone's watching you?"

"I think it's best to figure the Barrett's are being watched, and that we could have been followed when we left their house last night."

"He's right," C.J. said. "We have to protect his identity, and it has to look like he's home at night. I brought a timer for the lights upstairs."

"Jeez," Pat said. "Suddenly, I'm married to Mata Hari."

C.J. gave him the razz berries, kissed me on the cheek, and said, "Good luck, and be careful, Yankee Tom."

"Thanks for everything, C.J."

"Hey," Pat had a hurt look on his face, "I'm the one giving you time off!"

*   *   *   *

About 10:30 p.m., I headed for the door behind a large party that was leaving the restaurant. Out on Peachtree, I made a quick right, crossed East Paces Ferry

Road, and headed north, but only to the next bar, one of the ones frequented by the younger crowd.

The place was called "Yellow Jackets," after the Georgia Tech mascot. It was painted with garish yellow and black stripes across the front. At the back of the restaurant was an outdoor bar and patio through which I planned to leave after I was sure I had not been followed. I went up to the bar, and took a seat at the end facing the front entrance. There were maybe thirty customers, but none blocked my view of the front door.

I nursed a draft beer for twenty minutes. At precisely 11 p.m., I used the men's room at the rear of the place to turn my reversible jacket inside out, left the bathroom, and headed for the patio.

The weather was holding for October, and three tables were occupied outside. I took another beer to a table at the wooden railing closest to the street. At 11:30, I took a last sip from my glass and walked off the patio, heading back to East Paces Ferry Road.

I walked about three blocks to an apartment building with a double glass door entrance, and a dark lobby. Once inside, I punched the "down" button on the elevator panel, stepped in quickly as the doors opened, and went down into the underground parking garage.

On the 'P2' level, the elevator door opened to a dimly lit area which smelled vaguely of gas and motor oil. There were ten or twelve cars visible, but I was alone. Walking to the left of the elevator, I found stall eight with the silver Dodge Durango SUV there as expected. It was parked with its back end to the rear of the stall. I glanced around, standing as still as I could for about a minute. No one came down the elevator.

I went around to the rear of the Durango. The hatch was unlocked. I climbed into the cramped space, lying up against the back of the third row seats to pull the hatch down. And, then I waited, for what seemed a very long time.

At midnight, I heard the bell of the elevator door ring. A moment later I heard footsteps on the concrete, not loud, but footsteps just the same.

Just for a moment, it flashed in my mind that I was defenseless, lying on my back in a two-foot wide space with no weapon. My .38, still unused, was in a drawer in my bedroom. I hoped I wasn't about to need it.

The driver's door opened and the truck's weight shifted as someone sat down and closed the door.

A low voice whispered, "Tommy, you there?"

"I'm here, Bobby," I said, feeling a flood of relief.

"Jesus, I've been a nervous wreck, man!"

"It's okay," I said. "Let's get out of here but don't rush, Bobby, keep it natural." He started the Durango, put it in gear, pulled out of the stall, and I felt us go around to the right, then right again, and up the ramp toward the exit.

A few minutes later, we headed north on Peachtree to Lenox Road, took a left, and left again onto Route 400, southbound. Three minutes later, 400 melted into I-75/85, taking us through downtown Atlanta. From my position on my back, I caught the tops of the tallest office buildings along the freeway. Neither of us had spoken since we left the garage. I was stiff and in pain from lying in the cramped space. We took the I-75 branch where the two highways split. Finally, Bobby said, "we're crossing I-285, Tommy." We were outside the beltway of Atlanta now.

I said, "Pull off the Route 138 exit at Stockbridge, Bobby. Find a gas station or fast food place. I'll move up front with you when we stop."

"Okay. Hey, Tommy, what's this all about, man? My sister said someone's following you?"

"Get us out of town, Bobby. I'll explain later, okay?"

At a Wendy's, Bobby drove up to the drive-thru window and got us a bag of burgers and a couple of sodas. We were alone in the line so I climbed out of the rear hatch and joined Bobby up front.

"What do we do now?" He sounded eager and wide-awake.

"We'll stay on I-75 to the Florida Turnpike," I said. "From there, we'll head to Orlando. We should get there right around eight in the morning. We can lose ourselves in town, get a motel room, and grab some sleep. We can sleep several hours and still reach Miami by tomorrow night. We'll reach Mrs. Barrett's sister as soon as we get in."

"Sounds like a plan," Bobby said and pulled away from the pick-up window.

"By the way, who is Mrs. Barrett?"

CHAPTER 13

▼

6:00 P.M., 13 October 2002
Miami, Florida

We hit the outskirts of Miami. I pulled out a map of the city that I had bought at a gas station outside of town. Bobby Hemphill yawned as he drove. We were both tired, having driven until morning, catching too little sleep at a motel in Orlando.

"You okay?" I asked.

"Yeah, just a little tired, I guess," Bobby answered. "Let me see if I got this straight, man. So you got this lady whose daughter got kidnapped. She wants you to get information from somebody in Miami, so she can give it to the kidnappers. She gets her daughter back and all's right with the world?"

"That's about the size of it," I said. I had given Bobby the bare bones of the situation without telling him that this case was personal. C.J. had evidently told her brother that this was just another job, and had kept my relationship with Abby out of it. I figured that was the smart way to leave it.

"But if they know who has this information, why not just call 'em on the phone and get it?"

"We can't take a chance that the bastards will go after the source of the information directly. If they did, the girl's life wouldn't be worth a damn to them," I said, the words choking up in my throat. I wanted to shout out Abby's name. To scream out that I'm crazy about girl and that she is important to me, Bobby, so don't let me screw up and get her killed!

"So what happens when we find out what they want to know? Do we get to go save her? Do we get to be the heroes?" Bobby was practically bubbling over with enthusiasm. I was getting angry that he was having fun with this.

"'We' don't do anything, Bobby. In fact," I added trying to soften my words, "if the parent's have any sense at all, they'll get the cops, and FBI involved right away. This thing involves the Cuban government and could draw the Feds into a real mess. I don't belong anywhere near anything this dangerous."

"Hell, Tommy, we could do it, man! That's how you build a business, you know, show 'em what you can do!"

"What we can do is our job. That's it, that's all. There," I said, pointing out the window, "take the next exit."

*   *   *   *

Calle Ocho, Eighth Street, is one of two main commercial streets running through the center of Little Havana. The neighborhood, once the domain of the Cuban refugees who escaped Castro's regime, and now is the home of Latin's from all over Mexico and Central America, is still the heart of anti-Castro sentiment and demonstrations. The strong Cuban flavor of the area shows in the store names and colorful architecture. Restaurants, shops, and cigar factories all carried signs in Spanish.

Maria Barrett's sister, Anna Ortiz, lives to the south within the boundaries of Little Havana, and operates a gift shop on Calle Ocho. I had both addresses from Abby's mother. I looked at my watch, it was still early. The best bet might be to contact Anna Ortiz at her place of business.

I looked for the store sign while Bobby drove slowly down the street. Finally, I spotted the address I was looking for, high on the front of a two-story brick building which was painted yellow. There were two storefronts on the street level, one being *El Pinar Citrico*-The Citrus Grove. We had found Anna Ortiz. Bobby drove a little farther down the street and pulled into a parking space.

"Wait here for me," I said. He started to protest, but I stopped him. "I need you to keep an eye out for anyone who might be looking for us. If you see anyone suspicious use your cell phone to call me on the number I gave you," I said, showing him that I was carrying the phone Richard Barrett had given me. "Bobby, it's important that no one sees me talking to Mrs. Barrett's sister. Keep a sharp eye out."

That mollified him for the moment, and I climbed out of the Durango, took off the sling on my left arm, and threw it onto the passenger seat. I moved my arm around a little to get the blood flowing, all the time trying to figure out what to say when I met this woman. I left Bobby, and headed back down the block, Maria Barrett's letter in my back pocket.

A young girl, sixteen or seventeen with deep black hair, sat behind a cash register about half way back on the right side of the store. She didn't look up as I entered. When I reached her, I could see she was engrossed in one of those teen fashion magazines. The text, I could see, was written in Spanish.

Either I was invisible or the article she was reading was a 'doozy' because she never looked up until I cleared my throat. I was the only customer in the place.

"*Hola, senor,*" she said, finally.

"Hi," I said. "I wonder if you could help me. I'm looking for Mrs. Ortiz? Anna Ortiz?"

"My mother, senor, she has stepped out. She will be back soon to help me close the shop for the night. Would you like to leave a message or to wait?"

"I'll wait," I said. I thanked her and wandered around the store. The shelves were lined with expensive objects with a decidedly tasteful Latin flair. Nothing looked touristy. There was some real artwork around, including some things I really liked, but I wasn't here to buy antiques, I wanted to get this over with.

About ten minutes later, I heard a door back in the rear of the store close, and someone was rustling around back there. The girl looked up from her reading.

"Just one moment, senor." She left the register and disappeared behind a curtain that separated the sales area from what I figured to be the stockroom. She was gone several minutes, and then returned to her reading without giving me a glance.

A moment later, the curtain parted and a woman bearing a striking resemblance to Maria Barrett and Abby came out. She spotted me and came over.

"I'm told you are looking for me?" She looked at me closely, as if considering whether she knew me or not.

"Mrs. Ortiz," I started. "My name is Thomas Patrick. I'm here from Atlanta. I wonder if there is some place private we could talk?"

She glanced at her daughter and back at me. "Follow me," she said. "We can speak in my office." I followed her through the curtain into a brightly lit storeroom. The narrow hallway lined with boxes of merchandise led back to a door which opened to a tiny, uncomfortably warm office. There was a desk, two chairs, and a bookcase which appeared to hold catalogues, phone books, and such.

Anna Ortiz sat behind the desk, and motioned for me to take the other chair. "Who are you and what is it you need to see me about, young man?" she said.

"Ma'am, as I said, I came here from Atlanta. I came here at the request of your sister, Maria Barrett......"

She interrupted me. "I have not spoken to my sister recently. Maria has not informed me that I would be receiving a visitor." Her face took on a look of distrust.

"Yes, I know." I reached into my pocket. "I have a letter for you from her. It was not prudent for her to let you know I was coming. I think the letter will explain why I'm here."

She took it from me warily, opened it, and began to read. By her face, it took only moments for her to get the picture. "My God," she said softly, looking at me questioningly. "Abby has been kidnapped? How did this happen? Why?"

"Mrs. Ortiz," I said. "Now that you know why I'm here, can you help me? I've got a very short time to help Abby and her family."

"Why you?" she asked. "I do not wish to offend you, young man, but why has my sister not informed the authorities?"

I smiled ruefully. "Believe me, I asked her and Mr. Barrett the same thing. Frankly, they are afraid that the perpetrators of the kidnapping will get the information they seek from a source in Miami without our help. That could be dangerous for Abby and you, too, ma'am."

"Yes, I see that." She was quiet for a moment, her brow furrowed. "But, you can help? Are you qualified to help? If you are not that may also be dangerous for my niece, could it not?"

She was reading my mind or my age, but I said, "I am a private investigator, Mrs. Ortiz. But, as I said, the timing is urgent. I need your assistance if you can provide any." I took the list of names Maria Barrett had given me from my pocket and handed it to her sister. "Your sister said these people might be able to help us."

She took the paper from me and studied it. "I know very little about this buried treasure you seek. I heard many stories about el tesoro as a child growing up among the children of the very same families who came to America with my father." She shook her head. "Papa never told us whether the stories were true or just legends.

"Mr. Patrick," she said as she rose from her seat, "Again, I do not wish to offend or doubt you but I must speak of this with my sister."

"Sure, I understand." I rose with her. "It's not safe to call her on her home phone. I'm sorry for the cloak and dagger stuff but we have to be careful." I handed her the Barrett cell phone. "Use this. Your sister or her husband will answer, and you can speak freely. I'll wait out in the store, if that's okay?"

*   *   *   *

About twenty minutes later, Anna Ortiz came into the sales area and handed me the phone. "My sister would like you to call her later when you are settled in at a motel. I need some time to contact a few people. It is not easy to get to some of the old ones. Their children are very protective of them." I started to speak, but she cut me off. "I am very aware of the importance of time," she said. "You must believe me, Mr. Patrick, if these people are approached in the wrong way you may never obtain the information you seek. Some of them belong to secret paramilitary groups, like 'Alpha 66.' These people would kill you for trying to gather this information rather than help you."

"Yes, ma'am, I understand." I said. "How should I reach you?"

"I will use my daughter's cell phone to make inquires. I will reach you on your phone if you will give me the number. If you do not hear from me before 2 p.m. tomorrow, meet me here at three," she said, and abruptly turned and went back behind the curtain.

I wrote the number on the back of a business card and handed it to her. I went out to find Bobby Hemphill. I was not sure if I had accomplished anything, but I felt less alone.

CHAPTER 14

▼

2:00 P.M., 14 October 2002
Miami, Florida

The weather had been warm and muggy all morning, and now the usual after-noon showers had arrived. Bobby and I hung around the Seacrest Motel all day. I had been anxious to hear from Anna Ortiz but the phone had been silent. Our two o'clock deadline was about to pass so we prepared to head over to the store. It was futile to try to guess what her silence meant. Either she had not reached the people she wanted to speak with or she hadn't found anyone willing to speak to me. I hoped it wasn't the latter.

We were only ten minutes from El Pinar Citrico so I paced the worn, brown carpet of our room and willed the time to pass. Bobby kept busy watching HBO.

I had tried to reach the Barrett's twice during the night with no success. I decided to try again, before we went to see Mrs. Ortiz.

The phone in Atlanta rang twice before Richard Barrett answered. "Thomas, my boy," he said without preamble. "Are you making any progress?"

"I hope so, sir. I'm about to have a second meeting with Mrs. Ortiz. She was going to try and make contact with the people on the list."

"Yes," he said, "Anna called us yesterday. Poor thing, she is quite worried for us."

"Of course," I said. I always find speaking with Barrett a little unsettling but I'm not sure why. "Is Mrs. Barrett in?"

"I'm sorry, Thomas. She is attending a school function with our younger daughter. We feel it is best to keep things as normal as possible for the other chil-dren until we can resolve this matter."

This matter. I kept waiting for him to show fear, anguish, any of the feelings I felt like showing myself. "I will inform Maria of your situation. Please keep us informed. We have only a few days left."

"I will," I said and hung up.

*   *   *   *

We were nearing Little Havana when my phone rang.

"That you, Hoss?" The booming voice on the other end belonged to Max Howard. "Your brother gave me this number. Got a minute?"

"Sure, Max. I'm on my way to a meeting. Is everyone okay?"

"Yeah, they're fine. I just wanted to check in with you, see how your doin' down there, Tommy."

"Too early to tell Max, but I hope to know more, later today."

"Tommy, you're watchin' out for yourself, right?"

"We're fine, Max. You sure everything's okay back home? You sound concerned about something. Are you?"

"I just don't want to see you wind up hurt again," he said, sounding like a father.

I tried to make light of Max's concern. "Why would I, Max. John Edwards, or whoever he is, seems to be the only person looking to ring my bell, and I doubt he's hanging around Miami."

"You're probably right, but I got a call from Jake Berger over at the 14th Precinct."

For some reason, I tensed up a bit. "What did he say, Max?"

"Well," he answered, "seems like we were right when we told you we had finger prints from your truck that matched up with the guy who called himself John Edwards…"

"But?"

"But," he said, "what we didn't get told was those prints were all on the passenger side of the vehicle. There were no prints but yours on the drivers' side where you were attacked."

*   *   *   *

A few minutes later, I hung up with Max. I was taken aback by the information I had just received, but I couldn't think about what it all meant right now.

There would be time to sort it out when I got back to Atlanta. Right now, it was all about Abby.

Bobby dropped me off a block from the Ortiz' store and went off to park. He went for the 'lookout' job again, but I could see that his curiosity was getting the best of him. No time to worry about that, either. The store was busy, and several customers walked the aisles, studying the merchandise expertly. They were not tourists as much as they were patrons of the arts.

Anna Ortiz was taking care of some customers, but she saw me come in and motioned me to go back to her little office.

I went to wait for her. The room was still overly warm so I left the door open to circulate some air through the little room.

She finally joined me a few minutes later.

Anna Ortiz sat down across the desk from me. She looked tired, worried, a little frazzled.

"Your visit has brought many unhappy memories back to me," she said.

"I'm sorry, ma'am. That was not my wish."

"It is of no matter, young man. My dear sister and niece are the ones' we must worry about now."

"Yes, of course," I said. "Were you able to make any contacts last night?"

She hesitated for a moment before answering. "You must understand that what my sister is asking opens up old wounds."

"I don't think I understand." I thought I did but I needed to know more, I hoped she would fill in some blanks.

Anna Ortiz took a deep breath. You know about the defection…escape…what ever you wish to call it? My family, the five others, and the circumstances of el tesoro, the belongings that they left in Cuba?"

I nodded.

"Are you aware that my husband's family was one of the five?"

"No," I answered.

She shook her head slowly. "The Ortiz family was second only to the Martinez', that's my father's name, in wealth and influence. At the time my father put forth his plans to the others, they all knew he was right to suggest what he did. They all believed that Castro could not remain in power. They truly believed that the Cuban people would get rid of him so quickly that the families would return to their homeland and rebuild their plantations within a year."

Anna Ortiz smiled ruefully. "It was a stupid thing to think. History had shown that our people have never been willing to throw off the yoke of any oppressor. First came the Spanish, then Batista, and now, for over forty-five years, Fidel Castro.

"In any case, as the years went by, Castro kept his iron fist over the people and some of those who had come here with my father began to harbor ill feelings toward him. They missed their families and friends. They blamed him for a decision they had all made together. In the end," she said, sadly, "it broke his spirit."

"Did your husband's family feel that way?"

"Oh, it has meant little to my husband. Like my sister and I, he was but a child when we left Cuba. But yes, eventually my father and his old friend, my father-in-law, broke over this."

"I think you are trying to tell me that there is not a lot of help for us out there," I said, feeling sick to my stomach.

"These were rich families, Mr. Patrick. Most of them have not fared well here. Some that are left would be hard pressed to give up even the remotest chance to recapture the wealth their fathers left behind. Some lost family members at the Bay of Pigs. Most of the young ones were more concerned about recovering their family valuables than in overthrowing Castro. His disposal was to be but a means to an end."

I felt a devastating sadness envelope me. What could I do without help from these people?

"There is something else." Anna Ortiz said, and I fought to follow her words. "It does not help that my sister has gone outside our community to remarry. We are a very close-knit group, and there are some among us who were upset by her choice."

This seemed a bit archaic to me, but it interested me too. "Why is that, if I may ask?"

"Maria's first husband was a leader of our community. He was a spokesman against Castro. He is Abby's birth father, as you know."

I nodded.

"Ramon Castillo." She said the name fondly and reverently. "He was a wonderful man, a leader of our cause. His family had also followed my father to America. He was killed in an auto accident. That is what they called it, anyway. There are those among us, including my sister that doubt that it was an accident, but we could not prove it. The police were only too happy to call it such, in ending their inquiry. Then Richard Barrett came along. He and Maria were wed within nine months of the funeral." She smiled slightly. "We are very Catholic, Mr. Patrick. Propriety, such as a year of mourning, is very important to us."

"And this was considered an impropriety," I mused. "Were you upset about the marriage, too?"

She was quiet again. Then she said, "I love my sister, Mr. Patrick. I only want her happiness. She did it for the safety of the children."

I'd had enough family history. This was not going to save Abby. I couldn't remember ever feeling so helpless. I rose to leave. "I appreciate your trying to help, Mrs. Ortiz. I know your sister feels the same. I need to get back to Atlanta, and speak to the Barrett's about what to do next."

I offered her my hand, but she said, "I am sorry, Mr. Patrick, I fear my musings have given you the wrong idea. We are not out of options quite yet."

I sat down heavily. "What do you mean, ma'am?"

"There is one person on the list Maria gave you that I believe would help us," she said. "There is an old man; Jose Garcia is his name, who would do anything for the Martinez family. He ran the plantation for my father. Plantation El Pinar," she said wistfully.

"Like the name of your store?"

"Yes," she said. "It means 'the grove.' It was in the very center of the rich tobacco growing area of Cuba. Oh! The tobacco was magnificent, the land so beautiful!" she said, smiling for the first time. "My father loved El Pinar with his whole heart. And, Jose Garcia loved it just as much."

"So he remained loyal to your father?"

"Through the very worst of times. I believe he would have given his life for us."

I began to feel the weight lift. "So he is still alive? Did you speak to him? Will he help us?"

"Please, let me explain. Jose is a very old man. I believe he would help, but the question is, will he be able to."

I caught her meaning. "His memory," I said. "Alzheimer's?"

"I know only what I hear. Jose Garcia has been a leader of our community for many years, but he has been missing from meetings and anti-Castro demonstrations for some years now. His eldest son, Juan, has taken up his place."

"Did you speak to the son?" I was growing restless.

"I did," she said. "You will meet the Garcia's tonight."

My heart leapt. I felt like I was back from the dead.

"But," Anna Ortiz said. "I must warn you. You will have to convince them you can be trusted. They will be very wary of you, of your interest in all this."

*   *   *   *

At precisely 7:30 p.m., Anna Ortiz pulled up in front of our hotel room. I had told Bobby that I was meeting with family members tonight and that it might make them uncomfortable if I brought in an unknown person to this meeting.

"Hey, man," he said as I was walking out the door, "let me come along, Tommy. I'm bored stiff, sittin' around this damn room!"

"I'll be back soon," I said. "We'll go out, hit a few bars." I didn't mean it, but it seemed to mollify him.

"Where are we going?" I asked as Mrs. Ortiz pulled out onto the highway.

"The Garcia home is just three blocks from my shop," she answered. "I will drop you there, and Juan Garcia will call me on my cell phone when I am to retrieve you."

"You won't be at the meeting?"

"This is a business for men," she said quietly. "I have told them nothing but that my sister has asked them to meet with you on an urgent matter. It will be up to you to convince them to help you and Maria."

I thought about how to best do that. I had no idea who these people were. I remembered Mrs. Ortiz' comment that there were those in the Cuban community who were not ready to give up a chance to retrieve this treasure for themselves—if it even existed.

"Do you think this treasure exits?"

She was quiet for a long time. "I find it hard to believe," she said finally, "that my father and his friends would just walk away from their wealth. If they had, wouldn't the Castro government have taken anything of value that was left in the plantation houses?"

"That seems reasonable," I said.

"At this point, I hope that I am right for my niece's sake."

I thought about that for a minute. "Mrs. Ortiz, why was Abby in Miami?"

"Please," she said, "call me Anna, and I may call you Thomas?"

"Yes, of course."

"Abby's paternal grandparents are quite elderly. They are taking care of their assets, you know, giving many things including properties they own to family members now, rather than after death. Many of our old ones' do this. The Castillo family has more wealth than most."

"And Abby was here because…?"

"The Castillo family no longer recognizes my sister as a member of the family. Abby was here to represent herself and her brother, Carlos. Little Nina is Richard Barrett's natural daughter. There will be no Castillo inheritance for her, I'm afraid."

"That's kind of sad, isn't it?" I remarked.

"Yes," she said, "it is, but understandable too. The old ones see the anti-Castro sentiment dying off as our children become more American through marriages outside our community. They fear that soon our own people will no longer care about their Cuban heritage. Much the same thing has happened over the last three generations of Europeans who came to this country." She sighed. "Cuba has disappointed us, but it is still our home."

I smiled. "You obviously don't know many Irish people."

"There's always the odd duck," she smiled and said, as she pulled over to the curb, "this is the house." She opened her purse and handed me the letter Maria Barrett had sent to Miami with me. "This may help convince them to help you."

✳   ✳   ✳   ✳

The Garcia's house was small, but well maintained, just as most of the residences on the street appeared to be. There was an obvious pride in the appearance of the neatly cut lawns and painted fences.

I walked up the porch stairs, my damaged left leg stiff from lack of physical activity over the last few weeks, but my ribs and shoulder had continued to improve. I was able to go for longer periods without my sling and wasn't wearing it now.

The front door opened as I approached, and I was met by a heavy-set man in his early fifties, maybe five-eleven with a slim, salt and pepper moustache and wavy hair. He stood aside as I approached and motioned me in without a word.

He stared at me, still without speaking or offering me a hand. His face was set and unsmiling. I took this to be Jose Garcia's son, Juan, and I followed his lead back through the house into the dining room, feeling more than a little uncomfortable.

There were two men, one most certainly Jose Garcia, old, thin, and worn looking, the palms of his hands locked on the top of an ornately cut cane, and the other, a young man in his early twenties. His resemblance to the other men was striking. He was certainly family, likely Juan Garcia's son.

The man who had greeted me motioned to a chair at the end of the table, and sat down as I did.

There was a momentary silence, and then he said, "Now, senor, who are you, and why has Maria Castillo sent you to see my father?"

"Her name is Barrett, now," I said, realizing, even as I said it, that he knew this.

"Old habits die hard," he said. "Now, please tell us what this is about. My father is quite weak and I do not wish to burden him for very long."

"You are Juan Garcia?" He nodded slightly. "Then you were just a child when your family came to America with the Martinez family?" He didn't respond and I didn't wait for him to. "Mrs. Barrett's daughter has been kidnapped. She was in Miami on family business, and was taken while on her way to the Miami airport to fly back to Atlanta." I glanced at the old man, but he gave no sign that he was even listening to our conversation. The boy's face registered what I thought might be shock, or certainly surprise.

"Mr. Garcia," I said to Juan, "do you know an Abby Barrett?"

"I knew her when she was a child. She was a playmate of my son's," he nodded at the younger man across the table. "We have not seen her in many years. Not since her mother moved her and the boy, Carlos, away from Miami."

"I saw her, just last week," the boy said. I suddenly realized that he and I were about the same age. His father was caught off guard by the statement, his face showed surprise, and I thought a touch of anger.

"She called me," the boy said, almost defiantly. "We had lunch together near her grandfather's home."

"I am sorry for the girl," Juan said, ignoring the boy. "But this has nothing to do with us. I do not understand why you are here."

"We know who the kidnappers' are, or at least we think we do." I gave them the story. All of it, that is, except for how the thought of Abby in danger was tearing my heart out. I knew that this could be my only chance to help save her.

I finished my story, and sat back waiting for a response. The son of Jose Garcia continued to speak for his father, who seemingly remained unfazed by my story.

"So, Maria now comes to my family and demands our help to rescue the girl by giving up the valuables of others?" His short laugh was bitter. "Why? To enrich that pig, Castro?"

"She is not demanding…"

He interrupted me. "You are wasting your time, senor. It is a myth, this treasure you seek, this el tesoro. It does not exist. You have no business coming here."

The breath went out of me. Anna had seemed so sure that the story was true.

"Who are you, a stranger, to come here? How do we know you are not part of some conspiracy, who has come to help someone steal what is not theirs?"

"Father!" the boy yelled out.

"Quiet! You keep secrets from me, you disobey me, but you will speak only when I tell you to!"

The exchange angered me. "Are you accusing Maria Barrett of endangering her daughter for financial gain?" His bitterness toward the Barrett family was unfathomable.

Juan Garcia sat silently for almost a minute as if trying to gain control of his anger. "We do not know if the girl is truly in danger," he said calmly. "It does not matter. This treasure, this…el tesoro, is nothing more than a dream. My father has never given validation to this story and believe me senor, I spent many years trying to find the truth. Others died trying to return to Cuba to seek the treasures of these rich families and the meager valuables of a few families like ours who followed Pedro Martinez to Florida. It does not exist." He got up from the table and left the room. The old man and his grandson remained. The young man appeared to want to ask me a question but he didn't.

Juan came back into the room, holding a small cask, maybe one foot by two. It was made of a rich, dark wood, but scuffed and scratched, with rust coating the ornate hinges. He put it down on the table, his hands moving slowly over the rough spots on the lid.

He opened the lid, and the pungent odor of raw tobacco escaped into the room. "This, senor," he said. "This was the wealth of Cuba! This was the wealth of the Martinez family, the Castillo's, the Ortiz', all of them! This is what we left in Cuba." He shook his head sadly. "Everything else was worthless."

"So," I said, "what do you think happened to the paintings, the money, statues, and icons, everything else the families owned?"

"I do not know. For all we know, the Fidelistas already have those things or other looters do. It was forty three years ago!"

I looked from him to the old man. "Can your father speak about this?"

"My father," said Garcia, his voice bitter, "had many years to speak about this, and now," he looked at the old man, "he cannot even remember his son much of the time."

"The Cuban government seems to think the story is real. So does Anna Ortiz."

"She is mistaken," he firmly answered. "And I do not care what the Cuban government thinks."

"Father," the boy said, "we have to help Abby."

"There is nothing we can do." Juan was much calmer now. Then, to me he said, "I do not trust you, senor. After Anna called last night, we tried to reach

Maria for several hours. We did not reach her. I do not know who you are working for......"

I started to respond, to tell him about the cell phones, the letter to Anna Ortiz, and the list of names, but he stopped me.

"It does not matter. El tesoro does not exist. We cannot help you. Goodbye, senor," he said with finality. "I must put my father to bed now. My son, Tito, will see you out."

I tossed Maria's letter to her sister and my business card onto the table. "We have only a short time to help the Barrett's," I said. "If you think of anything…"

"Go back to Atlanta, or wherever you came from, senor. There is nothing for you here. Not in Little Havana."

CHAPTER 15

▼

2:00 A.M., 14 October 2002
The Seacrest Motel

I was tired, but I couldn't sleep. The room was lit by the glow from the TV, but the sound was turned all the way down. Bobby slept soundly in the other bed; a half dozen empty Coors beer cans littered the floor between us. The six-pack was my consolation gift to him for breaking my promise to go out drinking after my meeting with the Garcia's. There wasn't anything to celebrate. I was going home empty-handed.

The drive back from the meeting had been a somber one. Anna drove, wiping tears from her eyes several times, as I told her what had happened.

"Boy," I said. "You warned me they would be hard to convince......" I left the sentence unfinished.

"What if Juan is right?" she said. "What if it is all a myth? Whatever will you do then?"

"Try to convince the kidnappers that their demands will be fruitless, and hope they won't risk an international incident by harming Abby."

We were silent for a while.

"Except," I said, finally, "except, they won't believe it, and *I* don't believe it. Your argument that those rich families wouldn't just walk away from their things, especially since they truly expected to go home again, is too reasonable."

I took out Richard Barrett's cell phone and dialed the number of the other phone in Atlanta. I hung up after the ninth ring, surprised that no one had answered, but I didn't want to tell them what had happened in a voice mail message.

When we arrived at the motel, Anna said, "When will you leave?"

"I can't do anything else here. We're running out of time. We'll leave about six a.m., I guess."

She leaned over and kissed me on the cheek.

"God bless you, Thomas Patrick. I will pray for my sister and for Abby…and for you. I do not know what else to do."

*   *   *   *

Neither did I.

Abby's face ran through my head as I lay in my bed. I was staring at the TV, but wasn't really seeing it. I thought about the days events. I was confident that the means to save Abby were out there. I knew, in my heart, that the treasure existed but I was just as confident that I had no way to force the cooperation of the Garcia's or anyone else. I was going home empty handed. I had to try to convince the Barrett's to seek help from the authorities. I knew that wouldn't be possible.

I couldn't completely understand the ill will that these people; the Castillo's, the Garcia's, even the in-laws of Anna Ortiz seemed to harbor against Maria Barrett. Could this all be because of her marriage outside the Cuban ex-patriot community, as Anna seemed to infer? Why was Juan Garcia so obviously upset by a simple lunch date between two childhood friends?

There were two things, I was sure of: I had failed completely, and I was out of ideas. I was never surer of the uselessness of pursuing a livelihood in this business. I was totally out of my depth. This was not skip-tracing, or following the wanderings of an unfaithful spouse, or tracking down a wayward teenager. This was life and death, and the person who might die was important to me. Still, I couldn't think of a way to save her.

Sleep was never going to come. I decided to take a shower, pack, and wake up Bobby, who was out like a light. I needed to get back to Atlanta, to try to convince the Barrett's that it was a mistake not to get a real law enforcement team on this case. I didn't see any reason to wait another four hours to get on our way.

I got the water as hot as I could stand it, letting it beat on the back of my neck and shoulders. The dark areas of broken blood vessels around my wounds were disappearing, which was good, but sudden moves or long spells of inactivity were still causing some pain and stiffness, especially in my old knee injury. I had been able to go the last few days without pain medication but we were staring at fifteen hours in a car on the way back, and I'd need some tonight.

I soaped up, rinsed off, but remained in the shower a little longer. I had been in the bathroom about twenty-five minutes when I finally dried off, collected my shaving kit, and went out to get Bobby up.

The room was still dark, except for the silent TV picture, but Bobby was awake, and he was not alone. The sight of three men, all holding guns, caught me off guard.

Bobby was sitting on the edge of the bed. One of the men was kneeling behind him with his hand over Bobby's mouth, a gun pointed at the back of his head. Only the wide-open eyes of my designated driver could be seen over the big hand covering most of his face. All three of the men were dressed in dark clothing; had moustaches, and dark skin. The one who seemed in charge stepped forward, never taking his eyes off me, and reached over to the open closet. He grabbed a pair of slacks and a shirt, and tossed them over to me.

"It is such a lovely night for a drive, senor. Get dressed, there is someone who wants to see you," he said, without a trace of malice, but with a commanding presence in his voice.

"Your friend could come here," I said. "We've got Diet Coke, plantain chips; sorry the beer's gone but…"

"I do not think so, but I do insist you get ready to leave quickly."

I tossed the clothes on Bobby's bed. "Those are his."

"Your companion will not need them," he said. "He will be remaining here with my friend," he motioned with his gun hand at the man who was behind Bobby. He must have seen alarm in my face. "Do not concern yourself about your friend's safety," he said. "Unless, of course, you do not intend to cooperate with me, in which circumstance, you should worry about yourself as well."

I went to the closet and grabbed some slacks and a shirt. While I dressed, the thought that ran through my head was, unless we really had been followed from Atlanta or the Garcia's or Anna Ortiz' store, the only people who would know I was here were the Garcias. Maybe the other people on the list that Maria Barrett had sent to her sister were summoning me.

But if my late night meeting was to be with the kidnappers,' I didn't have a damn thing to tell them even if I was willing to, but they would never believe that.

I finished dressing and the man in charge motioned toward the door. "I will not tie your hands, senor, but my other friend and I will keep an eye on you. I would not like to shoot you," he motioned at Bobby, "or your companion. But I will not hesitate to do so."

I looked at Bobby Hemphill as we walked out the door. He was sweating and looked terrified. I was terrified, too. I just tried not to show it. "Don't worry." I said to him, "I won't do anything stupid. He won't harm you, Bobby," I said, watching the expressionless gunman. "We'll get out of here as soon as I get back."

I didn't know if I was lying to him.

*   *   *   *

A heavy hand pushed my head down and shoved me into the back seat of an old Cadillac sedan. The other rear door opened and my third new friend climbed in and shoved a short-barreled .38 into my side. A shock wave went through my damaged rib cage, but the pain subsided quickly.

The leader of this little group got into the front passenger seat, next to a fourth man who had been waiting in the car.

My new friend tossed a black cloth bag into my face. "Put this on, senor. It is not necessary for you to see. We know where we are going." He snickered, and said to my rear seat companion, "Watch him closely."

I felt the gun pushed deeper into my side. "You heard me say I would cooperate," I said, as I slipped the bag over my head. I was in total darkness and feeling very vulnerable. "Would you mind telling me where we're going?"

No one said a word.

We wound around the streets of Miami making it impossible for me to keep track of our direction. It seemed to me that the trip had taken maybe fifteen minutes, when we made one last sharp left turn, and rolled to a stop. Still, no one said a word. The car doors opened and I was pushed out. The other back seat passenger stood close to me keeping the gun against my side.

The doors closed and my guard pushed me forward. I heard another door open, this time a door to a building. As we went in, I was hit with the pungent, overpowering smell of cured tobacco. I figured we were in Little Havana warehouse.

We continued down a ramp and I stumbled over a raised wood slat, but I kept my feet. The dark was disorienting. I tried to use my other senses but to no avail.

Finally, light began to seep under the bottom of my headgear and we shuffled to a stop. The black bag was pulled off and it took a minute for my eyes to adjust.

I could see I was in a large room, a storage room of the warehouse maybe, most of which was dark. In front of me was a workbench covered with small stacks of tobacco leaves and hand tools. Overhead, a single, hanging bare bulb lit the table and the close-in surrounding area. There were two men, one to each side of the workbench. With surprise, I realized that the one to the right was Abby's friend, the son of Juan Garcia. The other man, I didn't recognizė.

Behind the bench sat the wizened form of Jose Garcia. His hands grasped a tool with a blade pointed at the end. No one said a word while the old man used the blade to cut the veins out of a leaf of tobacco. The hands that had looked so useless holding onto a cane only a few hours ago flew across the leaf, cutting the meat from the skeleton.

Everyone kept silent while the old man worked and I decided to do the same.

Jose Garcia continued his work, placing several long pieces of the leaf lengthwise in a little dugout piece of wood.

"This is the 'rolling' process," he said, matter-of-factly without looking at me, or even acknowledging my presence. "A fine cigar," he lifted the wooden mold and inhaled deeply of the heady aroma, "is always made with the finest long leaf filler, wrapped in only the best Cameroon, *Corojo*, or maybe, Connecticut Shade wrapper." His voice was strong, belying his frail appearance. He still hadn't looked at me.

Garcia picked up a box nearly full of newly made cigars. "This one," he looked at the leaves in the mold, "will be like these. A 'double corona,' we call this shape. He shook his head slowly, and smiled a rueful smile. "I grew tobacco like this for many years for Senor Martinez, and for his father before him. These leaves come from that very seed, but it was grown in the soil of Florida. Good, but it is not the same." He sighed audibly and finally looked up at me.

"Oh, but the soil of El Pinar! Such beautiful soil we had. The tobacco, it had so many flavors. Vanilla, black cherry, chocolate, leather," he shook his head, sadly. Then he spoke again, as if he had put his musings aside, and his wistful manner was abruptly businesslike. "Who are you, senor?"

"My name is Thomas......"

"I know your name, Senor Patrick. What I want to know is, who are you, and who do you work for?"

His English was nearly perfect so I was sure he understood the language perfectly, too. "Mr....Senor Garcia, you were present when I explained my purpose for meeting with you and your son earlier tonight, weren't you?"

The man behind me suddenly drove his fist into my right kidney; my body erupted with a shooting pain that traveled up my spine. I dropped to my knees, unable to catch my breath, tears flooding from my eyes.

"Please allow me to ask the questions, senor," I heard Garcia say in that same matter-of-fact tone. "I believe our guest would like a chair."

One of the others pushed a wooden chair over to where I was kneeling on the ground. Everyone was silent and motionless while I caught my breath. Eventually, I pulled myself up onto the seat. Only the hands of Jose Garcia had continued to move as he rolled the cigar.

"You know, I'm getting just a little tired of getting beat up."

"I have not made a cigar in a long time," he said, ignoring me as I tried to get my wind and my composure back. "I had forgotten how satisfying it is to make something of value." He looked at the man next to me. "Give my grandson your gun, Julio. Would you and your men wait outside, *por favor.*" It was not a question, but a command.

"Senor..."

"It is all right, Julio. My grandson will protect me."

The gunman handed over the revolver to the young man, and the five left us. I glanced at Tito, who seemed more than a little uncomfortable, but he held the weapon in my general direction.

"I found your story to be of great interest," Garcia said. "I would very much like to know who told you about this treasure trove that does not exist, Senor Patrick."

"Like I told your son, Juan," I said, squeezing the words out through gritted teeth, "Maria Barrett's daughter has been kidnapped by one or more men who say they represent the Cuban government. They want the treasure. They are convinced Pedro Martinez and his friends buried it in Cuba. I'm just trying to help Mrs. Barrett save her daughter. That's all I can tell you."

"Yes," he said, calmly. "It is terrible about the girl, but we cannot help you. Juan has told you that this story is but a myth."

"Yes," I answered my breath coming easier, "except I don't believe that."

"So?" he said, as if surprised. "And why do you not believe us?"

I let him wait a little before answering. "Because, I was a few hours away from being out of your hair. Why pull me down here like this, Senor Garcia? You're trying too hard to convince me that the treasure doesn't exist."

The boy looked like he wanted to say something, but his grandfather spoke first.

"You have told us twice that Maria sent you, but, senor, we cannot confirm your story. We cannot reach her. So, you see, I cannot help but be suspicious of your motives." He smoothed the tobacco in the mold. "You see my point, do you not?"

I was back in control of my breathing, but my kidney was still screaming. "I tried to tell your son that I could arrange for him to speak to the Barrett's," I said. "It is simply too dangerous for her to speak to you from her home telephone."

"And, why is that?"

"If the kidnappers,' and I'm only assuming they are Cuban nationals, not that it really matters who they are; if they knew you had the information they want, you'd have nastier people than me down here to talk to you." I gave him a minute to think about that.

"I can prove to you that I'm here for exactly the reasons I gave you earlier today, but I think you already know that I haven't lied to you. We are running out of time, Senor Garcia, I need to know. Does the treasure exist, and will you help Maria Barrett use it to get her daughter back safely?"

Jose Garcia took one of the cigars from the box, struck a match against the workbench, and held it under the end of the cigar, toasting the end before taking a deep drag. Then, he sat back in his chair. "How is Maria?"

"She's very worried…," I said, beginning to lose patience.

"I understand her fear for her child," he said, steadily. "But how is she otherwise?"

"I'm not sure I understand," I said. "Her husband is a successful business man; she seems to be in excellent health. She is a very beautiful woman. But right now, she is in trouble. We all are," I added.

The heavy, blue smoke hid the old man's face in the dimly lit room. "The treasure exists, Senor Patrick. It is where it has been hidden for these many years."

The boy said "Grandpapa," in a whisper.

"Does your son, Juan, know this? Was that all an elaborate act this afternoon? I'm a little surprised he would let you meet with me without him."

"My son has a home near mine. Tito came to stay with me and take care of me about a year ago." He smiled warmly at his grandson. "He is a good boy, senor. I asked him to come with me tonight. Juan does not know we are here.

"Juan's interest is in a fortune hidden underground. To him, it is not about ridding our homeland of a tyrant. It is about great wealth." He stood up and came around to the front of the workbench.

"My son feels cheated, senor." There was sadness in his voice. "He feels that we gave away our heritage, our future, when we followed the Martinez family to America. He feels that I betrayed him." He motioned to his grandson; the boy put the gun on the bench. "Have no doubt, senor. I know we will never retrieve the valuables for the people they belong to. Most of them are gone anyway. Maybe something good may come of it yet, if we can get the girl back."

My heart leapt and I felt a thread of hope well up in me.

"But, I do not believe you can tell them where to search, and expect to get the girl back alive," Garcia said.

"Neither do I."

"I must be careful. I do not want to involve my son in this."

"In forty-eight hours, the man who says he represents the Castro government is going to be in Maria Barrett's living room, demanding to know where to look."

Tito brought a chair over, the old man sat down in front of me. "I have an idea," he said. "Does this man know you?"

"I don't know for sure, but I don't think so."

"Then, Maria must tell him that she will send a representative to Cuba. That will be you. You will make contact with this government official, if that is what he truly is. You will agree to take two of his men to the treasure site. When it is found, you and one of his men will go back to Havana, meet him, and then take the Barrett girl to the airport." He stopped to make sure I was following his train of thought. "When you and the girl are airborne, the men you have left behind with the kidnapper's other man will leave him with their ill-gotten gains."

"What men?" I asked. "And, how do I get into Cuba? Isn't it illegal for American's to go there?"

"A common misconception, senor. It is only illegal for American's to spend money in Cuba. You will fly into Cancun, Mexico. There are several Atlanta flights to Cancun every day. From there, you simply fly into Havana. The Cuban authorities will give you a travel visa, but they will not put a stamp on your U.S. passport. American Customs officials will never know you were in Cuba. It is an old trick."

I looked him over. "You've been thinking about this for a while, haven't you?"

"I am sorry about our first meeting," he said. "I am afraid it was necessary to deceive you, and my son. I understood all that you said and I believed you. But it was still necessary to bring you here tonight."

"What do we do now?" I asked.

"Go back to Maria. Make your arrangements with her visitor. Be in Havana within twenty-four hours after she meets with him. There will be a room in your name at the Hotel Sevilla, on *Avenida Tajadillo*, in Central Havana. You will be contacted there by friends of ours within twelve hours. They will say that they were sent by the 'old one.'"

"And the location of the burial site?"

"The men who contact you will know where to take you. Each will know a part of the directions. That is all I will tell you for now." He took another pull of the strong tobacco. "Let us say that this is my way of protecting the girl......and you, senor."

*   *   *   *

Tito drove me back to the motel. He said nothing the entire way and I left him to his thoughts. As I got out of the car, he said, "Please save her, senor." The door to my room opened, Bobby's guard walked out and jumped into the car. They sped away, and I ran to the room to check on Bobby. He was in bed sitting up against the headboard. "Jesus Christ! You okay, Tommy?"

"Yeah. You?"

"I damn near shit myself, man! That fucker just stared at me for two hours. Never said a word. What the hell's going on?"

"I'll explain in the car. Get packed, Bobby, it's time to get outta Dodge."

CHAPTER 16

▼

11 A.M., 14 October 2002
I-95, South of Jacksonville, Florida

Bobby's fear had turned to bravado as we drove further north from Miami. He pumped me for information as to why some bastard had been able to stick a gun in his face for two hours and get away with it.

I had no choice but to tell him about my meeting with Jose Garcia, leaving out details that I didn't want to explain more fully, such as my relationship with Abby, or my pending trip to a Communist country. The more I talked about what had happened in Miami, the more surreal it all seemed. What was I doing? All I wanted was to get Abby back safe and sound. Now, I was on my way to Atlanta to meet with a shadow that says he represents Fidel Castro, a shadow that uses kidnapping, and maybe murder, to possess the property of others, all in the name of a dictator.

And at the center of it all for me, is a girl that I have fallen in love with.

"I owe that fucker," Bobby muttered.

"You're never going to see him again, Bobby. Just forget it." I glanced over at the odometer. We were hitting ninety-five miles an hour. "Slow down," I said. "We can't afford to get stopped. I need to be in Atlanta tonight without fail."

I needed to reach some people. Now was as good a time as any. My first call was to the cell phone belonging to Anna Ortiz' daughter.

"Yes, Senor Patrick, I will get my mother for you."

Anna came on the line and I gave her a brief outline of what had occurred without mentioning names over the phone. I was either paranoid or becoming more careful, but I thought it best to err on the side of caution.

"I do not understand," Anna said after I had filled her in. "Why does the old one pretend to be in ill health?" she asked, taking her cue from me. "Why does the whole family participate in this charade?"

"I don't know for sure, Anna. But I've been thinking about it since last night. Could it be that others have been making inquiries about the location of the treasure? Or, could it be that the father is trying to fend off the pressure of his son's greed?"

She was silent on the other end of the phone.

"Anna, something else has been bothering me," I said.

"Yes?"

"The first meeting with the family," I said. "It wasn't just that Juan couldn't tell me anything about the past, but he seemed to be more than a little hostile to your sister and her husband. In fact, when his son, Tito, admitted to having met with Abby during her stay in Miami, Juan Garcia was obviously upset about it. Do you have any idea why?"

She was quiet for a while, as if deciding what she could tell me. "Do you remember when I told you that some of our people were upset by my sister's remarriage, Thomas?"

"Yes, I remember," I said.

"Juan was one of those," she said, finally, "but it went deeper than that. I believe the old one's son was in love with my sister. At least that is what he said, and he may have been." There was a pause.

"Is there a 'but'?"

"It may be just me," she went on. "But I think he somehow saw marriage to my sister as a means of becoming a successor, if you will, to her dead husband's roll as a leader of our community, our anti-Castro movement. I think the father may have thought this was in his son's mind too."

"Would he risk Abby's life because of unrequited love?"

"I cannot answer that, Thomas. Maybe the father is right. Maybe greed has consumed what the son once thought was love."

We talked a few minutes more, I promised to try to keep her informed, although how I would accomplish that if I somehow wound up in Cuba was beyond me.

My next call was to the Barrett home. On the third ring, Abby's mother answered. "Yes?" she said breathlessly, "Thomas? Is that you?"

"Yes, Mrs. Barrett. I tried to call you yesterday, but there was no answer."

"I am so sorry, Thomas. It was my fault. The battery ran down on the phone. I'm afraid I forgot to check it." She was calming down a little now. "Are you all right?"

"I'm fine, ma'am. I'll be home very late tonight, and I need to see you early tomorrow morning, if that's okay?"

"Of course," she said. "What is happening, Thomas? Did you get the information we need?"

"I think so. It's complicated, Maria. I need to ask you to wait for an explanation until I get back, okay?" It was the first time I had called her that, it was just a reflex action, but she didn't seem to notice or mind.

"Time is so short," she said. "I heard from the man who came to see me. He reminded me that time is running out. Thomas, I'm frightened for my daughter!"

"I know," I said, with much more calm than I felt. "I just need to put a few more parts of the puzzle together. Just a little more time…please."

"Yes," she said with resignation. "Of course, Thomas, when will you come?"

"I don't think I should come there. I'll explain later, but I need to meet you away from your house." I thought for a minute. "There's a restaurant on Peachtree in Midtown called Jimmy's Bayou. Can you meet me there at 9 a.m.?"

"Yes, Jimmy's Bayou, 9 a.m., I will be there."

"Thank you. I'll see you there. And try not to worry," I said. I'd do enough of that for both of us.

"Thomas, the ten days are up tomorrow."

"I know," I said. "I'll see you soon." I hung up, and then placed my last call.

I was heartened by the jovial voice of Max Howard.

"Where you at, Hoss," he boomed.

"On my way back, Max, and I need a favor." I said. I told Max what had happened, and filled him in on my plan to deal with our Cuban official when he showed up to confront Maria Barrett.

"You think the lady and her husband will go along with this?"

"I hope so, Max. Listen," I added, "do me one more favor. Can you have someone in your office do a little research on Richard Barrett? You know, what he does, where he came from? The usual stuff."

"The girl's stepfather? What's on your mind?"

"I'm not sure, Max. Probably nothing, but can you do it?"

"Sure, son."

"Thanks. See you at Jimmy's," I said.

* * * *

We got back to Atlanta late into the night; Bobby dropped me at the parking lot behind Ireland's Own. I promised to keep him informed as to what was happening, and trudged upstairs to try to get a few hours sleep.

Of course, a million thoughts were rummaging around in my head, and sleep didn't come. As I lay in my bed, Abby's face flitted across my mind's eye again, and again. It seemed only a short time ago that she lay in my arms in this very room, and gave my life meaning.

And yet, the nagging thoughts came back again; what did I really mean to this girl who had become so important to me? We had been intimate just that one time, and yet I knew I was in love with her. But, did she feel the same? Did she just need that intimacy at that moment in time, and was I lucky enough to be there to revel in her closeness, her warmth, the smell of her?

How could I know?

And yet, unless her parents came to their senses, her life was in the hands of a slightly gimpy ex-jock who was most definitely in love. I was scared stiff that my feelings for Abby would cloud my judgment, and make me do something that would cost her life.

Maria Barrett must feel that there is something between her daughter and me. Otherwise, she would have to see the fallacy in putting me in charge of this beautiful girl's future.

But Richard Barrett bothered me. I'm not sure why, but he did. I'd have to worry about that later. Jose Garcia bothered me too. He was too ready with a plan for my Cuban 'invasion'. Could he really make all the plans he told me about a reality? Did he have those kinds of connections in his homeland? If not, I could be left defenseless in a hostile foreign land. And the visitor Maria had to face in a very short time. Was he really connected with the Cuban government? If not, then who? I set all this aside as best I could. Now I needed to get straight in my head what I wanted to say to Maria.

I glanced at the alarm clock next to my bed. 4 a.m. I tried to shut my eyes. Again.

CHAPTER 17

▼

9:00 A.M., 15 October 2002
Jimmy's Bayou, Peachtree Street

Max and I had been discussing our meeting with Maria while we waited for her. I was on my second cup of coffee, and Max was on his second plate of beignets.

"You wear the same tie every time you come in here, you'd never have to buy powdered sugar again. Just brush it into a bowl when you get home."

Max barked a laugh and a powdery cloud blew off the doughnut he was just about to take a bite from. "Some things are worth getting messy for," he said. "I do miss New Orleans, Tommy," he said wistfully.

"You lived there?"

"Was born there," he said. "Grew up in the area they call the Garden District, right next to the area where everybody parties today. You know, Bourbon Street and all."

"I didn't know that. Pat never mentioned it."

"Not sure he even knows," Max said. "Anyway, I've been here a long time now. Long as some of these other folks who call themselves Atlantans. My great granddaddy just fought under a different Confederate state flag."

I took a drag of the coffee, which was laced with chicory, Louisiana style. The coffee was strong but smooth.

"Max, you are full of surprises," I said.

He snorted, "You kinda' been creatin' a few surprises of your own, Hoss."

"Yeah, well, I've been waiting for the other shoe to drop ever since I got my ass whipped in the parking lot."

He motioned for more coffee. "Let's talk about that for a moment." he said. "What do you figure this finger print stuff means?"

My answer came easy. "I haven't got a clue, but I bet your cop friend has an idea."

"Yes, Jake does, and it's so simple he's surely right."

"And that would be?"

"Well, one, your attacker, who we presume to be this John Edwards or Melvin Udall or whoever he is from Chicago, may have been casing your truck while you were out at Junior Kline's place. Maybe he was bare handed then, and he was trying the door on the passenger side to see if he could get into the glove box. You know, to check out who you really were."

"And then he used gloves when he attacked me. Sounds logical," I said.

"It does. But Berger had one other scenario," Max said.

I shook my head questioningly.

"Maybe," he said slowly, 'Your attacker wore gloves, but he wasn't the guy we think he was."

"Not Edwards?" I let that sink in for a minute. "But who else would it have been? I mean the guy said I was messing in someone's business. I wasn't working on anything else."

Neither of us had an answer, so we just sat there thinking it over, getting nowhere.

It was nearly 9 a.m. I tried to concentrate on the situation at hand. "Were you able to get anything on Abby's stepfather?"

Max sat back and reached into the inside breast pocket of his sport coat, finding a small note pad. "Richard Barrett," he read, "born 1943, in Tampa, Florida, Miami University for a B.A. degree, then an M.B.A. in business. He went to work for a consulting company specializing in foreign trade. Founded his own import/export business, 1976, called 'Barrett/Americas' Group, Inc.'." Max stopped for a bite of beignet. "From there it gets a bit murky. No info on the kind of stuff he was bringing into the country, or exporting out. Married Maria Castillo, in Miami in 1984, not that long after her first husband, Ramon, died in a car accident. It happened," he flipped the page. "About a nine months before he married Maria. He adopted her two kids, your young lady, and a boy, Carlos, and moved the family and his business to Atlanta in 1986. Had a child, a girl, with Maria that year. He maintains an office in Miami."

I took this in. "Any idea how his business is doing?"

"Nope, but according to his credit card charges over the last five years, the man does a hell of a lot of traveling."

"Where does he go?" I asked.

"Don't have that list yet," Max said with a smile, "but I will."

I glanced at the door just as Maria Barrett walked in looking around for me. She saw me and came over to the table.

We stood to greet her and she gave me a hug and a peck on the cheek. The perfume, for a moment, brought memories of Abby, pressing tightly against me, her arms around my neck, and I felt heat rising in my face.

"I am so glad that you are back safe and sound," she said, and then she stole a glance at Max, and she tightened up a bit. She looked at me questioningly.

"Maria Barrett, Max Howard," I said.

"Ma'am," Max said, taking her hand and bowing slightly. "I am honored to make your acquaintance, dear lady. I only wish it were under happier circumstances." Max motioned to a chair, Maria sat down, still looking a bit tenuous.

"Maria, Max is an attorney as well as a good family friend. I've asked him to help us out when you get your return visit from the man who has Abby. You can say anything in front of Max."

Maria looked at both of us. "He is coming tonight at eight. He insisted, I am afraid, and he does have her, Thomas." She opened her purse and took a photo out and handed it to me. "This came yesterday by courier." My heart nearly exploded. The picture was of Abby, standing in front of an ornate building on a clear day, a tall, rugged looking man standing to each side of her.

The man on the right had a barely visible gun against her side. The look on Abby's face was a mixture of fatigue, fear, and defiance. I handed the picture to Max.

"Do you know this building, ma'am?" he asked.

"Yes," she said, in a small voice. "That is the Cuban Presidential Palace. It is in the center of Havana."

"Well," Max said, "it doesn't prove these guys represent the government, but it sure looks like they have the girl in Cuba."

Maria said, "Thomas, please tell me, will we get help from Miami?"

I filled her in on the trip to Florida. I tried to keep the more hurtful comments and attitudes out of my report, but I did give her a full breakdown on the two meetings with Jose Garcia.

Maria had a slight smile on her face when I told her the old man had offered to help. "Jose loved my father," she said. "He was like an uncle to me."

"I'm afraid his son, Juan, doesn't have much regard for his father." I explained that Senor Garcia would help, but that he was keeping his assistance a secret from his own son.

"How very strange," she said, looking puzzled. "Did he say why?"

"No," I said. There was no sense in explaining. "But I think we better honor his wishes. We shouldn't speak to Juan about this."

"Yes, of course."

"Ma'am, Tommy here has a plan that he's kinda' worked out with this Jose Garcia. We need to talk about that, and make some decisions."

She looked at me expectantly, and I gave her a rough outline on the plans for my trip to Cuba. Maria's face took on a horrified look.

"You can't!' she said. "You would be in terrible danger, Thomas! I can't let you take that risk."

"We can't count on these guys releasing Abby once they have the information they want, and certainly not after they have the treasure. Garcia and I agree on that," I answered. "I need to be there to simultaneously give them what they want, and get Abby out of the country. Besides," I added, "Jose Garcia won't help unless we do it his way. Please remember, you may certainly send someone else in my place. In fact, I strongly recommend calling in the big boys, Maria. After all, this is your daughter we're talking about."

"No, Thomas," She said without hesitation. She touched my face. "You are the right one. I believe it, and Richard agrees."

We were silent for a long time.

Maria snapped back first. "How can you help us, Mr. Howard?"

Max looked at me, and I nodded, afraid my voice would crack if I tried to speak.

"Well, we don't think the Kidnappers know who Tommy is. When this guy shows up at your home, I will be there with you. You can introduce me as your attorney." He stopped. "I'm so sorry, ma'am. Let me get you something to drink."

"Some water would be fine, thank you," she smiled, and Max waved to the waitress, quickly ordering some water and more coffee for the two of us.

"Tommy will be hidden, but its' important he sees what this guy looks like. Is there a way we can arrange that in the house?"

She nodded.

"Good. I'll explain that I'm not there to challenge him or negotiate with him, but only to make sure he understands how he will receive the information in exchange for the safe departure of Tommy and Abby from Havana"

"So we will cooperate, as long as he does his part?"

"That's right, Maria," I said. "You didn't contact the authorities as he instructed, but you're letting him know that someone else knows what is going on, that someone else knows that your 'representative,' that's me, will be in Cuba. It might just keep him from doing something stupid."

"I understand," she said. "Thank you, Mr. Howard. Thank you for your help." Then she looked at me. "I can't help but fear for your safety, Thomas. I will never forget this."

"We'll make it work," I said with more confidence than I felt.

"Would you feel more comfortable if we discussed this with your husband first, Mrs. Barrett?" Max asked.

"I'm afraid my husband is away until tomorrow evening." Maria said.

Max averted his eyes, and looked at me. The same thought was going through both our minds.

I shook my head slightly. Neither of us said a word.

CHAPTER 18

▼

7:00 P.M., 15 October 2002
The Barrett Home

"I know I'm repeatin' myself, Tommy, but I want to be sure you're hearin' me," Max said.

After our meeting at Jimmy's, I had lain hidden in Maria's car until she had pulled into her garage. Now, Max and I were alone in Richard Barrett's study. Maria was in her bedroom rehearsing her part in the upcoming meeting with the mysterious Cuban, who was due to arrive in an hour and a half. Max had been setting up the room so that I would be able to see our visitor without being seen. I would need to be sure who I was dealing with once I was ready to make contact in Havana.

"You got to take someone with you. You're still not a hundred percent, and you need to know you got someone you can trust backing you up."

"Yes, Mother Goose, I hear you, but how can I ask somebody to put themselves at risk, when they aren't even involved in this mess in the first place?"

"Don't make no never mind," he answered, emphatically. "Look at it this way. If, God forbid, anything happened to you, someone has to look out for the girl. We got no one else to trust down there."

He was right, of course. "Maybe I can get Pat to come with me," I said.

"That's not going to work," he said, shaking off the idea. "Not with two kids and Charlotte June back here, it's too dangerous."

"I know," I said resignedly, "I don't know why I even suggested that."

We thought about it for a while. "How about the Hemphill kid," Max asked. "You said he was okay down in Miami, right?"

"Yeah, but I kept him kind of on the outside of everything. He can be a bit of a loose cannon, Max." I sighed, knowing that there probably no choice but Bobby. "Maybe he won't want in," I said.

"You better hope he does," Max said, quietly.

"Max," I said, changing the subject, "does it seem strange to you that Abby's stepfather would be out of town on business while her life is in mortal danger?"

"It's been bothering me since I heard it. But either Maria Barrett is one great actress, or she isn't bothered by it."

Just then, the door to the office opened, and Maria walked in, followed by Patrice, who was pushing a cart loaded with pitchers of iced tea, water, glasses, a silver ice bucket, and a plate of sandwiches. Max jumped to his feet and brought a chair over for Maria. She smiled at us, but her hands were tightly clenched.

"How are you doin', ma'am," Max said soothingly.

"I am afraid my nerves are a bit jangled. But I will be fine," she said bravely. "I must be ready to do this, for Abby's sake, no?"

"Now, don't you worry, I'm gonna' handle everything'," Max took her hand. "You know where Tommy is going to be. I want him to get a look at this man, and we're going to try to figure out if he knows who Tommy is. You have to make sure you listen for anything the man says that might be different than he said to you before."

She nodded. "I understand."

"Outside of that, just introduce me. You don't need to say anything else." Max got up and poured tea for everyone. "Just relax," he said, smiling. "We're ready."

His confidence was heartening, but I noticed he didn't eat anything.

*   *   *   *

"Did you get a good look at him?" Max Howard asked me after the Cuban had left. We were waiting in the study for Maria to return from showing the kidnapper of her daughter out of the house.

"I don't think I'll ever forget him. I wanted to come out here and beat his brains out."

"I know the feeling, but that wouldn't help Abby."

Max was visibly calm, but it was obvious to me that he was relieved that the confrontation was over, for now. Maria Barrett came back into the room, and dropped into a chair. She was dabbing at her eyes, and seemed exhausted. I rang the servant bell behind the desk, and when Patrice answered asked her to bring water. The maid was ringing her hands, obviously concerned for her employer.

"Well done, Mrs. Barrett," Max said as he patted her hand.

"I was scared to death," she answered.

"Did he say anything to you when he left," I asked.

She wiped her eyes again. "Only that he hoped we would not mistake their resolve, and do something that would endanger Abby." She took the water from Patrice. "I thought it best not to reply."

"Good," said Max. "We made our point. Let him stew about it for a while."

"I couldn't hear much," I said. "You need to fill me in."

"No problem there," Max said, and reached under the lip of the desktop. He felt around and pulled out a miniature recorder.

"Jeez, Max. You took a hell of a chance! What if he had looked for a recording device?"

"Not very likely," he said, as he rewound the tape. "He knows we don't have his name, but he knows we have the information he wants. You could see the greed bleedin' outta' his eyes. He wasn't interested in protection. He's got Abby."

Maria stood and set her glass on her husband's desk. "If you will excuse me, I don't think I can listen to this again. I would like to go to my room for a while."

We both said that would be a good idea. When she was gone, Max said, "You can't get body language on a recording, but I'll tell you, this was one cool character."

The tape began to roll:

I could hear Maria and the Cuban enter the room. I remember my first look at the tall, slender man through the slightly open door to the adjacent room where I was hiding. His hair was full and black, with grey around the temples, and streaked through out. He was dressed expensively in dark blue, like the government official he claims to be.

(Maria's voice) *"May I present Mr......."*

"Senora Barrett, I assure you, we are quite serious about your daughter's safety. I would strongly advise you consider that renegotiating with me at this time is not..."

"Now hold on, sir (Max's voice broke in) *"Let me assure you that I am not here to renegotiate with you or threaten you. I am Mrs. Barrett's attorney, and I am not with any government agency. My, only purpose for being here is to explain how we will deliver the information you seek, and arrange how you will deliver Abby to us. I want to make sure there is no mistake on your part about OUR resolve to safeguard the girl. So, why don't we have a seat and talk about this?"* (Silence)

"So, you have the information I have requested on behalf of my government?"

(Max) *"Do you have proof the girl is alive?"*

"I believe this photograph will relieve your fears"

(Nearly a minute of silence, but I think I hear a sob from Maria.)

(Max, again) *"For the time being, this is acceptable."*

"Then, senor, if you will provide me with the data I requested, I will arrange for Senora Barrett's daughter to be returned upon verification that the former belongings of the defectors are secure. Yes?"

"No."

"Senor, this is a very dangerous game you play."

"And you stole a young American girl for profit, sir. If you don't think what you are doin' is dangerous, you are kiddin' yourself."

(Silence.)

(Max) *"Now, you get your treasure, or ransom, or whatever you want to call it, but you do it our way. You understand?"*

"What are your terms, senor?"

"Mrs. Barrett is going to send a representative to Cuba. Once there, he will call you, and you alone. You will give me a number where you can be reached in Cuba, forty-eight hours after you leave here tonight. This man and two others will take two 'associates' of yours to the location you seek. When they reach the spot, and your men verify that it is the right place, our man will bring one of your men to the Havana air-port, where you will meet him with the girl. When they are out of Cuban airspace, your man can take you to the burial site."

(The Cuban) *"And why should I trust you, senor? What if you, 'pull a fast one', I think you Americans' say?"*

"You have the girl. We are forced to trust you. Remember, Mrs. Barrett doesn't care about the stuff you want. She wants her daughter. I suggest you deliver her safely. If you don't, your government, if that is who you really represent, is gonna' have one big time international incident on its hands."

(Silence, again.)

"Very well, I will accept your terms, but we must conclude our business within one week. I would be most happy to assist your representative in getting into Cuba."

(Max) *"We'll make our own arrangements, if you don't mind. One other thing, our man will not know the exact location you are seeking when he contacts you. He will be told where to go by others as he reaches certain points. So, please don't interfere with his progress."*

"And, how do you know we will let your man and the girl leave the country?"

"Because, sir, if you don't follow the script, a very good Cuban marksman will drill a very small, but deadly hole, into your skull. Now, if you will give me a number to reach you at in Cuba, we can conclude this sordid business…"

✳   ✳   ✳   ✳

I called Bobby Hemphill later that evening and found him much too happy to accompany me to Cuba. I told him to meet me at my place around midnight with some clothes and his driver's license and passport.

I didn't know if it was a useless gesture or not, but I went out the back door of the Barrett house around 10 p.m. and through their backyard and the yard behind theirs, to the neighboring street. Pat was waiting for me there. If we were being watched, we couldn't tell.

"What's the deal?" Pat asked. I filled him in on the way back to Buckhead. "Christ," he muttered. "Maybe I should go with you. Bobby can be an asshole when he sets his mind to it."

"Forget it," I said. "Max and I agreed we weren't putting somebody's daddy at risk. But," I added, "thanks for volunteering."

"Yeah, yeah," he muttered. Then, in a serious tone, Pat said, "This thing is getting more dangerous by the minute, Tom. I'm worried. If something goes wrong over there, you can't count on help from anyone."

"I'll be okay," I said trying to sound confident. "Bobby will work out. I just hate to have C.J. worrying about him."

"Hell, she does that anyway."

Back at Ireland's Own, Pat went to check on the kitchen while I went upstairs to pack. My plan, which might not make any difference, was to go to the airport tonight and wait there, and leave on the first flight out to Cancun in the morning, hopefully, without being recognized.

Max hadn't been able to figure out if our Cuban visitor had any idea who the Barrett "representative" was going to be, and we both had our doubts as to whether it really mattered if my identity were known. They would find out soon enough anyway.

I took a shower, threw some clothes in my duffle bag, and sat down on the edge of my bed, cell phone in hand. It was late but I called Anna Ortiz in Miami. She answered on the second ring, sounding wide-awake.

"Thomas?"

"Yes, Anna. Sorry it's so late. I need you to get a message to the Old One."

"Yes, of course. Do not worry about the time. I brought the phone to my room so I would not wake my daughter if you called."

"Please tell him that my vacation starts tomorrow, and that I should be at my final destination within thirty hours. Do you understand?"

"Yes," she answered simply. "I will do as you ask, Thomas." And then she added softly, "God be with you."

I hung up. There wasn't anything else to say.

*   *   *   *

Bobby called from his car in the lot behind the restaurant. I grabbed my bag, stuffed some of the cash the Barrett's had given me into my back pocket, and went down to join him. As I went out the back door, I heard Pat's voice behind me.

"Tommy," he said, quietly, "you be careful, okay?"

I gave him a 'thumbs up' and a smile, all the while fighting the bile that was suddenly at the back of my throat.

Bobby was like a caged animal as we drove down the Interstate toward Hartsfield International Airport.

"It's payback time, Tommy! Those fuckers are gonna be sorry they ever fucked with us!"

"Cool your jets, Bobby," I said, trying to calm him down. "We're going to be on their turf, and there's a lot more of them than there will be of us."

Thankfully, he was silent after that. We were just about to enter the long term parking area outside the Red terminal, where Aero Mexico's ticket counter was located, when my phone rang.

"Thomas, this is Richard Barrett."

"Yes, Mr. Barrett," I said. My tone was unintentionally cold, but he didn't seem to notice.

"Thomas, Maria has given me a rundown on this evening's events. Certainly, we both appreciate the risks you are taking." He was quiet, waiting for a response.

"Yes, sir," I said simply.

"I'm sorry I could not be here for the meeting. I had no choice but to take care of some extremely important business."

Important business? More important than his own daughter's life? I didn't ask that question.

"Can you tell me your next step?"

Suddenly, I had the gut feeling that it was best to keep Richard Barrett in the dark. In that one second, my plans began to change.

"My plan? My plan is to go get Abby," I said, and hung up, turning off the power on the phone.

CHAPTER 19

▼

Midnight, 16 October 2002
Hartsfield Airport, Atlanta

I reached behind my seat and grabbed my duffle. Opening it, I pulled out my .38 Smith & Wesson, and put it on the seat between us.

"Shit," Bobby said. "What are you going to do with that? You'll never get it on the plane, man."

"It's not going on the plane, it's for here, in case any unexpected 'friends' show up before we leave."

"Nice friends you got," he said sarcastically.

I stopped looking through the bag. "Look, Bobby, I want you to listen very closely. Okay?"

"Yeah, sure," he answered.

"I'm not going to tell you that I know what I'm doing. This thing might blow up in our faces. But, Max and I worked out a plan, and I think its best that I try and follow that plan as best I can."

I stopped talking long enough to make sure he was listening. "I'm going to need you to follow my lead as closely as possible. You're going to be much more involved than before. Can you do that?"

Bobby looked at me for a moment. Then he stared straight out at the sea of parked cars. "Look, Tommy, you don't have to sugar coat what you're sayin'," he said slowly. "I know I'm ninety per cent bullshit, and I know everybody knows it. I just want to help. I'll do whatever you say."

"I appreciate that, but I just want you to understand," I said. "This isn't going to be like Miami. Those guys down there? Those guys were *friends* compared to the people waiting for us in Havana."

"I repeat, nice friends you got."

I sighed. "Look," I said, "I gotta' be honest with you, Bobby. The girl we are going after? I know her. I care about her. This is personal as well as business."

He looked at me closely. "You mean, like, she's your girlfriend? Jees, that must be rough on you, man."

"Yeah, well, I'm telling you this because I want you to know that I will do anything to save her. It could get very dangerous. You understand? So if you want to back out, it's okay. No hard feelings. I have to do this, Bobby, you don't."

"So, what you're sayin' is, this could get more dangerous than windin' up in a hostile country, with bad guys after us, lookin' for a buried treasure while relyin' on some old fuck in Miami to plan for our safety. And we'll be trying to rescue a damsel in distress, with no planned way out of the country if anything goes bad, right?"

I chuckled. "That's about it," I said, realizing the inanity of it all.

"Then, let's go get your girl," he said, with a finality that gave me hope.

"Okay," I said. "Thanks." I opened the duffel again, and fished around until I found a cloth sack with a drawstring at the opening.

"What the hell is that?" Bobby asked.

"A little care package from Max Howard."

I opened the sack and reached in. I pulled out two cell phones and handed one to Bobby. "Max got these for me. They're brand new and set up with international calling chips." We turned the phones on. "You push '1' and it will ring my phone. My '1' will ring you. On both phones, '2' will call Max in Atlanta, '3' calls the Barrett's, '4' calls a cop named Berger, who's a friend of Max'." We turned the phones off. "Both are set to vibrate instead of ring, have text messaging, and the longest lasting battery available. We won't be able to charge them up down there, but they should last way longer than we will need them to if we're careful."

I reached in again and pulled out two maps of Cuba with a detailed section on Havana, and Cuban guidebooks. Inside the rear cover of the guidebooks were blank pages marked 'NOTES', and I took out a pen.

Opening a book to the pages on Havana hotels, I found two near the Hotel Sevilla where I would be staying until I made contact with Jose Garcia's troops, and handed Bobby the book. "From Cancun, you know how to get to Cuba, right?"

"Yeah, I got it."

"Once you do, check into one of these hotels......"

"Whoa," Bobby interrupted. "What happens to you? What are we separating for?"

"I have no idea why, but I've got a sense about this. I got it into my head that we should separate until we get into the country, so that we can meet with the Garcia people before we have to contact the kidnappers. I may be full of it on this, Bobby, but I need you to go along with me."

"So, how do we meet up?"

"When I get to my hotel, I'll contact you by cell, we use only the cells, and we will arrange where to hook up."

"And if I don't hear from you?"

"Then, you just head for the airport, and get your ass back to Cancun. You're just a curious American tourist checking out Havana, okay?"

"Just leave you out there somewhere?"

"That's exactly what you are going to do."

He thought about that, and was obviously unhappy with that prospect. "Where are you going to go first?"

"Better I keep that to myself for now. Don't worry, man. I'll make it in okay. You just keep a low profile 'til I call you, okay?"

After a minute, Bobby said, "You're the boss. Just make sure you make it, or my sister will do far worse things to me than those asshole Cubans could ever dream up."

I chuckled. "I promise," I said. "Get some sleep. I'll wake you in about three hours. Then I'll sleep for a while. About seven, we'll go in and get our tickets. By the way," I said, as I reached into my pocket, "Here's fifteen hundred. Buy your ticket for cash. Use only cash. Credit cards are instantly traceable."

"Okay. Hey, by the way, this is an awfully big fuss for some old buried stuff. Any idea what it's worth?"

"I asked Jose Garcia that same question. He said that there are several paintings that the art world thinks disappeared a long time ago. Masters, you know? Garcia said the whole thing could be worth two, three hundred million."

Bobby whistled. "You know, that stuff has been underground a long time. We could be digging up a pile of mush. Then what?"

"I try not to think about that." I tossed my duffel onto the rear seat, picked up my .38, and laid it on my lap. I stared out the windshield.

*   *   *   *

I awoke with a start when a car door slammed closed nearby. Other doors and trunks followed in close order. It was just before 7 a.m.

"It's okay," Bobby said. "No one's paid any attention to us. I don't think any-one even noticed us sitting here, and they all have baggage."

I shook the cobwebs out of my head, put the revolver in the glove compart-ment, turned on the cell phone Richard Barrett had given me, and saw there were messages. I tossed it on the floor. The battery would go dead in a few hours, and I would be cut off from the Barrett's, unless I reached them on Max' phone. I still wasn't sure why Richard Barrett made me uncomfortable, but for now, I didn't want him to be able to trace my moves. We locked up and headed for the termi-nal. When we reached the garage entrance, we split up, looked around to see if we were being followed, and crossed the eight lane driveway to the Red terminal entrance. Inside, I milled around, watching, until Bobby was able to buy his ticket. When he turned away from the Aero Mexico counter, he nonchalantly drew a circle on his stomach with one finger. One hour. He would be leaving for Cancun in an hour.

I wandered around for a while, stopped to get a breakfast sandwich and coffee at one of the main terminal's coffee shops, and then wandered over to the Air Jamaica ticket counter. Above the counter, screens showing Arrivals and Depar-tures showed all the flights to Kingston, Jamaica for the day.

There were no passengers at the counter. I walked up and the woman behind the counter finished some computer work before looking up with a bright island smile.

"Last minute trip," I said. "Any seats available on the 9:30 to Kingston this morning?"

She punched information into the computer, and checked the screen. "Just one person traveling today, sir?"

"Yes."

"Window or isle?"

"Isle, please."

"Returning on?"

"Can I buy an open return? I'm visiting some friends, and I'm not sure when I will come back."

"Of course," she said brightly. "It is a great time to be going to the islands, for business or pleasure. You should stay as long as possible. My I see your proof of citizenship, please?""

I paid for the ticket, and wandered around for a while, then went through security as quickly as possible.

At 9:10, I boarded the Boeing jet, and took a seat in the rear of the plane.

I watched every face as the passengers got on.

CHAPTER 20

▼

16 October 2002
Air Jamaica Ft # 2660

My shoulder was giving me hell.

Cramped up in the coach section on my flight to Kingston. I was stiff and tired, even though I had gotten a few hours of restless sleep in the car at the airport.

We had arrived on schedule after a two-hour trip from Atlanta. The full plane had taken forever to unload, but since I had carried on my duffel, it took only minutes to get through customs and leave the airport building. I flagged down a cab outside.

"Welcome to Paradise, Mon," my cabbie had said, as if repeating a line used a thousand times. "Where we going this fine day?"

"Is there a nice hotel nearby? Maybe, a Holiday Inn?"

"Yes, Mon. Just down the road a little."

"Let's go there," I said.

Even in October, the heat and humidity was making me sweat. Or was it nerves?

The hotel was nice enough, not that it mattered, and I paid cash for four nights lodging and went up to my room. The room was stuffy, so I put on the air, double-checked the two door locks, threw off my clothes, and set the alarm clock for three hours. I was asleep in minutes, for a change.

When I woke, I felt better physically, but I was still a little groggy. I spent nearly a half hour in the shower, dug out some fresh jeans and a short-sleeved sport shirt from my bag and dressed.

I found the Air Jamaica number in the phone book and called to check times for flights to Havana.

An hour later, I put the "Do Not Disturb" sign on my door, grabbed my bag, and headed down to the lobby level to catch a cab to the airport.

$$*\qquad *\qquad *\qquad *$$

The pilot circled to the south as we left Jamaican airspace and stayed well to the south as we approached Cuba, keeping us away from the restricted airspace above the U.S. Naval Base at Guantanamo. How odd, It seemed to me, to imagine American troops stationed on an island nation, surrounded across fence lines by soldiers of a government sworn to hate us. It hit me that I was going to be in the same position.

Before leaving Jamaica, I had checked my cell phone for the "OK" text message that I had arranged for Bobby Hemphill to send me when he was safely in Havana. There was no message on the phone. It didn't mean anything at this stage, but it still made me a little nervous.

The flight was about half full. There were Americans on board, for sure. That should help take any suspicion off my traveling to Cuba.

The pilot banked the plane into a starboard turn, and the Cuban coast came into full view in my window. I pulled my sling out of the duffel under the seat in front of me, and slipped it over my head and around my arm, hoping to make myself look even less conspicuous.

From the map I had brought with me, I followed our approach to the airport outside Havana. As we passed over the island my made a wide sweeping turn towards the runway at Jose Marti Airport, I could see the mountainous area around Havana. We went lower and lower, until the ground came up to meet us, and the wheels squeaked against the tarmac, jumped back into the air, then settled down for good. Moments later, we pulled up the gate.

I was on Cuban soil.

We quickly gathered our possessions, and the plane was cleared of passengers in minutes. I was greeted by the same damp heat that I had felt in Jamaica, but also by the sight of armed guards stationed around the airport. I was sure they were waiting for me, but we all passed by them to the Immigration area without incident.

I held on to my passport, and it took a few minutes to fill out the Immigration paperwork we had been given before leaving the plane. I moved on to a uniformed guard who gave my duffel a cursory investigation, then passed me on. I took a deep breath and approached one of the three narrowing lines that led to armed-guarded booths, with a wide-open area on the other side.

That open area led to the main lobby, ground transportation...and Havana. My checkpoint was manned by a short, dark skinned, pudgy woman.

If I were being watched, this was where I was going to be stopped. When it was my turn, the disinterested female took my passport, and finally glanced up. She looked me over, matching my face to the photo. I had to fight the urge to take off through the airport. Seeing as how that would have got me a bullet...or several...in the back, I was able to fight the urge successfully. Instead, I gave her my most engaging smile.

"Norte Americano?"

It took me a second to realize she was speaking to me. "Uh...yes, American," I said, trying to sound as if I was saying something totally reasonable.

"Why do you come to Cuba?" she said, pronouncing the word "Cooba." Her tone wasn't that of an interrogator, but that of someone reading a question from a form. I glanced around as I answered, but no one was paying attention to us. The soldier seemed oblivious to my inner panic.

"Uh," I stammered, "I, uh, just wanted to see Havana. I was vacationing...uh, you know, *vacaceonas*, in Jamaica......"

She had lost interest. *"No estampilla,"* she said, handing me my passport, and a slip of paper written in Spanish, on which she had stamped *"Siete"* in a blank space. "You must leave Cuba in seven day," she said, pointing to the word. "You should no use *tarjeta de credito, s*enor."

I looked at her, my expression blank.

"The card," she said, forming a square in the air with her finger. "The *credito......"*

"Oh! The credit card, yes?"

"Si, senor, do not use," she beamed at me. "Is okay," she said, and pointed me toward the lobby concourse.

I tried not to break into a run.

*   *   *   *

Outside the airport, I caught a cab, a vintage Chevy like one my dad had years ago. It was in great shape, but had been repainted a hideous purple with yellow lettering on the sides.

I got in, and said "Centro Havana," the driver took off. The ride into town was made in silence, which was fine with me. The fewer people who heard me speaking English, the better. We covered the 25 kilometers in less than half an hour.

Havana, or what I could see of it, was a mix of old and new. Some magnificent buildings, beautiful gardens and parks, neighborhoods full of people sitting on steps outside their homes, and hundreds of old American cars from the fifties and maybe 1960 or '61. It looked like a Hollywood movie set.

I wasn't sure where the cabbie was planning to drop me. I didn't want him stopping at the Hotel Sevilla. I looked at my map, and found a restaurant a few blocks from the hotel.

As we drove up the *Avenida de las Missiones*, the driver looked back at me and raised his hand in a 'where to' motion. I took the cue. *"Restaurante El Patio, Avenida Empedrada,"* I said, as if I knew exactly what I was doing, but he seemed happy with my response. "Si, senor," he said, and turned right at the next intersection.

I waited a few minutes after the cab left and then consulted my map. I was only a block from Tejadillo. I reached the hotel in less than ten minutes.

The building was quaint and tropical. I guessed it was maybe thirty or forty years old. The lobby was filled with plants; ferns and such. Ceiling fans were everywhere, and guests lounged in overstuffed chairs. Some other time, I would have been charmed by its comforting look. At the registration desk, the man behind the counter asked me for my identification papers, and took a minute to write down some of the data on a card that may have been for the hotel's files, or for the governments.

I nearly jumped out of my shoes when, as I waited, the cell phone in my pocket began to vibrate violently. I ignored it, and it finally stopped. No one seemed to notice my little dance in the busy lobby. I took my key, smiled at the man and headed for my room.

I opened the door of room 410, looked around quickly, and walked in. The room wasn't very large, but it was nicely furnished with cream-colored walls and prints of Old Havana everywhere. I half expected to see scenes from "Godfather II" on the walls-like when Al Pacino comes to Cuba with all the other Mob bosses. I wondered just what constitutes extreme paranoia, anyway.

I threw my bag on the bed and pulled out my cell phone. The text message was there. Bobby was in Havana.

We had made it through step one.

There was a balcony outside the two sliding doors of my room's outside wall. It was barely big enough to stand on, but provided a nice view on the small courtyard garden and pool. I opened the door, stood out over the threshold as far as I could, and pressed the '1' on my phone. Bobby answered on the first ring.

"Don't say where you are!" I said quickly. "Any problems?"

"Just a plane delay," Bobby said a little excitedly, "you?"

"I'm fine."

"Man, this place is something else. You looked around yet? It's like 1950 here. Kinda' cool."

"No, I just arrived," I said.

"They got some beautiful senoritas here," he said.

"I know," I said a bit agitatedly. "I'm trying to find one."

"What do you want me to do?"

I had thought about this a lot. "Keep a low profile. Stay in your room and check your phone for messages on the hour, okay?"

"Yeah, sure," he answered, a touch of disappointment in his tone.

"This isn't a vacation. I need you to remember that."

"I hear ya', chief."

I checked the clock on my phone. "It's a little after three. At 8 p.m., leave your room. Meet me at a restaurant named O'Reilly's at the corner of O'Reilly and *San Ignacio.*" I hated saying the name over the phone, but had no choice.

"I saw it," Bobby cut in. "It's close…and very appropriate, I might add."

"Don't forget to check your voice mail, okay?"

"See you at eight."

*   *   *   *

The time passed slowly. I had half expected to hear a knock on the door from Jose Garcia's friends, or, maybe a phone call but nothing happened.

I was hungry. I stayed in the room. With only a little trouble, I ordered a burger, fries and bottled water from room service.

The TV channels were all in Spanish, and I dozed off for a little while. But I was wide-awake long before it was time to meet Bobby at O'Reilly's.

I had forgotten to let Max Howard know I had arrived as we had planned, so I sent him a text message that simply said "OK."

At ten minutes to eight, I put on my shoes, took a moment to put my few belongings in certain places so that I would be able to tell if they had been moved while I was gone.

I checked the hall, walked down the stairs to the lobby, and walked out of the hotel.

The area of town where O'Reilly's Café was located seemed to be where a lot of the hot nightclubs and restaurants were. I felt safe on the streets, but I couldn't keep myself from checking the sidewalk behind me a few times just in case.

O'Reilly's was full of colorfully dressed patrons and a jazz group was performing on a small stage at the back of the room.

The man at the podium by the entrance started to speak to me, but I spotted Bobby sitting against the wall about mid-way into the room. It was a beautiful night, and it would have been nice to sit on one of the second floor balconies overlooking the street, but Bobby had used good sense picking his location so that the entrance was in view.

I walked over and sat down. There were four beer bottles in front of Bobby, all empty.

"Been here a while?" I said, accusingly.

"No," he said. "Relax, Tommy, they haven't even cleaned off the table from the last customers. But I could sure use a beer, man."

"Sorry," I said. "Just a little nervous, I guess."

"You hear from the old man's boys?"

We were able to speak without whispering with the quartet playing. "No, not yet. I was hoping they would have contacted me by now. I'm supposed to reach the kidnapper's tomorrow." We ordered two beers when a waiter stopped by to remove the empty bottles.

"Any trouble getting into the country?" I asked.

"They kept us on the ground after we pulled away from the gate in Cancun for almost an hour, but once we got on our way, everything was cool." We each took a long pull of the Cerveza's Pacifico, a nice Mexican brew that the waiter delivered on his way to another table. "I gotta' tell ya', Tommy, I thought I was gonna' shit myself going through customs."

I smiled. "Yeah, me too, but I won't tell anyone back home that you were scared if you don't tell anyone I was."

"Deal," he laughed. "Honest to God, man, I can't believe we're here, you know?"

"Yeah, but I bet we're going to believe it starting tomorrow."

Bobby's face got sober. "What's next?"

"Well," I answered, "we can't do much 'til Garcia's men contact me. Truth is, I don't even know if they're aware that I'm in Cuba. I figured by the time I saw you tonight, they would have contacted me."

"What're we gonna' do if they don't contact us?" Bobby asked.

That, was the question I didn't want to consider for the moment.

"If I don't hear anything by early tomorrow, I guess I'll have to try to contact somebody in Miami. I hate to get Anna Ortiz involved anymore than I already have, but I know she can at least reach Garcia."

We ordered from the waitress and ate pork, rice, black beans and grilled plantains in silence for a while.

"Tommy," Bobby said as we were finishing, "I know Abby is your girl, and I
know she's in big trouble. But I gotta' tell ya', man. If we don't get some help
pretty quick from this Garcia, or whoever, we better get our asses out of Cuba in
a hurry!"

I started to answer angrily, but he cut me off.

"Hey, I ain't getting chicken, man, but we are hangin' way out there on a limb
here. Without help, there's nothing we can do. Being tied to a chair next to Abby
with a rag stuffed in our mouth and a gun pointed at our head ain't gonna' save
her, you know?"

He was right, I knew, but the idea of being this close and not rescuing Abby
was too bitter a thought to contemplate.

"Hey," I said, trying to lighten the mood a little. "Don't worry. I haven't lost
my mind yet."

"Okay," Bobby said. "You're the boss. I'm just sayin', you know?"

I let it go. We had been at O'Reilly's over an hour. I thought it best that I get
back to my room to await a contact that I hoped was coming soon. Reaching into
my shirt pocket, I cupped my hand over a small piece of paper, took it out and
slid it across the table to Bobby, who picked it up without looking at it and pock-
eted the note.

"That's where you should meet me at eight tomorrow night if you don't hear
from me beforehand. Don't forget to check your cell every hour," I said. He nodded. I called for the check, paid it in Cuban money I had exchanged some U.S.
cash for at the hotel.

We got up to leave. On the way out, I noticed two men watching us intently.
They looked to be in their fifties. I tried not to show interest in them. The one
closest to the aisle leading to the exit, a stony looking man, with grey-hair and
deeply tanned, leathery skin, never took his eyes off me. His stare sent a shock
wave through my nerve endings.

On the sidewalk, Bobby nodded and turned westerly up the busy street. I
waited a minute, then followed him to the intersection of Cuba Street. I glanced
around and headed north toward the Hotel Sevilla.

The street was quiet with few pedestrians around. I kept a hurried pace, thinking that maybe I should have gotten a cab. A block ahead, walking toward me,
two men kept up an animated conversation gesturing and laughing wildly at
some joke. No one paid me the slightest attention.

As I reached the two men, they parted way to let me pass between them.

Suddenly, I felt both my arms being grabbed, twisting in vice-like grips from behind, and I was forcefully turned and driven into the wall of the building I had passed. My face was slammed into the wood siding. I felt blood wet and warm on my skin. I couldn't tell if my mouth or nose was supplying the blood. My forehead seemed to explode as I was pushed against the wall again, and again. My breath was driven out of me, and pain shot through my ribs and shoulder.

I felt a strong hand grab a fistful of my hair pulling my head back. I was too startled by the attack to feel fear, at least for the moment, but thoughts flashed through my head of that night in a parking lot in Atlanta.

I heard the roar of a car engine and the screech of tires behind me. A door opened and my captors wrenched me backward and threw me into the back seat. Someone else got into the car quickly. It jumped forward tires squealing down the street. I tried to pull myself to an upright position, the man behind me kept his weight on me as he frisked me.

Finally, I was allowed to struggle to a sitting position. I fought to clear my head. The man in the front passenger seat leaned back and tossed a rag at me.

"Clean up your face," he said. I realized that it was the same grey-haired man from the café who had been watching Bobby and me.

We were taking high-speed wild turns through the streets of Havana, as if trying to get rid of a tail. They left me alone for a few minutes.

The man up front said, without looking at me, "You are Senor Thomas Patrick, yes?" His English was perfect.

I realized he was thumbing through my wallet. "I know who I am," I said through swollen lips, "and so, apparently, do you. The question is, who are you?"

He ignored me for a minute, then said, "We have been sent by the Old One, senor."

"You guys really need to come up with a friendlier way to say 'hello'. I've had so many guns shoved at me, I feel like a holster."

"You see," the obvious leader of the group said to his companions. "This is what I find so endearing about Americans, my friends. They can keep their sense of humor even in the face of impending death."

"Bullshit," I said, wiping blood from my split lip. "Why would you want to kill me? We're supposed to be on the same side, in case no one told you."

"You were told to enter Cuba from Mexico, but you did not. Is this not so?"

"Cancun was only a suggestion. I thought it best to change my port of entry."

"Why so?" he asked suspicion in his voice.

"What difference does it make? The choice was mine. I'm here, right?"

"Why did you not stay at the hotel until contacted?"

"I was there all day. Where the hell were *you*, and how do I know you are even who you say you are?" I said.

He finally looked over his shoulder at me. "That is easy, senor. You are still alive, are you not? The question is, for how long."

Suddenly, I remembered that there had been two men at his table as Bobby and I left. Where was he? Had I put Bobby in jeopardy by meeting him tonight?

"You are in serious circumstances, senor. It is best you allow me to ask the questions, although I will answer your last one. My friends and I also had to change our 'point of entry,' I believe you called it. But our change was caused by Cuban naval patrol boats that were blocking our original landing location."

That threw me. "You mean you came by boat from Florida?"

"It is easier to do so than most would think." he said. "Imagine our concern when we found our way blocked by Castro's police. Then we find *you*, senor, conversing at great length with a stranger that we did not expect to see with you." He threw my wallet into the back seat. "Could it be that you were the cause of our discomfort off the coast?"

"That's ridiculous," I said, anger creeping into my voice. "I'm here to save the Barrett girl! That's it and that's all! I had no idea who was meeting me, or where they were coming from."

"Then, who were you with tonight?"

"You might have just asked. He is a friend from Atlanta. The same person who traveled with me to Miami. Senor Garcia's men held him at gunpoint at our motel while Garcia and I met at the cigar factory the night we hatched this plan."

"So? And why is he here? He was not expected."

"Because I had no way of knowing if Garcia could produce help for me. And, even if he did, what if something happens to me down here? I needed backup to go after the girl if I couldn't."

We drove around and around in silence for a few minutes.

"What you say makes sense. But you understand, senor, we are not in a business that allows for surprises."

"Yeah, well," I said, "I'm not used to getting the crap beat out of me every couple days either."

"I can see where that might be annoying," my captor said in a lighter tone.

He spoke to the driver in Spanish. We stopped our aimless driving, and headed off toward what seemed to be an exact location. Minutes later we pulled up in front of my hotel.

The grey-haired man turned back to me. "It seems you have stopped bleeding, Senor Patrick. Good. We shall go upstairs now. Please do not make a commotion in the lobby. Miguel would become quite distressed should you do so, eh Miguel?"

The man next to me cocked the hammer on his revolver while showing it to me and put it back in his pocket.

I was still a little woozy and I could feel the mouse growing above my left eye. My upper body ached, but I made it through the lobby to the elevator. My new found companions and I went up to the fourth floor. As we approached, I noticed that the door to my room wasn't closed all the way. Miguel pushed it open without hesitation.

Bobby Hemphill was sitting on the edge of the bed holding a towel to the back of his head. The other man from the grey-haired man's table at O'Reilly's Cafe was standing at the balcony door with his arms crossed, a gun pointed lazily at Bobby. The room was a mess having obviously been searched, with no apparent attempt to be careful. Bobby Hemphill gave me a look as if to say, "Are we a pair or what?"

"You okay?" I said.

"Yeah," he said sheepishly.

"Please sit down, Senor Patrick."

I did. "So, now what?" I said.

"I will choose," the grey-haired man said softly, "to believe what you have told me this evening. But you and your friend," nodding at Bobby, "will not leave this room again tonight. Do you understand, gentlemen?"

We nodded.

"You will speak to no one, yes?"

We nodded again.

"Tomorrow I will come here at ten in the morning. We will call the man who has the girl. In the mean time, I suggest you sleep." He smiled, and opened the door. "You will be watched," he said, and walked out trailed by his men.

"Hey, Miguel," I said. "You better put the hammer down on your gun before you shoot yourself in the ass." He sneered and walked out, closing the door behind him.

Bobby looked at my split lip, the bump on my forehead, checked his towel for blood, and pressed the towel back on his wound. "You having fun yet?"

CHAPTER 21

▼

17 October 2002
Early Morning

I let their footsteps recede down the hall. When I couldn't hear the Cubans anymore, I got up, and locked the door, not that the lock had mattered to them when they broke in earlier.

I turned out the light and walked over to the balcony door. I stood to the side and moved the drapes slightly. My old friend, Miguel, was sitting on a chair at a table next to the pool. His view of the window of our room was perfect.

I figured it was a sure thing that someone was watching our room from the hall as well. "We aren't going anywhere tonight," I said to Bobby.

He stretched out on the bed, being careful with his head. "How'd they get you?"

"I walked right into them. Before I knew it, I was face down in the back seat of a '54 Chevy." I said slouching into the old chair.

"I never knew what hit me." Bobby gestured a hit on the head. "The guy just came up behind me, whacked me on the head, but not hard enough to knock me out, stuck a gun in my back, and brought me here." Bobby lay quietly for a while. I stared at the fan on the ceiling. I had nothing to say. I had never felt more like a fish out of water.

Bobby turned to me and in a near whisper, "Were you scared, Tommy?"

"It's okay to be scared," I answered. "I damn sure was."

"Yeah," he said. "So was I."

"You feeling any better Bobby?" He sat up and inspected the bloody rag on his head. "I guess so," he said.

"Hey, they take your cell phone?" I felt my own still in my front pocket.

"No," Bobby said, pulling his out. "That's a little strange, isn't it?"

"I don't know, but I'm not looking a gift horse in the mouth," I said. "Watch the door. I'm going to try and reach Max."

Bobby got up and went over to the door, pressing his ear up against the wood. He made a face as if to say, "All's quiet." I went into the bathroom, put down the toilet seat top, and sat down. There was certainly a chance our Cuban friends had bugged our room, but I didn't think so. Anyway, I had to take a chance. Max answered on the second ring.

"Telling you that it's great to hear your voice would be a very big understatement," I said as quietly as possible.

"You okay, Hoss?"

"A little banged up, but otherwise fine."

"Banged up? Why you banged…"

I heard a "give me that," "ouch," and the phone being ripped out of his hands. Suddenly, Charlotte June, was talking in an excited half-scolding tone.

"Thomas Patrick, are you hurt? What's wrong? Are you two all right? So help me, if you don't come back in one piece, I'll kill you both myself!"

"C.J., hold on! Really, Bobby and I are fine. We just had a little bit of a rough first meeting with our welcoming party, but everything is fine now," I insisted. There was no sense in worrying her more than she already was. "Bobby's fine and he is keeping an good eye on me, so don't worry, okay, sis?" Bobby rolled his eyes and said "just great" under his breath.

"I guess…," she started as Max retrieved his phone. "Times short, sit down…What's happening Tom?"

I filled him in on what had happened, and my guess as to what was likely to happen next.

"What do you want me to tell Abby's parents?" he asked.

I thought about that a minute. "There isn't much to tell them right now, Max. Just say I made contact with our Miami friends. We expect to talk to the bad guys in the morning."

"Whatever you say."

"Max, if anyone tries to keep me from talking to you, I'll try to punch in your number and keep the line open. You might be able to follow what's going on."

"Who might do that?" he said matter-of-factly, probably so he wouldn't alarm C.J. and Pat, or explain to them what I was concerned about.

"Probably no one. Just a contingency plan, nothing more."

"Be careful, Tommy."

I went back into the bedroom, Bobby abandon the door. I told him what Max said.

"Best try and get some sleep," I said. "I'm sure our friends will be here right on schedule and I personally feel like a punching bag on stilts."

*   *   *   *

I woke up in a cold, drenching sweat, my breathing coming fast, and deep. I sat up and tried to get hold of myself in the darkness. Bobby slept soundly in the other bed.

The nightmare had come quickly and vividly. Abby was in the chair, tied tightly with surgical tape across her mouth. Yet, I could see her lips through the tape, soundlessly begging me to save her. I looked down at my feet, which were moving toward her, as if on a conveyor belt, no steps being taken. My arms were pointed at her, long knives protruding from more tape that secured the blades to my hands.

My body moved ever forward toward the figure tied to the chair. I couldn't stop myself, I couldn't stop moving toward her. I couldn't move my arms away from her. I heard myself saying to Abby as I was about to kill her, *I told you I couldn't do this! I told your mother you would die! I told her…I told you!"*

That was when I woke up, sweat pouring from every pore, tears welling up in my eyes, pain in my rigid body, a scream, no bile rising in my throat.

I got out of bed quietly and barely made it to the bathroom. I stripped my damp tee shirt from my body and splashed cold water over my face and on the back of my neck.

I looked at myself in the mirror. My dream had confirmed what I had tried to tell myself wasn't true. I was consumed by the fear of failure. The consequences of Abby's death would be due to my failure. I was a well trained athlete. I had dealt with fear my whole career. But that was a fear based on athletic performance which was within the realm of my control. If I failed, I only lost a game. There was always another game. I felt invincible.

Many lives would change forever, if I lost now. I was unequal to the task. I was sure of that. Yet, with no one else in a position to step into my place, I was cornered in a situation beyond my ability and beyond my control.

I calmed myself as best I could. The room was still in darkness. Shards of light were coming through gaps in the drapes. I glanced at the clock. 7:50 a.m. Peering through the drapes, tilting the shutter, I saw that Miguel was still at his post in the garden watching the balcony. I closed the drapes.

I lay down again, but couldn't sleep anymore. Frankly, I didn't want to sleep. I didn't want to relive my dream. I figured I'd let Bobby sleep a little longer. I wanted to be sure we were up before the grey-haired man, and his merry men returned.

He had said we would contact the kidnapper together when he returned in the morning. I had to try to control that call. I wanted to be sure that I continued to be the contact with the people who had Abby. I couldn't trust that the man from Miami did, indeed, have the same motive as I. How to stay in control was the problem, since we were unarmed and outnumbered.

I tossed around for a while. I was trying not to aggravate my already aggravated ribs and shoulder. Thankfully, my knee was holding up okay. Bobby will have a headache today. What a pair of cripples we are.

Right about nine, I poked Bobby in the back as gently as I could. He finally stirred.

"Oh, shit," he moaned. "Is it morning already? Oh, my head, a hang-over would be kinder."

"Yeah. Remember, we got company coming. Better get dressed."

He headed for the shower as I paced around the room. At exactly ten, the door rattled as a key slid into the lock and the door popped open. Nice knock I thought.

"*Buenos Dias*," the grey-haired man said as he walked in followed by his posse. He looked around. "Your friend?"

I pointed to the bathroom. He walked over to the drapes opened them and adjusted the light through the shutters. This was probably Miguel's signal to join us.

"And, how was your evening. I trust you are not still hurting from our little encounter last night?"

"Is that what you call it down here?" I said flatly. "Back home we call it a mugging."

He smiled and pulled a chair over from the little two-seat dining table and sat down in front of me, just as Jose Garcia had done in Miami. Miguel joined us, the ever-present gun in his hand.

"Oh, senor," said the grey-haired man, "that was not a 'mugging.' In Cuba, muggings are usually deadly. And here you are! All safe and sound, no?"

Bobby came out of the bathroom with a towel wrapped around his waist.

"Please, senor." he said to Bobby, "If you are to be part of our little enterprise, you should hear of our plans, yes?"

Bobby looked at us tentatively, and then sat next to me on my unmade bed.

Grey Hair looked at one of his men. "Café, Eduardo," he ordered. "Ah! Would you like some breakfast?" he said to us as if it was an afterthought.

"Let's see how the morning goes," I answered.

"Please yourself," he said. Eduardo went for the coffee.

"Now," Grey Hair said, "let us dispense with the small talk and get to the matter at hand."

"Before we do that," I said. "Let's dispense with the bullshit. Just who the hell are you?"

"You may call me Jesus," he answered, "Hay-zoose," he repeated giving us the Spanish pronunciation. "It may or may not be my name but it does not really matter, does it, senors?"

"Did you really come here by boat from Florida?" getting to the point myself.

"As I said last night, it is not too difficult if you have good intelligence and a very fast but quiet boat."

"And," I said, "just what are your instructions for this little 'enterprise', as you call it?"

He sat back in his chair. "Why, senor, I thought everyone knew what we are all here for."

That was a useless answer in my present state of mind. "I'd like to hear it from you, if you don't mind Jesus."

"Of course," he said calmly. "I do not take offense that you do not trust me." He leaned forward. "Be assured, senor, that I do not trust you either." He leaned back again giving an engaging and totally put-on smile. "I have been asked to perform a service for a man that is revered by many who yearn to return to our homeland." He shrugged. "We may not see that day, my Miami friend and I, but our children…," he shrugged again. "In the mean time, I have been asked to help you find some objects very special to my people. It is wanted by some very dangerous people as ransom. We are to help you rescue the girl and escape from Cuba to America. She will be protected at all cost to us. She is the daughter of a man who was my dearest friend."

"You knew Abby Barrett's father?"

"I knew him," he said reverently, "and I would have followed him into hell, itself."

"Hopefully," I said, "That won't be necessary."

"Amen to that," Bobby said in a near whisper.

The door opened and Eduardo wheeled in a cart loaded with carafes of coffee, cups, and pitchers of cream and bowls of sugar. We were quiet while the coffee was passed around. It was powerful stuff, dark and hot. It was like a tonic.

"If we are to make this work well, we are going to have to put aside our doubts about each other," Jesus said. "Do you not agree?"

"I do," I answered. "I just wish I knew who and what we are up against."

"Oh, but we do know, senor."

I was stunned. "What do you mean, we know?"

"We know the man who came to Senora Barrett's home."

"How?" I stammered. "Who is he?"

"The 'how' is simple. You told Jose Garcia of the meeting you were to have with this man in Atlanta. We simply had a man watching the house. He followed him after the meeting. The 'who' is also simply answered, his name is Gregorio Asparza. He is, as he said, a member of the Cuban contingent to the United Nations, in New York." Jesus took a long drink of coffee. I was too busy absorbing this information to speak.

"But we seriously doubt that he is representing the Castro government in this dirty little deal." Jesus added.

"Then who *is* he working with?" I said. "He didn't plan and pull off this kidnapping and extortion by himself!"

"Most assuredly not," Jesus said, "but we are not sure who is involved with him, That," he added, "is something we are most interested in knowing. For those of us who want to return Cuba to its people, knowledge is necessary for our protection."

"Just as long as the first order of business is Abby Barrett," I reminded him.

"But of course, Senor Patrick." That sly smile came again.

$$* \qquad * \qquad * \qquad *$$

"You have the number which we are to use to reach this man?"

It was a few minutes before 11 a.m. "I do." I said. "But what am I supposed to say to him?"

Jesus handed me a piece of paper. On it were written the words "*Consolacion del Sol,*" and "*Guarida de los Leons.*"

"This," he pointed to the first words, "is a town in the tobacco region of Cuba. The second is the name of a small hotel in that town. Your contact will know the location. Tell him to have his two men there at midnight tonight." He let this sink in. "They are to stay in their vehicle," he continued, "in front of the hotel. Then they must follow you and me to the next stop. Eduardo, Miguel, and Jaime," pointing to the men who had not been introduced before, "will meet us there."

"All right," I said, "but what if he doesn't agree?"

"I believe he will," Jesus said. "Now, you may make your call."

I took out my cell phone. Unlike Bobby's, there was a number listed on my phone which I accessed by pushing the number "5."

I took a deep breath and awaited an answer. My throat was tightening. It would all start when a man answered.

"I have been expecting your call," the silky voice on the other end said.

"Well, you got it," I answered, trying not to strangle the words in my throat.

"You have instructions for me?"

I wanted to shout, "*I know who you are, you bastard!*" I kept control somehow. Jesus said nothing but listened intently, as I spelled out the instructions for the enemy on the other end of the phone.

When I was finished, the man agreed immediately just as Jesus had said he would.

"There's one more thing," I said, looking at Jesus as I said it. "I want to see the girl before I take one step out of Havana."

Jesus tensed but didn't speak.

"That is not possible, senor," said the man on the other end of the phone.

"Make it possible...*senor*," I said, angrily. "'Not possible' is an answer I will not accept!"

There was an angry silence on the other end. I could feel the hair on the back of my neck bristling. If he hung up now, I might have lost the game before it started.

"Where are you?" The voice said, finally.

"The Hotel Savilla," I said breathing again.

"Stand outside......just you...in exactly thirty minutes," he said. "You will see the girl, senor. If you attempt to go near her, even one step, you will see her die!"

The line went dead.

"That was quite a chance you took," Jesus said, quietly. He turned to Miguel. "Make ready to leave."

"One other thing, Jesus, I want weapons for Bobby and me."

"As you wish, senor." Jesus looked at me hard.

*   *   *   *

Thirty minutes later, a big, late model sedan pulled up in front of the hotel directly across the street from the entrance where I stood.

She was there; sitting in the back seat, next to a man who stared right at me, and held a snubbed nosed gun pointed at Abby Barrett's temple.

She was wide-eyed and vulnerable, hair falling in her face, just like in a movie. She saw me and our eyes locked. Her look was one of disbelief. I could only guess what she read in my face. The car accelerated and she was gone, both of us turning to get a last look.

The phone in my pocket vibrated. It shocked me back to reality. "Hello," I said trance like.

"I trust you are ready to proceed as planned, senor?"

"You son of a bitch…" I started and he hung up.

CHAPTER 22

▼

17 October
The Havana Road

"Who is this Asparza, anyway? What is he?" I demanded.

We were outside Havana heading southwest on the Havana Road. Outside my window, ramshackle huts, each painted in faded bright colors, with the natural wood showing through, lined the narrow road. Jesus was driving the old truck which he had borrowed from someone in town. He didn't say who, and I doubt he would have told me had I asked not that it would have made a difference.

A second truck had left town before us, with Jesus' men, and Bobby Hemphill. After talking about it, Jesus and I had decided it would be best if Asparza's men didn't see there were six of us, especially two from Atlanta, until we were far enough away from Havana that they would have a hard time calling in reinforcements of their own. I couldn't argue with my companion's feeling that we were less likely to have trouble with the bad guys once they realized they were outnumbered, and out of range of Asparza.

Jesus kept his eyes on the road, but said. "Gregorio Asparza is an emissary of the Castro government in New York. His job is to develop trade opportunities for Cuba through his United Nations contacts. It is hard to say what 'opportunities' he makes for himself, as well."

"Wouldn't that tend to piss off Castro?"

He gave a disgruntled laugh. "In el Presidente's government, a little taste of the profits is always spread around to keep his minion's active in their pursuit of more and bigger profits." He looked at me with anger barely contained below the surface. "Of course," he said, "Castro and his brother, Raul always get the biggest cut."

We were working our way into the countryside. Children along the side of the road watched us pass by, blank looks on their faces.

"They," Jesus pointed out the window, "are the one's who do not see benefits from his work, Senor Patrick."

"Call me Thomas," I said, not knowing why I was suddenly willing to get on a more personal level with this man with the false name.

I changed the topic. "You said you knew Abby Barrett's birth father. Did you know her mother, Maria?"

"Everyone knew the children of Pedro Martinez," he said. "El Patron was the leader of our community for many years. Maria married the man who was to be his successor."

"Until he died?"

"You know this story?" he said, eying me with surprise.

"Some," I said. "I was told his death was suspicious."

"To some, yes," he answered. "But, what does that matter now. He is dead many years, and nothing will change that."

We were quiet for a few moments.

"Was your family one of the five who escaped from Cuba with Martinez'?"

"You are very well informed. There were other families that came with the six patrons. Not all of them were wealthy but they all followed Senor Martinez for other reasons."

"And your family?"

"It is not important to our mission," he said with finality.

"All right," I said. "You say you don't think Asparza is working for Castro in this situation. How do we find out who he *is* working for?"

"That is a part of why I am here," he said. "How, indeed?"

*   *   *   *

The day was heating up. A sticky dampness was settling in. Jesus appeared to be dry and comfortable, even with the windows open and the warm air rushing into the truck's small cab.

I was sweating profusely. "What happens after Consolacion del Sol?" I asked.

He glanced sideways at me. "I will tell you after we arrive there."

Impatience and stress were getting the best of me. "Jesus, or whatever the hell your name is, I'm getting tired of this horseshit! We're supposed to be on the same side, and I need answers." I said, trying to calm myself. "You need to stop treating me like I'm the enemy, and I mean now!"

He drove on for several minutes as if I hadn't spoken. Then he said, "We will meet Asparza's men outside the Guarida de los Leons, the Lion's Den. It is a small Inn."

"How far away are we from there?"

"About one hundred fifty kilometers," he answered. "Once there, we will have them follow us to a small village on the southern coast, called, *Cortes*."

"Okay, then what?"

"I do not know."

"You don't know?" I said. "What the hell do you mean, you don't know?" I could feel the heat rising in my face again.

"Do you not remember the instructions of Senor Garcia? You were told that the men who would meet you in Havana would each have knowledge of a portion of our route. Were you not?"

"Yeah, I guess so," I said. "But since you are the leader of your little group, I figure you should know the whole story, right?"

"I do not believe the word 'leader' has come up in our conversations," he answered.

"Well…no. I guess I just assumed so since none of your pals has said a word the whole time."

"Each of us is a *soldado,* a soldier, each with a job to do. Mine is to speak for Senor Garcia" he said. "We will do our jobs……Thomas," he added, finally using my first name. "And my name really is Jesus," he said, smiling.

I thought that over for a while. I was being asked to trust that their "jobs" coincided with mine, but with no way to confirm it.

"I'm curious," I said. "I get the impression that this is not your first trip into Cuba?" He didn't answer, so I went on. "If it's so easy to get in and out of the country, why haven't you, or others, slowly taken the treasure out of here before now?"

"I never said it was easy to come here, or, for that matter easy to get back out," he said slowly. "A few men, two, or three, in a very small, very fast boat can usually sneak into some desolate cove and evade a government gun boat if necessary. But it would be impossible to remove any large objects that way. Dangerous, very dangerous, senor"

"I guess so," I said.

"You must understand this, Thomas. Although there are children of the six families who would be happy to have those things their fathers' left behind, after many years, the patrons' came to understand that the chance of recovering their valuables in the near future was gone." He sighed. "They began to realize that the treasures they left in Cuba, a wealth of artifacts, jewels, and precious church icons and art, had taken on a new meaning. It was best left there until the Castro government and the communist leaders were gone. Then the great hidden wealth would be used to help rebuild a democratic country."

"But why is Garcia now so willing to give that possibility up for this girl?" I said.

He looked at me with sorrow in his eyes. "Because we have also realized that the children of the patrons and the others of their generation have little interest in the future of Cuba. They have no wish to go back and the treasures put them in great danger like this girl. It has been too long. This generation lives as Cuban-Americans now. Even if they were to get their belongings back, too many want the wealth for themselves, not for the future of Cuba as intended."

"Like Juan Garcia?"

"My old friend's son cares for nothing but the future he believes his father gave away almost fifty years ago."

"And," I said, "what about you?"

Jesus smiled. "My father gave me his love of our homeland," he said. "I will never stop fighting for a free Cuba!"

It didn't sound to me, like a fight that could be won.

$$* \qquad * \qquad * \qquad *$$

I was tired from an almost sleepless night. The stress of seeing Abby so close that I could nearly touch her but not rescue her, made me exhausted. The over-whelming exhaustion and the unrelenting humid heat constantly slapping me in the face, made me drift off.

I don't know how long I was out, but the nightmare about me being responsible for Abby's death came back. I snapped out of my coma-like sleep. I sat upright, and Jesus glanced over at me. "Where are we?" I said.

"About seventy-five kilometers from our destination," he answered.

I rubbed my eyes and looked around. It was like we had driven into another world. Gone were the shacks and dusty roadsides. Gone were the urchins standing along the road with vacant stares. The old truck was pointed through lush fields of green, perfect rows of plants and, in the distance, well kept barns and shed-like buildings. All this surrounded by hills and low mountains.

Jesus caught my eye. "This is my homeland," his voice containing an emotion I hadn't heard from him before.

"Yeah," I said.

"No, I mean this is where I was born, not far from here."

"Oh. It's beautiful here," I said. "Those are tobacco plants?"

The finest in the world," he answered proudly. These are young plants, always put into the fields each fall in October. They will be harvested in about four months. Now it is the Castro government who owns the fields."

"Did the Martinez family live near here?"

"No." he said. "The patrons lived south of Consolacion del Sol, in the very heart of the tobacco region. This place is just the beginning of the plantations. It is mostly sugar cane that is grown here. The rice plantations are found along the western coast, which is very marshy. The biggest tobacco growers have their fields south of the provincial capital of Pinar del Rio."

As we spoke, Jesus continued to check the rear view mirror every few minutes.

Finally, I said, "You know, they might be in front of us. They could have left Havana before us."

"Si," he answered. "That is why I told Miguel to wait at Consolacion del Sol and watch the town until we arrived. I wish to stay out of any traps."

I needed aspirin for the headache I could feel heading up my spine to my brain. Jesus yawned. "Do you want me to drive for a while?' I asked.

"I am fine," he said.

"Do you know this Asparza? I mean personally?"

He was quiet for a moment. "No, we never met."

"Did his father know Pedro Martinez?"

"It is possible but we do not really know. The patrons, their families, and the people who worked their fields, were part of a very tight community. Everyone knew of everyone, of the tobacco and sugar cane plantations. We were a family community."

Jesus checked the mirror again. "The Asparza's were not one of the six families; the Martinez' and the others."

"Why weren't they?" I asked.

"Jose Garcia once told me that there were many who were very vocal in his approval of the rebels led by Fidel. Maybe this Asparza was one of them."

"So the Asparza's stayed and became part of Castro's inner circle?" I asked.

"So it would seem."

A thought struck me. "Could the Asparza's have known about the valuables left behind all along? I mean, it wouldn't be logical to think the six patrons could have taken everything of value with them to the U.S."

"We do not think so," he said. "But we cannot be certain. Besides, he was not from our region, so we are not sure of his beginnings."

"Shit," I said, realization hitting me, "You guys have been watching Gregorio Asparza for a long time, haven't you?"

"Longer, we hope," he said with a smile, "than he has been watching us."

The cell phone in my pocket started to vibrate. Bobby's voice was scratched by static.

"Where are you, Bobby?" I looked at my watch as I spoke. It was nearly 6 p.m. We had been on the road a long time.

"We're at the town where we are supposed to meet you."

"We're getting close. Maybe, an hour, or so. Any sign of our guests?"

"I don't think so. You think they're ahead of you?" he said.

"No way to tell for sure, but, if they're behind us, they're not pushing us. Just keep your eyes open, pal." I glanced at Jesus. "You doin' okay, Bobby?"

"Yeah, sure," he said. "But, these guys don't talk much, you know?"

I laughed at that. He sounded fine, no distress in his voice. "Keep cool, Bobby. We'll see you soon, okay?"

"Yeah, listen, Miguel wants to talk to his boy."

"Okay," I said, and handed the phone to Jesus. They spoke in Spanish for a few minutes, then Jesus hung up and handed me the phone.

A look of concern passed over his face.

"What's up?" I asked.

"You feel how heavy the air is against your face, Thomas?"

He was right. Even with the sun dropping in the sky, the air was still, sticky, hot and damp. "What about it?" I said.

"Miguel said the people in the town are preparing for a very bad storm. It is coming across the Caribbean Sea toward Cuba. It is coming very quickly now."

"Is that going to bother us?"

"It will surely not help us," he said.

CHAPTER 23

▼

17 October 2002
Consolacion del Sol

"Man, am I glad to see you!" Bobby Hemphill said, as I got out of the truck and tried to rub feeling back into my legs. It was only the third time we had gotten out of the truck to stretch the whole trip. "I'm not used to being quiet for that long a time. Those guys are made of stone."

I punched his arm. "Lots of people wish you would be quiet more often."

"Nice talk," he said. Bobby pulled the front of his shirt away from his body. "Jeez, I thought it got muggy back home."

"Must be this storm that's coming."

"Yeah, people been boardin' up their windows all day long."

Later, we were sitting outside of the cantina of the Inn. "Bobby, I don't know if we're going to be able to maintain the cell phone signal much longer. I got a feeling we're going to the coast for more than just a look at the water."

"How'd you find out we were going to the coast, Tommy?" Bobby asked.

"Ol' Jesus decided to confide in me driving down here in that sweat box of a truck."

"Don't complain to me," he said. "There were four of us stuffed in that old Ford."

He chuckled. "But, anyway, it may not matter. Miguel has a phone, and I think it might be one of those GPS thing-a-ma-jigs." That surprised me.

"A global positioning phone? What makes you think so?"

"I don't know for sure, but it's bigger than a regular phone. I think he was gettin' weather reports or news or something, 'cause he kept using the phone but didn't talk to anyone."

I didn't like not being part of the plan. Whatever was about to happen, Jesus and his pals were keeping us on the edge of what was going on. I was willing to bet Jesus had a GPS phone, too. I had to tell myself to be on guard and to not take Jesus' openness for a reason to trust him completely.

"If anyone asks where I am, just tell them I went for a walk to loosen up. I had better try to reach Max and tell him where we are. If these phones go dead, I want him to at least have some idea where we are going, okay?"

"Okay," he nodded.

I went down the town's main road a ways. I turned down a side street full of worn out houses with threadbare kids playing in the front. I tried to connect with Max three times but the signal kept cutting out. I moved around to try and strengthen the signal. On the fourth try I got through but the static was making it hard to hear.

"Tommy? Tommy? It's Pat. Can you hear me?"

"Pat?" Just hearing his voice made me feel better. "Yes, I can hear you! Pat?"

"Yeah! Go ahead," we said together.

"Pat, listen. I think the cell phones won't be working very much longer. Get something to write with."

Within ten seconds, he said, "Yeah, go ahead."

I gave him the name of the town we were in. "About midnight, we're going to leave here and head to a town named Cortes," I said, suddenly realizing the kids in the street were watching me yell into the phone. I ignored them. "It's on the southeastern coast. I don't know where we go from there. If you don't hear from me in a reasonable time, tell Max to get a hold of Mrs. Barrett. She's to reach her sister in Miami." I looked around the corner of the building, and up the main street of Consolacion del Sol. I couldn't see any of Jesus' men out looking for me.

"Tell Maria to tell her sister to reach the Old One. She'll know what you mean. Have her tell him that we are out of contact. We know his men have a GPS phone with them." I let Pat get all that down.

"Okay," he said expectantly.

"If he refuses to contact his men…and us," I said slowly, "then, you have Max contact his cop friend, Jake. He'll know what to do. Got it?"

There was silence on the other end of the line.

"Pat?"

"Tommy, you guys okay? It sounds……"

"We're fine, bro," I said, trying to sound upbeat, "just planning ahead, in case I can't call you."

We were both silent for a minute. I sensed Pat trying to feel what was truly going on over the airway. I was hanging on to the life I knew, not wanting to go back to the reality of the situation.

"I saw her," I said finally.

"Who, Abby? You saw Abby?"

"Yeah," I said, a lump forming in my throat. "I made them let me see her. They drove by me in Havana. This guy...this bastard had a gun pointed at her head and just like that they were gone."

"Christ," Pat swore.

"I need to get back, Pat. Listen, tell C.J. that Bobby's doing great, okay?"

"Take care, Tommy," he said finally. "I'll tell her. And, get back here soon, man. I'm having a hard time holding off mom."

He was gone, the connection dead.

CHAPTER 24

▼

Midnight, 18 October 2002
Consolacion del Sol

Gusts of hot, water soaked wind rippled across the deserted streets of Consolacion del Sol. I felt like I was in a constant state of sweaty discomfort.

I moved my watch under the dimly lit street light. Eleven-forty. Almost midnight. I moved back into the shadow of the Lion's Den and waited.

Miguel, Bobby, and the others had left long ago for the next stop on our journey. Jesus and I hung around the town, keeping an eye out, waiting for our visitors.

Within a few minutes, I heard the rutting sound of our old truck coming from a side street a short distance away. Jesus brought the truck, with its lights off, down the main street and parked in front of the Inn.

"This way, Thomas," he said, climbing out from behind the steering wheel motioning to me to follow him back up the road.

We tucked ourselves into a little alley about a hundred feet from the rear of the truck, with a perfect view of the road in both directions.

"Do you have your pistol?"

"Yeah," I said, feeling the weight in my waistband. I was thinking that I still had not fired a gun in the line of duty.

"Good," Jesus said. "When our friends show up, we will come up behind them. Be sure to have your pistol out but keep it at your side, unless they get out of their auto."

"Fine," I said, wiping the sweat from my face. "How the hell do you stay so calm?" I asked.

Jesus gave a low laugh. "You will be fine, my young friend," he said. "This is not the place that they will want to start trouble. Tomorrow, once they see that there are more of us than them, we will be able to control them."

I looked at my watch. "It's time," I said. "Where the hell are they?"

"Patience, Thomas, they will be here soon enough. I would not be surprised if they have been waiting outside the town, waiting for the proper time to come in."

"You know," I said, "we could have told them to be here a lot earlier. We could have been on our way long ago."

Jesus was looking up the road for any cars coming from the direction of Havana. "These people," he said, waiving his hand around in a sweeping motion, "and those who live in the valley, and work the fields, their days are long, and start very early......"

"I get it," I said, breaking in on his thought, "any other vehicle that follows us once we leave here tonight, for any distance, would be very suspicious, right?"

"And, very visible in the night."

We were quiet for a while, only the swirling wind making any kind of noise.

"I'm glad you're here," I said, and meant it. Fish out of water.

Jesus started to speak, then, suddenly, his head turned and his face changed. He had the look of an animal smelling prey on the wind.

"Listen!" he said.

I couldn't hear anything for a next minute. Jesus was squinting up the road now, watching, I guessed, for headlights.

"I believe our friends have arrived," he said.

He pushed me back farther into the shadows of the alley. I felt my heart leap into my throat. This is what I was here for, but somehow, I don't think I had ever believed that this moment was really coming. Abby's face flashed across my mind's eye. This was for her. I had to do this right for her.

Time seemed to stand still, until gradually the sound of a strong engine became noticeable in the distance. We waited. If these were the people we were waiting for, they weren't rushing into town.

Finally, the darkness in the road in front of us began to lighten as the headlights grew closer.

"Thomas," Jesus said, "once they pass us, and pull up behind our truck, stay to the passenger side, and keep as low as you can." The sound got louder. "Do not let the man on that side get out of the auto. Show your pistol if he tries."

I must have looked deep in thought, or distant. "Thomas!" Jesus grabbed my arm.

"I'm okay," I said. "I got it."

The light on the road increased until the car, an American SUV, a Ford or Lincoln, by the looks of it, passed slowly by.

"Where the hell did they get that?" I said.

In a low tone, Jesus said, "They are easily obtained through Mexico or Argentina. Be ready!"

The heavy, dark colored SUV approached even slower as they came up behind our old pick-up. Suddenly it stopped. Headlights went out pitching everyone back into darkness. I had clearly seen two people in the front seats as they had passed us, but I didn't have to warn Jesus that there could easily be three of four more hiding in the rear. Jesus motioned that I should hang back a little.

He moved behind the SUV, keeping in a low crouch, checking the cargo area to make sure no one was hidden back there, and then quickly moved along the driver's side of the vehicle.

Just then, the engine went dead, and the driver's door opened slowly. As the man started to get out, Jesus stepped out of his crouch, and put the muzzle of his revolver under the man's chin.

The startled giant, who hovered over the top of Jesus' head by well over a foot, and looked to outweigh him by a hundred pounds, stepped back abruptly as if he had seen a ghost. I took this as my best shot at surprising his passenger. I rushed up the right side, tapped my revolver on the side window to get the man's attention. He looked at me, shock on his face as well. I motioned for him to keep his hands where I could see them.

"Please sit back down, my friend," Jesus said loud enough for me to hear him, and the man stepped back up into the SUV. "Turn on the battery......*only* the battery…of your auto, senor, and put down the front windows, so that we can have a little talk."

The driver huffed loudly, as if offended by the necessity of obeying the man with the gun but he did as he was told.

The stale stench of tobacco and sweat rolled out of the cab as the windows went down. I put the barrel of my gun, a Smith & Wesson .38 like my own back in Atlanta, against his passenger's neck. Trying not to look as out-of-place as I felt, and hoped no one besides me could hear my heart banging against my rib cage. It was the knowledge that these men were connected with the others who had Abby that kept me from shouting out that this whole scene was crazy.

Pull yourself together! You did what you had to do with Junior at the nursing home, no matter how tasteless the whole mess was. This is much more important! Think about Abby!

"You will please put your hands out of the windows, you and your friend," Jesus said, flicking his gun hand at the man I was guarding. "Ah, *bueno*," he said as they complied.

My man gazed steadily and maliciously into my eyes.

I felt heat rising in my face. I wanted to smash the killing machine in my hand against that menacing face. "Turn around," I said, in a stronger voice than I would have thought possible. "You may want to hear what my friend has to say."

"I believe," I heard Jesus say, "you are looking for us?"

The man behind the wheel was nonchalant. "I do not know who you are."

"You may call me Jesus. And, who are you?"

Looking straight ahead, the driver remained silent probably casing the situation. Jesus tapped his gun impatiently on the door on the SUV.

The man looked at him with utter contempt. "I am called Hector," he said.

"And, your friend?"

With the same nasty look. "You can call him 'Hector,' too," spitting out the window, tobacco juice nearly hitting Jesus' shoe.

Jesus ignored the affront, and said, affably, "That will do for the moment." He looked at me, and his face was blank, as if he was thinking.

"There has been a change in plans," he said, finally.

I looked across the truck's cab at him, questioningly, but stayed silent.

"What?" the big man behind the wheel said, in a loud voice. "Bullshit! I know who you are, and you know who I am! We have a job to do, and there won't be any changes!" He was almost purple with anger.

"Well," Jesus said matter-of-factly, as if discussing where to have dinner, "I suppose we could all go back to Havana, yes?"

"Listen, asshole," the driver said, teeth bared, and lips snarling, "You fuck with me, the girl, she is dead!"

"So, kill her," Jesus said, stone-faced, and my heart skipped a beat. What was he playing at, I thought?

"She is nothing to me. I am just a hired hand. But I do not think those that hired *you* will be satisfied with killing the girl." Jesus let that sink in. "Do *you*...think so...Hector?"

Hector One was silent staring at the steering wheel. Hector Two, or whoever he was, hadn't opened his mouth. Jesus had struck a nerve.

"It is nothing to worry about," Jesus said calmingly.

Both men looked at him expectantly.

Jesus pulled a folded paper and pen from his shirt pocket. He wrote something on it. "You will not follow us to our next point. You will meet us there, instead." He handed the driver the paper. "You will stay here until precisely 7 a.m. and then you will leave and meet us at the Cantina Libre. It is in the village I have named on that paper. You understand, Hector?"

Hector was defeated and angry about it. "Why all this bullshit!? Why we don't go right now?!" he snarled.

"Because, my friend," Jesus said, with steel in his voice, "I will set the rules. The rules are mine. You must arrive at the cantina at exactly seven, tomorrow night." Jesus gave them a big, toothy grin. "It is not so far, maybe a three hour drive, so take your time. Enjoy the beautiful countryside on this fine day, yes?"

"You are laughing now," Hector said, menacingly. "Be careful not to be too smart. I am not finished with you, yet."

"So be it," Jesus said, no fear in his voice or face. "My friend and I will be taking our leave now." He motioned me to the truck. "Hector," he added, "do not do anything stupid."

I got into the truck on the passenger side, reached over, and turned the key. The old truck's engine kicked over as I reached back to the small, rectangular, sliding window behind the seats, opened it, and pointed my revolver at the front window of the SUV.

Almost before I realized it, Jesus was in the driver's seat, dropping the gearshift into "drive" and we were pulling away from the two Hectors.

$$*\qquad*\qquad*\qquad*$$

"God damn it!"

The town was rapidly disappearing behind us, with no sign of the SUV in pursuit. I put my gun on the seat between us and glared at Jesus. "God damn it!" I said again. "What was that back there? Why did you keep antagonizing that guy?" A cold sweat was snaking its way through the layers of my skin. I tried to calm down. "Why the change in plans? You had to know that was going to make them nervous!"

Jesus stared straight ahead, and spoke softly. "It is no good," he said. "It is too dangerous to have those men too close to us for such a long time."

"Yeah, well I wasn't too crazy about that either, but......"

Jesus wasn't listening. He reached under his seat and began working the buttons of the GPS phone I knew he had to have been hiding. He listened for a response. Somebody answered at the other end, and the Spanish flew back and forth. I sat there, brooding, while they spoke.

Jesus hung up.

"I wanted to talk to Bobby," I said, agitation in my voice.

"Your friend is sleeping," he answered. "They will be in Cortes soon."

"We'll be lucky if Hector doesn't have a helicopter full of bad guys waiting for us when we get there, too," I shot back, accusingly.

"They do not know where we are going, Thomas."

"But the location in the note......" My confusion was evident.

"...Will leave them thirty kilometers from Cortes." Jesus finally looked my way. "We will meet them and lead them to Cortes once we are sure there are no helicopters, or autos' following them. But, first, we will join Miguel and the others in the village, and make sure all is in readiness. Then we will backtrack, meet Hector and his friend, and lead them in."

I had calmed down now but I was still annoyed. "Why didn't you tell me you were going to change things around? That son-of-a-bitch could have called his boss right then and there. You could have cost Abby her life."

Jesus said, "I am sorry, Thomas, but I made the decision to change our plan only after our conversation started. But, you give these men too much respect. They are just hired guns and they know what their job is or they are dead." He shook his head. "These men who have the girl, they will not be satisfied with killing your Abby Barrett. They want the treasure and the Hector twins, they knows that. They will not sacrifice this mission because they are angry with us."

I had to concede his point, but something was still bothering me. "What else?" I said, finally. "Is there something else you're not telling me?"

Jesus was silent a long time. Then just when I thought my question would go unanswered, he said, "I know this man, this Hector One." He checked the rear view mirror. "I have seen him before, many times in Miami. I do not think he recognized me."

"He came here from Miami, too?" I said in awe. "Damn, this country's a fucking sieve!" And then, it hit me. "Wait," I said. "If you know who he is, that means you must know who he works for, right?"

Jesus' face was stone like. "We are not sure," he said, apologetically. "We do know he has connections with the Russians."

"Russians?" I said, mystified. "I don't get it. What do *they* have to do with it? The Russian military has been out of Cuba a long time, right?"

"Russian military, yes, Russian Intelligence, maybe." He looked hard into my eyes. "Russian Mafia? That is another story, my young friend."

"Mafia?" I couldn't believe what I was hearing. "You think the Russian Mafia is behind this?"

"I cannot say for sure, but it is a fact that this 'Hector' has been involved with them in Florida. The Russian's no longer care about world domination. But there are those among them who long to dominate crime. He moves drugs for them. He sells too, and it would take a lot of money to pull him away from his stinking business. Unless," he said, "he is serving the same master."

My head was swimming, trying to absorb this latest possibility. I wondered, would Castro deal with the Russians in kidnapping Cuban-Americans? Why would this possibility surprise me?

"Castro deals with whoever can enrich his personal treasury. But I do not think the Russian's would deal him in on something this big," Jesus said.

"So, you *don't* think the government is involved?"

"We must play against all parties until we know for sure, and that is what we will do." Jesus pointed to the GPS phone. "We may have a new ally," he said. "Miguel says the storm is getting stronger. It is moving through Haiti and the Dominican Republic, toward Cuba. Maybe God has given us this storm as a gift. We must find a way to put its strength on our side."

For the life of me, I couldn't imagine how *that* was going to work out.

CHAPTER 25

▼

Near Dawn, 18 October 2002
South of Pinar del Rio

Fear, worry, and pure exhaustion having taken a toll on me, I had dozed off. Sleep had been elusive since leaving Havana. Sometime later, a particularly deep pothole shook me back into consciousness.

I sat upright, and rubbed the sleep out of my gritty, red-rimmed eyes, sweat, and grime stinging my face. I looked sheepishly at Jesus.

"Sorry." I said. "You must be very tired. Do you want me to drive?"

"I am fine," he answered, and looked it. "I will rest when we reach Cortes. There will be plenty of time before Asparza's men arrive tonight."

Dawn was a while away and the road was empty.

"There," Jesus said suddenly, pointing out my side of the windshield.

"What?" I said, fully alert now, and following his site line. "What is it?"

"These fields, they are the lands of Pedro Martinez. This is where Maria Barrett was born."

I stared out the window at the dark fields. There were buildings in the distance, points of light coming from their windows.

"The workers will be going to the fields soon," Jesus said, "just as they have done for generations."

I was silent, staring at the quiet land, imagining Maria and Anna and their brother, Carlos, walking among the perfect rows.

"Pull over a minute, please," I said. He did as I asked, and I jumped down from the cab. I bent down and scooped up a handful of the rich soil. "Maria might appreciate this," I said as I climbed back into the truck.

We got back on the road. "She is your woman, is she not?"

I heard Jesus' voice, but not his words.

"What?" I said. "Sorry, I was thinking about something…"

Jesus glanced at me. "This girl you have come to save. She is your woman, yes?"

I looked back out the window. "She is…very special to me." I gave a short, despondent laugh. "Honestly, I'm not sure what I mean to her. But I think we had…maybe have, something between us." I looked at him. "And, I know I have to save her."

He nodded. "Mostly," he smiled, trying to break my mood, "it is the woman who must 'save' her man. We shall have to see it goes the other way this time."

*   *   *   *

We had turned off the road we had been following since leaving Havana. We were now on a narrow, two-lane snake of a road, heading toward Cortes. As we drove, the hill-and-valley landscape was giving way to flatlands heading towards the coastal plains.

We finally reached a small village called *Guana*.

"There," Jesus nodded at a small cantina as we passed through the village square, "is where the 'Hectors' will end up. We will meet them here tonight."

Forty minutes later, the marshy outskirts of Cortes were in our sight.

We drove through the sleepy town. After a few twists and turns, we wound up at a small cove where I saw the truck Jesus' men and Bobby had been driving parked next to a dock. Two old fishing boats that appeared to be converted sport fishers were tied up, one on each side of the wooden dock. A heavy layer of moist air floated around us.

The place was empty.

"Stay here, Thomas. I will find Miguel and the others," Jesus said. "They may be at the owner's shack."

He hopped down from the cab, and headed up the drive to an old wooden structure about the size of small room in a matchbox house.

When he was almost there, I pulled the cell phone out of my pocket and pressed the on/off switch. I waited for the screen to come on, which seemed to take forever. I watched for Jesus to come back out of the building.

Finally, the phone lit up, but the signal bars never popped up. As I had expected, the phone did not pick up a signal. I couldn't reach anyone back home anymore.

I had made the right decision to try to reach home from Consolacion del Sol, for whatever good it did. At least Max and Pat, and Anna Ortiz, would know that we were going to Cortes.

I resolved to tell Jesus that I would need to contact Max Howard on the GPS. His response to my request would confirm or deny my lingering doubts about his real intentions.

As much as I hated doubting if we were on the same team at this late date, I had to keep my eye on the prize, which was finding el tesoro, the treasured goods of six families, and trading it for Abby, the treasure of the Barrett family.

I repeated to myself, *err on the side of caution,* all the time knowing that if these men wanted to kill Bobby and me, and make off with the riches, there was little we could do to stop them.

The door of the little shack opened. I saw Bobby come out and head for the truck. He had a big smile of relief on his face. I immediately felt the relief myself.

I got out of the truck and grabbed his outstretched hand as he reached me.

"I am never going to forgive you for sticking me with that bunch of zombies," he said, his voice sounding relaxed and calm.

"I would gladly have changed places with you," I said, smiling at him, and truly happy to see him. "The bad guys are coming and they're a little scary looking. Listen, Bobby," I said in a more serious tone. "The cell phones don't work here…"

"I know," he interrupted. "I tried myself when I was away from those guys. What do we do?"

I told him my plan about asking to use the GPS. "They give you a hard time at all?"

"Naw," he answered. "Pretty much ignored me. I didn't let on I could understand them when they spoke to each other in Spanish."

I raised an eyebrow in surprise. "It never crossed my mind to ask you if you spoke Spanish!"

"Not a lot," he said, "But, C.J. and I grew up with Mexican maids our whole lives. I caught some from them."

"So, what do you know from listening?"

"I acted like what they were saying was goin' right over my head, but I'll tell you this, we are goin' on a long boat ride. There is one hell of a storm headin' right at us. I think they are makin' this trip no matter what."

I thought about that. "Did you hear a conversation between Jesus and Miguel on the GPS last night?"

"Yeah," Bobby said. "That's where I got the storm report."

"And you're sure it was Jesus that Miguel was talking to?"

"Oh, yeah. I'm sure."

We were quiet for a while, and then Bobby said, "I don't know who the other call was made to, though."

"What other call?" I felt my nerves respond to his words. "What other call, Bobby?"

"Miguel made another call right after talking to Jesus. He was talking fast in a low, whispered monotone. I couldn't catch anything." He saw the worry on my face. "Sorry, Tommy."

I squeezed his arm and tried to smile. "You did well, Bobby. Keep letting them think you don't understand them. Let's see what happens, okay?"

"Sure," he said, "whatever you say."

Behind us, the door to the shack opened. Jesus and the others headed our way.

$$*\qquad*\qquad*\qquad*$$

"So," Jesus said, "do we understand what each of us is to do?"

It was nearly ten in the morning. We were sitting around an old table, on rickety benches, eating *Ajiaco*, a meaty vegetable stew, heavily laced with garlic, which had been leftover from the last night's meal. The smell of the marshes around us was strong enough to wipe out the smell of the stew, but I was very hungry. I spooned the savory food into my mouth, feeling the heat of it coursing into my stomach. Not bad I thought.

The brilliant sun that we had enjoyed every day since arriving in Cuba was nowhere to be seen this day. A heavy overcast had come in from the east, and it was as deep and far as could be seen, and the wind was gaining strength.

"I understand your plan," I said. "But tell me about this storm that is coming?"

Jesus took a pull on the beer that he had taken from a cooler at the end of the table.

"It is coming soon," he said, with no visible change of expression. "It is coming quickly, and it is a very strong storm. It will bring winds of more than fifty miles an hour, and much heavy rains. Maybe six or seven inches, if the speed of its movement does not increase. If it does, then more rain will fall." All this was said without the least concern on his part.

I looked around the table before speaking. Everyone else, except Bobby, who was looking at me, stared at their empty plates. "And just how is this of benefit to us?" I said. "You plan for us to cross over fifty kilometers of wide water to an island that might be a mud pie before we reach it?"

"That is correct, my friend. It may very well be a dangerous crossing, and the island we are going to may be a, mud pie, I think you called it? But we know what we are going to do on Isla de la Juventud. The Hector twins do not." He drank again. "And that is our edge."

Miguel got up from the bench and started clearing the plates.

"I think we are ready," Jesus said, and rose. "I think we should get some rest, Thomas," he said. "There will be much to do later."

I followed Jesus up to the shack. As we entered, I said, "I need to use your GPS to contact home. I need to tell them where I am, and where I am going."

He didn't look at me, but said, over his shoulder, "That is not a good idea, Thomas. There may be a chance the wrong people will pick up information from your message."

I walked around in front of him. "What does it matter," I said. In a few hours the bad guys are going to know where we're going."

"We may need those few hours, Thomas. Besides, the bad guys will not know where we are going until we get there, or if it will even be our final destination." He squeezed my arm in a friendly gesture. "You must trust me on this."

"Why?!" I said, shaking his hand off. "Who the hell are you and those other guys, Jesus? What reason do I have to believe you aren't in this for yourself?"

My anger was rising, and I was saying too much. I wasn't ready for a confrontation with this man.

"What reason," he said in a quiet voice, "have I given you to think otherwise?"

I stopped before I could say any more, and took a deep breath, then another, and felt the tightness in my throat ease. "I have to save her," I said, barely getting the words out.

"I know this," he said. "And I must help my country. I think we may be able to do both."

I wasn't sure of his meaning and he didn't give me a chance to ask him.

"You should sleep," he said pointing to the cots against the wall. "You and I must meet our friends in Guana in a few hours."

*   *   *   *

At 7:10 that evening, after we had circled the town looking for any unexpected visitors, and convincing ourselves there were no other players around, Jesus pulled the old truck into a tight U-turn on the main street of Guana. He pulled in front of the waiting SUV, stuck his hand out the window, and motioned for Hector to follow us. We pulled away and headed back toward Cortes. I kept my eyes on the big Expedition and on the sky above.

CHAPTER 26

▼

Evening, 18 October 2002
Cortes

The village was deserted. The windows of the houses boarded up and the streets empty of the few old American cars and trucks I had seen earlier in the day.

"They have taken their children and livestock to higher ground," Jesus said, guessing my unasked question.

"Even the animals are smart enough to get away from the storm, but we're going into the teeth of it, right?" I said, shaking my head.

"These people," he answered, nodding at the clapboard houses. "Their business is only to survive. We have much more to do."

I looked behind us again. "Are we going to leave right away?"

"Yes. The wind will slow us on our journey."

I looked up at the sky, which was deepening in color almost every minute, and peppering our windshield with spotty rain. The drops hit the glass with a "splat" that was louder than I thought possible.

We pushed on through town and pulled up alongside the dock. I glanced down to the two boats, which were bobbing up and down, stretching the ropes that held them to the dock's pilings. The water was deep black and angry looking.

Jesus turned off the engine and jumped down from the truck.

The same Hector was driving the Expedition as the night before, and he pulled up almost to our rear bumper, turned off the SUV's big engine, and, swinging the door open, jumped out and rushed toward where Jesus was standing.

"That is enough, you bastard!" Hector One yelled, "Enough of this bullshit!"

He looked like he was about to grab the smaller man by the neck and choke the life from him, but he pulled up suddenly, when Miguel came out of the cabin of the closest fishing boat, and Eduardo, one of Jesus' silent companions, came out of the owner's shack.

Both men were pointing double-barreled shotguns, which were aimed at Hector.

The big man pulled up short and stared at the two newest arrivals to our little group

"What the fuck is this," he snarled. "There was supposed to be only two of you bastards." He was purple with anger, but his body visible relaxed, and he did not advance any further.

"I am sorry, my friend," Jesus said to him, apologetically. Then, in a harder voice, "Tell your friend to join us, *por favor.*"

Hector One motioned to his partner without taking his eyes off Jesus. Hector Two got out and joined us. As I had expected, he was as big as his friend.

Bobby and the last member of our Cuban team, Jaime, were nowhere to be seen.

I knew they were hiding in the boat that Jesus, Miguel, and I would be traveling in. Eduardo would pilot the boat carrying the men sent by Gregorio Asparza.

Jesus had decided, and I had instantly agreed, that the four of us should be sufficient to give the bad guys pause, if they had any thoughts of causing trouble. We could risk keeping two men in reserve, to follow us and watch our backs, once we landed on the island and set off to find the burial location.

I was secretly relieved that Bobby Hemphill would be out of immediate danger for a while at least.

Except, of course, for the immediate danger of crossing some fifty kilometers of storm tossed seas.

In the distance, the dark skies emitted a low rumble of thunder, and the first flashes of lightning followed.

"If you do not mind, senor," Jesus said to the angry giant, "we have a trip to take." He pointed to the fishing boat on the left side of the dock. The boat bobbed up and down more violently, as the wind continued to increase in velocity.

Hector looked at him with a look that now was one of fear and consternation. His companion gave his first sign of any emotion other than meanness.

"Are you crazy?" Hector One said. "You cannot be serious! Are you blind?!"

"On the contrary," Jesus responded in total control, "I can see very well. But surely, a big man like you cannot be afraid of a little rain?"

"A little rain?" the giant answered, looking at his friend. "Do you hear this crazy son of a bitch? A little rain, he says!"

Jesus said, in a voice loud enough to be heard above the rising howl. "What you seek is out there," he said, pointing over the roiling water. "We go for it now, or we do not go at all."

He turned toward the dock and headed off for the boats. Eduardo followed him, while Miguel kept his shotgun trained on the Hectors'.

"Oh," Jesus said, turning back to the two men. "You will please leave the pistols I am sure you are carrying with my friend, Thomas."

The two men made to protest. Miguel raised his weapon to a shooting position, training his eye over the site of the shotgun.

I took my own .38 out of my pocket. I held it down at my side, but it was enough to convince them that they would never get their weapons out and ready to fire before they both died.

"Slowly, please," I said, the first words I had uttered since we had arrived back here. "Let's see if you are carrying anything else you won't be needing on our trip."

They grudgingly complied, and set their guns on the ground as I patted them down. I removed their cell phones, but found no other weapons.

Hector One snarled at me, but didn't try to stop my search. Maybe he was more worried by the shotgun still aimed at him and his partner. I threw the weapons; two very angry looking .45's, and the phones into the cab of their truck, and pointed to the dock. We started down the little slope towards the boats, Miguel and I trailing behind Asparza's two gunmen.

*   *   *   *

"Are you sure this is a good idea?" I said to Jesus, as Miguel loosed our boat's mooring ropes, tossed them onto the pitching deck, and nimbly jumped aboard. Miguel came into the pilothouse and took the wheel from Jesus, who had been holding the boat in place.

"We will use the storm to our benefit," he answered. "They will most likely be too seasick to cause Eduardo any problems," he said, smiling. "We will not see any government patrol boats, either."

"That's good, I guess," I said, rolling my eyes. "I just hate to throw up in front of other people. It's a shyness thing."

Miguel backed the boat away from the dock, turned into the wind, and we headed out of the little bay and towards the open sea. I looked back to see the other fishing boat following in our wake. I looked at my watch. It was a little before nine.

"How long?" I shouted over the wind and engine noise.

"We shall see," Jesus yelled back. "We shall see."

*   *   *   *

The boat carrying Eduardo and Asparza's men became a shadow in the driving rain, so Bobby and Jaime came up for air from the V-cabin up front. Surprisingly, neither seemed to be suffering motion sickness from their time below decks, while the seas had tossed us around.

Bobby grinned at me. "Nice shade of purple," he yelled over the wind and pointed at my face.

"You're enjoying yourself, aren't you?" I yelled back.

"Thank God Daddy had a sailboat down on the Gulf all those years."

"Bobby, you watch yourself when we land. You listen to Jaime, okay?" His face lost its smile, and he nodded.

The rain pelted down so hard that I thought the windows of the little pilot-house would shatter. I hung on for dear life as we got farther out into the wild water, and the bow of our thirty-eight footer plowed into the rising waves. The second boat was out of sight most of the time as the rain began to sheet, and one or the other of us dipped deep below the waves.

Some four hours of hell later, we had passed the halfway mark of our voyage over the empty seas. The weather hadn't changed; no better, but no worse, either.

I grabbed hold of the doorway and pulled myself out onto the tossing deck to where Jesus was holding onto a ladder that went up to the fly bridge high above the pilothouse. He was staring into the heavy rain behind us.

"There," he shouted, and pointed over our stern. "Eduardo is just behind us, maybe two hundred yards."

I followed his line of sight. I could see the other boat plowing into the waves we had just passed. "The storm," I said into his ear. "I figured it would get worse as we got closer to the core winds."

He turned his face and said, "It has turned north, just as had been predicted. We are following around the edge of the storm, and we should see the winds come down soon." He paused and looked for the other boat again. "But there will be much rain before this is over."

"How did you find out about the storm's change in direction?"

He patted his pocket where the GPS phone bulged. I was at once glad that Jesus was so well informed, but I also realized that weather reports were chancy, at best. We could be in far worse trouble than we were in right now.

I was suddenly curious as to whether sharks lost their appetite in stormy weather. I certainly had.

*   *   *   *

Dawn approached. Jesus had been right. The storm was slackening and we could see much farther through the rain. Eduardo, piloting the second boat, had closed the distance between us as the waves had calmed. Bobby and Jaime stayed in the pilothouse so that they could quickly duck down to hide in the V-cabin when we docked.

At the stern, Jesus was working his way around a half dozen ten liter cans filled with diesel fuel, to take picks and long handled shovels out of the transom box where bait usually resided, and lay them on the deck. He closed the lid and worked his way around the starboard side of the boat to the bow.

When I joined him, he was staring off into the distance, shielding his eyes from the rain with his hand.

"I always meant to ask you." I said. "Since Cuba hasn't done so well under Castro, how has he been able to keep control for so long?"

"You must understand, young Thomas," Jesus said. "It is most important *who* you control. Castro keeps his finger on the criminals like Asparza, by allowing them their ill-gotten gains. They are the ones who keep the rest of the people in line for him." He shook his head, a sad smile on his face. "It is quite a system, no?"

There wasn't much to say to that, so we just watched out over the waves for a sight of land.

A few minutes later, Jesus shouted, "*There!*" He motioned at the pilothouse for Miguel to come starboard about ten degrees.

"That is where we are going," he said. "That bay, she is called *Ensenada de la Siguanea*, Siguanea Inlet. It is the entrance to the lower part of *Isla de la Juventud*." He pointed and I followed his gaze. "There are many little coves in which to hide the boats," he said, guessing my unasked question.

"This is the place?" I asked.

He nodded. "Si, Thomas. This is the place."

I couldn't read the distant look on his face, but there was something there. Something that remained unsaid.

"Is the island uninhabited?" I said, trying vainly to wipe the rainwater from my eyes.

"Oh, no," he answered, not taking his gaze away from the seas ahead. "There are many thousands of souls living there."

"Christ!" I said in a suddenly worried tone. "What are you telling me? How could the burial ground remain safe all this time? There could be a resort or something on top of it by now."

He smiled. "Do not worry, my friend. The area we must go to is a…how you say…a reserve, a nature reserve, called *Lianura Carsica del Sur*. There are no buildings, no housing, and certainly no tourists in this weather." He patted my arm. "We will be very much alone while we do what we have to do."

He turned and went back into the pilothouse, leaving me to contemplate what was to follow. As usual, facing my own insecurities, my thoughts turned to Abby.

I will find you, Abby. Just hang on a little longer.

CHAPTER 27

▼

Dawn, 19 October 2002
Isla de la Juventud

Miguel cut the engine and tossed the bow rope over the side to where Jesus had jumped down.

We had been working our way slowly up the swollen waterways between small spits of land off the Ensenada de la Siguanea.

Jesus grabbed the bow rope and tied it to a foot-wide palm, then did the same with the stern rope. The ground squished beneath his weight and his boots sunk into the water soaked soil.

Eduardo brought his boat up behind us, switching the barely running engine from forward gear to reverse gear to keep the boat in place, until Jesus could get back to him and tie off his boat's lines. I was left to stay on board and keep my weapon on the second craft while it was secured to the trees.

Bobby and Jaime were back in the V-cabin awaiting our departure. They would follow us at a safe distance.

Miguel came out of the pilothouse carting his shotgun. It was evident as the two Hectors' pulled themselves off the deck where they were lying; they were in no condition to offer us any problems.

Eduardo opened the transom bait box and took out more tools. He put them into the hands of his passengers and jumped overboard.

Hector One jumped off the fishing boat, a massive look of relief on his bluish tinted face. "You are crazy, you bastard," he said, weakly to Jesus. "You could have killed us all."

"That may be," Jesus answered, easily, "But surely it was safer than answering the questions of a Cuban naval officer, yes?"

Asparza's men looked at each other, but said nothing.

"Come, we must go. There is much to do and little time."

Everyone grabbed shovels and picks and headed off after Jesus. The Hector twins were followed by Miguel and me. I looked behind at the gently bobbing boats. There was no sign of Bobby or Jaime.

We had walked, or I should say pulled our feet, step by miserable step, from the sucking mud, for about a half mile or so. Jesus stopped and put his arm up. No one said a word as he looked around for some unknown and unseen talisman. After a minute or two, he motioned us forward, taking a slight tack to the right of the trail we had been following. The trail began to quickly change to an over-grown patch of wet, shoulder high plants, which slapped at us as we worked our way forward.

Through it all, the men in front of me glanced around, as if looking for ways to mark their route. Or maybe, they were just looking for danger. I had to remember that these men were killers. They worked for kidnappers' and if Jesus was right, might be members of the Russian Mafia. They weren't going to be caught in a trap if they could help it.

The sun was starting to peak through the breaking cloud cover, as the storm moved farther away. There was still a heavy rain falling as the steamy heat was rising from the ground. The back of my shirt and pants stuck to me adding to my soaked misery.

Jesus changed course again a few minutes later. I figured we slogged through another mile or so in the ankle-deep mud. I didn't know how long I would last. My bad knee was feeling the pressure of my exertion as I pulled my legs from the spongy ground.

Jesus raised a hand and we stopped again. He motioned us to wait while he went up ahead about thirty or forty yards. A minute later, he waved us forward.

When we reached him, he was standing in underbrush and behind a large tree.

"That," he pointed out to a clearing a few yards away, "is the road to *Caleta Grande*, a small village on the coast. We are almost to our destination." He looked down both directions of the two-lane road, crossed over it with all of us following on his heels, and headed inland.

Jesus appeared to be unaffected by the efforts we were putting out, and bounded up ahead. For me, a growing sense of trepidation fought an inner battle against the realization that our destination was minutes away. The excitement of that thought made my heart beat faster. We had followed him another hundred yards, when he stopped suddenly in an open area about thirty yards square.

He turned and looked back at our little group. The Hectors were a little winded, and I was a little sore, but we had made it. Here in the ground below us was what we sought. Ill-gotten gains for the cretins who stood before me. Hope for my Abby safely returning to me.

"Just a little longer." I said out loud, accidentally.

*   *   *   *

The shovels made a squishing sound as we dug deeper into the water soaked ground. It was my turn, along with Miguel and Hector Two, to get into the pit that contained riches put here almost fifty years ago by men who had not seen this place since, except in their dreams.

Each sloshing shovel-full was piled higher and higher above the gaping hole.

Finally, the soil seemed dryer and more compact, and we bit into it with the picks, and then shoveled it up onto the mounds that now surrounded us. The torrential rains had not soaked down this far.

We were clearing an area about ten feet square. The moist heat had made the little clearing feel like an oven, and we were tiring more quickly with each shift.

Miguel was the first to hit the hard surface of the layers of thick, oiled planks. We could see the outline as we dug of a large concrete coffin with oil skins stretched over the tops of the planks to preserve the treasures of six families. The "thunk" of the shovel against the wood reverberated in the little clearing. Miguel swore at his stinging hands.

Hector Two scrambled over to where Miguel stood. With an excited look crossing his face, he pushed Miguel away and buried the head of his pick into the wood. He ripped away a section of the planking, which came away too easily, I thought. We were all too caught up in what was happening to give any attention to anything but the rising and falling of the tool in the pit as he continued to slam it into the wood.

I hadn't even notice the light rain that had begun to fall from the rear edge of the storm which I thought had long passed us by.

Hector One moved closer to the pit's edge. "You two," he said, pointing to Miguel and me. "Get out. I do not trust you in there!"

I looked at Jesus standing a few feet away. He shrugged his assent and we scrambled up the side of the pit, using a knotted rope that we had tied to a tree and run into the pit as a ladder.

The rain came down harder. I moved under the cover of the closest tree. I waited, not needing to watch, just waiting for the first word that the pick had broken a big enough hole through to see el tesoro.

When it came the words struck me like an electric shock.

"I can get in!" I heard Hector Two say excitedly from down in the hole. Jesus was standing near me. I looked back at him as I moved closer to the mound of mud at the edge of the pit. He didn't move closer and neither did Miguel.

Suddenly, there was a commotion at the edge, and the other Hector, standing along the top was swearing, and screaming, "What do you mean they are empty?!"

"Everything is rotted!" I heard from the pit. "The stinking water is a meter deep! The crates have fallen apart and they are full of rocks! Nothing but fucking rocks!"

His partner spun toward Jesus. I looked at him too with a look of shock and confusion on my face.

"You son of a bitch!" the giant yelled.

And, just as suddenly, Hector One twisted to the right as his left leg gave way and the mound of mud began to slip quickly from beneath him. All around the pit, the slithering mass of soaked dirt was sliding back toward the gaping hole. Faster and faster, the mounds gave way. I half heard the strangled cry from deep down in the pit as Hector Two tried vainly to claw his way out of the hole. The mud moved faster and faster. Within seconds, his cries disappeared and so did most of the pit.

We all stood immobile, shocked. All except for Hector One, who scrambled to his feet, grabbing the shovel he had dropped when the ground gave way beneath him.

Screaming with a rage that barely invaded my conscious, Hector whipsawed the flat of the blade against Miguel's leg as he tried to rise from the mud. Miguel blurted out a scream of pain as he went down again. His crazed attacker spun around letting loose of the shovel as he came around to face Jesus.

The shovel edge made a whacking sound like a machete blade as it sliced deep into Jesus' side, burying itself six inches into him. I stared at Jesus. As if by magic, blood began to coat the blade outside the wound. Jesus looked down at the wooden handle sticking out of him as if looking at a spot of dirt on his clothing. He looked at me. His face was strangely calm, fearless. Without a word, he slumped to the ground.

I was thunderstruck. I had never seen a man die violently before and now death was all around me.

I was rooted in place, unable to move, when suddenly the giant came at me with his full force. Hitting me head on, he drove me back against the tree behind me, throwing me into a low limb.

Pain shot through my spine as he bent me back further. The air shot out of my lungs. I could feel the monstrous hands closing around my neck, and his thumbs pushed against my windpipe. My ears began to ring, and I thought my head was going to explode as he pushed his full weight against me. I couldn't force my chest to expand so that I could get air into my lungs. My mouth was open but no air...no air...air...I struggled, but couldn't get a foothold in the soaked ground.

There was pain in my neck and my muscles, and my vertebrae felt like they were turning to sandpaper. I tried to push him away from my body to try to break his hold on me. If I could just get a little air.

I lifted my face feeling the rain beating down on me. He tightened his grip. I was losing consciousness and I knew I was going to die in this swampy hellhole. My Abby was going to die too. I let Maria Barrett down...all because of the lies of old men.

"You...YOU!" I heard him say, his voice roaring in my ears. I could feel his hot, stinking breath against my skin as he squeezed harder, "I should have killed you in Atlanta!"

And then I knew the truth. This man had tried to kill me in the parking lot at Ireland's Own.

It had always been about this.

I knew this would be my last thought, my very last known truth.

I struggled to bring my hands up against the rock-hard chest of the maniac above me. It was useless. I had lost all feeling except for the cool rain on my face when I felt, rather than heard the loud explosion and felt the hot liquid hit my face. I willed myself to open my eyelids which felt like they had been glued shut. When I could finally see, the eyes that stared back at me were dark, vacant, looking through me.

I felt the great pressure on my neck loosen as my eyes focused on Hector. The hot liquid on my face was his blood. The top of his skull was flipped over onto his forehead.

Globs of the grey matter dropped in slow motion down onto my face from the huge hole in Hector's head. The big hands fell away from me but his dead weight still pressed against my chest pinning me over the heavy branch. I was too weak to try to push him off me anymore.

Just as suddenly, the weight was gone. The killer's carcass fell sharply away from me and slumped to the ground in a heap.

Bobby Hemphill's face, splashed with mud looked pained and frightened and dumbstruck all at the same time. He stared at me in shock. I pushed my head forward, grimacing in pain. I looked at his left hand outstretched towards me.

The .38 in Bobby's right hand hanging at his side, slipped to the ground.

CHAPTER 28

▼

19 October 2002
Isla de la Juventud

The rain had stopped again. I could not make myself move.

Bobby pulled himself together, wiped the gore from my face, and helped me over to where Miguel knelt next to Jesus. He was trying to dry the wounded man's face with a small piece of cloth but nothing we possessed was very dry. Jaime and Eduardo stood over their fallen leader and friend, deep sadness in their eyes, but their faces were strangely stoic.

I nearly collapsed as I sat down heavily next to Miguel. Jesus was conscious but breathing shallowly. His face was colorless, his lips nearly white. No one had touched the shaft of the shovel for fear removing it would cause more severe bleeding and excruciating pain for the badly wounded man.

It didn't matter. We knew Jesus was dying and nothing we could do would change that. He knew it too.

*   *   *   *

A few minutes earlier, I had been near death myself, yet, in my recovering mind, rage began to build. I had entrusted the fate of Abby Barrett to this man. I had been betrayed and used. Now, Jesus was dying and I could feel no pity for him.

"I am sorry, Thomas," he spat out the words with what air he was able to draw into his lungs. "You will have to rescue your Abby without me."

"Why?" I croaked through my bruised windpipe. "Why did you do this to us? You knew this place, this treasure, all of it was a lie, didn't you?"

"I...knew," he wheezed, his voice becoming weaker. "You...must...understand...what is...at stake, Thomas." He stopped and forced air into his lungs. "We had to...know who knew about the treasure, and...where their information came from. We failed."

"Bullshit! What treasure?" I said, half sobbing as I spit out the words. "There is no treasure. The lies of Jose Garcia are going to kill that girl!"

Jesus raised his hand off the ground and wagged a finger in my face.

"No!" he said with as much force as he could muster. "No! It...el tesoro...exists...listen...it was my job to rescue the daughter of Maria Barrett *and* safeguard the treasure...for the return of..."

"......There's no more time for lies!" I said forlornly.

"Listen to me! There is...no time for this now," Jesus spat the words at me. "Listen to Miguel...he will take you...a man...he will help you." The voice was drifting now, as blood continued to pump from his wound. "Miguel, you know...what to do!"

Miguel took Jesus' hand. He was still holding it a moment later when the dead mans fingers relaxed their grip.

Miguel gently put the hand on Jesus' still chest, made the Sign of the Cross over the body, and pulled the shovel from the gaping wound.

"We must bury that pig," he said slowly glaring at Hector's corpse. "But we must hurry. We must get back to the boats and leave before patrols begin again. I will take you where you have to go."

"Listen to me," I said. "Asparza is going to expect to hear from these guys soon."

"Not since the storm hit Cuba," he said emphatically, "Asparza will expect that the storm will have knocked out Hector's ability to call for a while. Havana will be having troubles of its own with the storm's winds."

I sat back on my heels. "So that's what Jesus meant about using the storm to our benefit. He knew it would buy us more time."

Miguel said nothing. He rose to his feet wincing from pain, and rubbing the swelling growing in his leg where he had been hit with the shovel. Bobby and the others were already digging into the mud where the pit was still visible.

When we finished smoothing the mud over the Hector twin's grave, we tossed some bushes over the disturbed ground. We had buried all the tools but two shovels in the same hole.

Miguel said, "It is time to leave." I looked at my watch. It was nearly dusk.

Bobby and I made sure nothing was left behind, while Miguel gathered up Jesus' body and hefted it up over his shoulder. "We must go right now," he said again, and the four of us headed off in the direction from which we had come only a few hours, and a lifetime before.

∗   ∗   ∗   ∗

We arrived back at the cove and found that the boats had been undisturbed during our absence.

While Miguel stowed Jesus' body, Eduardo put fuel into the tank of the first boat, I went into the pilothouse where Bobby stood looking out over the bow. He hadn't said a word since he had fired the gun into the head of the man who was about to kill me.

"You all right?" I said quietly not wanting to startle him.

He looked at me for several seconds before nodding. "You saved my life back there, Bobby. You know that, right?"

He nodded again. "Yeah, I know. But I was almost too late." He looked at me hard. "I just stood there, man. I must have stood there a whole minute trying to get my finger to squeeze the trigger, you know?"

I nodded, I know.

"He was *killing* you, Tommy. And I couldn't pull the trigger." Tears weld up in his eyes. "I'm sorry."

I wasn't sure what to say, but I tried. "Only a stone-cold killer can kill without thinking about it, Bobby. You and me, we aren't killers. We've got ourselves tied up in something neither one of us would choose to be a part of, if we had any choice."

"Yeah," he said, "but we had to know something like this could happen." He wiped a hand across his eyes. "I thought I was ready, you know. If anything happened I could...but I wasn't."

I knew the feeling. "When the time came, Bobby, you did what you had to do. I just stood there and let Jesus die. I couldn't even move to defend myself."

He sighed. "Man, it all happened so fast! Jaime and me, we stood there while people were dying. When I saw Miguel hit in the leg?" He shook his head. "It was like watching a movie from the front row of a theatre."

"If it's any help," I said, "I just keep thinking about Abby. Whatever happens, it's all part of getting Abby back."

Bobby looked at me and finally gave me a small smile and nodded.

The door opened and Miguel came into the pilothouse. He looked at us as if he understood the conversation we had been having without hearing a word of it.

"There may be patrol boats out to inspect the damage on the coast. We will wait a little longer until it is fully dark and run without lights."

"Okay," I said.

"There is much cloud cover tonight. There will be little moonlight."

"Are we going to take both boats back?" Bobby asked.

"Eduardo will bring the other one back after we are long gone. He is carrying papers for the boat and a forged commercial fishing license in case he is stopped."

Some thirty minutes later, we could hardly see our hands in front of our faces. Miguel fired up the diesel and with only the lights of the instrument panel to see by, he slid the boat around the small spit of land that had shielded us from the channel.

After a half hour, we were approaching the wide expanse of water that stood between us and the mainland.

Miguel kept to his word leaving the running lights off. At *Capo Frances*, the point of land at the edge of the island, we hove to and waited about fifteen minutes without seeing another craft. Miguel put the engine back into gear, and left behind the nightmare of Isla de la Juventud, the Island of Youth, which would forever be the Island of Death to me.

CHAPTER 29

▼

Before Dawn, 20 October 2002
Cortes

The seas were calm and pitch black like the sky.

We made the crossing to the mainland quickly and safely without seeing another boat. Miguel docked us just before two a.m.

I breathed a long sign of relief as we stepped ashore. Our trip was a failure but we were still alive, with one last chance to save Abby.

I thought about using Miguel's GPS to call Atlanta but I didn't ask him to let me. Besides, Jesus would have said that it would be dangerous to call anyone. My anger at Jose Garcia and his insane followers left me fearful of their knowing what had happened.

But I couldn't stop Miguel from informing them if he wanted to anyway. That worried me. At some point, I would be able to use my cell phone again and that would be the time to decide about calling home. Right now, I had other questions.

"What do we do now?" I asked Miguel after the engine died and the ropes were secured.

He pointed up to the little owner's shack. "Wait for me up there," he said. "I will return soon with food and water. You can rest there in safety."

I felt my impatience welling up in me again.

"There's no time for games," I said as forcefully as I could. "Jesus said you would get me to someone that could help me. That's what I want, Miguel. And I want that now!"

He turned to me. "I promised Jesus I would do his bidding!" There was anger, yet a touch of sadness in his voice. He quickly softened his tone, and spoke tiredly. "The help you seek is very close, senor. Please, go change into the dry clothes you left here. Rest for a while. I will bring food and drink soon." He wiped his red-rimmed eyes with his sleeve. We were all exhausted. This was the first time Miguel had showed it.

"Are you going to check in with Miami?"

He thought about that.

"I think not. Not for a while, anyway."

I sighed from exhaustion and relief. "Okay," I said. "We'll play it your way for now, Miguel. But only for a little while."

I knew my threat, if he even took it for one, was baseless. Without his help, I would never find Abby.

He said nothing, nodded, and started up the little hill towards his truck.

I was suddenly overwhelmed with a fatigue unlike any I had ever experienced before.

*   *   *   *

She straddled his body and kissed his chest, once, twice, her cool lips brushed against his neck, and she smiled at him. He hadn't known this kind of happiness, this kind of peace before. He looked deep into her eyes and saw the moon and the stars, and the future.

"I love you," he said.

The noise woke me from a fitful sleep...a car door, footsteps. Many footsteps.

I sat up abruptly, the dream gone. Abby's face gone. I looked over at Bobby, who was sound asleep, on his side, facing the wall. The door opened and Miguel came into the shack. He was alone.

"I have food," he said without preamble, and tossed a bag on the table. The smell of the food hooked me immediately. I realized how long it had been since I'd had a hot meal.

But I was still tired too. "What time is it?" I asked.

"Nearly four a.m.," he said.

"No wonder I feel lousy," I said, rubbing my eyes. "We've only been asleep about an hour and a half."

Miguel nodded at Bobby. "Shall I wake him?"

I shrugged. "No, let him sleep a little longer. Is the other boat back? It thought I heard other people out there."

"I brought some friends to take care of Jesus' body. They will take him to be buried." There was pain in his voice. "You should eat something," he said. "It is time to take you to the man of which Jesus spoke."

"Good," I said. "Then I better wake Bobby, if we're leaving."

"That is not necessary. We are going up to the village. Just a short distance."

"The man who can help us is *here*? Here in Cortes?" I couldn't believe what I was hearing. "Why didn't Jesus take me there before, for Christ's sake?"

Miguel ignored my question. "I am going to help with......" He opened the door and looked down to the dock.

"Yeah," I said in a calmer voice. "Let me eat something real quick and I'll be right out."

When he was gone, I went over and sat on Bobby's bed and gently shook him awake.

He rolled over on his back, his eyes wide, but confused.

"You awake?" I asked.

"Ahh...yeah," he said, fighting sleepiness. "Uh, what's going on?"

"I'm going into the village with Miguel, to meet someone."

He rose up on his elbows. "You want me to go with you, Tommy?" He yawned, struggling to come fully awake.

"Naw, you get some sleep. There's food over there when you want it."

"You sure?"

"I'm sure. Listen, there are some guys down at the boat. I don't know if they are going to stick around or not, so just be aware, okay?"

"I gotcha, but you gonna' be all right?"

I sighed. "We have to trust Miguel, I guess. God knows we're lost without him."

Bobby nodded.

"But I'm only going to give him so much rope. So, if anyone comes to you and says that I want you, that you to follow them to me. You ask them for the code word. 'C.J.' They say that and you come running, okay?"

"'C.J.' is the code word."

"Good," I said. "You got your .38?"

"Right here," he said, looking down at his side next to the wall. He seemed to have made peace with what he had done to Hector One.

"I'll be back soon," I said, patting him on the shoulder, and got up. Bobby rolled over and went back to sleep.

✳   ✳   ✳   ✳

"We will walk," said Miguel. "It is best we leave the truck here."

"Whatever you say, let's just get to wherever we're going." I said flatly.

In less than ten minutes, we were at the village square, which was deserted at this hour. Miguel kept an eye open for anyone who might be out, and about, but the sensible villagers were all asleep. If there were any strangers in town, their vehicles were well hidden. I didn't think there were any but we had to remain on guard.

Calle Angelica ran along side the little "Church of the Angels," the only building on the eastern side of the square.

Miguel turned onto the street and I followed close behind.

He kept to the side of the road until we reached a stoned wall which enclosed a plot of land behind the church. He found an unlocked gate which led us into a field of headstones and bent trees.

"This way," Miguel said in a low voice. He headed away from the church, winding his way through the graves, trying not to trip in the darkness. I followed but I was getting edgy. I grabbed Miguel's arm and stopped him. "Where are we going? Tell me now!"

He did not pull away, instead pointing at a small building at the far left hand corner of the yard. I let go of his arm and stayed close behind as we reached what I then realized was an open-structure with benches with a topped with a wooden cross seven or eight feet above the seats.

Miguel stepped aside. In the shadows, I could make out a shapeless figure sitting on one of the benches.

Miguel stepped farther away and motioned me forward. Miguel turned and walked back toward the church, leaving me alone with the shadow waiting to talk to me.

"The family of *el difunto*, the deceased, comes to this place after the burial to remember their loved one. To say their final goodbyes to those who came to mourn with them."

The tones were elderly and peaceful and calming. I said nothing, waiting for more from the disembodied voice.

"I come here at night when I cannot sleep…for the peacefulness, you see," the voice said. "I do not sleep very well anymore, I am afraid. Please, my son," he said, patting the seat next to him, "come sit by me. I cannot see you very well."

I had no choice if I was going to find out how and why this person, whoever he was, might be able to help me. I took a quick look behind me. Miguel was not in sight. I walked over to where the shadow was sitting. As my eyes focused, a saw that he was wearing a dark robe, with a cowl over his head, which obscured his face.

"Are you a priest?" I asked as I painfully sat down next to him.

He chuckled. "For many more years than you have been on this earth, my son. But I regret, not for much longer."

"Who are you?" I asked, peering under his hood. "I don't understand why I was brought here."

"I am Father Ignacio, Senor Patrick. I know precisely why you are here," he said in a soothing voice. I was intrigued and confuse at the same time.

"Then, please tell me," I said. "I have a very important task to take care of and not a lot of time." I leaned forward and tried to look at his face. He turned and looked straight at me—eye to eye.

He put his hand on my arm. "You seek el tesoro, senor, as others have before you." He smiled. "But the treasure you truly seek is a young girl who is a descendant of an old friend of mine."

"You know about Abby Barrett?" Then it came to me. "So you knew her grandfather, right?"

"The Patron," he said gravely. "Oh, yes, I knew the Patron very well. He was a great man and a good man. He put his faith in the Cuban people believing that they would rid themselves of Castro and his followers quickly. They would see through Fidel Castro. He was just another selfish leader, a tyrant, a good actor, that was supposedly for the common people, but in truth a user of the Cuban people for his own purposes. I am afraid the Patron was right. Before God, I wish it had not been so."

"So you know the whole story?"

"I am very much a part of the whole story," he said. "I was told what the Patron was considering by my friend, Jose Garcia, at the very early stages of the idea to hide their wealth from Castro."

"Garcia!" I spat the name out. "He lied to me, he sent me on a wild goose chase to find some fake treasure and gave false hope to me and to a mother whose daughter was kidnapped." I tried to calm down but found myself becoming more agitated.

"Listen, Father, Jesus told me the truth after we found out too late that this el tesoro doesn't exist. We have three men dead including Jesus, from this madness. And the treasure was a lie so no ransom for Abby."

It was my turn to look *him* in the eye. "How do I save her now? Answer me that! There is nothing to trade for her life."

"Jesus Estrada," he said, his voice suddenly older and full of fatigue. "Do not judge him too harshly. He was a good man, senor. Our cause will miss him."

I glanced over at Father Ignacio. "Cause? What cause?"

"Many years ago, my son," he said quietly, "the Patron made a decision that changed many lives including mine." He said sadly. "Those were terrible days. Our whole way of life was changing. The men who were responsible for an old way of life that had come to be over many generations were powerless to stop the madness. They realized they were not without fault. They elected the wrong man and he did not do as they demanded. Without control of the army, it became too late to repair the situation."

I wanted to talk about Abby, but I sensed this man needed to say these words, so I kept still.

"So a drastic decision was made to leave Cuba. Can you imagine how respected this man was that these people would leave their heritage behind to follow him to America?"

"I guess so," I said.

"Yet, you do not believe el tesoro exists, yes?"

"I did," I sighed. "I don't now. But I'll tell you what I do believe."

"Those men, the patrons, they were smart, very wealthy, and the objects that made up their wealth did exist. So what happened to that stuff? Without it how do I get her back?"

The priest sat back and said, "What do you think became of their treasures, Senor Patrick?"

I thought about that for a while. "Jose Garcia said everything was brought to this town, crated up, and delivered to the burial site. So who took them off the island? Who would have stolen the treasure? Who could build fake crates and put them into that hole as if it was the real treasure?"

"Who, indeed?" he said in a barely audible voice.

And suddenly, I think I knew and the truth felt like the weight of dead Hectors' body pinning me again to that tree on Juventud.

"My God," I said. "The treasure never made it to the island. The patrons thought they were burying their precious possessions but they were burying rocks." I shook my head sadly. "It's here, isn't it Father Ignacio? El tesoro is here in Cortes, isn't it?"

The priest nodded. "Yes, my son, it is just as it has always been."

I felt the exhaustion, the mind-numbing exhaustion, washing over me again. "Three men are dead and more may die before this is over. And it was here all the time." I rubbed my eyes as if all this would magically make all this go away. "What's your part in all this? Why was the Church involved?"

"The Church was not, Senor Patrick. *I* was. When the plans were set by Pedro Martinez, Jose Garcia came to me and told me what would be required. I asked the Bishop for permission to come here from Havana to replace Father Vitorio, who was deathly ill with the cancer. I remain here for the Patron and the future of Cuba."

He shrugged. "The people of the town needed a spiritual leader, you see. My request was immediately approved and that is how Cortes became important to the Patron's plan. This is why Cortes is important to the treasure, it holds the future."

He stopped talking to let me absorb the story.

"Because you would be here to help him, right? And?"

"Jose brought the valuables here. The crates were made and everything was readied for the island." He wagged a finger at me. "But twice as many crates as were needed were made, senor."

"The extra crates were the ones made to hold the rocks, right?"

"That is correct."

"So you came here to watch over el tesoro," I said.

"You must try to understand, my son. The Patron wanted to believe in his heart, that the people of Cuba would throw the communista out quickly, but he knew that this was not the history of this people. They had never stood their ground against the powerful forces that have controlled Cuba."

"So he gave up the dream of coming back home?"

"Oh, no! But the dream eventually changed from coming back to claim the treasure of his ancestors for his children and their children yet to come." He shook his head again. "No, Pedro Martinez began to understand that el tesoro would be needed someday to help rebuild a free Cuba. But," he said sadly, "he never expected to die so young. He never expected to die before he could come back home."

I began to understand. "And he couldn't let anyone else know where the treasure really was in case they decided to get greedy. Even the other patrons may have tried to return to get the treasure."

"That is so," he answered.

"But what if *you* die? What if el tesoro just disappeared from memory?"

"Ah, now you see the problem! The Patron made sure that Jose Garcia and one or two others who could be trusted, knew the truth, the true location. It is up to our little band to tell the younger ones in pieces to be put together later as we got older. Those who would keep the truth and the love of Cuba in their hearts until the time for action was upon them." He laughed quietly. "We are much like the knight's of old, who protected the Holy Grail, you see."

"Christ, Garcia won't even tell his own son."

He sighed again. "Yes, it is true, my son. Too many of the younger ones, they no longer care about their homeland. But those that do must have a chance to some day reclaim Cuba!"

Now a further realization came to me, and my heart felt heavy.

"They never intended to let me trade the treasure for Abby Barrett, did they?

He put his weathered hand on my arm again. "I am sorry my son, but the greater good of the Cuban people is at stake."

The feeling welling up in my chest was a mixture of sorrow and anger. "So, why this absurd charade? They kept me from looking for Abby!"

"Do not misunderstand, Senor Patrick. We had every intention of helping you rescue the girl. She is an innocent! She knows nothing of el tesoro we believe, but her father…her natural father *did* know. He was to be a leader of our people in Miami, and in a democratic Cuba, and he was told the truth about the treasure of the six families. We believe he was murdered because he would not tell what he knew. They say his brakes failed causing a terrible accident, but we know his auto was tampered with."

"And they are using Abby to get her mother to turn over the treasure, yes, I know."

"They cannot believe Ramon Castillo did not pass on the information to her before he died."

"All this was a trap to catch whoever is after the treasure, right?"

"Si," he answered. "And afterward we would have rescued your Abby for you."

"And now?" I said. "Jesus told Miguel to bring me here, to you, and he did. But can I trust him now that Jesus is gone to help me?"

"Senor," the old priest said, "Miguel would never sully his brother's memory by not following his dying order."

"Brother?" That shocked me. "I didn't know they were brothers. Miguel never said anything, or showed any sorrow or anger when Jesus died."

"That does not surprise me, my son. These men are soldiers. A soldier cries for those who are lost only when the battle is over. There is no time to grieve at the moment of death."

"Well the whole thing's gone to shit and Abby is still in danger. So what do I do now, Father. Why did Jesus send me to you? What do you know that can help me?"

"Why, Senor Patrick," he said, rising to his feet, "I know where your Abby Barrett is being held."

CHAPTER 30

▼

20 October 2002
Cortes

My blood was boiling up into my face, and I could feel the heat rising. I jumped up off the wooden bench. "What are you saying?! You sick bastards have known where Abby is all this time and you kept it from me?" I was purple with rage.

It was the priest's turn to speak forcefully. "And what would you have done with such information, senor? Would you have stormed the castle with your guns blazing?! This is not your Old West!"

He made an effort to soften his words. "There are many forces at play, my son. We are not even sure of all those who may be involved." He sat down, heavily. "Please calm yourself, Senor Patrick. Sit down and I will tell you what you wish to know, in due course."

I was powerless to do otherwise. For all I knew, Miguel could be training his revolver at my head. How simple it would be for them to kill Bobby and me. And all their problems would be over.

After all, who would make a fuss over the death of a girl that no one could even prove had been in Cuba.

I sat down next to the old man. "Who is behind all this?"

"We are not sure who is pulling the strings of Senor Asparza, but we have a good idea," he said. "Asparza is well known to our people who keep abreast of these things…"

"Wait a minute, Jesus said he only knew *of* him."

The priest shook his head again. "I am afraid that Jesus Estrada may have been less than truthful about that."

"Why? We were supposed to be working together."

"We will speak of that later. Time is getting short, and the sun will join us soon." He went on. "Gregorio Asparza is not a Cuban by birth," he said. "He was born in the Soviet Union, and came here as part of the Russian forces, although he was a civilian, that were here during the 1960's."

He stirred on the seat. "When the Russians left, he stayed to operate his own little 'business'. I am being clear?" He looked at me questioningly.

I nodded, wondering where this was all going, and he continued with his story.

"By cutting the Castro brothers' in on his more profitable ventures, he gained the protection of the government, and was even given 'official' duties that put him in a position to make further ill-gotten gains for them all. Of course, for this, he had to 'become' Cuban."

"So he changed his name?"

"His real name," the priest said, nodding that I was correct "is unknown to us, but we are sure he is Russian."

"So you think he is working for the Castro's now?"

"Truthfully, we are not sure. We believe that Asparza is a member of the Russian Mafia, which has become very strong in my country." He looked at me again. "There is a very real chance that someone in *los lideres,* the leadership, of the Mafia, may have alerted him to the existence of el tesoro."

"And that's who you've been trying to trap," I said.

"Si."

I stood again. "Well, Father, I don't give a damn about all that. I want the girl safe, and away from this craziness. That's all I care about. Now that I know the treasure is here, why shouldn't I just find this Asparza and tell him?"

The priest stood and took my arm. "That, my son," he said, "you will never be allowed to do."

So there it was; the implied threat. Whatever chance remained to find Abby and get her back did not include giving up the treasure.

The old priest led me toward the church, as I contemplated the threat that had finally been delivered. "Come," he said. "Let us discuss instead, what we must do to save Maria Barrett's daughter and get you all safely out of Cuba, yes?"

*   *   *   *

An hour later when I opened the door of the shack, Bobby Hemphill was sitting at the little table wolfing down the food Miguel had brought us earlier.

Eduardo and Jaime had arrived from the island safely and were taking their turn sacking out on the cots.

I motioned to Bobby to join me outside, and we walked down to where the two fishing boats sat bobbing gently.

"You okay?" he said, through bites of crusty Cuban bread stuffed with roasted pork. He handed me a wrapped sandwich from the bag.

"Yeah, I'm fine," I said. "I guess." I took a bite.

"Well, that sounds positive." He chuckled.

"Do you realize the position we're in?" I asked in frustration. "We're in the middle of Cuba where the government hates us, and people are trying to kill us. We're trying to rescue a kidnapped girl we can't tell the cops about. We don't know if we can trust the people who are supposed to be helping us."

"I try not to think about it," he said.

"Those two say anything?" I nodded up toward the shack.

"Those zombies?" He huffed. "Not a word, man. Just came in and hit the sheets."

We ate a little more.

"What happened up there, Tommy?"

I shook my head in wonderment. "These guys have been lying to us all along, Bobby. That trip to the island was nothing but a waste of time. Just a dangerous, murderous, bullshit, waste of time."

"The treasure wasn't ever there, was it?'

"I'm sorry I got you involved in this, man."

Bobby grabbed one of the cans of beer he had taken from the cooler in the shack and tossed it too me. He opened one for himself. "A little early," he said, 'but I know I could use one."

"Jesus, this whole thing was just a trap to protect their precious treasure. I'm sorry, Bobby," I said again.

He took another swig. "Know what's funny? I've been trying to think of a way to *thank* you."

I didn't understand what he meant by that. "Thank me? For what, nearly getting you killed?"

"No," he said. "I mean for bringing me along, for trusting me. Look, Tommy, I told you I know what everybody back home thinks about me."

"You're wrong, man," I said, shaking my head.

"No," he shook his head. "I'm not wrong. Its okay, you know? It doesn't make me angry. I've had my share of fuck-ups." He smiled. "More than a few and I'm sure you had a lot of second thoughts about bringing me along on something this important. I know C.J. asked you to."

"They would be proud of you, Bobby. Believe it."

"Thanks," he said, "but let's face it, we gotta' save that girl of yours or none of this means anything."

"Yeah," I said, quietly.

"Point is, do we still have a chance?"

I told him about my meeting with Father Ignacio.

When I was done, he said, "So they got somebody watching this guy Asparza's house, and they think Abby's been there all along?"

"That's about it."

"Jeez, I can't believe they let her stay with those guys just to keep their little secret."

I sighed. "It's a pretty big secret, I'll give them that. They say they're going to help us get Abby out."

"What's the plan?"

"Damned if I know, but one of Jesus' men, one we never met, has been shadowing Asparza all this time. When we get back to Havana, we go in and get her out, and hope we don't alert Castro's police while we do it."

"How do they know what's been going on while we were down here?"

"I figure the GPS phone. You remember you said Miguel had made calls that didn't seem to be to Jesus?" I asked.

He nodded. "All makes sense," Bobby said. "But Asparza has to have expected a call from one of his boys by now. They gotta' be wondering what's been going on, you know?"

"That's worrying me, too. Jesus was counting on the storm as a cover to buy us time, but you're right, Bobby, we have to get back."

"So, they get a hold of this guy watching the house?"

"They were trying. I told them I was coming back to get you."

We threw our leftovers in an old trashcan at the top of the dock, and headed back to the shack to collect our meager possessions.

A few minutes later, we heard the truck that had carried the remains of Jesus Estrada away to the church burial ground come racing up to the shack. It's tires sliding on the gravel drive to a dead stop.

Almost immediately, Miguel slammed through the doorway.

"Come! We must leave, immediately," He was nearly breathless as he spat out the words. "The girl, she has escaped from Asparza!"

"What!" I nearly screamed out the word. Jaime and Eduardo scrambled off the cots, pistols in hand.

"What do you mean, escaped?!"

"She got out of Asparza's house. That is all we know."

"That can't be," I said. "If she's out of there, you must know where she is!"

Miguel was apologetic. "I am sorry, senor. We do not know where she is hiding. But we must find her before they do."

I was excited and fearful at the same time. "Let's go," I said, wondering how in hell I would find Abby Barrett in Havana. If I did find her, how would I ever get the three of us out of the Cuba?

The only thing she knew for sure was that she had seen me in the street, in front of my hotel. If Castro was involved, it was possible an army would be looking for us. If it was the mafia, that could be even more dangerous.

"Let's go. *Now!*" I said, and ran out the door.

CHAPTER 31

▼

Evening, 20 October 2002
Ciudad de la Habana

The strain on my body from past injuries as well as the digging I had done on Isla de la Juventud, and the attack by Hector One, had taken its toll on me mentally as well as physically.

By the time Miguel reached the outskirts of Havana, I could hardly contain my impatience. The trip had taken many hours, although we had cut the time by taking the *Autopista* highway that runs alongside the slow two-lane road that Jesus and I had taken on our way to Cortes.

I was stiff, sore, agitated, and could barely stay in my seat as we turned onto *Paseo de Marti*, a divided boulevard bounded by a mixture of grand to marginally attractive buildings.

"Do you know exactly where to go?" I asked Miguel, who had driven the entire way back.

"Si," he answered. "We will be there soon."

I glanced out the back window, happy to see that the second truck, with Bobby, Eduardo, and Jaime on board right behind us.

"We could have all come back in the Hectors' SUV," I said. The keys had been left in the vehicle when we had departed on the fishing boats.

"It would be easily spotted if Asparza's men were looking for it," he said, shaking his head at the suggestion. I knew Miguel was right. For all we knew, every giant, American SUV in Havana could belong to the Russia Mafia.

On the way back, I had quizzed Miguel about the people that were probably frantically looking for Abby. I figured the more I knew about them, the better chance there would be for me to find Abby Barrett before they did

"There is always someone who is prepared to take advantage of a troubled country, senor. In Cuba, the only openly communist country in this part of the world, it was an easy place to get a…how you say, foothold."

Miguel seemed willing to talk so I pursued it. "But who is 'they'?" I asked.

He seemed to be trying to put his thoughts together.

"In Russia, there is a group of men who were *afiliado,* members, of the old KGB, and *los militar…* "

The army?"

"Si, the Red Army. And, Putin, the president of Russia, was one of the KGB. The organization is called in Russian, the '*Siloviki*' and it very strong and power-ful in every part of life in Russia."

"I know something about their move into the States," I said. "They are being blamed for a lot of the crimes that the Italian mob families and black gangs used to control."

"Si, senor, they have done the very same in Cuba. There is much *interactivo* between the Mafia cells in America and Cuba."

"And cutting the government, or at least the Castro's, in on the money makes it easy for the Mafia to operate here, right?"

"Fidel Castro has a great love of money for a comunista," Miguel said. "He gives much freedom to the Russians. But I think he also has much fear of them too."

"That's why they might try to pull off something like this without fear of interference by the government?"

I thought about that. "So the best bet is that it isn't Castro that started this mess. Am I right, Miguel?"

"We think so, yes." He took his eyes off the road and looked at me. "The man who has been watching the home of Gregorio Asparza, said that no soldiers or police have come near the house since the girl escaped." He paused again. "Si, senor, we think it is the Russians."

We drove in silence for a long time.

I, for one, was lost in thought. The fearful feeling was coming back. Could I pull this off? Could I trust Miguel and his friends to do whatever was necessary to find Abby and get her out of the country?

Father Ignacio said I could trust these men. But why would I believe him? Yet, why couldn't I? He had wanted to come to Havana with us. Miguel insisted that this would be too big a risk.

"We can not allow that, Padre," Miguel had told the priest. "If this goes wrong, there can be nothing to tie you, or this place to el tesoro. It would not take long for the truth to come out if you are thought to be involved."

Father Ignacio had finally agreed. "We have kept our secret for a very long time, Senor Patrick," he told me, "Miguel is correct. I must remain here, in Cortes." And he sent us on our way.

"So," I said, finally, "what do we do? How do we find Abby? She's all alone in an unfriendly foreign country, with no money, no identification, and no friends. What do we do? You need to tell me, Miguel, because I have no idea."

"We will decide that when we know all the facts," he said. "We will decide that when we know everything. There!" he said, suddenly. "That is the street we are looking for."

✶   ✶   ✶   ✶

You can trust Miguel, senor. He would never sully his brother's memory!

I knew that I had no choice but to depend on Father Ignacio's words. But I couldn't shake a nagging distrust.

When we stopped to gas up the trucks, I told Miguel I needed a few minutes to stretch my legs, and got out of sight of the others. I turned on my cell phone, and to my relief, immediately picked up a strong signal.

I suddenly felt less alone and back in at least a little bit of control. I rang Max Howard.

"Where the hell are you?!" the familiar and welcome voice boomed, without preamble. "Tommy, you okay?"

"I'm fine, Max. Christ, it's good to hear your voice."

"We all been worried sick, Hoss. Where are you?"

"I gotta' make this quick, Max, so listen carefully. Bobby and I are okay, but it's been crazy and I don't have time to explain. I promise you'll be the first to know the whole story when we get back."

"All right Tommy," he said, I could sense his curiosity running rampant. "Tell me."

"We're halfway back to Havana. We got word this morning that Abby was at Asparza's home. Max, we think…no, we're sure, that Abby somehow escaped her captors."

"What?!"

"You heard me. But we have no idea where she's hiding, or where she might be trying to get to. Abby knows she can't go to the Cuban police, or the airport, I'm sure, and there's no consulate where she might be safe."

"Damn, Tommy, how the hell you gonna' find her?"

"I don't know, Max," I said, 'but that's where you come in. I need you to get to Maria and see if Abby's been able to contact her."

"How long you figure the girl's been on the run?"

"I'm not sure…"

"Look," he cut in, "I was with Maria 'til about ten last evening. I know she hadn't heard from Abby then. You know, I hate to have her sittin' there all by herself, worryin' and waitin' for word…"

It was my turn to stop him. "Alone? What do you mean, alone? Where's her husband?"

"Took off again," said Max, a hint of displeasure in his voice. "He's in Miami. Said he couldn't take sittin' around, and thought he might be able to pressure someone down there to get information on where Abby might be being held."

How could he leave Maria again at a time like this, I thought. We put Richard Barrett aside for the moment.

"You got help down there?" said Max sounding concerned.

"Yeah, at least I think so. We're on our way back to try to find her before they do. Listen, Max. Garcia's men say they can get us out of Cuba but I want a backup plan."

"What do you want me to do, Tommy?"

I thought about that for a minute, trying to clarify in my own mind what I had been thinking about.

"Max, go back to Maria. We need to know if she might have someone we could contact in Cuba who might help us if we need it. An old relative, a family friend, anyone that we could trust. If these guys can get us out, fine. If not, I'll need a backup, fast."

"Okay, I understand."

"Go to her, Max. No phones and if she needs to discuss this with her sister use the niece's cell number. No one else though Max, okay?"

"Got it. How do I reach you?"

"I'll call you sometime in the middle of the night, tonight, so keep the phone with you."

"How's the battery capability on your phones?" he asked.

"I'm okay, maybe half, but Bobby's is almost full."

"How's he doin,'" again the concerned tone.

"Better than me, Max. He saved my life."

"What? What the hell happened?"

"Later pal, but it's true. How is everybody back there?"

"They're fine, other than worryin' about you two."

"Max," I said, seriously, "move fast. There are already people dead, and we have to end this quickly. I'll call later."

∗   ∗   ∗   ∗

I awoke about 2 a.m. after taking my turn sacking out in the small bedroom off the *cuarto,* or what I would have called the living room, back home. The small apartment was located on the fourth floor of a residential building on *Avenida Consulado,* about six blocks from the National Capitol building.

Miguel Estrada and the man I had been told was named Carlos were kneeling at the window. The shade was up about six inches and the two were staring across the dark road at one of the large estates that ran along Consulado. Most of them housed foreign diplomats and consulate personnel. All were dark at this hour. One particular house, the home of Gregorio Asparza, was brightly lit. Carlos said late-model American cars were arriving or leaving every hour or so.

Carlos had been the one watching Asparza's place while we were on our quest to Cortes and the island.

Bobby was by now, fast asleep, and Jaime and Eduardo were somewhere on the street below watching from different angles, trying to catch license plate numbers as the cars pulled up to the gated entrance across the street.

We had kept our lights off so that we could watch the activity on the other side of the street without being seen. The small room smelled strongly of leftover food and what I figured was the natural scent of neglect. I yawned and made my way over to where the two were crouched down and peering through the small opening.

"See? There he is again," Carlos was saying in an unnecessarily quiet voice. "That man, he had made many visits here yesterday and today. But he does not stay very long." Miguel followed Carlos' gaze, while I got down to their level to look. The house we were watching was close enough for us to see some faces as their owner's went in and out of the lit doorway. Dark shadows hid some of the others. Carlos did have a set of binoculars, and we took turns using them.

"Recognize anyone?" I asked.

"No, senor," Carlos answered. "But these men, they are not of the *policia,* not of Castro's men."

I gave the glasses back to him and touched the pocket of my shirt. I could feel the folded slip of paper which contained the information I had asked Max Howard to get from Maria Barrett.

As it turned out it was Anna Ortiz, who had been a couple years older than her sister, who had the best memory of their escape from Cuba. She remembered the fishermen, brothers of their mother, who had hidden the families accompanying Pedro Martinez to America until all the refugee's had arrived for the departure. Her uncles, would help, she was sure.

"The place is called *San Rafael*. It's on a river across from a nature preserve called *Cayo Coco*. You got a map?" Max had asked.

"Yeah," I said. "Who am I looking for?"

"There're two related families, two brothers of Maria's mother who we *think* are both alive and are still living there."

"Shit, we're not sure?"

"Pretty sure, Hoss. But there ain't much chance for talkin' regularly to relatives in Cuba."

He was right, of course. "What do we do, Max?"

"When you get there, you look for either of the two 'Hernandez' houses. They're both right down by the family dock where they keep their boats. Their names are Benito and Pedro. Now, they're gonna' be old, but they both had sons who should be living there, and they'll be around Anna and Maria's age or a little younger. The played together."

"They won't know Abby and they sure won't know me."

"I know, but Anna said when you find them, Abby should say that she's the granddaughter of the Patron. Jose Garcia has sent her to seek their help. You got that?"

"I hate getting Garcia's name involved in this, Max. I still don't trust him" I said ruefully.

"Hoss, I'm just the messenger but I expect you should follow the lady's advice."

We talked a few minutes more. Max reminded me to memorize the information about Abby's family and get rid of the notes I had made. When I hung up, that feeling of being cut off from my only support was back in a heartbeat.

I had gone in to sleep after that, but it was a struggle, it took a while, even though I was exhausted.

I had the dream again. The one about causing Abby's death, tied up in that chair, with me unable to keep the knives away from her. Eventually, I beat back the nightmare and got a couple hours of solid sleep.

✳   ✳   ✳   ✳

Miguel and Carlos were still watching Asparza's house intently through the binoculars when I woke up.

"Look at them." Miguel said. "They are running around like fools. This girl has escaped right under their noses. They cannot find her in over a day's time." He smiled at me. "They have no idea where she is."

"Neither do we," I said, "but we had better figure it out before they do. There can't be that many places Abby could be hiding. Maybe she could go somewhere nearby? They have a lot more people looking for her than we can put on the street."

Miguel sat back against the wall next to the window while Carlos continued to watch. "You must think, senor. There is some connection, yes? Something the girl and you have in common? Something or some place that you have talked about or something that can lead you both to the same place. Where she might go to wait for you?"

I thought for a moment and sighed. "We haven't been involved with each other that long." I shook my head. "I don't know."

"Think hard," he said. "There may be something."

"Maybe," I said, "if we go over what we know about her escape again......"

Carlos picked up my train of thought. "It was when the big rains came, you know, the *tormenta,* yes?" he said.

I nodded.

"The street was empty." He continued, "There were no *guardia* around the house." His face took on a sheepish look. "I am sorry, senor," he said. "I was having some of the food that my brother Manolito brought me..."

"Its okay, Carlos," I said, looking at Miguel for support.

"What did you see then?" Miguel asked.

"The rain, she was very strong and it did not stop for many hours. In the late night, over there..." he pointed to the other side of the house, away from the door Asparza's people had been using tonight. "...in the *relampago...*"

I glanced at Miguel, questioningly.

"The lightning from the storm," he said.

"Si," Carlos said, nodding his agreement. "The lightning, she is very bright, and it comes, bang, bang, bang, very fast. I see something over there. I get the *gemelos,*" he said, picking up the binoculars. "I must wait for the lightning, but I see someone crawling from the *sotano,*" he looked at Miguel.

"The basement," Miguel said. "From the window at the basement."

"Si," Carlos continued. "I see this, but I am not sure what it is that I see, and…" He looked us both in the eye, a hint of embarrassment in his face. "I am sorry, senor, but it was too far for me to understand what I am seeing. When I do, I run down to the street, but I cannot see the girl on the property of Asparza. Somewhere on the *finca,*" he pointed out the window and I understood that he meant the estate. "She found a way out, into the city. I could not find her when I go around the back."

"How long was it before anyone came out of the house to look for Abby?" I asked.

"Oh, not until the storm is past," he said. "And then the place is *loco.*"

"And there was never a sign of the girl?" I said.

"No, senor," he said. "I do not know the girl's face, so I stay here to watch."

I put my hand on his shoulder. "You did the right thing," I said with a smile. But, inside I was sick to my stomach. How close Abby had come to walking right into safety.

Miguel and Carlos continued to keep an eye on the goings-on across the street, while I spent the next few hours trying to come up with a plan for our search. We had to wait until daylight when the streets would be busy with Cubans living their lives. It was too dangerous to be out at night amid the police patrols and Asparza's men.

That also meant Abby would be in hiding, making her even harder to find. Where would she expect me to look for her? Would she even think I *was* looking for her?

After all, she had seen me only for a moment at the hotel, as her car passed.

Bobby came out of the bedroom as light was beginning to come through the window.

"You should have stayed in bed," I said.

"I'm okay," he said, yawning and scratching his two-day-old stubble. "You, on the other hand, look like shit."

"Well, good," I said with a smile. "I would hate to look inconsistent with how I feel."

There was a soft knock on the door. I nearly jumped out of my chair.

"Is okay, senor," Carlos said. "Manolito, he brings food."

Carlos let him in. He was a smallish, younger man, but, otherwise, the spitting image of his older brother, dark and thin.

The room quickly took on the smell of the food, which Manolito passed out. Carlos took his food with him back to the window.

Bobby and I were famished. We stuffed our mouths full of a stew…Manolito called it a *fricase*, full of pieces of lamb and vegetables. We ate it with fried plantains, in a sweet, brown sugar glaze, and rice. I'd have killed for a pot of hot coffee. A look from Bobby told me he had the same idea but we washed it all down with barely cool beer.

But we weren't complaining, far from it. For the first time in a while, our bellies were full of good, hot food.

"Miguel!" Carlos said, excitedly. He pointed across the street. "Asparza!"

Miguel and I went quickly to his side, kneeling next to him.

There he was, the man I had last seen through a doorway in Maria Barrett's living room. This man had changed my life, maybe forever.

Gregorio Asparza was standing at the door to the house surrounded by his henchmen. He was dressed in a suit with a dark tie.

"What's he doing?" I said.

"I do not know," Miguel answered, without looking at me.

We continued watching but nothing happened for about twenty minutes. I began to fear that he might be waiting for one of his patrols to bring back a recaptured Abby Barrett.

At about eight, a dark SUV like the one the Hectors had driven approached the gates, which opened automatically, and the SUV pulled up to the house exactly where Asparza stood. The front doors of the vehicle opened and the driver and a heavyset passenger got out. Another man got out of the back seat. He was shorter and older than the others. He looked around before walking over to stand in front of Asparza.

"Oh, God," I said in a small voice. "Jesus Christ, no." I stared in disbelief. My nerves were on fire, seemingly ready to break through my skin. I felt a cold sweat forming on my brow, and soaking the back of my shirt.

"What is it?" Miguel asked, rushing over to stand beside me. "*Dios mio,*" he said quietly, "that is Juan Garcia!"

I couldn't say anything for a moment, finally, I found my voice. "Yes, the son of Jose Garcia and the other man," I said. "That man is Richard Barrett, Abby's stepfather."

CHAPTER 32

▼

21 October 2002
Havana

I was dumbstruck. I sat on my knees, unable to move and rooted to that spot in front of the window facing onto Ave. Consulado.

Bobby Hemphill was standing beside me, his hand on my shoulder.

"Tommy, you sure, man? You could be wrong."

I could only shake my head. Finally, I said, "No. It's him, Bobby. It's Richard Barrett. He is supposed to be in Miami, looking for information about where Abby is being held.

"Holy shit," Bobby strung out the words. "Look, maybe he got some info and showed up to negotiate…"

I finally looked away from the window to Bobby. "Forget it," I said. "There's only one reason for him to be here. He's part of this, Bobby. He's one of them."

"You think so." It wasn't a question. He knew it too.

"Remember how he left Maria alone a couple times since this all started? Max said he took off again the other day. Who does that? Who leaves a grieving wife alone while her daughter-and his-is in mortal danger?"

I took another painful glance out the window. The group of men standing around the door no longer included Asparza, Garcia, or Richard Barrett, who apparently had gone inside. "Hell," I added, "even Max was upset that Maria was left alone while he supposedly went to in Miami. Now I know what's been bothering me about that guy. I just never put it all together 'til now."

"Senor" The word came from Carlos, still kneeling at the windowsill. "I think I see that man before," he said. "Not about this girl, but sometime, at another place."

"Donde?" Miguel said. "Where?" It was the first time he had spoken since the car had arrived.

"I am not sure," he said, apologetically, "But I have seen him. He limps, no?"

"What did you say, Carlos?" I said, startled.

"The hair, it is *plateado…*"

"Silver, right?" I said.

"Si, and the man, he limps. His leg, it is…"

"…Shorter than the other." I said, "Shorter."

Carlos nodded agreement. Barrett had been here, in Cuba before. There was no time to guess why he would have come here. I had to assume the worst.

"You must try to remember where you have seen this man," Miguel said. If he was shocked by the site of Juan Garcia's arrival, he was not showing it.

"We've got to get going," I said, shaking off my disbelief. "Their search is going to intensify now that it's daylight. Bobby, you stick with Miguel. Get the other guys and make sure they get another good look at Abby's picture."

I wasn't sure how this would work since I hadn't come up with any great plan. I was sure things were going to get worse with Barrett here.

"Split up into two teams," I continued, "but I want you and Miguel together. If you see Abby or I find her first, I want to be able to get away from here fast."

They both nodded.

"You gonna' let them know about this back home?" Bobby asked.

I thought for a minute. "I'm not sure. Maybe Max, but I want to think about it. I don't think Maria should know just yet. It might put her over the edge." My mind was racing. "Keep your phone close, and check it every half hour, Bobby. Keep going up and down the streets. Miguel, can Carlos reach you if he needs to?"

"Si, he has a phone and my number."

I looked at Miguel. "What are you going to do about Juan Garcia?" I asked.

"For now," he said, "I agree with you. I will wait to talk to Jose Garcia for a while."

"Okay. Then have Carlos stay here and keep us informed, especially if Barrett or Asparza leaves the house. Everyone understand? Good. Let's get out of here."

*   *   *   *

I found myself out on the street, staring at Gregorio Asparza's estate, and unable to decide where to go first. Armed with the worn map of Havana, which I had taken since the others knew the city, I headed east, back toward the boulevard.

I wanted to walk for a while. Partly to clear my head and partly to try to gauge how far Abby might have gotten on foot that night. She had a two-day lead on us but I was sure she would have stuck around Havana. She had probably gotten as far away from Asparza's home as possible. Abby is very smart. I believed she would head to safety, if it could be found. Somewhere where she could think rationally and calmly.

The key was money. If she had some money, she could be holed up in any hotel trying to figure out if there was a safe haven, where she might go for help. Not the airport, nor the police. A foreign embassy? Doubtful. That might cause an international problem for any country that took her in. If I only knew how she had gotten free. It would have been too dangerous to be on the streets or try to get a cab that night. With so few people out, I was sure she had stayed on foot for as long as possible.

After about two miles, I worked it out in my mind that she would head for *Viejo Habana,* the old town where there were many restaurants, and shops, where she could hide during the day, with cheap, nondescript places to stay in at night.

With my mind made up, I hailed a cab, an old '60's Chevy painted a bright green. I asked to be taken into the Old Town, and kept quiet the rest of the trip.

A few minutes later, I was standing at the corner of Tejadillo and Habana Streets.

By now, it was nearly ten, and the streets were filled with people shopping, selling their wares, and visiting with their neighbors. I looked around and felt the enormity of the task I was facing.

Maybe, I thought, it might make more sense to let Abby find *me.*

The day was sunny and warm even at this early hour. I shed my jacket and tied the sleeves around my waist, and went looking for a prominent corner where Abby might see me if she were walking the Old Town. I found a spot and stood around for almost an hour. The savory smell of cooking food permeated the air, and I was getting hungry. There were several mobile food stalls nearby.

I bought some *tapas* being sold from a cart, the way we sell hot dogs on street corners back home. I'm sure the little triangles of meat-filled pastries were good, but I hardly tasted them as I watched the faces of people passing by for another hour or so. In my mind's eye, every young woman looked like Abby, but it was all in my imagination.

At noon, Bobby checked in. They weren't having any luck either. I told him to keep looking and tried to decide where I should look next.

I decided to go back to walking the streets of the Old Town, this time block by block. I was struggling to zero in on a common thread with Abby but I wasn't getting anywhere.

A thought hit me. The Hotel Sevilla. That's where Abby had seen me standing in the street watching, as she was driven past by Asparza's men. I headed there, trying not to run. A few minutes later, I stood before the Hotel Sevilla, looking up at the fourth floor. It had only been a few days since I had informed the front desk that I would be taking a sight-seeing trip through the countryside and paid additional nights to keep the room available for my return. It seemed like the distant past to me, but I had never checked out.

I took my wallet from my back pocket. I could feel the outline of the heavy key resting against the leather.

Would Abby try to find me here? Would Asparza's men be watching my room? If they were, they would be watching the hotel's entrance, too. I had certainly given them ample time to spot me on the street. I thought it might be safe enough to check the room out.

I figured that it was best not to use the elevator and risk being trapped in it, I worked my way through the lobby trying to look like I wasn't sneaking around. Finally reached the stairwell on the building's west end, and I went up.

At the door leading to the fourth floor hall, I took a deep breath and opened it an inch as quietly as I could. I could see my door. The hall was empty. I stepped out into the hallway and headed for my room trying not to make noise as I walked. I put my ear to the door for almost a full minute but heard nothing.

My heart was trying to bust through my ribcage as I slipped the key into the lock, opened the door, and stepped into the room, quickly closing and locking the door behind me. I half expected to have a gun shoved into my face but the room was empty and utterly silent.

The air in the room was still. I took a quick look out the same window to the spot below where Miguel had sat that first night, watching to make sure we stayed in the hotel. There was no one there.

I used the bathroom, trying not to mess up anything. Once I left again, I wanted it to appear that the room had not been recently used.

I stood in the center of the room. Was there a scent of her perfume lingering in the air, had Abby stood in this room, in this very spot, waiting for me to walk through the door?

No. I knew I was projecting a wish, not a fact. She wouldn't take a chance on being seen by a maid or anyone else.

As carefully as I could, I checked around the room, looking for any possible clue that someone else might have been around, but found nothing.

A weird feeling was working its way over me, and my nerves were firing up again. Maybe it was the deadly quiet of the room, but I suddenly had the feeling that I needed to be away from here. I had been here too long.

I was about to step out into the hallway when I heard a door open near the stairwell I had used earlier. I took a quick look, my hand reaching for the .38 that I had stuffed into the waistband of my pants which I covered with the jacket that was tied around my waist.

It was a maid, coming from another guest room.

I closed the door and walked toward the stairs, expecting to see Asparza's men come busting through the doorway.

"*Buenos tardes*, senor," the maid said as I passed.

I smiled as I hurried by, then something made me stop and look at her.

"Do you speak '*Ingles*'," I said, in as natural a voice as I could muster.

"Si, senor," she said, "*un poco*, a little.*"

"My wife was to arrive yesterday while I was away," I said. "Have you seen a lady in 410?"

"No, senor. No lady has come, I think."

"Gracias," I said opening the door to the stairwell.

"Just the man, senor," she said, taking towels off her work cart, and stopping me in my tracks.

"Man? What man?" I tried not to sound alarmed.

"The big man, who comes *por la manana,* this morning. He is a friend, yes? He say so!"

I needed information but I was afraid to sound like I hadn't expected my visitor. "Oh, yes," I said. "Of course he waited for me."

"Si senor, *un rato,* for a while, then he leaves."

"Did you let him in my room?"

"Oh, no, senor!" She sounded genuinely horrified. This is not *permitir*. This friend, he have a key to the room!"

So Asparza could reach into the manager's office of the hotel for assistance. I had to leave, and now.

"He say he come back, senor. You wait, yes?"

"Uh, yes, but I need to stop at the desk downstairs first. Gracias, senorita."

I went down the stairs as quickly as I could, stopping to check the lobby before hurrying through and out onto the street.

Keeping my head down hoping to make it harder to recognize me, I walked across the street and into a small coffee house. There, I took a seat close to the window and watched the entrance to the Hotel Sevilla.

My instinct told me I should be far away from here but I had to see who was looking for me. I couldn't hang around for long, but I'd give it a little time.

I didn't have to wait long. Less than a half hour later, one of the big Ford SUV's pulled up in front of the hotel. I slid back in my seat as if that would hide me, as Juan Garcia hopped out of the rear seat and went into the Savilla. He wasn't in a hurry and I figured he had come back to check the room.

The sight of Juan Garcia still stymied me. What purpose would Asparza and Barrett have for involving him? Had he been part of this when I had met with him in Miami? It didn't make sense unless Garcia had known more about the treasure than he had let on. I didn't believe he did.

At that moment, as my mind tried to wrap itself around the sudden appearance of Juan Garcia, he came rushing out of the hotel, running this time, and spoke rapidly to the driver of the Ford.

The driver jumped out. They spoke for a couple of minutes, looking up and down the street as they did. They seemed excited and confused, unable to decide what to do.

I knew then that I had been foolish to come here. Even more foolish to have stayed here at risk to myself. If they decided to start searching the shops and restaurants close to the Savilla, I would be trapped in minutes.

Suddenly, they seemed to make up their minds. Both men jumped back into the SUV, and the big truck shot away.

I took my first full breath since Garcia had come out of the hotel, threw some money on the table, and left the coffee house, quickly heading away in the opposite direction from where Asparza's men had gone.

CHAPTER 33

▼

21 October 2002
Havana

I spent the next several hours walking the streets of the Old Town, ducking, from time to time, into stores and restaurants just to get a break from trying to be invisible.

I had taken it upon myself to put a plan into effect to find Abby. We had no success at all. I checked my watch. It was nearly 6 p.m. Soon the streets would be less crowded and more police patrols would be patrolling the area where I had been looking for Abby. I wondered if Asparza and Barrett might somehow involve the government or the police to help them search for us. They were certainly aware that I was in Havana and they would be looking hard for me, too.

I was at the plaza at the end of Empedrado Street standing in front of the Cathedral of Havana. Could Abby be hiding in one of the many churches in the city?

I walked up the long stairs to the massive front doors, and went in. I hadn't realized how tired I was, or maybe I had just been juiced up since escaping the clutches of Juan Garcia and his friends. But now I sat down heavily in the last pew and closed my eyes.

It was nearly an hour later when I woke up, startled by the sounds of other people coming into the church for evening mass. I walked out into the darkening night and wandered south down San Ignacio, totally at a loss as to where to go or what to do next.

The cell phone in my pocket started to vibrate.

"Tommy, where you at?" Bobby said.

"Just walking," I answered. "Anything?"

"Naw, sorry. Listen, Miguel says we had better get off the street. He thinks we should go back to the apartment. Tell me where you are and we'll come get you."

I looked up as I reached the corner and checked the street signs. And I stopped in my tracks.

"Bobby," I said, urgently. "You remember the place you and I first met after we got to Cuba?"

"Uh, yeah, sure. You mean…"

"Don't say the name," I said quickly, suddenly worried that the phones might have been traced. "I want you and Miguel to go there and screen the front entrance. Keep an eye out. I have an idea I want to check out. Just wait for my call!" I hung up without waiting for a response.

I took off running down O'Reilly Street, toward the O'Reilly Café.

The common thread-Ireland's Own, an Irish Pub. I knew that the Café had nothing to do with being an Irish pub; it was a Jazz club, but the name was Irish. I knew in my heart that this was a long shot but I had to get there fast.

*   *   *   *

I stood in front of the restaurant trying to get the courage to go in. Bobby and Miguel had not arrived yet, but I couldn't wait. I could feel the perspiration forming on my face, and I took a deep breath and went in.

The room was dimly lit just as it had been the first time I had come to O'Reilly's. The place was busy and there were few empty tables. A quartet was on the little stage, working their way through Dave Brubeck's piano classic, "*Take Five.*" I looked around, wondering if I should sit and watch for a while. I scanned the room, looking for any sign of recognition.

"Senor?" The hostess was speaking to me.

I held up a finger, as if to say that I was waiting for someone, when a dimly lit figure at a corner table caught my eye. There was no overt sign, just a form in the shadows that caught my attention.

I squinted to get a better look amid customers and waiters crossing through my line of sight. The face I was trying to see moved slightly forward into the light, and my heart nearly stopped. Abby Barrett was staring back at me, a smile that I would have recognized among a thousand faces radiating at me. I wanted to run to her, grab her in my arms and shout out my joy. But, I didn't.

Abby put a finger to her lips as if to say, "Be calm, Thomas. Remember where we are."

I forced my feet to move forward. I walked over to her table. I sat down next to her, unable to tear my eyes from her face. The smile was still there, but little rivers of tears ran down each cheek.

"I knew you would never stop looking for me," she said. It was my turn to smile.

"Until I heard your voice just then, I was afraid you were a mirage." I said.

"I'm right here, Thomas," she said, touching my face with her cool finger tips.

"I never thought I would find you," I said. "I…didn't think I could."

She put her hand on mine. "When I saw you on the street that day…"

Abby didn't finish the thought, but I knew what she meant.

"I could have reached out and nearly touched you, and then you were gone. Abby, are you okay?"

"Tired, but, yes. I'm fine, Thomas," she said. "How on earth did you get here? How did you know where I was?"

"Later," I said. "I'll tell you everything later, I promise. Tell me how you got away from those guys."

The waitress came over before Abby could speak, and I ordered a beer for me and another for her.

When she left to get our drinks, Abby said, "It was very strange, Thomas. These men treated me very well. They didn't hit me; they didn't even tie me up. Pepe…that's the name of the man who brought me food…he even called me 'carino,' which means 'sweetheart.'"

The waitress set the beers on the table.

"I couldn't understand why someone would kidnap me, and then treat me kindly." She shook her head in wonderment.

I thought I knew why, but this was no time to discuss Richard Barrett.

"They kept me in the basement. I saw no one but Pepe. He brought me food and drinks three times a day..He even brought some books to read." She took some beer. "There was a window high up on the wall, where I could see outside. There were always people…guards I guess, walking past."

"Then how did you get away?"

"Pure luck" she said. "It was pure luck. The storm knocked out the electricity and it was pitch black down there when Pepe brought me some food."

The jazz quartet ended their song. Abby moved closer so I could hear her speaking softly so she wouldn't be heard by others. The scent of her filled my head and my heart.

"Pepe is old and very fat. I think he's the cook for whoever owns the house. He had a flashlight, but I guess he lost his balance or tripped in the darkness, and he fell down the stairs. Luckily, the thunder must have kept the others from hearing. He was unconscious. I thought he might be dead!"

I took her hand in mine. "What happened then?"

"I was stunned for a minute, but he didn't move. I actually thought about calling for help, but I finally calmed down and thought about what was happening. I went through his wallet and took his money. He had enough for me to live on for a while, so I pulled the table over to the window, put a chair on top of it, and climbed up."

"What about the guards?"

"I guess the rain kept them inside. The wind was strong, and the rain very hard. I don't think they expected any trouble from anyone while all that was going on. Anyway, it took me a while to work the lock free, I was about to smash the glass, but once I giggled it the window just popped open."

"So you climbed out and got over the fence," I finished for her.

She looked at me quizzically.

"I'll explain later." I wanted to ask her a million questions. I wanted to take her in my arms and kiss every inch of her beautiful face. "Right now, we need to get away from here." I took out my phone, and thought about going to the restroom so I could hear as the band started another song but I wasn't about to let Abby out of my sight for a second.

"Bobby," I said when he answered on the first ring. "We're coming now. Get ready to move out..."

"Hey!" he said, excitedly. "You've got......"

"We're coming out now," I said, again, as I threw some money on the table and took Abby's hand. We got up from the table and walked out of O'Reilly's Café.

*   *   *   *

Miguel Estrada drove the car down a side street about two blocks from O'Reilly's Café and pulled over to the curb and flicked off the lights. I was glad he had thought to bring this old 4-door Buick instead of the pick-up.

We got in and waited a full minute. No other vehicles turned down the street. Miguel pulled back into the lane and we shot off.

Minutes later, we were heading into Central Havana, and out of the Old Town.

I had introduced Bobby and Miguel to Abby and no one had said a word since then. Bobby and I kept an eye out for Asparza's men, and Miguel concentrated on his driving. I had not let go of Abby's hand since we left the table at the café.

"Where're we going?" I asked Miguel from the rear seat as he headed east along *Avenida de Italia*. The area looked like the central business district of any large city. We had been driving around for about twenty minutes. There had been no sign of a tail.

"There is a house," Miguel said, "a place where we will be safe for the night. We can decide what to do next."

I wasn't in the mood to take any chances. "How do you know it's safe?" I asked pointedly.

He didn't answer, but instead pointed up ahead. "We are here," he said.

I left it alone. After all, he had gotten us away from the Old Town without being followed. I had to keep trusting Miguel.

He turned into an underground garage which sat beneath an apartment building. We piled out of the car.

"This way," he said, leading us toward the stairs, away from the elevator. Bobby brought up the rear watching for any other cars coming into the garage. On the street level, we went out a door leading outside and then back behind the apartment building to a bunch of two story, row houses.

Miguel took a key from his pocket and opened the door to the third house from the corner. We were inside with the door locked behind us before I had time to wonder if it was smart for us to be following him so blindly.

The place was dingy and sparsely furnished, but with several cots set up in the two bedrooms. Some food was in the refrigerator. This was obviously set up to be a safe house, probably for Jesus and his friends when they made their forays into Cuba.

"You should rest, Senorita Abby," Miguel said, pointing to a bedroom. "We will be here until the morning."

"Gracias, senor," Abby said. "I think I will."

I followed her into the little room, which had three cots set up in it.

Abby turned and took my face in her hands. I put my arms around her and kissed her for the first time since that night up in my room above Ireland's Own. For a moment, it seemed that nothing had happened to us since that night. It was as if nothing had changed.

"Thank you, my darling, Thomas," she breathed against my ear. "Thank you, my love."

My heart was full of love for this girl. Yet, I knew she was anything but safe and that she knew it, too. I kissed her again, longer and harder. "I thought I had lost you forever," I said.

"I thought I had lost you, too."

We stood there holding on to each other for dear life.

*   *   *   *

I closed the bedroom door and joined Bobby at the table in the small kitchen. Miguel was making café cubano at the stove, which he served in espresso-type cups. Bobby was slicing roasted pork for sandwiches. A bottle of Havana Club Rum had also found its way to the table.

"Is the girl sleeping?" Miguel asked.

"If not, she will be soon," I said. "She's pretty worn out."

"She's not the only one," Bobby said with a yawn. "I can't decide whether I need food or sleep more."

"We have the girl and now we must get you out of Cuba," Miguel said as he poured an inch of the golden colored rum into three glasses.

I took a hit of the strong, but mellow, liquor and poured another. "Bobby, you should get some sack time." I said.

"That's exactly what I plan to do, soon as I finish this sandwich. But you guys need sleep too, sport."

"There will be time for sleep before we leave," Miguel said. "First I must make arrangements for your escape. I must let those who will help us know when we will be ready to put to sea."

I put down the sandwich that Bobby had made for me without tasting it. "I know we can't fly out of here but I think we should make other arrangements anyway," I said.

Miguel looked perplexed. "I do not understand," he said. "What do you mean, senor? What other arrangements?"

"There are a lot of people looking for us," I said. "It's going to get worse by morning. Your escape route by sea is near Havana, right?"

"Si. But I do not understand what it is you wish to do?"

"Miguel, we aren't going to stay around here. Asparza knows we can't leave by air, and that means a boat. He's going to have his men out on the water looking for us, and if they find us, we're going to be defenseless out there."

"So, what're you thinking?" Bobby asked.

"You are right that we must leave by sea," Miguel said. "There is no choice!"

I drank some of the Havana Club. The fiery sweetness burned its way down to my still empty stomach. "We will go by sea, yes," I said, "but not from around here. Abby has relatives living in a small fishing village. We can hide out there until it's safe to put to sea. We'll be far enough away from Havana to avoid easy detection by any of Asparza's hunters."

Miguel looked skeptical. "And where is this village?"

"The place is called San Rafael, in the province of *Ciego de Avila*." I said.

"No," Miguel said in a strong tone. "No, senor! That is much too far. We would be in much danger for a very long time! There is no good reason to go there when we can get away from much closer."

"And what if your escape route has been compromised?"

He shook his head, emphatically. "There is no reason to assume so," he said.

"Miguel, I would probably have said that you are right before I knew that Juan Garcia and Richard Barrett were involved," I said. "We are taking too big a chance if we don't consider that they may have gotten information in Miami that might have put your route out of here at risk."

"I do not think…" he started to say.

"Miguel," I said, cutting him off. "I will not take that chance with Abby's life!" I lowered my voice and leaned in closer to him in case she could hear us. "If Richard Barrett finds her, he will realize that there will be no way he can let her live. He will certainly know that he can never go back to Atlanta. He won't send Abby back, either. And remember, you guys saw patrol boats near your landing area when you came here from Miami. It's smart to assume that your route might have been compromised. Isn't it? Especially since you had trouble landing on the coast when you arrived in Cuba."

He was silent thinking about what I had said.

"Holy shit," Bobby said. "I never thought about that. Hell, there'd be no reason for him to let *any* of us live!"

"I'm afraid not," I said, with more calm than I felt.

"San Rafael is a very long way from Havana," Miguel said, but with resignation in his voice. "It will still take much planning."

"The fewer of your people who know what we're doing, the better off we'll be."

"It will be very dangerous for my contacts to bring a boat to us that far away."

"They won't have to," I answered. "Abby's relatives are fishermen. They'll help us get a boat. "All right, senor," Miguel said finally, "we will do this your way."

"Thank you," I said, and meant it. I couldn't afford a fight with Miguel right now. "How do we get there?"

He sighed. "We will drive the Autopista to *Santa Clara*. From there, we will have to take roads through the countryside. Many hours," he said, still unhappy at the turn of events. "We must leave very early."

"Tommy," Bobby said, "what about Abby? You tell her about her old man?"

It was my turn to sigh. "No, there hasn't been time, but I'm not looking forward to it."

"What about her mom? We gotta' let her know we have her daughter, man."

I poured more coffee. "We can't," I said.

"What? Why not? She's gotta' be worried sick, man!"

"Don't you think I know that?!" I snapped. I tried to soften my tone a bit. I knew Bobby wasn't wrong. "Look," I said, "if we tell Maria that Abby is with us, the first thing she is going to do is try to reach her husband to let him know. That's exactly what she is going to do, unless we tell her that Barrett has been involved in the kidnapping of her daughter. We can't let him know we have Abby, and I'm not ready to tell Maria what a bastard her husband is. Beside Maria would be in grave danger if Barrett thought she knew."

"I think you are right," Miguel said. "But I must decide what to tell Jose Garcia about his son. It is nearly time for me to contact Miami."

"I think," I said, "that you have the same problem."

"You mean..."

"...I mean that if there *has* been a breakdown in security around Jose Garcia, someone might alert Juan that we know he's here." I let that sink in. "Maybe it would be better if we are far away from here before you report this."

Miguel was silent for a long time, his eyes staring at the table. "I will wait," he said, finally.

CHAPTER 34

▼

Early Morning, 22 October 2002
Havana

Abby was still asleep at 5 a.m., when I brought her fresh coffee and some food. I brushed her jet-black hair from her face gently, and she stirred awake. "Good morning," I said, and she treated me to her beautiful smile. "How about some coffee?"

"Umm, that smells good!" she said.

"Sorry, but we're a little short on room service."

She sat up and I sat down next to her. I handed her a plate with some bread, cheese, and roasted pork slices, and she ate hungrily.

"Did you sleep?" she asked between bites.

"A few hours," I said. "Bobby and Miguel are sacked out in the other bedroom."

Abby yawned, as she ran a hand through her hair. "Are we leaving now?"

"A little later," I said. "There's time."

Abby leaned against me and drank a little coffee. "I haven't felt this safe in a long time," she said. "But, we're not safe, are we?"

"No," I answered. "I'm not going to kid you, sweetheart. We have a ways to go before we're truly safe." I kissed her forehead.

She showed no fear and I wished I could be so calm.

"Do we have a plan?"

"Yeah, and it might not be the smartest thing to attempt, but we're gonna' take a chance on an idea of mine."

"What do you mean, Thomas?"

I explained my conversation with Miguel.

"You mean my mother's uncles and cousins who hid my family and the others, until they left Cuba, right?"

"Yup, that's who I mean."

She nodded her head. "That seems like a smart thing to do," she said, and my spirits were buoyed. "I'm sure they will help us."

"I hope so, or Miguel's going to be pissed"

"Thomas," she said, seriously, "do we have a way to reach my mother?" The look on her face was hopeful.

This, was the moment I had dreaded. I had been thinking long and hard about how to tell Abby about her stepfather. At some point, I knew she would have to ask about her mother.

"Abby," I said. "You know why you were kidnapped, right?"

"Yes," she nodded. "It was made clear to me that I was being held for ransom, but winding up in Cuba was a surprise."

"Do you know what the ransom was to be?"

"You mean, how much?"

"Not exactly, although we do know the amount was estimated to be, maybe, three hundred million dollars."

Abby looked at me, and dropped the cheese in her hand onto her lap. "Thomas, what are you talking about? My family doesn't have that kind of money!" She stood up, abruptly, and the cheese on her lap headed for the floor. "My God," she cried, "for three hundred million dollars, you kidnap the Queen of England, not a Georgia Tech student!"

I took her hand and she sat down again. "Abby, I've got a little story to tell you."

And I did. The whole story, up through the drive back to Havana, to the apartment across from Gregorio Asparza's estate. I told her the whole story, except for the true hiding place of el tesoro. If we were captured, I didn't want her to be tortured for that information.

Abby sat in rapt silence as I laid out what had happened since that day in Miami when she had been kidnapped. I told it all. Her response to the existence of the treasure, and her family's involvement in the fifty-year-old mystery, surprised me a little.

"So others have tried to find this el tesoro before with no luck?"

"It would seem so," I said.

"And they…whoever 'they' is…tried to force my mother to give them the location of the treasure, using me for a hostage," she said, with awe in her voice.

"Yes," I nodded, "but she had no idea if it even existed."

She shook her head, slowly. "My God," was all she said.

We sat still for a while, holding hands. The room was barely lit by the small table lamp, the darkness was like a cocoon around us.

"What else, Thomas," she said finally.

I turned my eyes away, not ready to hurt her with the rest of the story.

She leaned over and searched my face. "Thomas, there is something you aren't telling me, I think."

I tried to smile my way out of it. "Nothing that's important enough to talk about right now, Abby."

"Thomas," she said, taking my face in her hands and turning my head until she could stare into my eyes. "I love you very much. You know that, don't you? And, you love me, too."

"More than you know," I said, simply.

"I don't know what will happen to us," she said, "but for however long I have your heart, I want you to know that you don't ever have to hide anything from me. Trust me, my dear Thomas, I am very strong. Tell me what is bothering you, and we will deal with it."

I sighed. "I wish I had your strength," I said, and meant it.

"You are much stronger than you know," Abby said. "Now, tell me, please."

"Okay," I said. She had a right to know.

I told her of my horror at seeing her stepfather get out of that SUV in front of Gregorio Asparza's house, of the obvious reason he would have for being here in Cuba, and of the association he had with Juan Garcia, a man who desired the riches for himself.

Abby was outwardly calm as I told her what had happened in Havana after her escape. I neglected to mention that Carlos had tried to catch up with her after he saw her come through the basement window, as that information would serve no purpose now.

She took a deep breath here and there, but there were no hysterics. I realized I was learning an awful lot about this woman.

"That's why I haven't called back home to tell them we're together," I finished. "It's not fair to Maria, I know, but I can't take a chance on your...uh, on Richard Barrett finding out I have you before we're ready to get off the island. Let him keep looking for us in Havana."

She was silent, but nodded her understanding.

"You okay?" I asked.

She just looked at her hands, folded in her lap. "My poor mother," she said.

"I'm sorry to have to be the one to tell you all this sweetheart, but I need you to understand why I'm doing what I'm doing. It's why I think we need to try and reach your relatives in San Rafael."

"I think you are right, Thomas. I'll do whatever you say, of course."

She seemed deep in thought. "Thomas," she said, "I had lunch with Juan Garcia's son, Tito while I was in Miami. You don't think he is involved with this do you?"

"I don't think so," I said. "I met the young man while I was there, and he seems to be much more on the side of his grandfather, and he knows Jose Garcia is not senile. No, I think he's okay."

"I'm glad," she said and kissed me again, and I held her tightly against me, not wanting to let go.

A few moments later, there was a soft knock on the bedroom door, and I heard Miguel asking to see me in the other room.

"Carlos reports that both men from Miami were at Asparza's all night. He thinks that they have called in more men to search now that Garcia has told them that you are back in Havana."

"Wouldn't surprise me," I said, ruefully.

"I think you are right, senor. We must be far away from here as soon as possible. Jaime will be here at seven, with another auto," he said, and I checked my watch.

"That's a little over an hour."

"Si. Let the senorita know, and I will wake up your friend," Miguel said.

I knocked on Abby's door and went in. "We leave in an hour or so," I said.

"I'll be ready," she said, and gave me a reassuring smile.

CHAPTER 35

▼

8:30 A.M., 22 October 2002
Matanzas Province

We were traveling eastward on the Autopista along the edge of the swampy marshlands of *Peninsula de Zapata,* an hour and fifteen minutes out of Havana, a place that I was more than happy to leave behind.

Abby and I were in the rear seat of the '59 Chevy Impala. The immaculate Impala which obviously Miguel drove with pride had a well-tuned and powerful engine for its age. Bobby was up front with Miguel and Jaime was behind us in the big Buick, covering our tail.

I was poring over my frayed and torn map, checking to see how much progress we had made in an hour and fifteen minutes. With a sour feeling building in my stomach, I began to realize what Miguel had meant. It was going to be a long trip.

We had no sooner left the city that the pure rural nature of Cuba was back in full force.

The six-lane highway ran through sleepy villages with their dilapidated, thatched roof dwellings scattered amid dusty fields.

Abby caught me gazing out the window. "Those shacks are called *bohios,*" she said. "These people are very poor. Many years ago, generation after generation of these families worked the fields of the patrons. Now they work the government fields every day for a pittance." She shook her head. "Once they had dignity, Thomas, now they have none."

I watched the countryside go by. "Is that sugarcane over there?"

"Yes," she said. "This was once the main crop of Cuba, but now the sugar industry is much less profitable, since the embargo by the U.S., ordered by President Kennedy."

"Looks like we Americans haven't done these people any favors," I said, watching the peasants traveling by horse and bicycle along the highway.

"The Kennedy embargos were meant to get rid of Castro. They were to be short-term, but the Russians saw a way into the Western Hemisphere through Cuba, and that was that."

"But the Russians are gone," I said.

"Yes, but Castro is not." Abby took my hand. "These are the people my grandfather wanted to help someday."

✳   ✳   ✳   ✳

Some time later, we were about forty kilometers outside the city of Santa Clara, near the center of the island. The swampy marshlands had given way to long plains of growing fields.

I glanced back through the rear window to see our back-up car about a hundred yards behind us. The traffic on the Autopista was still light, and Jaime was following us without trouble. It was nearly 2 p.m., and we were chewing on the sandwiches and drinking bottled water from the canvas bag that Jaime had brought with him in the morning.

I had offered to drive, but Miguel said he was fine, and that was fine with me, since I preferred to stay in the rear seat with Abby snuggled up against me. The farther we got from Havana the more relaxed I became. I began to think we might be in the clear, and that we had successfully fooled Asparza and Richard Barrett, who, I hoped, might believe we were still in the city, looking for Abby.

I checked my map again. We were passing a village called *Aguado de Pasajeros.*

Bobby, glancing at his side view mirror said, "Jaime's flashing his lights. Something must be wrong."

Miguel looked at his rear view mirror just as the Buick pulled off at a service station. "He is getting fuel," he said. "We will keep going. He will catch up soon."

I didn't like losing our cover vehicle, but it shouldn't take long before Jaime caught up to us again.

Ten minutes later, I was thinking that we were in pretty good shape, when the first bullet smacked through the rear window, just inches from my head, and lodged in the back of Bobby's seat.

Abby screamed as the second and third shots hit us, and Miguel started to take evasive action, weaving the big Chevy from lane to lane.

"Get down!" I yelled, pushing her down onto the seat. I turned to get up on my knees, facing the big Ford Expedition that was barreling down on us, and fumbled for the Smith & Wesson in the waistband at the small of my back.

As Miguel weaved, the SUV followed, and I caught sight of another Expedition just behind the first.

"Shit, how'd they find us?!" Bobby yelled over the sound of the Chevy's big engine and screeching tires.

"Can you get a shot at them from your side window?" I said, ignoring his question. How they had gotten here didn't seem very important right at that moment. "Miguel, there's two of them! Try and keep steady for a few seconds."

I fired my weapon in anger for the first time, trying to hit a tire, and then I went for the grill, desperate to knock out at least one of our pursuers. I missed both times, and guns poked out from the first vehicle's side windows. I yelled for Miguel to zigzag and Bobby and I ducked down.

More bullets 'thunked' into the trunk, each sounding like a mule kicking the car, and we came up firing again. I hit the windshield of the SUV in front, and the driver took his own evasive steps. That opened up a little more room between us, but only for a short time.

"I'm out!" I heard Bobby say.

"Here!" Miguel said, and handed his .45 to him. "There is ammunition for both pistols in there," He pointed to the glove box, and Bobby found the shells, and tossed me a box for the .38.

Abby was face down on the seat next to me, and she grabbed the box of bullets and opened it, handing me some shells. There was no outward sign of fear from her, and I didn't have time to think about the danger I had put her in again. I loaded quickly and put two more shots into the big Ford, but it kept coming.

Suddenly, the lead car picked up speed, heading for the inside lane. They were probably going to try to knock out Miguel. If he were injured at this speed, we would surely crash. Miguel was in the center lane, then the right, then back again.

"They're coming up on the inside," I called back to Miguel. "When I say 'now,' pull to the left sharp as you can!"

He didn't answer, but he nodded, and I knew he had understood me.

"Bobby, when he does that, this guy will probably pull to the right real fast. Let's see how many shots we can put into the cabin. Got it?"

"Ready!" he yelled back.

I took a quick look back at the racing truck, watching it get closer and closer. They weren't shooting either, waiting to get along side, I guessed. The second SUV was hanging back, letting the guys up front do all the work.

I felt Abby's hand on my arm. Her fist was balled up, full of .38 shells that she was ready to hand me if the need arose. I looked down at her, and she gave me a serene smile, as if to say, 'whatever happens…'

The Ford was maybe thirty yards away, close enough for me to see three gunmen, weapons at the ready. I could see their faces clearly, and neither Richard Barrett nor Juan Garcia was among them, not that I had expected them to be. These guys were plain old gunslingers.

I estimated we were doing eighty-five or ninety, but they were faster, and would close the gap in about fifteen seconds. If I waited too long, they would have us. Strangely enough, the emotions I was feeling didn't include fear. Concern, certainly, apprehension, undoubtedly, but I was not afraid. I never had an adrenalin rush like this on or off a football field. I knew what I had to do, and I only hoped I would do it right.

They were coming on now, guns trained on us, waiting for their chance.

"Miguel, get ready, and when you go over, throw on your lights so it looks like you've hit your brakes!"

He nodded again, concentrating on his driving. I took a quick look ahead to make sure there were no cars in our path, and then took one more look at the Ford. I ducked down, counted to five as I heard the big engine coming up along side us.

"Now!" I yelled at the top of my voice, and Miguel swerved sharply into the inside lane and turned on his rear lights.

The speeding Expedition's driver, taken by surprise, slammed on his own brakes, and the SUV pulled to its right, turning the driver's side toward us, and slowed down a bit.

This was our chance. "Slow us down, now!" I yelled to Miguel, and he did, keeping us close to our pursuer. "Now, Bobby!" I was screaming like an Indian, as we both came up from our kneeling positions, firing as quickly as we could at the truck's cockpit.

We both pumped bullets through the open windows and the driver threw up his hands in front of him, the horrified expression on his face burning into my memory. But I didn't stop firing until all six shots were gone.

I wasn't sure which of us hit the driver, but suddenly he was thrown violently sideways. We watched in fascination as the left front tire seemed to buckle under, and the Expedition was on its side, then its top, and flipping over, and over.

"God damn," Bobby yelled, "did you see that?!"

The truck wound up on its smashed-in top, still sliding across the road. The second Ford whipped around its stricken partner, and never slowed down, as it came hurtling after us.

"Reload!" I said, as I bent down to check Abby.

"Are you all right?" she asked, breathlessly.

I touched her face and smiled. She opened her hand and I took the shells from her. "Stay down," I said.

The other vehicle came on fast, as if angered by what we had done to the other truck. I knew we weren't going to get a chance like that to stop these guys.

"Miguel, you okay?" I yelled over my shoulder, unable to take my eyes off our pursuer.

"I am fine," he shouted back at me.

"They're coming! How's it looking up there?"

"We are nearing some traffic, but I think I can get around it."

The gap between the two vehicles was getting smaller.

"Can't you get any more out of this tub?!" Bobby said.

"Senor," Miguel shot back, "this 'tub' is twice your age!"

He maneuvered the Chevy around the slower traffic, slipping in and out of the three lanes, and even using the shoulder along the outside lane. We clipped an old truck as the driver tried to get out of our way, but Miguel brought us under control quickly. The stares and looks of sheer terror on the faces of the other drivers would have been comical if we hadn't been about to die.

A round of shots came from the Ford, and we ducked instinctively, the bullets hitting the trunk again, and I cringed, waiting for our gas tank to explode but, luckily, they did no damage, and the chase continued.

Our attackers were now among the other traffic we had just passed through, and had lost their constant view of us. For the moment, that kept their gun sights off the Chevy, and Miguel pushed the big car forward, opening the gap again.

A thought struck me. If Asparza's men had found us, what chance might there be that we were heading for a roadblock? I pushed that thought out of my head. We had to deal with the enemy we knew. We would worry about roadblocks if, and when, they happened. A drop of perspiration found its way into my eye, and I wiped it away, realizing, for the first time, that I was sweating profusely.

The remaining Expedition swerved left and then right as it came out of the traffic, and the driver tried to give his pals a shooting lane, but Miguel did the same, keeping them at bay for a few more seconds.

Our tires gave out an agonizing screech as Miguel pulled the car violently back onto the outside lane as the shoulder narrowed to nothing. We were on a section of road that sat like a bridge about twenty feet above a sea of cane fields to our right. The Ford was flying toward us now, with no other vehicles between us, and was going to catch us in less than a minute.

I saw a gun emerge from the Expedition again, but this time, it was bigger, and I knew we were about to tangle with an automatic weapon.

A fusillade of high caliber bullets smashed into the Chevy, literally taking my breath away. I heard a loud grunt from the front seat. As I turned from my crouched position, I saw Bobby Hemphill thrown back against the dashboard, blood spurting from a wound in his shoulder, just inches from his heart.

Before I could react, another round of shells came at us, and the rear tires of the Chevy exploded, with rubber torn from the wheel spraying across the highway.

We fishtailed out of control as Miguel fought the steering wheel. The high speed of the vehicle fought him for control, and we spun around, finding the edge of the road, and plunged down the embankment. Out of the corner of my eye, I saw Miguel let go of the wheel and grab for the unconscious Bobby, who had slumped toward the open window.

Somehow, we remained upright as we skidded downward, most likely because the slope down into the sugar cane field was not steep. The big car slid into the cane stalks and came to rest about a hundred feet into the field.

I pulled Abby off the floor where she had fallen, and tried to open the door. The cane stalks, which were taller than the car and very thick, pushed back against the door, and I had to shove hard to get it open enough for Abby and me to get out. Miguel was fighting the same battle on the other side, and, once out of the car, turned back to search the floor for the guns Bobby had been using. Bobby remained slumped against the door, and I got it open and pulled him to the ground.

Through the broken cane, I could see the Expedition slide to a stop above us. Two gunmen with automatic rifles and the driver, who was carrying a pistol jumped out and ran to the road's edge.

Sporadic fire pumped into the top of the Chevy meant they weren't sure if we were still inside the car. We had worked our way around to the front of the car, and tried to stay low.

Abby was trying to staunch the flow of blood from Bobby's shoulder. His shirt was drenched with red on his right side, and his face was ashen. I prayed to God he wasn't dead.

The attackers were milling about on top of the road, trying to decide if it would be safe to come down after us.

Miguel took a chance on dissuading them from doing so, and shot the driver in the chest. He went down like a rock, and the others ducked back behind the Ford.

They got their nerve back quickly and, stepping away from the SUV, let loose a withering hail of automatic fire that began to disintegrate the busted up Chevy. The bullets slammed into the car and the ground around it, and Abby screamed as the shots got nearer and nearer.

I was trying to get off a few shots of my own to break the pattern of their unanswered fire when out of the corner of my eye, I saw the Buick, our cover car with Jaime at the wheel, come flying across my field of vision aiming right at the two men. They continued shooting, oblivious to the speeding car, and gave us all of their attention.

The first turned toward the Buick just in time to catch the full weight of the vehicle squarely in the gut. Jaime never took his foot off the gas as he hit the gunman, who flew over the top of the car, landing in a disjointed heap, some fifty feet away.

The second gunman never knew what hit him, as the Buick severed his legs with a spray of blood that we could see from down below, and threw his torso thirty yards up the road. He never had time to scream.

Cars catching up to the scene started to stop. Jaime jumped out of the Buick and fired three shots into the air. The gawkers, probably intending to help, scrambled back to their vehicles and sped off.

Jaime came running to the edge of the road, shouting Miguel's name at the top of his lungs.

Miguel jumped up and waved back. "Are you alright?" he said to us.

"Yeah, but Bobby's hurt pretty bad," I said, examining his wound. "Looks like it went clean through."

"He's bleeding an awful lot, Thomas." Abby said her voice heavy with concern.

"Are you okay, Abby?"

"Yes, I'm fine, Thomas," she said, brushing hair away from her face with fingers dyed red with Bobby's blood.

"Let's try and get him up top," I said, trying to lift the dead weight of Bobby Hemphill.

Miguel took hold too, and we worked our way over to the slope. Jaime scurried down and helped us get Bobby up the hill. The front of the Buick was smashed up pretty bad, and the radiator was leaking steam. The car was useless.

Miguel took one look and said, "The SUV!" and we put Bobby in the rear seat.

It had taken us almost fifteen minutes to get everyone up to the road and ready to travel. Abby sat next to Bobby in the back, trying to keep pressure on his wound, and I got in next to them.

"We better get out of here," I said to Miguel, who was standing outside the car.

"Wait a moment," he said, and ran to each of the corpses and dragged them to the roads edge, pushing them over. Next, with Jaime's help, he pushed the Buick towards where our Chevy had gone over. It went over the top of the hill in slow motion, burying itself among the sugar cane.

Miguel Estrada picked up the dead men's weapons and threw them on the front passenger's floorboard of the Expedition.

He was barely in the truck as Jaime floored it, and we headed toward San Rafael, and whatever lay between us and Abby's relatives.

CHAPTER 36

▼

6:00 P.M., 22 October 2002
Near San Rafael

We got off the Autopista at Santa Clara and picked up the two-lane to *Remedios* and then through several small villages along the coast, to a dirt road which would take us to San Rafael. And, I hoped, to safety.

Bobby's bleeding had slowed to almost nothing, but he had come to in a lot of pain. Like Mexico, drugs are readily available without prescription in Cuba's socialist medical program. Jaime had gone into a *farmacia* in Santa Clara for bandages and an arm sling, and he was able to get some codeine-laced painkiller, and more bottled water without questions being asked.

Miguel drove the Expedition to a secluded grove of trees outside town, and we got some pills down Bobby's throat before he passed out again while Miguel and Abby dressed the wound.

"He is better off if he stays asleep," Miguel said, and I knew he was right.

We headed east again and passed through the town of Remedios. We took turns trying to catnap, except for Miguel, who refused to give up the wheel. Abby had fallen asleep next to Bobby. As for me, the rush I had experienced during out battle with Asparza's men was long gone, and I was exhausted, but couldn't sleep for very long.

Now, as I had feared it would, my mind turned to thoughts of the dead bodies we were leaving in our wake. I was finding it very difficult to correlate the experiences of the last few days with my life up to then.

It was slow going on the two-lane as we kept running into road construction. The Cuban government was spending a lot of money turning this into a four-lane highway, and our slow progress was beginning to unnerve me. "What the hell is going on around here?" I asked under my breath to no one in particular.

Jaime turned in his seat to face me. "*La playa*," he said.

"What?" I said, realizing he was answering me.

"The beaches," Miguel said. "On the other side of the *Bahia de Santa Clara*...the waters off the coast...there are many islands, which we call the *Archipielago de Sabana,* and then comes the *Archipielago de Camaguey...*"

"You mean the barrier islands on the map?" I interrupted.

"Si," he answered. "They are islands that are between the mainland coast and the Atlantic. The foreign investors, they are planning many hotels and resorts. Some are already started. Castro must improve the access for the *turista* to these places to keep the foreigners investing."

"A lot of big American developers are going to be sorry they missed out on that," I said.

"That is the point, senor."

"I don't understand. What do you mean?"

"These developers and others who wish to invest in the future of Cuba after the Castro's are gone, they are the ones who are trying to force the American government to end the embargoes and trade and travel restrictions against Cuba." He laughed, ruefully. "They say it is not fair to punish the Cuban people for Castro, but it is money that drives those who protest these restrictions as 'unnecessary.' It would be a disaster for our cause," he said.

"Because it wouldn't help get rid of Fidel Castro," I added.

"Worse than that, senor," he said. "It would legitimize his government after all these years. He would have his capitalism, without being forced to give up his socialism."

We were quiet for a while, and I was dozing off again when Bobby stirred, and moaned softly. Abby was instantly awake and checking his wound. She smiled at me and shook her head. "No new bleeding," she said, and checked his forehead. "No fever, either." He didn't wake up.

"Good," I said.

"Where are we, Thomas?"

"Miguel?"

"We are near," he answered. "Maybe, one hour away."

"How are you feeling," I said to Abby.

She stretched as best she could in the crowded rear seat of the Explorer. "I don't think I will ever catch up on my sleep."

I took her hand. "You were unbelievable back there," I said, quietly.

"I won't say that I wasn't afraid," she said, "but, somehow I knew we were going to get through it."

"I wasn't quite that sure."

She was serious again. "We *will* get home, Thomas, but I am very worried about my mother. She must be frantic about both of us."

"I know," I said. "We will reach my friend in Atlanta tonight, after we speak to your relatives in San Rafael. I promise we will. I need to talk to my friend before we contact Maria. I want to be sure your stepfather didn't go back there. It wouldn't do us any good to have him standing next to your mother when we call. Max Howard knows your mother well, and he's keeping an eye on her. If he thinks it's safe, I'll have him let her know what's happening." I wanted him to let Pat and C.J. know we were still breathing too. By now, they would be frantic.

"Of, course," she said. "I understand."

"Have you thought about what you will say at San Rafael?"

"Yes. I will make it very simple. I just hope that their politics haven't changed over the years."

I hadn't thought of that possibility. What if the brothers of Maria Hernandez-Martinez, Abby's grandmother, had become socialists? What about their children? Maybe they had been so indoctrinated by fifty years of communist rule that they would condemn the Americans on their doorstep, and alert the police.

After the carnage on the Autopista, it was safe to assume that some driver who had witnessed our bloody gun battle would have called the authorities about what they had seen. The entire Cuban police force—or worse, the army, could be turning the country inside out looking for us.

Also, our travel visas were now invalid, which was another reason for the police to be looking for Bobby and me, even if they knew nothing about Abby Barrett.

I was beginning to understand how Custer had felt at the Little Bighorn.

*   *   *   *

It was already getting dark when we arrived at *Moron*, a little village at the bottom of a small lake, where the dirt road turned off towards the coast, and San Rafael.

I almost got Bobby killed, and Abby too, but we had to follow the course we had decided on, and I couldn't think about whether we should have taken Miguel's route out of Cuba instead. After all, he'd been doing this for a long time.

"There!" Jaime said, pointing to the turnoff, and Miguel headed toward San Rafael.

The lake was on our left, and as we continued northward in the dark, the clear water began to be swallowed up by long shoots of marsh reeds, until the water was only visible when the moonlight touched the small, wet clearings.

The smell of the sea and the salty-sweet, decaying marsh odors got stronger as we went on, and my trepidation grew. We were about to make either the best or worst decision of our lives, and strictly on my say so. But I knew there was no turning back now. We were about to meet the relatives that Abby had never known.

As we got closer to the village, Miguel slowed down, and finally turned off the Expedition's headlights.

Up ahead, only a hundred yards or so were the lights of the village. Miguel stopped the truck.

"What do you wish to do, senor?"

I'd been thinking about what we would do when we reached San Rafael for hours, but I still wasn't sure. Finally, needing to make a decision, I said, "can you get through the village without your lights?"

"I believe so. There does not seem to be anyone around, and the moonlight is strong."

"Okay, let's see if we can find the waterfront. The Hernandez' houses are supposed to be near the docks."

Miguel started the Ford up again, moving forward slowly.

Abby was wide eyed now, far more ready to meet the Hernandez' than I was.

It took only a few minutes to find the little bay where eight docked fishing boats of thirty or so feet each, rocked gently. We stopped again. No sound except for the gentle lapping of water against the boats and the docks could be heard. No one was around, but two houses sat less than fifty yards away. One was brightly lit; the other had only an outdoor porch light on.

We got out of the Expedition, making sure that Bobby was comfortably braced in the seat, so that he wouldn't fall over on this injured shoulder and reopen his wound. The codeine had done a good job of keeping him knocked out. I didn't think he would wake up for a while, but I couldn't afford to leave anyone with him. We were going to need Miguel and Jaime to keep an eye on us in case things went badly. We started for the house with the blazing lights.

I took Abby aside for a moment. "Sweetheart, you say whatever you think is best," I said, "and I'll be right by your side if things get out of hand…"

"No, Thomas," she interrupted. "This, I must do myself. These are my people. They will help us, but I do not wish to frighten them."

"But…"

"No, my darling," she said, and there was a serene look on her face. "Please, let me talk to them. Just stay nearby, but out of sight. Please," she said again.

Okay," I said after a few seconds, realizing as I did, that I was always going to have a hard time denying this strong-willed girl anything she asked of me. "I'll be around the corner," I said, and gave her hand a squeeze.

I got in position, and waived to Miguel, who was on the ground behind a stand of palm trees. Jaime was behind an old truck parked next to the house. Both had clear views of the front door.

Peels of laughter came from inside the house, as if a party of some kind was going on. I could hear children's as well as adult voices.

Abby stood in front of the door and gave me one quick glance before stepping forward and knocking on the door.

I held my breath as she knocked again, and the voices inside went still.

The door opened, spilling light out onto the porch, and Abby looked up slightly into the face of someone I couldn't see clearly.

"*Hola, abueltio,*" she said, speaking to her granduncle. "I am *la nieta,* the granddaughter, of *tu hermana,* your sister, Maria Martinez. I've come from Miami."

It was all she said, and I wished I could see the reaction on the man's face. My hand moved to my gun, and I held my breath and waited.

After what seemed like an eternity, I heard an old, but strong voice, speaking perfect English say, "I thought I was seeing the face of my dear sister as a child again. She would be pleased to see what a fine young woman you have become." He said this as if the appearance of his American grandniece, Abby Barrett, on his porch here, in the middle of a communist Cuba, was the most natural of occurrences.

"I need your help, granduncle," Abby said.

"And, you shall have it, my dear! You must come inside. We are having a birthday celebration for one of your cousins."

"There are others," Abby said quickly.

"Then, you must bring them in," The old man said, without hesitation.

*　　*　　*　　*

Benito Hernandez introduced us to his wife, Carmella, his widowed brother, Pedro, their sons, daughters, and combined ten grandchildren of various ages. They were all enthralled to meet their American relative and her friends. No one questioned how she had wound up on their doorstep in the middle of the night, with four men, one seriously wounded. It was as if they were content to wait for us to explain our arrival.

Carmella and her eldest daughter took charge of Bobby, getting him cleaned up, his dressings changed, and putting him to bed. Through it all, the strong pain medicine kept him groggy, and although he had fought to wake up, he was deep asleep again minutes after they finished working on him.

We joined in the celebration of cousin Theresa's twenty-first birthday, but Abby had become the center of attention. I had to fight the urge to check outside, but the faces in the room showed nothing but pleasure at our arrival, and, in any case, Miguel had kept his eye on the yard outside the window. Abby's face showed pure joy, and I finally relaxed a little. I couldn't believe we were not peppered with questions about how we had arrived out of the blue.

Around ten, the grandfathers took control of their respective broods, and after everyone had said good night to us and nearly squeezed Abby to death, Pedro's family went home to the house next door, Benito's headed to their rooms, and we found ourselves sitting around the big dining table with the two brothers and their four sons. The house fell silent, as if not to interrupt our talk.

"Now my child," Benito said to Abby. "Tell us why you are in Cuba, and what we can do for you and your friends."

Abby glanced at me, and I nodded. She began with the kidnapping in Miami, and told the story.

She told it all, including Richard Barrett's part in it. None of the Hernandez' broke in on her recital.

When she was through, Benito said, "It is a miracle that you have reached this place."

"Yes," I said. "I suppose it is, but we couldn't think of any place else to go. I hope this will not bring you trouble, senor." I wanted them to know that if we had brought them trouble, it had been my idea, not Abby's.

"You did the right thing, senor," Pedro Hernandez said. "Family must help family, no matter the consequences, and right now, you are all family."

I thanked him for the sentiment.

"Are you absolutely sure about your stepfather? He has truly done this to you?"

"We are sure, granduncle." Abby said. "That is the worst of all this."

"Many years ago, our dear sister and her husband, Pedro Martinez, asked our help, and we gave it gladly," Benito said. He shook his head, and added, "Maybe we should have gone with them to America, but fishing was all we knew, and our lives were here. Now it does not matter. Ask of us what you will."

It was my turn to speak again. "I must get Abby out of Cuba. There are many people looking for us, so we must leave soon."

"You will be able to arrange for a boat to meet you in international waters, yes?" Pedro asked.

I looked at Miguel. "It can be done," he said.

"Then, we will take you outside the twelve mile limit." Benito said.

"No," I said, quickly. "That will be too dangerous for you. We need to do this without bringing suspicion on you. Can you get us a boat that you will be able to do without? We need an unmarked boat, with no registration numbers that can be traced back to you."

Pedro spoke in Spanish to his eldest son, Rico, who answered him, and the two seemed to have a disagreement about something. The conversation went on for a couple of minutes, while we waited in silence.

"My son feels that honor calls for him to deliver you to your destination outside Cuban waters, but I have convinced him otherwise. You are right, Senor Thomas. My brother and I, we do not have so long, but my sons must raise their children here. Rico will find a proper boat for you."

Rico grunted an unhappy assent.

"You must forgive him," Pedro said, with a smile at his son. "He is a good boy, but stubborn, like his sainted mother," he said, as if Rico was but a child.

I smiled at that.

"What then?" Benito asked.

I sighed. "I hate to ask this of you, but we need a day for my friend to stabilize, and make sure he is okay to travel. And, I think we should leave in the early hours of morning." I looked at Abby. "If you can allow us, we need to stay here through tomorrow."

Benito sat back. "Of course," he said. "That will be best. There is much boat traffic from here to Cayo Coco, across the *Bahia de Perros,* during the daytime, because of the building of the hotel. You will need to stay in hiding."

"Yes, I understand."

"Also," Pedro said, "we will need to think about the route you must take to get to the open sea."

"The auto we came here in," Miguel said. "We will need to hide it. We took it from the wrong people."

"It is better to get rid of it," Pedro Hernandez said. "May I have the keys?"

"They are in the truck, senor."

Pedro spoke in Spanish again, and two of his sons got up from the table, and went out the front door.

"They will dispose of the auto," Benito said.

"How?" I asked.

"The water you passed on your way here, the *Laguna de Leche,* it is very deep, he said, not needing to say more.

"I see," I said. Abby took my hand and squeezed it.

"Granduncle, would you mind if we take a walk down to the water. We have been in the car all day."

"Of course," Benito said. "Carmella will get places ready for you and my niece to sleep, senor." Then he said to Miguel, "will you and your friend honor my brother by staying with his family tonight?"

"Si, senor, with much thanks," Miguel answered.

Abby and I left the table and went out into the cool evening air. I was glad things had gone well, and for the kindness of Abby's family, but I was happy to be alone with her in the still night with only the sound of water lapping against the dock pilings.

I put my arm around her waist and drew her close. We stood on the dock looking out at the water, and I was thinking of the safety that was on the other side, only ninety miles away.

"We will be home soon, my darling." Abby said softly, as if reading my mind.

"Of course we will be," I said, trying to sound confident.

Abby took my hand and turned away from the dark water.

She walked over to the closest of her family's fishing trawlers, kicked off her shoes and climbed down the steps to the deck of the spotless old boat. I followed her to the captain's cabin, which was as well kept as the deck.

She took my hand and pulled me down to sit next to her on the cabin bunk. Taking my hand in hers, Abby looked at me, like a teacher looks at a bashful child. "Thomas, are you worried?"

Her face was so set with an attentive look that it was almost comical, and I nearly laughed. She didn't deserve bravado from me. "Yes, I guess I am," I said as honestly as I could. Then I smiled, trying to lighten my own mood. "What about you?" I asked. "Are you worried?"

She thought for a minute. "Hmm...concerned, yes, but afraid...no. After all, we are together." she said.

And, again, I smiled. "You amaze me," I said, with true admiration in my voice.

Abby put both arms around my neck and said, "I know we will get home, Thomas, but if something should happen, I don't want to die without one more chance to give my love to you. I wouldn't want you to doubt how much I love you."

She kissed me lightly on the lips, and began to unbutton her blouse, slowly, but not to excite me. She wanted me to know that she was mine, without question, without reservation. Abby took my hand and placed it on her breast. My heart was so full of love, and fear, and emotions I couldn't explain, but I knew I was with the woman I loved, and that I had to get her home safely.

Abby pulled me down to the cushioned bench, and kissed me long and deeply. The rich smell of her made me woozy. There had been so much doubt in my heart that I would never have the chance to hold her this close to me again.

"Make love to me, Thomas," she said, and I felt her warm breath against my neck. "Now, my darling. Make love to me."

I prayed to God that He wouldn't let me let her down.

C H A P T E R   37

▼

Morning, 23 October 2002
San Rafael

Morning broke clear and sunny over the small village.

The sons of Benito and Pedro Hernandez were up and at work on their little fleet early, with their fathers offering advise from the dock on things the boys had done a thousand times.

Carmella had started breakfast for her hardy fishermen at 5:30 a.m. She served a second round of *revoltillo* and *salchicha* and grilled *pan* for the rest of us at eight. The scrambled eggs and spicy sausage reminded me of home, and Abby's great aunt treated us to cup after cup of café cubana.

Abby was already answering a ton of questions from her female cousins and the older grandchildren, and all were obviously having a wonderful time.

I checked on Bobby and was surprised to find the village doctor stitching up and dressing his wound, which luckily had manageable, clean holes. I could see now, that this was why we had been able to control the bleeding right after he was shot.

Bobby was awake, sipping a broth of some kind, and was being fawned over by the newly twenty-one, Theresa Hernandez.

He saw me in the doorway and gave me a tired smile. "This is gonna' slow me down with the chicks."

"Doesn't look like it." I said, happy that he was doing better.

Benito came up behind me and said, "Do not worry, Senor Thomas. I would trust this man," he pointed to the doctor, "with my life. His two brothers came from Florida with the Bay of Pigs invasion force. Castro kept them in jail until they died."

I nodded, and thanked him for helping Bobby.

"It is I who should thank *you*, senor, for saving my grandniece. I think there is much love between you two. You are both very lucky."

He put his hand out to me, and I shook it, solemnly. There was a tear in the eye of Benito Hernandez, as he left me and went down the hall to his bedroom.

I went outside to find Miguel and Jaime. They were helping the fishermen set the boats up for the day's activity.

"Are they going out?" I asked as I approached the dock. This was the boat where Abby and I had been last night, sharing our first moments alone together since that night in my room, so long ago in Atlanta.

"No," Miguel said, "but it is best to make things look normal."

I knelt down on the dock alongside the boat.

"How is Senor Bobby?" Miguel asked.

"Doing better, I think. The doctor is getting him fixed up to travel. Any word on our boat?" I asked.

"Rico said he will have a boat here by this afternoon."

Just then, I was startled to see several men in workman's clothing walking down the path to the harbor, and they proceeded, without paying a bit of attention to us, to load onto two boats at the end of the dock. Within minutes, the boats pulled away and headed across the water to the barrier island of *Cayo Coco*.

"They are the workers who are building the hotel on the island," Miguel said. "Many came through this morning before you came out. The boats run back and forth from here."

I nodded. "I see the SUV is gone."

"Yes, since last night," he answered.

"I'll be up at the house if you need me," I said. "After Rico brings the boat, we can make our final plans. This is our last day in Cuba, Miguel."

*   *   *   *

Rico Hernandez brought the twenty-two footer up the Bahia and docked her along side the fishing boats. It was almost 4 p.m.

One of the younger of Benito's grandchildren came running into the house with the news of Rico's arrival. I looked out the window and saw the boat being tied down.

Rico joined us a few minutes later. He spoke to his father, Pedro for a few seconds.

"The boat was bought from a boatyard nearby. We have ten days to register boats here in Cuba. I am afraid this one will be lost at sea before that time." Pedro smiled. "You will make sure of that, yes?"

"I will," I said. "I will have to arrange to send you the money you paid for the boat, senor."

"That is not necessary," Pedro said, gravely. "This is something we are proud to do." Benito nodded.

I thanked them. "If you will excuse us, my friends and I will make our plans for tonight."

Abby was helping her grandaunt and cousins prepare dinner. Miguel and I went out to take a look at the boat that would take us home.

"It's kind of small for five people on the open sea," I said.

"The seas will be calm for the next few days," Miguel said. "You will have no trouble with this boat. The engine is also new, and you will not need much extra gasoline."

Something in his words bothered me. "You talk like you aren't coming with us, Miguel."

"That is right, senor. We cannot go with you."

"What?" I asked, puzzled and suddenly worried. "Why not? I don't understand, Miguel. Our job is not done until Abby is safely home in Atlanta!"

Miguel shook his head. "Your job will be done, but my job is to protect el tesoro. I must settle accounts with Gregorio Asparza, and this Richard Barrett and Juan Garcia, if they are still in Cuba. That is the only way the treasure will be safe."

I sighed. "This is about your brother, Jesus," I said. "This is about retribution, isn't it?"

Miguel shrugged. "My brother and I, we knew our lives belonged to the Patron. We expect death, senor, and every day we are alive to do our duty is a *regalo de Dios,* a gift from God."

"How will you get home? If you kill Asparza, the whole Cuban police force will be after you."

"Yes," Miguel smiled, "but only for a little time. There are other 'Asparza's' who will line the pockets of Fidel Castro. They will forget him after a while. Then, I will come home from our usual route."

"I can't convince you to forget this and come with us?"

"Jaime will be with me, and Eduardo and Carlos will meet me in Havana."

"How will you get there? The Explorer's gone, remember."

"Rico will take me back to Havana," he said.

I smiled. "You've been thinking about this all along, right?"

"It was always my plan, senor," he said. "If I am able to deal with these men, all my friends in America will be much safer."

"Well, what do we do now?"

"We must arrange for you to be met by our men at sea. I will call Jose Garcia and take care of this for you."

I didn't like hearing that, but I knew there was no choice but to trust in Jose Garcia, something I had trouble doing since I had seen his son in Cuba. "How will they reach us from Miami?"

"The people who will meet you are already located in Key West. They will reach you in good time."

*   *   *   *

"I'll be a sorry son of a bitch!" Max Howard was responding to the news about Richard Barrett. Abby and I were sitting at the edge of the dock, dangling our legs towards the calm water. She was sitting close against me, and I had my cell phone tilted out so she could listen to our conversation.

"I gotta' tell ya,' Hoss, I knew something wasn't right about that guy, but I never saw *that* one coming!"

"Any chance he's come back to Atlanta, Max?"

"I was with Maria until about nine tonight, and she talked to him at eight. He said he was 'makin' progress' in Miami. No, he's not here, or if he is, he's not lettin' her know." Max was obviously disgusted by the turn of events.

"I wanted to be sure before we said anything to Abby's mom," I said. "I hate to keep her in the dark, but we didn't want to alert her husband if he had gone back home."

"Look, it's up to you, and I'll go talk to her if you like, but if you want my opinion," Max said, "I don't know that it does anyone, especially Maria Barrett, any good to be tellin' her that her husband had her daughter kidnapped for money." He let me think about that. "If I got to tell her that her marriage has been a lie, I'd like to be able to start the conversation by tellin' her that Abby's safely out of Cuba."

Abby took the phone from my hand. "Mr. Howard? This is Abby Barrett. I want to thank you for helping my mother. Please don't feel badly about this. I think you are absolutely right." She touched my hand and said, "Thomas will have me away from here by tomorrow afternoon, and we will contact my mother then. Is that alright?"

"I think that is best, dear lady," I heard Max say as Abby brought the phone back to my ear so I could listen. "And I look forward to meeting you in person, Abby, and very soon. As for Maria, I've been honored to be of service to her."

Abby got up, kissed me on the forehead and headed back up to Benito Hernandez' house.

"It's me, Max," I said into the phone.

"Sounds like you got yourself a real prize there, Tommy."

"You have no idea, Max, and I'm scared to death I'll screw this up. I can't let anything happen to her."

"You'll do fine," he said, with conviction. "Is Bobby really okay?"

"Yeah, but I almost got him killed," I said.

"Right way to say it is, he almost got killed doin' what he signed on to do. We just lucked out, that's all."

"I guess you're right, Max."

"So, tell me how you're getting outta' there," he said. I hadn't told Max earlier, because I hadn't told Abby about Miguel staying in Cuba. I didn't want to worry her.

I told Max about the call Miguel had made to Miami. "I get the boat out beyond the barrier islands and keep the compass on the straight and narrow towards the Keys. I'm supposed to keep going until we run into Garcia's men," I said. "We should be fine once we get twelve miles out."

"Son, don't count on Castro's navy leaving you alone just 'cause your twelve miles from Cuba."

"I know, Max," I sighed. "I know."

✳   ✳   ✳   ✳

It was midnight and we were sitting around the big dining room table with the Hernandez brothers and their sons. Benito Hernandez was unfolding a maritime map of the San Rafael/Barrier Island area. It showed Cayo Coco looming across the Bahia de Perros.

"There," Benito said, pointing to a small channel passage between two islands east of Cayo Coco. "This is where you must cross out into the Atlantic. There is too much risk of patrols guarding the construction site on the bigger island for you to cross there."

"I hope I can find it in the dark," I said, glancing at Abby.

"Just before the passage, there is a sign in the water," Pedro said. "It is a white triangle on a wood piling with the number '3' painted on it in red. Once you pass this marker, count ten seconds, and turn north, and you will be in the channel."

"I understand," I said.

"From there, the compass setting must be kept as close as possible."

"350 degrees, North," I said.

"Si, Thomas, you must run slowly until you are out in the open ocean, and do not use the running lights, so that no patrol boat will see or hear you. That will take you home."

Benito got up from the table and brought back a small silver tray with ten thimble-sized glasses and a bottle of rum.

"Now," he said, "one drink, and then you should rest. You must leave by 3:30 in the morning to get far enough out into the ocean before it is light enough for you to be seen."

*   *   *   *

Miguel and I got Bobby comfortable on a mattress we had fixed up for him on the deck of the little boat. Abby was saying goodbye to her family and the tears were flowing. I had already said my goodbyes, in order for her to have the last few minutes alone with them.

Benito Hernandez walked down the dock and stood above the boat. I stepped out to stand next to him.

"She is called '*Esperanza*,'" he said, nodding at the boat. "She will serve you well."

"I don't know how to thank you, Senor Hernandez. You and your family have been very kind, and I know Abby has enjoyed her time with you."

"You are welcome, young man. Abby is very lucky to have you for her protector."

I hoped he was right as we watched Miguel finish tying down the two extra gas cans to the transom, and Mama Carmella, worrying after us like she would her own brood, brought a basket of food and a jug of bottled water from the house.

"It is time to leave," Pedro Hernandez said, as he delivered his wife's basket. He shook my hand. "It does not please me to see you on your way, but it is best to wait no longer."

"Thank you for everything," I said. "I hope we will meet again."

Miguel finished his work and came up to me as I hopped back down onto the deck.

"Go with God, senor," he said as we shook hands.

"Are you sure you won't come with us?" I had hoped he would change his mind, but I knew in my heart that he wouldn't.

"I will see you in America," he said, solemnly. "My path is clear, and I must follow it."

"I'm sorry this has cost you so much, Miguel." I said, sadly, thinking about Jesus Estrada. "Come home safely, okay?"

He smiled without saying a word, gave Bobby a slight wave, and climbed up onto the dock. He met Abby on her way down to us and tried to pass with another wave, but she stopped him. He must have been telling her he was not coming with us, because she suddenly gave him a hug and a kiss on the cheek. Miguel gave her a little bow, and walked away. I knew he was walking into danger.

I helped Abby down onto the deck, and went over and started the engine. It coughed into life, and Rico slipped the ropes from the pilings and tossed them aboard. I slowly eased *Esperanza* away from the dock.

When we had backed some fifty feet from shore, and had waved one last time to the Hernandez family, I turned the wheel, and put the transmission into forward gear.

We were on our way.

I ran us northeastward to bring us closer to the barrier islands, so that I wouldn't miss the passage turn-off in the dark. There, we would turn northward.

Abby stood beside me, silently watching as we moved farther away from San Rafael. I gave her a smile, and she smiled back, but we did not speak.

The boat moved smoothly through the calm waters of the Bahia and it took us barely thirty minutes to reach the big, white sign on the piling. As we passed it, Abby counted; a thousand one, a thousand two…, and we made the turn at precisely the tenth second.

There was just enough moonlight for me to see the two shorelines and the open expanse of water between them.

Heeding Pedro's words of caution, I kept us as close to the center of the narrow channel as I could so as not to hit any of the shifting sand bars.

I figured we were moving at about eight knots, which I felt was fast enough until we could work our way out a mile or two into the Atlantic. Rico had said that the engine would give us thirteen to fifteen knots if the ocean was calm. Once we were out a ways, we could make a run for the twelve-mile limit, and take our chances from there.

"Bobby is asleep," Abby said after checking on him.

"Good," I said, "I made sure he took some of that pain medication in case it was rough out on the Atlantic."

She pulled a sweater on over her head. "A little chilly out here," she said.

"It's the humidity. Thank God, the wind is down. I think we'll be okay weather wise till we get picked up."

"Can you see all right?" Abby asked.

"Yeah, in fact let's speed it up a little," I answered, and pushed forward on the power. The twenty-two footer's nose came up out of the water a few inches, and I had to remind myself to stay within the guidelines given to me by Pedro and Benito Hernandez. This was no time to make a mistake. I was fighting my need to be away from here.

We had been in the channel about forty minutes when we both noticed small swells coming at our bow from the Atlantic. We were nearing the end of the passage. I slowed us down so we wouldn't go flying out into the ocean before we had a chance to check the barely visible horizon for patrol boats.

As the shorelines of the two small islands began to recede and the channel widened, I brought our craft nearly to a stop, giving the engine barely enough power to keep us from being pushed backward by the incoming tide. We waited like this for twenty minutes, both Abby and I looking for a telltale glimmer of light coming from searching patrols running the coast.

We didn't see anything, and I made my decision. With Abby sitting on the deck next to Bobby, I gave the engine some juice, and we moved out into the Atlantic.

$$*\qquad*\qquad*\qquad*$$

By 5:30 a.m., the wind was building a little, but the sky was clear and star filled, and an expanding ribbon of dim light was building on the horizon. We had been running at about eight or nine knots into the incoming tide for about thirty minutes. With every yard we passed, I grew a little more hopeful that we had pulled off our escape. But Jose Garcia's men were a long way from us. I glanced at the compass. We were right on track.

Abby was still with Bobby, and the lives of these two people were in my hands. One was a volunteer looking to give meaning to his life, and I had put him in danger, and the other was the woman I loved. I could feel myself trying to urge the boat forward through the light swells. There was more power that I could give to the engine, but I kept repeating to myself what the Hernandez' had said to me. Keep it slow for a few miles, no wake, and no excessive noise.

It was then that I came out of my reverie and noticed that Abby was on her knees, holding on to the side of the boat, and looking back towards the islands. She was pointing off the port side at an angle from the route we had followed out of the channel.

I squinted into the dark in the direction she was pointing. Off in the distance, I thought I saw something, but I couldn't make it out for sure. Instinctively, I pushed forward on the power stick, checked our direction on the compass, and kept an eye on the water behind us.

I felt Abby come up next to me. "There's something out there," she said in my ear.

"Are you sure?" I asked.

"Yes…no…I'm not really sure, but I think so." She was speaking loudly to be heard over the sound of the engine.

"Abby, take the wheel, just keep us on a 350 degree heading, okay?" I said.

She nodded and took the wheel from my hand. I looked deep into her eyes, and saw only utter calm. I went back to the transom and steadied myself, trying to keep my gaze centered in the direction Abby had indicated.

My eyes were fighting wave action, the movement of the boat, shadows from the island shoreline, and my imagination, but I couldn't turn away.

The minutes passed by-maybe five minutes altogether before I knew the truth.

We were being followed, and at high speed. Even in the dark, a form was taking shape in the distance, and my blood ran cold. I scrambled back to the wheel. "Someone's heading our way, Abby! Get back to Bobby and lay down on the deck. Quickly!" I said, grabbing the wheel.

I waited agonizing seconds until she was in place then I slammed the power stick forward, and *Esperanza* skipped forward, rising up at the bow as the propeller blades dug into the water.

I took my .38 out of my waistband. Bobby's gun was in a canvass bag alongside his mattress. I waived my gun at the bag and Abby caught on immediately. She dug the Smith & Wesson out and put it on the deck between her and Bobby.

The ghostly form on the water behind us was coming closer, and I knew for sure that we were facing a bigger and faster craft. I also knew, in all probability, there were several men on board her, too.

I tried to will the little boat to go faster, but I knew in my heart that we were many miles from help, and our pursuers would not stop at the twelve-mile limit. I looked back again, and they were still gaining on us. We weren't going to be able to outrun them.

"Abby!" I yelled, "Is Bobby awake?"

She shook her head.

"You have to try and wake him up!" I didn't know what good it would do, but if we had to fight, I would need Bobby to try to help us.

Now, I could see the white hull of the boat, maybe a mile away, and coming on. She looked to be about the size of the Hernandez' fishing boats, and appeared to be coming from Cayo Coco. It could be one of the boats carrying workmen to the island from San Rafael, not that it mattered. They were not friendlies, of that I was sure.

Bobby was struggling on his good arm to rise from the mattress with Abby's help, and was able to get to his knees, where he could see over the railing. Anna was pointing at the craft following us.

I could hear the roar of the other boat's engines now, but it was impossible to see who was on board her. She was closing quickly, and her outline was clearer now, at a quarter mile distance. I motioned for Abby to get down on the deck again, and Bobby waved to me that he was armed and watching the craft coming at us. I could see that it had a fly bridge, which meant that she was a sport fisher of some kind. The pilot was certainly high up on the bridge which probably helped him spot us as we ran north from the channel passage.

I looked at the gun on the chart table next to the wheel, and I knew it was practically worthless unless the other boat was right on top of us.

The first shot from what was now clearly recognizable as a sport fisher hit the wheel pedestal inches from my leg, with sufficient power to convince me that they had rifles on board, and I zigged to the left and then zagged right, over and over. This would make it harder to hit us, but would also pull us off the course we had been following. I had no choice.

Several more shots hit us while the pilot on the fly bridge kept the sport fisher just far enough off our wake to make our weapons useless. I thought about the gun battle on the Autopista. The shooters in the SUV's weren't firing warning shots, weren't just trying to stop us. They had been shooting to kill, and so were these guys. There wasn't going to be any attempt to capture Abby and Bobby and me alive. They meant to kill us, here and now.

Bobby fired off a shot, but I waved him off. "They're too far away," I mouthed, and he ducked down again.

Now, the sport fisher moved off to starboard in an attempt to circle us and force me to turn us farther off our course. I knew their superior speed would make the trick possible, and that I couldn't let them get in front of us, where they could spray the bow with rifle fire.

As the boat came across our bow, I made a hard turn, not to port, but to starboard, bringing us behind its stern. I was able to stay closer on course this way, but I knew that this maneuver was only going to work once.

Sure enough, the boat made a tight turn and came back directly at us.

Her direction would bring her on a parallel line toward us, and I turned to starboard to bring us back on a perpendicular course. We got another fusillade for our trouble from a semi-automatic weapon at about sixty yards. The shots missed us, but a spray of wood splinters stung my face, and I felt blood trickle down my cheek.

As the sport fisher ran past our stern, the shooters changed tactics and began firing at the engine and the gas line, and it was obvious that if the couldn't blow us up, they were going to try to disable us. I turned hard to port again and tried to keep space between the two boats. The heavy caliber shells were turning our boat into driftwood.

I wasn't going to be able to keep them off us for long, and my mind raced, as I tried to do something I had never had to attempt before.

The sport fisher shot past us, and our engine was still working, so the last attack had failed to put us out of commission. Now they were turning and heading straight for us again. With Abby's help, Bobby slid across the deck to the other side of the boat and took aim on the fly bridge, getting off three shots as our pursuer bore down on us.

Once again, I waited until the last second and then spun the wheel hard to starboard.

Whether on purpose or because the sport fisher's pilot lost us in the dark, or maybe because Bobby might have got lucky with one of his shots, the larger boat kept coming, sliding into a starboard turn just as we did.

The bow struck us just behind of the wheel pedestal and rode up the side railing of our boat and came down hard, bringing us to a dead stop, and nearly cutting the twenty-two footer in half, wood against wood grinding and then screeching loudly.

I was thrown back into the transom as, out of the corner of my eye, I saw Bobby up in the bow thrown overboard by the force of the collision, and Abby, without a moment of hesitation, dove into the water to help him.

The sport fisher loomed high above me and I could hear the whining sound of its propellers spinning out of control as I struggled to get to my feet. I could feel a warm wetness on the back of my head. I touched my head and my hand came away red with blood. I hadn't even felt my head strike the rear of the boat, but my blood stained the wood.

Our boat was trapped under the bigger one and the sound of cracking planks came one after the other. *Esperanza* was dying. I shook myself to clear my head, pulled myself up the slanting deck, and grabbed the lifesaving donut off the side of the wheel pedestal. I threw it overboard in the direction of the splashing sounds where Bobby and Abby had gone over.

Finally getting to my feet, I fought off the lightheadedness caused by my wound, and reached up to grab hold of the side rail of the sport fisher high above me. With a great deal of difficulty, I hoisted myself up and over the railing, falling in a heap onto the deck. My heart screamed for me to help Abby and Bobby, but I had to make sure no one was going to start spraying us with automatic fire while I went to their aid.

Juan Garcia lay on the deck. It appeared he had been piloting the sport fisher, and had fallen from the fly bridge when the two boats collided. Suddenly, there was a loud *crack!* And the deck shifted under me, throwing me down again against the starboard sidewall.

This time, when I got to my feet, I was staring into the face of Richard Barrett as he came up from the forward V-cabin. He held a revolver in his hand, and there was a crooked smile on his lips. Grabbing hold of the cabin door, he struggled up the steps to the tilted deck and trained the .45 at my chest.

"You have a tendency to complicate my life," he said with the cold smile as he stepped over the prostrate Garcia to the deck wheel, and turned off the useless engine. The sudden silence was deafening. "For an untrained, incompetent, inexperienced, young man, you have made a complete nuisance of yourself. I don't know whether to hate you or congratulate you on your efforts, Mr. Patrick."

"I'm not looking for any praise from you, you sick son of a bitch!" I spat out at him.

"No," he sighed, "I don't suppose you are, Thomas, and I suppose I could make an attempt to explain my actions to you, if it were the least bit important to me that you understand why I have undertaken my recent actions." He smiled. "But I do not car one whit what you think. You have made my life difficult for the last time." The smile had turned to a sneer.

"She's your daughter, God damn you! How can you do this to her? How can you do this to Maria?!" I cried out in exasperation, feeling impotent, and defenseless. After all this, I had failed just as I had feared I would. I wanted to cry out to Abby, and tell her how sorry I was.

He ignored my outburst. A savage look crossed his face, and raised the gun toward me again, and surely would have pulled the trigger except for the loud crack below us, and the deck dropped to starboard, some fifteen degrees, which threw a surprised Richard Barrett in a heap. He rolled down the deck taking my legs out from under me, and we went down together, as the big revolver flew out of his hand.

Barrett struggled to get out from under me and I pushed his face hard against the deck. He screamed as blood gushed from his nose, but it was a scream of anger, not pain.

With a show of strength I would not have expected from an older man, he gyrated violently to throw off my weight and scampered away on his hands and knees as I slid back down toward the transom.

I bounced up, my head raging with pain and dove for him as he was reaching for the .45, and it skittered down the slanted deck.

Barrett flipped over and grabbed me by the neck with both hands. I tried to break his grip, but he was out of his mind with hatred, and I couldn't break his hold. I could feel his finger nails puncturing my skin, and I arched backward to try to lessen the horrible pressure. I threw a roundhouse punch into his right ear, and with a startled grunt, he went slack for a few seconds. But he recovered quickly and pulled back his withered foot and kicked out at me, catching me in my gut, and throwing me backward.

I landed on my back and cracked my head on the deck again. I shook off the pain that was shooting through my neck, and fought to catch my breath. Our fight had taken it out of both of us, and Barrett's next attack had less steam. He grabbed at me again, his breadth hot and heavy against my ear. I forced myself to imagine the old brown punching bag hanging in my small living room above Ireland's Own, and managed another punch to his face, and this time, he went down hard and didn't move.

I bent down, my hands on my knees, trying to catch my breath. When I looked up, Juan Garcia stood before me, his revolver in his hand.

Without a word, he raised the gun, and I heard the boom and simultaneously felt the searing pain in my shoulder. It was as if I had been kicked by a mule, and I was twisted over to the left and fell backward, barely keeping from tumbling over the stern and into the water.

I struggled back up, my left arm useless, and faced Garcia.

"You will not have what is mine!" He roared, and the pistol came up again, aimed at my chest.

Sweat and blood coursed down my face, blinding me. I thought of Abby foundering in the water with no one to save her, and waited for the kill shot.

As Garcia began to squeeze the trigger, there was an agonizing, earsplitting groan, as the damaged deck planking gave way beneath him.

With a look of complete surprise stamped forever on his face, Juan Garcia dropped through the splitting deck, finally firing off his second shot as if in protest at this last joke upon his life by an unfeeling God. The round struck me in the thigh, passing through flesh but missing bone, and I went down hard, reeling from the sudden impact.

As Garcia dropped into the cabin below, the wood splintered around him, and a jagged plank thrust upward catching him under the chin. It drove itself against his falling weight, up through his neck, severing his spinal cord. He was dead before the force of the plank rammed it through his brain and ending up against the top of his scull, stopping his fall. Only his head and shoulders were above the deck, and crimson blood poured across the deck from the wound below his chin.

I sat back heavily onto the floor, and I was getting weaker by the second as the blood flowed from my wounds. I must have been in shock, as the pain was still bearable, but I could feel consciousness slipping away.

I had raised my face up to the light breeze that had begun to track across the deck, when Richard Barrett, blood still flowing from his damaged nose, slammed his heavy boot across my face, and I was flat on my back again, pain bursting from my left eye. My hand flopped into the scupper under the transom, where water was meant to find its way off the deck area during heavy rain, and my fingers closed around the handle of the revolver we had fought over.

"What I shame, young Thomas," I heard Barrett say. "It seems that this baboon has done to you what I wished to save for myself. No matter, it will still be my pleasure to end your little life." He took a step closed, and I fought to keep awake long enough to take my last chance.

"She's...your...daughter," I stammered, again.

"Yes," he said, calmly, with no apparent emotion. "And I will miss her greatly, but she cannot return home for obvious reasons." Barrett reached back to the side of the boat where the grappling hook hung. He took it off the hooks and worked it around in his hands. Out of the corner of my swollen eye, I could see the sharp, barbed steel tip.

With a deep breath that I was afraid might be my last, I pulled the gun from the scupper, and through bloody, half-closed eyes, took aim at the chest of a surprised Richard Barrett. He lunged at me and I fired the big gun at him, the shock of the recoil nearly ripping the weapon from my hand.

The slug threw him back, and the look of utter astonishment on his face was quickly replaced by one of searing hatred. He was raising the grappling hook over his head, ready to thrust it at me, when I fired a second shot, catching him full in the chest again.

Richard Barrett's eyes seemed to lose focus as the crimson floret grew on his chest. He staggered backward against the slanted railing, hung in mid air for a moment, and tumbled backward, almost in slow motion, over the side. I heard him hit the railing of the wallowing *Esperanza* beneath us, and then fall into the sea with a loud splash.

I fought nausea and the bile rising in my throat, and lightheadedness growing in my head, and tossed the gun aside. It took me a minute to work my way onto my stomach, and I finally pushed myself against the stern, and somehow got to my feet.

The pain was coming on stronger now, and I was dizzy the moment I stood. I got to the side and looked overboard.

Abby and Bobby were in the water, each with an arm through the donut. Richard Barrett's body floated less than ten feet from his stepdaughter, his unseeing eyes staring up at me.

I picked up the grappling hook, which lay where he had dropped it when Barrett had gone over the side. Fighting against the urge to sit down and sleep, I reached over the side, guiding the hook with my good arm, and grabbed the donut, bringing it as close to the side as I could. Every movement sent bolts of pain surging though me.

"Abby," I hissed through swollen lips, "can you climb up?"

"Bobby first!" She yelled back. She got behind him and struggled to boost him up. It took almost five minutes, but he finally got his knees up onto our little boat, and once on his feet, fell onto the deck above, next to me.

Abby was up on the lower deck in a matter of seconds. I couldn't stay upright any longer, and collapsed again as she came over the side.

"Oh God, Thomas!" she cried, and was quickly beside me on her knees, peering into my face. "Thomas! Can you hear me?"

I could hear her, but I couldn't answer. Her beautiful, chocolate eyes were the last thing I remembered, as a light rain began to fall on my face.

CHAPTER 38

▼

Noon, 30 October 2003
Grady Hospital, Atlanta, Ga.

I was alone in my room at Grady Hospital for the first time in the six days since being flown back to Atlanta from the hospital at Key West, where Bobby and I had received emergency care after we were rescued.

It had taken two days to get me stabilized, and it wasn't until nearly the end of that time before I was coherent enough to understand what had happened after I had finally passed out on the deck of Richard Barrett's boat.

The first time I had regained my senses, I was able to make out Abby's face before me, and I could feel her light touch on my forehead.

I figured I was still lying on the deck of Barrett's boat bleeding to death in front of Abby.

But this boat was moving through the water at high speed, although that didn't register with me just then.

"Thomas? Can you hear me?" Abby was saying, "Thomas, we're going home, sweetheart."

"Sure we are, babe," I said, although my words may have come out sounding completely incoherent from my swollen lips.

We were going home. Two days later Abby told me how she and Bobby had staunched the bleeding from my wounds, and then they had lain there on the tilted deck for nearly three hours, hoping against hope that we wouldn't sink into the Atlantic.

Richard Barrett was dead. I had killed him. Jose Garcia was dead, but he had nearly killed me, before he died. As the sea rose slowly over the foundering pile of wood that had once been two boats dueling across the surface of the Atlantic, and as the horizon started to lighten into full daylight, Abby had spotted the distant speck on the water.

It was maybe three miles out, but coming from the north, not from Cuba. That was enough for her, and she took off her white sweater and waved it at the approaching vessel.

Jose Garcia's men had taken a chance, passing through the twelve-mile limit and into Cuban waters to look for us.

Bobby told me later that seeing that boat slide up along side us was the best thing he had ever witnessed. "We were sitting there while they got you onto a stretcher for about fifteen minutes, and that was the *worst* thing I had ever seen. I expected some Cuban gunboat to come along and blow us all out of the water!"

We had been on our way to Key West when I woke up that first time, and Abby had been right. We were going home.

*   *   *   *

My list of injuries was long and impressive: a broken nose, bruised eye, a cracked jaw, twelve stitches in my scalp, bruised ribs, a .45 slug in my left shoulder, and entry and exit wounds in my thigh, and multiple areas of pain were still a daily occurrence if I didn't keep up with my pain pills.

The door to my room cracked open, and the cherry-red face of Max Howard peeked around the opening. I smiled and motioned him in.

"Good to see you, Hoss," he said, as he pulled his bulk into the room.

"Good to see you too, Max," I said. "Believe me, there were times I wasn't sure I'd see any of you guys again."

"I can imagine. How are you feelin' Tommy?" He sat on the edge of the bed and inspected my bandaged head.

"I'm okay for a guy who is beginning to make a habit out of getting the crap kicked out of him," I said ruefully.

"Well," he chuckled, "maybe I can make you feel a little better by fillin' you in on what my kids have found out." That's what he called the young, energetic, and dedicated people in his office.

I braced myself for what was to come.

"Our friend, Mr. Barrett, had a brother, and his name was Victor..." He paused for effect. "Victor Yevshenko, but he called himself Gregorio Asparza."

I was stunned and confused. "What?! You are telling me that Richard Barrett and Asparza were Russian by birth, and brothers, to boot?"

"That, my boy, is exactly what I am tellin' you." He went on. "It seems that Richard, his real name by the way, was Vladimir, came to Cuba in 1958. He was only eighteen, but fully trained as a spy, and you couldn't tell him from an American."

"You mean, he was trained to speak and act like one of us," I broke in.

"Exactly. Like those Nazi's back in WWII who passed themselves off as GI's durin' the Battle of the Bulge. Only the Russians took likely prospects at a very young age, to make it easier to make these kids like us. He made several trips into the U.S. with forged papers, and spied for the Commie government back in the U.S.S.R."

I shook my head. "So, how does his brother fit in, Max?"

"Well," he said. "Best we can figure, Victor came over as an engineer with the missile forces that President Kennedy finally forced out during the Cuban Missile Crisis, back in '62. It seems neither of the brothers felt the need to return to Russia when the military left."

"Jesus," I said.

"Could be they were left there by Khrushchev to continue aiding Castro, but I think they saw the benefits of capitalism, stayed, and hid out 'til it was safe to reemerge into Cuban society." Max smiled. "And by that, I mean emerge into the society of the Russian Mafia, including kidnapping, murder, embezzlement, torture, smuggling, and other niceties of Mr. Castro's regime."

"No shit," I said, quietly.

"None at all," he said. "They knew about that treasure for a long time, and just couldn't get their hands on it, Tommy."

"But, how did Barrett find us when we finally left San Rafael?" I asked.

"That's easy, actually," Max said. "Turns out Richard Barrett knew the whole story of Pedro Martinez' escape from Cuba, and the help he got from his wife's brothers. I think finding you on the highway might have been a good guess on his part, or maybe just a lucky break. But once he did, he musta' figured where you were going"

"Why didn't he attack us in San Rafael?"

"Why take the chance that something could go wrong? Anyway, once he knew you were on your way to Abby's family, I think he just put it all together. After that all he had to do was have someone watch for you to make a break over the water, where it would be safer for him to grab you guys."

"The construction workers," I said, shaking my head. I had so much to learn. "Does Maria know all of this?"

"Abby told her," Max said. "We discussed it, and she thought it would be better if she broke it to her."

"I never saw a speck of fear in Abby, Max," I said, thinking about everything that had happened in the last few days. Maria had to put her life back together, and Abby would be a big part of that. I hoped I would be too, but how would Maria react to my part in killing her husband, no matter what he was responsible for.

"Maria feels she owes her daughter's life to you," Max said.

"Might be the other way around," I said, relieved to hear how Maria felt.

"You all are good for each other, Tommy. I surely do like those women."

"How do you think Juan Garcia got involved?" I said, dismissing the corrupt Yevshenko brothers for the moment. I had to figure out the rest of it.

"Well," he said. "I figure they were takin' advantage of his greed, but he probably saw it as one last chance at his dream of finding the treasure. Anyway you look at it, he was a minor player hired for his hatred for his father's part in hiding the wealth of those families. I doubt Seenyor Garcia would have ever got back to Miami alive."

That made perfect sense. "How's Bobby doing?" I asked, finally.

Max Howard laughed. "He's bein' treated like a hero at home. Something he hasn't been used to in the past, as you know. Even C.J. has been takin' care of him, and he's playin' it for all it's worth."

My sister-in-law had been caring for me too, right alongside Abby and my mom, and they were all getting along great. "I don't thing Bobby knew he had it in him," I said, "but, I'm glad he did."

"Me too, son," Max said, softly, "me, too."

"Thanks for everything, Max," I said.

He just looked at me and nodded. We didn't need to say more about it.

"Oh, say," Max said. "Almost forgot." He took another piece of paper from his pocket. "I thought you might find this interesting."

It was a cutout from the *New York Times* from two days earlier. The headline read: "Cuban Trade Minister to U.N., Found Dead." The article went on to say Gregorio Asparza had died of a heart attack while at his home in Havana during a trip to Cuba to report on trade negotiations, during a series of meetings with governmental authorities.

"I'll be damned," I said. "They did it! They got the bastard!" I felt a sudden relief for the people in Miami who had helped us save Abby. I knew Miguel was coming home. Maybe he was already safely in Miami.

"Seems like," Max said. "By the way," Max said. "While you were gone, Junior Kline copped a plea and rolled over on his compatriots, including Charlie Mitchell. He'll still do some time, and the lawsuits will bust him. His girl friend, Miss Ellen, will go to jail for a while too, but she'll get a chance to start her life over. Mitchell will be doin' some serious time. As we figured, that Edwards' guy disappeared into thin air."

"Good day all around," I said.

The door of my room burst open and the imposing sight of my brother, Pat, filled the doorway. "If you're finished with your vacation, I could use someone for the five o'clock bar shift!" he said.

I looked at Max, then back at Pat. "You know," I said "Mom always did like me better."

CHAPTER 39

▼

ENDGAME

Night, 3 January 2003
Peachtree Street

I was sitting in the old recliner in my silent living room. I had been there a couple of hours, as the room had grown darker and darker around me. The TV was off, but I was unable to put the noise of excited, yelling fans coming from Ireland's Own below me out of my head.

Knowing what they were watching on the restaurant's big screen and regular TVs, I couldn't help feeling a little low, even though Abby was back in the bedroom, just a few feet away.

The last college bowl game of the season was being played at the Fiesta Bowl, about two thousand miles from Atlanta, in Tempe, Arizona. The top ranked Miami University Hurricanes were playing the second ranked Ohio State University Buckeyes, for the national championship.

Downstairs, a few hundred people cheered on their favorite team as all forty televisions blared away. I couldn't bring myself to be there.

I felt the light touch of Abby's fingers on my shoulder, and reached back to cover her hand with mine. The simple move pulled slightly at the tightness in my shoulder, and I winced. I was still dealing with some of my injuries, but, all in all, I was healing.

"Come to bed, Thomas," she whispered in my ear. I could feel her body behind me; I could smell her hair and skin. I had come so close to losing her, it frightened me, even now, to think about it. Either of us could have drowned in the swirling sea, eventually washing up on the sands of the Cuban coastline. I think I could have dealt with my own impending death, but to think of losing Abby that way would be worse than death. As it was, I nearly cost Bobby Hemphill his life, and thought I had for a day or two after we were pulled from the wreck of the *Esperanza*. But he was alive and well and already bugging me again about joining me in the business. He's probably earned it, but I'll have to think about that a little more.

It was only a little past ten, but there was no use in staying up. I pulled myself up from the chair and followed her into the bedroom, feeling the relief I always felt, seeing her safe in our home.

✳   ✳   ✳   ✳

But I lay awake, unable to sleep.

Abby was nuzzled up against me, breathing softly, while I sat up against the headboard of my old bed. She deserves more than I can give her, yet she seems at peace with her life. What I want, more than anything, is to give her all of me. I know that to do so, I have to exorcise my demons. I need to be able to accept and believe that this is where I belong; that this is where my destiny has led me, and that all other places, at this time in my life, would be foreign to me.

I pulled away as gently as I could, and Abby didn't wake up. I got out of bed and went into the other room and over to the old chest of drawers that held my few belongings. Down below, in the bottom drawer underneath some old sweatshirts, I found my game program. The only game program my name had appeared in.

I held it against my chest, without opening it, and walked over to the TV, turned it on, leaving the volume down, and turned the channel to the ABC affiliate which was carrying the game. The light from the screen lit the room, and, sitting back in my old, tattered chair, I began to watch, mesmerized by the scene, unable to tear my eyes away.

I was alone with my demons.

Then, near the end, the Hurricanes running back was hit as he plowed through the line. His leg buckled at the knee, and he went down in a heap. A shot went through my body, every nerve exploding, again, and again, as the network replayed the moment of contact repeatedly. I realized, a few moments later, as the player was carried from the field never to return, his pro career now handing by a thread, that I had tears streaming down my cheeks. I knew then, that I could feel the pain of, and cry for, someone other than myself. In that moment I could swear, although it was most likely more in my head, that the nagging pain I had felt for so long in my left leg, was gone.

I watched, still feeling the sting of tears, as one of the greatest college championship games ended in a tie, and proceeded to two overtime periods.

After a Buckeyes running back scored from five yards out in the second overtime, Miami took their turn and pushed the ball to the OSU two-yard line.

The Buckeyes held for three downs, and as Miami came to the line of scrimmage on fourth down, my heart was in my throat, my breath shallow, and my grip on the chair's arms almost painful, I was holding on so tightly.

Cie Grant sliced through the offensive line within a split second after the snap and grabbed the Miami quarterback, spinning him to the ground as the desperately thrown pass arced, as if in slow motion, over the players battling at the line. And, in a moment, Matt Wilhelm, the Buckeye nose guard, stood looking down at the football, lying on the turf at his feet.

For a moment, there was a brief stop in the action, as if each person in the stadium was looking to others for conformation of what they knew they had just seen. And then, the floor of the playing field was like a roiling sea of Scarlet and Grey, along the Ohio State sideline, and fans swarmed the players on the field at the end zone where the game's last play had occurred.

I felt a sob escape me, and found myself standing without knowing when I gotten to my feet. National Champions!

✳   ✳   ✳   ✳

I was still standing in the dark room, still watching the screen a few minutes later, when Buckeye coach Jim Tressel stood on the hastily assembled podium next to ABC's Lynn Swann, the former Steeler receiver and Hall of Famer I had watched as a child, surrounded by the victorious team. The coach turned to the cheering crowd, and held high the cut-crystal football, the trophy symbolic of the championship. One by one, the players passed around their trophy, kissing it, holding it high. Finally, it passed on to one of the wide receivers who hugged it tightly to his chest, tears of happiness and pride streaming down his dirt stained face. My tears stopped, my breathing calmed, and I felt a flood of relief I would not have thought possible.

I went to the kitchen and found my bottle of Sauza, and poured a shot. Walking back to the TV, watching the celebration continue, I raised my glass and drank a toast to the victors. For the first time this night, I could smile. I felt pride. I might have been there with them, but I did not feel jealousy, as I might have thought. I could have been there. I should have been there. But then, what of Atlanta, of C.J., Pat, Max, Bobby, and the life I wanted, with all my heart, to build with Abby.

I put down the glass and picked up the game program that had slipped from my lap. I looked at the cover one last time. I went back into the kitchen and dropped the program into the trash.

I turned off the TV, and the room was in complete darkness again. I yawned, feeling suddenly spent. I went back to the bedroom and stood over Abby, feeling a sense of well being flooding my chest. I watched her sleep, and gently brushed a wisp of hair from her eyes.

I didn't know what was ahead for us, and I suddenly realized that it wasn't necessary to know the future, only, the present.

Abby is my gold, my silver, my artist's masterpiece, my treasure, and I suddenly knew that I was exactly where I was supposed to be at this precious moment in time.

I turned off the lamp on the night table, and lay down as gently as I could next to the woman I love. Abby stirred and put her hand on my chest and nuzzled against my arm.

It was time to sleep.

As I began to drift off, content in her closeness, my thoughts went to the weeks we had spent at the home of Maria Barrett after we were rescued from the waters off the coast of Cuba.

The two women tended to my recovery and, I suppose, the time Abby and I had spent there was a help to Maria, as she dealt with the betrayal, and death, of Richard Barrett.

My last thought was of the day I had spotted the bible on the piano top among the family pictures and remembrances. I had passed it a dozen times, but I guess its presence had never registered on me before.

Etched across the ornate, but worn cover was the name "Castillo," and the family crest of Abby's father. I had opened the cover, and found, written in English, the words, "For my Daughter."

The words were followed by a poem which Ramon Castillo had left as parting words for Abby. Was it meant as a clue? One that Richard Barrett, in his greed, passed every day as he walked past the piano in the home he shared with the family of Ramon Castillo? It didn't matter any longer, and I have kept the discovery to myself, not feeling that it was necessary to tell Maria and Abby what I had found. It was better to let the healing begin.

The last lines of the poem, which had been burned into my memory, were:

> *The little church by the sea,*
> *Long lives in our hearts,*
> *There is our life, our future,*
> *The treasure of our children.*

The End.

ABOUT THE AUTHOR

Sam Biondo was born and raised in Cleveland, Ohio, and attended The Ohio State University. He is a real estate developer and now lives in the Atlanta area with his wife, Susan, and near his two daughters. An amateur historian and writer since high school, he is now at work on the second volume of the Peachtree Chronicle's novel, *A Stained White Veil*.

978-0-595-36555-5
0-595-36555-8

Printed in the United States
45909LVS00007B/28-45

9 780595 365555